*SALVAGED: Tatia's Story –
Book #3*

SALVAGED: Tatia's Story - Book #3

Linda Brendle

Linda Brendle

DEDICATION

To the Good Shepherd who cares for the ninety-nine
but also seeks the lost one.

THANK YOU...

- To David Brendle, my husband and number one fan, for always being patient when I disappear into my writing for hours and days at a time; for always being my first reader; and for loving me like Johnny loves Maddie.
- To Gloria Moore-Cresswell for reading and offering comments and corrections on this very long manuscript.
- To JoLynn Robinson, my sister-in-law, who volunteered – again – to be a reader and editor, and who offered very helpful suggestions.
- To Audrey Wauson whose drawing captured the beauty and longing in Madison's face before she knew what she was longing for.
- To my friends and family who encouraged me to continue when writer's block set in and threatened to disown me if I didn't produce Book #3 soon.

Contents

Contents | xi

Preface

Friday - 9/22

"Madison, what are you doing with my phone?"

"Misty! I thought you were asleep."

The phone went dead.

Saturday - 9/23

After Joy's dramatic rescue and return to her parents, Detectives Tracy Martin and Adam Nelson spent the wee hours of Saturday morning at the Belmont Avenue Station sorting through witness statements, writing up reports, and finding a prosecutor to approve felony charges against Eric Hall and Victor Ellis, the two men who had allegedly snatched Joy Matthews out of her back yard the day before her ninth birthday and sold her to an anonymous buyer on the dark web. Once the paperwork was done, the detectives walked down the hall to Precinct Captain Carter's office and tapped on the frame of the open door.

"Yeah," said Carter in a tired voice. He took off his glasses and laid them on his desk before rubbing his eyes. "What ya' got?" he asked with a yawn.

Martin laid a file on his desk. "The arrest report, the criminal records of Hall and Ellis, a report for the pre-trial services officer, and a synopsis of all the fun we've had this evening."

Carter opened his mouth to say something, but Nelson jumped

in. "We made three copies so you could send one to the prosecutor, one for the pre-trial services officer, and have one left for your files."

"Good job," said Carter. The detectives exchanged looks of relief while the captain flipped through the file. "If I can catch all the decision makers in their offices and in a good mood, we may be able to formally charge these lowlifes and get bail denied in the next couple of days." He continued to peruse the paperwork and reached for his phone.

"Uh, sir," said Martin. "What can we do to help?"

"Oh, uh, right," stammered Carter. He rubbed his eyes again to clear his foggy brain. "Uh, nothing. This all looks good. Go home, get some rest. As soon as I see what's happening, I'll let you know when to be back here."

Martin started to say something else, but Carter had already dialed the phone. Nelson grabbed her arm and dragged her out of the office. "Let's get out of here before he changes his mind. He'll still be sitting there when we come in Monday morning – and I for one don't want to spend the weekend with him!"

1

Sunday - 9/24

The day after Joy's ninth birthday party she was sitting at the kitchen table with Grandma G, working on an illustrated account of her experience with Eric. Tatia had suggested the project as a kind of catharsis for Joy, and she knew that Deborah, the woman who had adopted her after pulling her out of the dark underworld of child trafficking and jumped on a plane from Texas the moment she heard that Joy had been taken, would be able to help Joy deal with the fear. The three of them were laughing at a picture Joy had drawn of Eric with horns and a tail when the doorbell rang. Momentarily forgetting to be afraid, Joy jumped up and ran into the living room.

"I'll get it," she yelled unnecessarily.

"Be careful," said Tatia. "You almost ran over your brother."

Daniel and Grandpa were in the middle of the floor, playing with several trucks and trying unsuccessfully to entice Harley, the cat, to play with them.

Joy opened the door and was shocked to see a tall, slender young woman in white jeans, white running shoes, and a white hoodie leaning against the door frame. Her black hair was pulled back into a ponytail, and she was wearing a pair of black wrap-around sunglasses that hid her eyes but didn't quite cover the edge of the bruise that spread out over her cheekbone and disappeared into her hairline.

"Madison?" said Joy. "Is that you? How did you get here?"

"I...uh...cab," she stammered, and then she collapsed across the threshold.

"Mommy!" screamed Joy. "It's Madison. I think she's sick."

Tatia dashed in from the kitchen. "What is it...oh!" She stopped short when she saw the young woman lying on the floor. She hurried to the kitchen, wet a hand towel, and rushed back, kneeling beside Madison. She began to bathe her face with the towel and speak soothingly to her.

From the kitchen, Deborah saw and recognized the symptoms of withdrawal. "Where do you want to put her?"

"In our bedroom."

"I'll get it ready."

As she disappeared, Tatia called after her. "The sheets are in the washing machine. You'll find clean ones in the cabinet in the bathroom."

"What can I do?" asked Joy, her voice full of concern.

"Grab a bottle of water out of the refrigerator."

By the time Joy returned, Madison was sitting up, and Tatia opened the bottle and encouraged her to take a sip. She finally swallowed a capful and promptly wretched, spewing clear, foamy liquid into her lap.

"I'm so sorry," moaned Madison. "Joy said you could help...I shouldn't have come."

"This is exactly where you need to be," Tatia said as she used the towel to clean Madison's lap.

Joy sat down on the other side of her friend and took her hand. "Mommy, this is Madison. She's the one that called you."

"Yes, and I will never be able to thank you enough, Madison. Now, do you think you can stand up? Joy, you help her on that side."

Joy slid Madison's arm around her shoulders and continued to hold her hand. She slipped her other arm around Madison's waist and said quietly, "Lean on me, Madison. We were strong before. We can be strong now."

Joy and her mother guided their unsteady friend into the bedroom where Deborah had just turned back the covers on the freshly made bed. The women helped Madison sit on the edge of the bed, and Joy knelt at her feet where she removed her shoes. Deborah supported her while Tatia slipped her arms out of the hoodie. "This will do for now. We'll get you into some pajamas later."

Tatia pulled the sheet and blanket up over Madison who had begun to shiver. She sat down on the vanity stool Deborah had moved to the side of the bed, and her mother continued to gather what they would need to help Madison through the next forty-eight hours.

"Joy," Tatia said, "Can you run over and ask Daddy to call Dr. Patterson? If you're afraid, Grandpa can go with you."

"I can do it Mommy. God has sent us a job, and He will make us strong enough to do it."

"You're right, Joy. It seems that God has sent us another fallen angel to care for."

2

Sunday - 9/24

"I wonder what happened to the million bucks," said Johnny as he hit the ON button of the coffee maker. He was one of the newest members of Jesse's Bible study. He had come with a friend he met at Recovery Ministry where he was dealing with a pornography addiction. He wasn't sure about the Bible part yet, but he enjoyed the camaraderie, and he had become the most welcome member when he used his computer expertise to save Joy. After that adventure, he was weighing his options between pursuing a position as a computer consultant with the Chicago Police Department or becoming the vice president in charge of a new computer service department in the Fallen Angel Salvage family. At the moment, though, his job was to pull a few mismatched mugs out of the cabinet and place them on the counter next to a tray of snacks Tatia and Deborah had prepared earlier in the day.

"What million bucks?" asked Brush who was preoccupied with setting up folding chairs around two molded plastic tables set end to end in the middle of the room. "Jesse, do you think this will be

6

enough chairs? We'll have the usual Thursday night group, plus the guys from the church group."

Johnny pulled an insulated coffee dispenser out of the cabinet and began filling another filter with coffee. "I'd better make another pot since we're having extras. Why are we having a special study tonight anyway?"

"Yeah, more coffee, extra chairs, and another table would be good," agreed Jesse as he placed a copy of his study notes and a Bible in front of each chair. "As for why, Pastor Jason, who usually teaches our men's group on Sunday afternoon, left after this morning's service for a pastor's conference. He asked if I'd sub for him, and Brush and I decided to change the venue and invite you guys to see if we might stir up some intergroup fellowship and interest."

"I see," responded Johnny with a grin. "Another way to try and 'encourage' me to come to church with you."

"Whatever works," said Jesse, looking around to check the preparations. "And what million bucks, Johnny? We could use a little capital infusion around here."

Johnny was now leaning against the counter with his arms crossed and a far-away look in his eyes. Brush picked up a sheet of paper off the table, wadded it up, and fired it across the room at Johnny's head.

"Hey, techno-wizard! We asked you a question."

Johnny jerked to one side as the flying ball of paper narrowly missed his ear. "You know - the money Eric and Victor got from the auction," Johnny responded. "Actually, it was probably more like a million and a half."

The atmosphere in the room went from playful to heavy at the mention of the men who had kidnapped and sold Jesse's nine-year-old daughter. Joy had been rescued, but the proceeds of the sale had not been recovered

"Yeah," said Brush with a dark look that flashed back to his days as an outlaw biker. "I'd like to get my hands on the lowlifes who bought her. They should be in the pen with the other two scumbags instead of out there somewhere shopping for more kids."

"Yeah," agreed Johnny. "But it would be nice to get our hands on that money."

"Especially if Brush wants to go furniture shopping," said Jesse trying to lighten the mood.

He rescued the crumpled notes as the bell on the shop door jingled, and the sound of male laughter drifted up the stairs accompanied by heavy footsteps. Jesse took a deep breath to clear his head of the memories that haunted his little family and looked at his business partners.

"An interesting discussion for another time," he said and added with a grin. "Right now it's time to see if we can teach these reprobates something about God's Word." Then he turned and shouted down the stairs, "Come on up, guys. Coffee's on."

"Daddy! 'Scuse me, 'scuse me!"

Jesse almost dropped the cup of coffee he had just poured when he heard the urgency in Joy's voice. He set it down and turned toward the stairs in time to see her push her way between the two men on the top step.

"Daddy!" she gasped. "Mommy said to call Dr. Patterson. Madison's sick!"

"Hold on, kiddo," said Jesse, relieved to see that his daughter was okay. "Catch your breath and slow down. Who's Madison, and what's wrong?"

While Joy took a couple of deep breaths, Brush spoke up. "Madison. Isn't that the one who lives with Misty? The one who called Tatia and tipped her off?"

"You're right. I remember the name now," replied Jesse. "Okay, Joy. Tell me what's going on."

"When I was with her I saw marks on her arm and I told her

Mommy could help her and I guess that's why she came. But she's sick. She fainted and when Mommy gave her some water she threw it up. She and Grandma are putting her to bed, but she's shaking real bad."

"Sounds like withdrawal to me," said one of the men who had just come into the room. Jesse looked at him with a question in his eyes. The man shrugged. "Been there."

"And lived to tell about it," said Jesse with a smile. He pulled his phone out of his pocket and began scrolling through his contacts while he gave instructions. "Brush, lead the guys in praises and prayer requests. My notes are right there, so you can get started on the study. I'll go see what's going on and get back as soon as I can." He hit a number on his phone and grabbed Joy's hand. "Come on, Joy. Let's go see how the ladies are getting along."

Halfway down the stairs, Jesse's call was answered. "Mrs. Patterson, this is Jesse Matthews at Fallen Angel Salvage. I'm sorry to disrupt your Sunday afternoon, but we've got what appears to be a young lady in withdrawal over here...thank you."

Grandpa G was sitting in the glider on the front porch with Daniel in his lap. The boy's face was hidden against his grandfather's chest, and Grandpa was patting his back reassuringly. "See," he said, pushing Daniel away a few inches. "Daddy's here, and the doctor will be here soon. Grandma and Mommy have done this before, and Madison will be fine. It's just going to take a few days."

Daniel turned his face toward Jesse and smiled tearfully around the thumb in his mouth. Jesse ruffled his hair and said, "Hey, buddy. It's going to be...yes, Dr. Patterson. We have a young lady apparently in withdrawal...Just a minute. I'm just coming into the house."

He made it into the bedroom in a few long strides. "Do we know what she's on?" he asked Tatia, putting the phone on speaker so the doctor could hear her.

"She's not real coherent, but from what I can piece together, she's on a variety of intravenous benzos. She hasn't had anything today, so it's probably been around fifteen hours. She's very thin and may be dehydrated – and she has a number of fresh bruises and an open wound on her forearm."

"Okay," responded the doctor. "I'll run by the clinic and gather equipment for an IV. I'm assuming you don't want an ambulance."

"That's correct," responded Tatia. "We want to keep her here if possible. We can make her feel safe here."

"For now, make her as comfortable as you can. I'll be there in fifteen minutes – twenty tops."

3

Sunday - 9/24

Victor Ellis was in a familiar setting – behind bars in a local lock-up somewhere in Chicago. He had spent years in and out of Texas prisons for multiple crimes including fraud and financial crimes, obscene or offensive content, drug trafficking, and solicitation of prostitution, but this was his first experience with the Illinois criminal justice system. He wasn't sure about the differences between the states, but he knew that the ink stains on his fingers from the arrest procedure and the view from inside the cell were the same.

He also wasn't sure how long he'd been there - there were no windows, so he couldn't tell if it was daylight or dark - but he was lying on a steel bench welded to the wall of the holding cell where he had been since his arrest. He was tired of lying on the cold, hard surface, but he knew if he got up, he'd lose it to one of the other men who had been added to the cell since his arrival. Cold or not, it was better than standing or sitting on the filthy floor. He kept his eyes closed, hoping the others would think he was asleep and leave him alone, but it didn't work. Suddenly he felt huge hands pick him up and drop him unceremoniously on the floor he had tried to avoid.

"You're on my bench," growled a man who looked a lot like the guy who grabbed him in the hotel room – the one he heard them call Brush.

Victor was a genius when it came to all things computer related, but sometimes he wasn't very smart when it came to real world situations. However, he was smart enough not to argue with a man who towered over his own 5'11" frame and had at least fifty pounds on him. And unlike his own unmarked features, the face of his tormentor was battered and scarred by more than a few barroom brawls. Deciding on discretion rather than valor in this situation, Victor slunk over to a corner by the bars where there was at least a little bit of air moving. He made himself as small as possible, hoping no one would claim his new space.

After repeatedly reviewing the last couple of days in his mind, Victor still could not figure out what had gone wrong. Even if the mother of the girl had recognized Eric in the van, she couldn't have known where they were taking her. They covered their tracks everywhere they went, and he was confident enough in his skills that he knew nobody could have tracked the online auction site back to him. And how did the cops find him – not just the right hotel, but the right room? And where was Eric? He left the room with the girl a few minutes before the cops showed up. If they caught him, too, where was he? What if he had set Victor up and then ditched him? At least he didn't know how to access the money. If Victor was going down alone, he'd go down rich.

From his position by the bars, Victor could see the door that opened onto the hallway in front of the holding cells. He glanced up when he heard the buzz of the electronic lock and the squawk of hinges that probably hadn't been oiled in years. To his surprise, Eric Hall walked through the door, escorted by one of Chicago's finest. He was even more surprised by Eric's appearance. He had two black eyes that stood out against the contrast of the white bandage that covered his face from the bridge of his nose to its tip and extended out onto his cheeks. In addition, his right hand was swathed in gauze.

Eric felt Victor's eyes on him and looked up. He glared at the man behind the bars as if this was somehow his fault. Victor was so glad to see a familiar face that he didn't seem to notice Eric's mood. By the time the cuffs were removed and the prisoner was shoved into the cell, Victor was almost vibrating with the tension of holding in his questions. As soon as Eric was close enough, words came tumbling out.

"Wow! What happened? Did the cops do that to you? Did you get..." His voice trailed off as he finally caught the warning look in Eric's eyes and became aware of the silence that had fallen in the cell.

"Shut up, you idiot!" hissed Eric under his breath. "The cops have ears everywhere, and we don't need you confessing before we're even formally charged." Besides, he wasn't about to tell Victor how he had been bested by a nine-year-old girl and her motorcycle-riding mom and dad.

Eric didn't speak again for a long while. He leaned against the wall with a disdainful look on his face, glaring around the cell and daring anyone to make a comment about his face. Victor finally tired of trying to look cool, so he slid down the wall onto the dirty floor, trying to land gently without catching himself with his hands. He crossed his arms on top of his knees and rested his head against his forearms hoping to catch a few winks. He had just drifted off when Eric nudged him with his foot.

"Hey, get up. We need to talk."

Victor heaved a sigh and rolled his eyes. "We couldn't have talked five minutes ago when I was still standing up?"

Eric scowled at him, and he shrugged and struggled to his feet, losing the battle to rise without putting his hands down. He gasped for breath from the exertion and made a mental note to work out more when he got the chance. When Eric didn't speak immediately, he said, "Okay. So, talk."

"Just keep your voice down. We don't want to share our business until we're ready." He looked around to be sure no one was eavesdropping before he continued. "You didn't say anything to the cops, did you?"

"Nothing except that I wanted a lawyer."

"Ok. That's good. Now, we don't want to settle for a public defender since we've got the cash to pay for better. You've been here a few months longer than I have. Do you have any idea who's the best criminal defense attorney in the area?"

"No. I didn't look into that since I wasn't planning to get caught. How did they find us so fast anyway?"

"I guess you're not as slick on that computer as advertised. Just keep your ears open in case somebody drops an attorney's name."

"This guy can help." At first Eric wasn't sure what the low, raspy voice had said or where it came from. Then he saw something drift to the floor as the man who was standing next to him pushed himself away from the wall and shuffled to the other side of the cell. Eric elbowed Victor and pointed to the small white rectangle between them.

"What?"

"Pick it up, you idiot!"

Victor didn't like being pushed around, but he was also familiar with Eric's temper and didn't want to attract any unwanted attention from either their cellmates or the guards. He leaned over, picked it up, and handed it to Eric.

"Grayson Vandoren, Attorney-at-Law, and a phone number," he read quietly.

"Where'd that come from," asked Victor who had been scanning the room in search of someone who might recommend a lawyer.

"That guy over by the sink must have overheard us. He mumbled something like 'he can help' and dropped the card."

"Why would he do that?"

"There's some numbers on the back of the card. Maybe he gets a kickback for recommendations."

"Is that legal?"

"Probably not, but if he's good, who cares? Sounds like our kind of man anyway. You know, not too worried about the rules."

4

Sunday - 9/24

Daniel looked into the older man's face with a serious expression that put a small crease between his eyebrows. "Grandpa," he asked, "what's with doll mean?"

"Withdrawal? That means that she has been taking some shots that are not good for her."

"Like drugs?"

"Yes, like drugs. And when she stopped taking them, it made her sick. Now the doctor is going to help get the bad drugs out of her body so she can get better."

"Would God help if I prayed for her?"

"Of course, He would, Daniel. I think that's a great idea."

When Dr. Patterson pulled into the driveway a few minutes later, he hated to disturb the scene on the porch of grandfather and grandson praying together in the swing, but they both looked up when they heard his wheels crunch on the gravel. "Sorry to break up your prayer meeting," he called as he climbed out of the driver's seat and headed toward the back of his old white SUV.

"That's okay," replied Daniel wiggling away from Grandpa and running toward Dr. Patterson. "We prayed that you'd be real smart and know what to do for Madison. That's my Grandpa," he said, pointing back toward Mr. G who was following him down the walk.

The doctor smiled down at Daniel. "Thank you. I can use all the prayer – and smarts – I can get. Hi, Grandpa." He looked up and extended his hand.

"Alexander Grochowsky."

"Bill Patterson."

"Can I carry your bag?" Daniel was standing on tiptoe, peering into the open cargo space.

"You sure can. I'll need some help carrying all this equipment I brought."

He handed Daniel an old-fashioned double-handled leather satchel that had seen better days. The boy struggled under the weight and began inching his way up the walkway, barely keeping the bag from dragging.

"Careful with that, Daniel," called Grandpa. "Let me know if you need help."

"I can do it," panted Daniel as he took another step.

"I'd hate for him to damage your bag. It looks like it's been around a while."

"Yeah," said Dr. Patterson, smiling after Daniel. "I'm the third Dr. Patterson to carry it. But seeing the triumph on his face when he gets it to the door is worth any scuffs it suffers. Besides, I only carry it because I'm too cheap to buy a new one."

The doctor turned back to the IV stand that was collapsed into what looked like a shipping carton stand continued, "If you'd like to help, too, you can grab that box of IV solutions while I make sure I have all the parts to this thing."

"Sure," said Grandpa as he hoisted the box onto his shoulder. "What's the treatment plan?"

"I'll start with a mild saline drip to help flush the garbage out of her system. I'll probably add a banana bag as well."

"Banana bag? What's that?" asked Daniel, who was sitting on the top step catching his breath. "Does it have bananas in it?

"No," laughed Dr. Patterson. "It's called that because it's in a yellow bag. It has vitamins and minerals that will make her feel better if she's been drinking alcohol along with her drugs. Of course, I'll know more after I examine her."

"I don't know about the alcohol," said Grandpa, "but she can probably use the vitamins. From what I saw, she's very thin and pale." He stepped around Daniel and opened the door, and the little medical parade continued into the makeshift detox center of the Matthews' home.

Daniel dragged the bag just inside the door of the bedroom where he dropped it and struck a pose with his fists on his hips. "I did it!" he crowed.

"Yes, you did," said Dr. Patterson. "And I appreciate it very much. Now, why don't you and your grandpa go find some refreshments while these ladies bring me up to speed. Then you can all take a break in the kitchen while I examine our patient."

Daniel grabbed Alexander's hand. "C'mon, Grandpa. I'll show you where the good snacks are!"

The doctor took in the scene with a practiced eye as he assembled the stand and prepared the IVs. "Even if I didn't know you'd done this before, I could tell by the way you've set things up. I couldn't have done better myself. Now, tell me what's going on."

Tatia looked at Joy who was sitting on the edge of the bed, wiping Madison's forehead with a damp cloth. "Since you answered the door, why don't you begin."

"I opened the door, and there she was. She looked kind of sleepy or something, and then she fell down. We tried to give her some water, but she threw it up. Not very much – just kind of foamy like after the cat throws up a hair ball."

Dr. Patterson busied himself with hanging the saline bag for a moment while he swallowed the laugh that threatened to disrupt Joy's serious account. "Tell me a little bit about when you first met Madison."

"It was when Eric and Victor stole me. They took me to Misty's house so they could make a movie to use to sell me. Madison lived with Misty."

"Did she look sleepy then?"

Joy thought for a minute. "I guess so – at first anyway. But when she took me to her little salon and fixed my hair, she was more awake and happy. That's where I saw the marks on her arm and told her that Mommy could help her."

Dr. Patterson looked up at Tatia, and she responded to his un-spoken question. "Yes, she has tracks inside both elbows and some on her upper thighs. She was lucid enough for a few minutes to tell me it was Benzos – mostly Valium, but whatever was available."

"Did she use alcohol as well?" he asked.

"I don't know. Joy, do you have any idea?"

"Well, when we went to the kitchen to get me something to eat, she had a glass of wine while I ate."

Dr. Patterson nodded. "I'll assume so. It won't hurt to give her some extra vitamins. Alexander said she's quite thin."

"Yes, she is," replied Tatia. "I think I could dress her in Joy's pajamas except for the length."

"I may have a couple of hospital gowns in my truck. They'll be easier to get on and off for the first few days." Tatia looked surprised, and he shrugged with a sheepish grin. "What can I say? Once a Boy Scout, always prepared. Now, Joy, if you'll switch places with me, I'll examine our patient and get the IV started."

Dr. Patterson gently took Madison's vitals. "Her blood pressure and heart rate are a little high, but that's to be expected. The levels aren't dangerous, but I'll want you to monitor them for a few days. You have a monitor, don't you?"

"Yes," responded Tatia. "We've done this before, but it's been a while. I'll want you to leave me with instructions about what to watch for."

"Sure, and I'll stop by every day for a while, just to see how she's doing. I'm ready to start the IV, so anyone who doesn't like needles might want to step out of the room."

"It's a little crowded in here anyway," said Jesse. "Come on, Joy. Let's go see what Daniel and Grandpa have gotten into, and then I'll get back to the Bible study."

Tatia gave him a grateful smile. "Thanks," she whispered.

Dr. Patterson rolled up Madison's sleeve carefully, and let out a tuneless whistle. "Wow! That's quite an ugly wound. Wonder how that happened."

"I did it," Madison whispered.

The doctor was surprised but pleased to see her eyes open and fairly clear. "Tell me about it – if you can," he asked gently.

"Microchip. Didn't want them to find me," she said with an effort. She looked at Tatia and added, "Or you, so I scratched it out."

"Oh, Madison!" exclaimed Tatia. "Thank you!"

Madison smiled weakly. "Least I could do."

"Okay," interrupted Dr. Patterson. "Let's save your strength, because after I tend to this, I'm going to need you to scoot over to the other side of the bed so I can put the IV into the other arm."

"What IV?" asked Madison.

"It's called a banana bag…"

"Because of the color," shouted Daniel from the other room.

"Sorry," said Tatia. "The walls in this old place are a little thin."

Dr. Patterson laughed. "But he's right. It's mainly to give you fluids until you can keep down enough to keep you from being dehydrated. It also has some vitamins and minerals that the drugs might have leeched from your system."

"No drugs?"

"No. I can give you something to ease the withdrawal if you need it."

"I'd rather do without if I can."

"Good girl. You have a great support system here."

"I don't know why," she whispered, wiping away a tear.

5

Monday - 9/25

At 10:00 a.m. Detectives Martin and Nelson once again sat in front of Captain Carter's desk looking refreshed and a bit amazed that Carter had not called them in over the weekend. The captain showed evidence of having been home to shower, shave and put on fresh clothes, but the circles under his eyes held no evidence of much sleep.

"Looks like you might have put in a couple of long days," said Nelson.

"You know this precinct," Carter responded. "Weekends are busy."

"Thanks for giving us the time off," said Nelson.

Carter waved his thanks aside, as he took a gulp from the ever-present insulated coffee mug on his desk and flipped open the file in front of him.

"Good news this morning," he continued without looking up. "All your reports have been reviewed, and everybody seems to agree with your conclusions. The prosecutor has approved charges against Hall and Ellis for aggravated kidnapping and abduction as a class X felony because of the victim's age. Also for sex trafficking which will be bumped up to an X because of the kidnapping. Each of those charges could carry a penalty of 6 to 30 years and up to $25,000, plus the trafficking could require restitution of all income from the victim's services - which in this case would be what they sold her for. They're also going for aggravated assault and battery rather than simple assault because of her age, because of the way Victor grabbed her in the initial snatch, and because Eric dragged her out of the car at the ball park. Also going for a weapons angle because of the knock-out drug they used on her. This would probably only add another three years and another $25,000 for Ellis, but a prior conviction for battery can add another 60 years. I think Hall's conviction for beating a woman to death in Texas might qualify."

Carter looked up from his desk in time to see Martin and Nelson exchanging grins and a triumphant fist bump. "I take it you're both in agreement."

"Yeah, boss," replied Nelson. "We'll get over to the jail and go through the formal booking procedure. What about a bond hearing?"

Carter flipped open the next file in his pile. "The pre-trial guy reviewed your reports and responded without requiring an interview. Because of their lack of ties in Chicago, lack of employment, and criminal histories, he considers both of them a flight risk. And the fact that Hall has violated parole makes him an even greater risk. The allegation that they probably have the money to go wherever they want adds to the mix, so he's recommended against bail. I'll let you know when we get the hearing scheduled."

"What about extradition? Will Texas fight us for Hall on his parole violation?" asked Martin.

"I wouldn't worry about that. With several felony charges against him here, no judge is going to release him to another state until after the trial – and I doubt Texas would push it anyway."

Detective Nelson was pushing up out of his chair when Carter continued. "Hey, I know you already mirandized at the scene, but do it again. And be sure they get their phone call. We don't want to lose this one on a technicality."

"You got it, boss."

"Oh, and good work."

"Thanks!"

"Hey," said Nelson to his partner as they walked down the hall. "Let's stop in the break room and see if there's anything in there to eat."

Martin shook her head and laughed. "The way you eat I don't understand why you don't weigh 300 pounds!"

Nelson laughed and patted his protruding belly. "I'm a blessed man!"

6

Monday - 9/25

Eric paced the cell until the man who had taken Victor's bench threatened to mess up the rest of his face if he didn't settle down. He continued to harass the guards, though, asking them every time they came within earshot when he'd get his phone call. The answer was always the same.

"As soon as you're formally charged. Now shut up!"

"I don't know why you're so anxious to make that phone call," whispered Victor. "If they don't charge us within seventy-two hours, they have to release us." He lowered his voice even further. "And I don't know about you, but if that happens, I'm outta here!"

"Neither of us is going anywhere if you don't keep your mouth shut!" snarled Eric.

Victor glared at Eric but kept quiet until a buzzer sounded and the door screeched open to admit three guards. All three stood back several feet from the bars, and the apparent spokesman called out in a no-nonsense voice, "All right, gentlemen! Everybody against the back wall. You, too, sleeping beauty," he called to the man who still maintained possession of the only bench. He must have known from past experience that protesting would be pointless because he grumbled as he rose slowly and joined his fellow inmates.

"Eric Hall, step forward, face the back of the cell, and put both hands through the bars."

Eric stepped forward and one of the guards stepped toward the cell door. Instead of turning around, Eric pointed to his bandaged hand.

Unimpressed, the guard responded, "Special needs, huh? I can use leg restraints if you'd rather." When Eric didn't respond, the guard continued. "That's what I thought. Now turn around."

Once he was cuffed and escorted out, the rest of the prisoners began to shuffle around.

"Hold it, ladies," shouted the spokesman. "I didn't tell you to move. Victor Ellis, step forward, face the back of the cell, and extend your hands through the bars."

Victor's hands were cuffed behind his back, and he followed Eric out of the cell block. After a few turns, he entered a hallway with a series of doors on one side. He saw the guard who took Eric coming out of one door, and he was escorted to the door next to it. Inside was a metal table and two metal chairs, all bolted to the floor. His right hand was uncuffed, and his left hand was cuffed to a bar in the middle of the table top. He was shoved into one of the chairs and left alone. He had been through this enough that he knew he'd be here a while, so he laid his head on his free arm and drifted off to sleep.

Victor woke with a start some time later when the door was slammed open and a man and woman burst in. He recognized them as the detectives at the hotel, the ones who took charge after Brush almost crushed his ribs. He wiped the drool from the corner of his mouth with his free hand and said, "I want a lawyer."

"Yeah, yeah," said Nelson with a grin. "We'll get to that. But first, I need to read you a little story." He pulled a card out of his pocket and began to read Victor his rights. "Do you understand these rights as I've just read them to you?"

"Yeah, now when do I get to see my lawyer?"

"After a little more business. Detective Martin is going to explain to you why you are now a guest in this lovely facility in the State of Illinois and to formally charge you with those crimes."

Victor's eyes widened at some of the charges and the possible penalties, but he remembered Eric's orders and kept his mouth shut. When asked if he had any questions about anything he had heard, he simply repeated that he wanted to speak to a lawyer.

"Eric has his name and number. I want the same one he has," he added.

Victor dozed off again, this time with his head lolling over the back of his chair and his mouth hanging open. The door crashed open again as Nelson and Martin stormed into the room, but this time Victor didn't stir.

"Hey, sleeping beauty!" bellowed Nelson as he pounded on the metal table. "That lawyer you've been squawking about wants to see you with your partner in crime."

Victor opened his eyes slowly and covered a yawn with his free hand. "You mean my alleged partner in crime?"

"See there," said Nelson, spreading his hands. "You don't need a lawyer. You already know the lingo. Now, put your right hand behind your back so I can hook you back up."

With his hands cuffed behind his back, Victor was led to a different section of the building and into a room that was larger but furnished by the same designer. The larger table was set up to accommodate two cuffed prisoners, one at each end, and two free people in the middle on either side. Eric was attached to the bar at one end with a characteristic scowl on his face. The only other occupant of the room was an armed officer who was leaning against the wall opposite the door.

"Where's the lawyer," asked Victor as Nelson pushed him to the chair across from Eric.

"On his way," replied Eric. "Now shut up until he gets here," he warned.

Nelson secured Victor to the table, and he and Martin headed for the door. With his hand on the doorknob, he grinned and turned back. "I'll see you two in court tomorrow. Enjoy your evening." He tipped an imaginary hat and followed Martin out of the room.

Victor wanted to talk, but he resisted the urge when Eric glanced at the guard against the wall and turned a threatening glare on Victor. There were no windows in this room either to provide a view or a clue to the passage of time, so Victor didn't know how long they sat in silence before the door opened again and a thin, studious looking man entered. Eric looked disgusted as the newcomer pushed his thick black-rimmed glasses up on his nose with his index finger. But Eric's eyes widened in surprise when the man spoke.

"Grayson Vandoren, Attorney-at-law here," he thundered in a voice that affected his listeners like a roar coming from the mouth of a kitten. He surveyed the room until his eyes settled on Eric. "You must be Mr. Hall and," shifting his gaze to the other end of the table, "that would make you Mr. Ellis. I'm pleased to meet you both." He pushed his glasses up again and peered at the name badge on the guard's chest. "And you, Officer Franklin, may wait in the hall while I consult with my clients."

After the officer left, Vandoren perched on the chair facing the door and opened his briefcase which contained a small laptop, a leather folder containing a yellow legal pad, and a gold Mont Blanc pen engraved with his initials. Once his mobile office was set up to his satisfaction, he folded his hands on the table in front of him. He smiled at each man in turn, or at least his mouth turned up at the corners.

"First, let's talk about my fee," he announced. "My billing rate is $350 per hour plus expenses. Of course, assistants and administrative personnel are billed at a lower rate. I require a $25,000 retainer to begin, and when billables reach that amount, I will require another $25,000. And, of course, since I will be dealing with your cases separately, I will require that amount from each of you. Do either of you have questions so far?"

Both prisoners were sitting with their eyes wide and their mouths open, but Victor found his tongue first. "Are you crazy?! My lawyers before charged maybe $5K total."

"Shut up, Victor! I'll handle this," said Eric. He didn't notice the anger that flashed in Victor's eyes as he focused his full attention on the attorney. "That is a lot of money, Mr. Vandoren. What do you plan to do for us that merits that kind of fee – and why a separate fee for each of us?"

"That's a good question, Mr. Hall, and one you have every right to ask. First, I plan to see that you both are cleared of all charges."

"I like the sound of that," said Victor under his breath. Eric shot him a vicious look and he looked down at the table.

"Go on," said Eric.

"I have reviewed the arrest reports, and our best chance of acquittal lies in requesting separate trials. Separate trials will require double the work and thus double the fees. Based on your previous records and the nature of the charges against you, I will most likely be unable to secure bond for you, but I will use my influence to see that the time you spend behind bars will be in a special housing unit on administrative detention status for your safety rather than in general population – and as long as you have the funds, I can see that you are very comfortable during your incarceration. In addition, I plan to help you recoup that expense by filing suit for each of you for the brutality you suffered at the time of your arrests."

Eric, who had been following Vandoren's monologue with

interest, looked at Victor in surprise. He shrugged. "Yeah, I think I got knee-shaped bruises from where that big goon knelt on me."

"I am sorry for your trauma, but it would be a good thing if his attack left marks. I'll request a doctor's examination to determine the extent of the damage you suffered, and I will want to take pictures of both of you displaying your injuries before we finish here. But first things first," he said, focusing on Victor. "In our phone call Mr. Hall said you need access to the Internet in order to wire transfer funds into my account?"

"That's right. I'm the tech savvy half of this operation."

Within thirty minutes, their initial business was completed and Vandoren summoned the guard. "Officer Franklin, we are finished for the moment. I trust your superiors have informed you that my clients are not to be returned to the general holding cell but are to be placed in private accommodations until their hearing tomorrow."

"Yeah, I got the message," sneered Franklin. "Special treatment for your special clients."

7

Tuesday - 9/26

"The chip led to a dumpster at a cab company northwest of the city. Every cab is cleaned out and sanitized between shifts by a crew that probably wouldn't pass immigration scrutiny. We got a lot of blank looks, and nobody had any idea what trash came from which cab. We showed Madison's picture to every cleaner and every cabbie, and nobody recognized her. I left a copy of the picture and my phone number if anyone had any information."

"Get out!" growled the man sitting behind a huge slab of beveled glass supported on one end by a titanium pedestal and suspended on the other end by a titanium chain. He was oblivious of the luxury that surrounded him in his penthouse office, of the view of Lake Michigan behind him, and of the bank of TV screens on the wall in front of him. Instead he glared at his second in command who sat across the desk from him. "Where do you find these idiots? Not only does he fail to find one young, inexperienced woman, but he also leaves his phone number!"

"I'll take care of it, Mr. S," Ian replied with a calm that belied the knot in his stomach.

"While you're at it, check this out," said Mr. S, throwing a newspaper across the desk. He had circled a small article about a child who had been rescued from kidnappers a couple of days before. "See if that's our kid. I want her or I want my money back – or both."

"Yes, sir!"

Mr. S stopped him as he stood to leave. "And, Ian, I want to talk with Misty to find out what part she played in this debacle."

8

Tuesday - 9/26

Tatia had finished cleaning the kitchen and was washing salad greens for lunch when Jesse came in the back door. She looked up with a surprised smile and quipped, "Did you miss me already?"

He strode into the kitchen and slid his arms around her waist while she dried her hands on a dish towel. "Of course I did," he said as he nuzzled her neck. "Where are the kids?"

"You really did miss me, didn't you," she said playfully. She turned around and slid her arms around his neck. "Fran was taking Cade to the park, so I let them go as long as they collected nature specimens for science class. What did you have in mind, big boy?"

Jesse laughed and kissed her lightly. "As tempting as that is, we need to talk. I just got off the phone with Tracy, and we have a decision to make about the case."

Tatia instantly turned serious. "Okay. Do you have time for another cup of coffee while we talk?"

"Now that's a temptation I have time for." He leaned back against the counter while Tatia took a clean cup out of the cabinet and popped a fresh pod into the coffee maker.

"Tracy and Adam met with the prosecutor this morning," he continued. "The bond hearing is set for this afternoon. The D.A. will request the preliminary hearing be waived and that they go straight to trial. They think the judge will go along with it based on the arrest report and that he will also deny bail. The prosecutor wants to know if they would consider a deal to avoid having a long, drawn-out trial. Tracy asked what we thought about it."

"You mean the kind of deal where they plead guilty to a lesser charge and get off with a lighter sentence?" Tatia's tone of voice let Jesse know exactly what her first reaction was. He nodded.

"Let's take this to the swing out front," said Tatia handing him his coffee. "This may take a little while."

The couple sat in silence for a while, Jesse sipping his coffee and Tatia sipping from the bottle of water she had picked up on the way out, both lost in their own thoughts. Finally, Tatia spoke.

"What are your thoughts?" she asked, reaching over and taking his hand.

He squeezed her hand and sighed. "Some of my thoughts about what I'd like to do to those two are not fit to be spoken. And after I've run them through the filter of my faith, I'm still torn. I want them to get every penalty the law can possibly throw at them with more piled on top for good measure. But I don't want to put our children and Madison through what you had to go through during Eric's prosecution and trial in Texas. Tracy said the defense attorney might even want to depose Daniel because of his part in identifying the kidnap vehicle. How can we put them through that?"

"It's as if you put my thoughts into your words," Tatia she said, giving him a tender look. "But that's what old married people do, isn't it?" He returned her look and wiped a tear that had strayed down her cheek. After a few more moments of silence, Tatia continued. "I think we should pray about it, and when the kids get back, we should have a family meeting. We've raised them to think for themselves, and even at their ages, they have a right to some input."

"I agree," Jesse replied as he bowed his head and began to pray.

"Hey, you guys," yelled Daniel a few minutes later. "Are you having family 'votionals without us?"

"You guys?" Tatia grabbed her youngest and tickled him until he howled with laughter. "You definitely need to spend more time in Texas."

Joy and Jesse joined in the fun, and it was hard to tell who was on which side. Jesse finally tried to restore order. "Enough!" he called out above the noise. "We have serious family business to discuss." The children sensed the serious tone behind the smile in his voice and settled down quickly.

"What business?" asked Joy, the tension of the past few days obvious in her voice.

"It's okay, sweetie," reassured Tatia. "There are just some decisions we have to make. Why don't you go grab a bottle of water for you and Daniel, and then we'll tell you all about it." Anticipating Daniel's next objection, she headed it off. "This won't take long. After we're done we can all have a snack and you can show me what you collected on your walk."

When Joy returned, the children sat on the floor in front of the swing and listened attentively as Jesse explained the situation. Then, he asked if there were any questions, and Joy spoke up first.

"So, we might not have to answer any questions or testify, but that would mean that Eric and Victor wouldn't be in jail as long. Right?"

"That's right, Joy."

"Before I blew out my birthday candles, I made a wish and asked everybody to repeat it with me – that no little girl would ever have to be scared like I was again. If they get out sooner, they might kidnap and sell somebody else, so I want to testify so that doesn't happen."

Tatia and Jesse exchanged looks of pride in their daughter, and Jesse took a deep breath to gain control of the emotion in his voice. "Daniel, I know this is probably a little confusing to you, but would you like to tell a few other people what you told the policemen about the van the men were in when they took Joy?"

Daniel nodded solemnly. "I want to help make them be in jail a long time."

"What about Madison?" asked Joy. "She might have to testify, so we should ask her what she thinks."

"Good point, Joy. If she's awake and feels like talking, I'll ask her about it. But among the four of us here, are we all agreed?" asked Jesse.

"Yes!" shouted Joy. "No deals!"

After finishing her snack, Joy checked to see if Madison was awake and then took her a small glass of apple juice diluted with water. She hovered by the bed while Madison sipped the juice, just in case she needed help. "Mommy said to sip it real slow so it doesn't come right back up."

Madison smiled weakly. "I feel a lot better today, and this tastes really good. Thank you for taking such good care of me."

"You took good care of me before. Now it's my turn." Joy sat down on the edge of the bed and the two girls shared a comfortable silence that usually takes years to develop. But their friendship had been forged under the pressure of a common danger, and their bond was already strong. After a few more sips, Madison handed the glass to Joy. "I think I'm done for now, but if you'll leave it on the nightstand, I'll have a little more later."

"Okay. Daddy needs to talk with you for a minute. I'll go tell him you're awake if you feel up to it." She saw the look of fear on the older girl's face and hurried to reassure her. "Oh, it's nothing bad.

It's just that we have to make a family decision about the case and all that, and since you're part of it, you should have a say in what we decide."

Madison reached out and took Joy's hand. "You hardly know me, but you treat me like one of the family."

"If you start getting mushy, I'm gonna cry. I'll go get Daddy before we both start bawling."

Joy came back in with Jesse and returned to her place while Jesse sat on the vanity stool that still sat beside the bed. Joy and Madison held hands while Jesse explained briefly the choice that had to be made as well as a little about Tatia's history with Eric. When he was finished, he leaned forward and put his elbows on his knees so he could look Madison in the eye.

"I know this is a lot to take in after everything you've just been through, but I have to call Detective Martin back before noon with our decision. What are your thoughts?"

Madison took her time in answering, but her eyes never left his. "Going up against those people scares me, especially the way I feel now," she said. "but I spent my life in a virtual prison because of men like Eric and Victor, and it sounds like they stole Tatia's childhood. She had the courage to speak up and take him out of commission for twenty years. If I can do something like that to put him away for good, I'll do it no matter how scared I am."

9

Tuesday - 9/26

Eric and Victor had passed the night somewhat more comfortably than the previous one in the holding cell, but it wasn't the luxury they had expected when they watched the balance in their numbered Swiss account rise during the online auction for Joy. After their meeting with their new attorney, they were returned to a different area of the jail. They were put into a cell with no other inmates so they didn't have to fight for seating space. The two benches were covered with thin sleeping mats and thinner blankets providing a place to at least lie down if not sleep soundly, and solid walls reduced the noise a bit and provided a little privacy. The door was barred, but the lone guard was at the end of the hall, so Eric felt comfortable enough to allow Victor some of the conversation he had squelched earlier.

"Ya' know, Eric," Victor yawned, lounging back on the makeshift pillow he had fashioned from his rolled up blanket. "Even if we don't get bail, this might not be too bad. I mean, just look at us. We've already got a semi-private cell, and that burger and fries we had for lunch was sure better than the slop we got yesterday."

"I guess you've got a point. This is better than sitting on that filthy floor, but we paid a lot of money for that burger and fries."

"What do you mean? They took everything we had when they booked us. How did we pay for it?"

"How do you think Vandoren is going to see that 'we are very comfortable during our incarceration'?"

"I don't know. I guess I thought he just knew some people."

"Yeah, he knows some people. And those people will charge a high price for our comfort, Vandoren will add a service fee to that, and all of it will come out of that retainer fee – those two retainer fees we paid to Vandoren. We have no control over what he's charging or what we're paying, and he'll be back for more before we know it."

"It doesn't sound like a very good deal when you put it that way. I don't guess there's anything we can do about it, is there?"

"Nothing right now. If we get bail, like you said, we're outta here. But if we get held over for trial and transferred somewhere more permanent, we'll let him use his influence to get us into the segregated area. Once we're in, we'll put out some feelers and see who can get things done around there. We'll go direct and cut Vandoren out of the deal."

"Is that really a good idea? What if he gets mad and leaves us hanging before the trial?"

"Good point. We should probably let him take care of a few basics but take care of the real necessities of life on our own."

"Yeah, I guess we can afford to have him grease the wheels at first. We've got plenty of grease." Victor laughed at his own joke before continuing. "And based on what that doctor said after he took a look at us, we should be getting plenty more after we sue everybody."

"Yeah, he seems like our kind of doctor just like Vandoren is our kind of attorney."

###

In spite of Vandoren's posturing and bluster, his clients were held over for trial – and his subtle probing about a possible deal yielded nothing but a scornful response.

"You've got to be kidding!" said the DA. "These guys have records that would make Guinness envious, and they were caught in the act."

Left without a plausible response, Vandoren snapped his brief-case closed and exited the courtroom with as much dignity as possible. True to his promise, he reached out to his contacts to ensure that his clients would be transferred to the Chicago Metropolitan Correction Center by police car instead of on the prisoner bus, and in handcuffs rather than belly and ankle shackles. He also requested that they not be subjected to the normal body search before being made as comfortable as possible in the special housing unit. Noting the hours already spent by himself and his staff as well as the cash inducements already offered, he made a note to draw down additional retainer funds at his next client meeting.

###

"I wonder if we can sue that judge for prejudice?" Eric speculated out loud. "Vandoren put on a pretty good show with some good arguments, but it seemed to me that the judge had made up his mind before the hearing ever started."

"I don't know," responded Victor, "but he did a pretty good job of smoothing our move over here. That was the easiest intake I've ever been through. And these tan scrubs are a lot better than the orange ones I had to wear the last time I was inside."

"Yeah," sneered Eric. "You're a real fashion plate. All I know is that I'm starved. I hope Vandoren ordered dinner and that it gets here before lights out."

As if on cue, the sound of boots echoed down the hall and the guard appeared in front of their cell door. "Back against the wall, ladies," he barked. Another guard approached the door carrying two sandwiches in plastic wrap, two small bags of chips, and two juice boxes.

"What do you call that?" Eric complained.

"Dinner. Kitchen's closed. You're lucky to get this, and you've got ten minutes before I come back to collect the trash and turn out the lights." He started back toward his chair at the end of the hall.

"Hey," yelled Victor. "I need a real mattress instead of this sponge – and a pillow."

"You can talk to the warden about that at the orientation meeting for newbies tomorrow. And any special requests that aren't available in the commissary or on the approved list of prisoner purchases have to go through another channel. Now, eat up. You got eight minutes."

10

Wednesday - 9/27

Mr. S was once again sitting behind his massive desk, drinking a cup of coffee, and reading through the stack of newspapers that was placed precisely on the corner of his credenza each morning. He scanned headlines and used his speed reading skills to check out the articles that interested him. He sat up straighter in his chair as one of those articles grabbed his attention. He read it twice more and then circled it with the marker that had been set next to the papers. He hit the intercom button on his phone and spoke quietly.

"Adrian, is Ian in yet," he asked.

"Yes, Mr. S," replied a soft voice with a slight British accent. "He just went into his office about five minutes ago."

"Send him in, please."

"Right away, Mr. S. Shall I come in and make you a fresh cup of coffee?"

"No, I need to get up and stretch anyway. I'll get it."

He pressed a button on the control console on his desk and a wall panel slid back silently to reveal a drink bar that offered everything from bottled water to a bottle of French cognac that had cost him $20,000. There was a fancy espresso machine with all the bells and whistles, but he used it mainly to heat water to exactly 200° so he could pour it over the grounds in the simple French press that he preferred. He had just pressed the water through the freshly ground coffee when Ian knocked on the door.

"Come," he said as he poured the steaming brew into his cup.

"Good morning, Mr. S," said Ian.

"Good morning, Ian. Can I make you a cup of coffee?" asked his boss who was already walking toward his desk.

"No, thank you, sir." Ian walked to one of two chairs in front of the desk and waited until Mr. S was seated before he sat.

Mr. S sipped his hot coffee as he looked at Ian thoughtfully. Everything about him was medium except his brain. He was medium height and weight, medium coloring with nothing out-standing except that he topped out every IQ test he ever took, had a photographic memory, and had a total grasp of every aspect of Saint International. Without speaking, Mr. S turned the newspaper in front of him around so it was facing Ian and slid it across the desk toward him. Then he sat back in his chair and continued to enjoy his coffee.

Ian read the article quickly, and then looked up at his boss. "An interesting development," he said. "It certainly sounds as if this could be your traffickers. It's very convenient that bail was denied so we'll know exactly where they are. I'll do some research into the activities of Mr. Hall and Mr. Ellis, and I'll contact our man at MCC to check them out."

"My thoughts exactly, Ian," said Mr. S with a chilling smile. "If these are indeed the two who thought they could walk away with my money without consequences, I want them to realize their mis-take as soon as possible."

"Understood. Is there anything else you need me to do today?"

"No. Make this your number one priority, second only to finding Madison."

11

Wednesday - 9/27

Wednesday afternoon Dr. Patterson walked out of the Matthews' master bedroom shaking his head and smiling. "That young woman is amazing," he said. "I've never seen anyone detox as quickly as she has. She's still got a way to go, but I've removed her IV. Give her electrolyte drinks for a few days, adult or child version, whichever she prefers. How's she eating?"

"Not a lot, but she hasn't thrown up since Monday evening. She likes chicken broth and oatmeal, and she drinks some juice."

"Good. Try adding a few noodles to the broth and other soft foods as she can tolerate them. We need to fatten her up a bit. How's she sleeping?"

"Not very well the first night, but then Joy insisted on sleeping in the bed with her. I'm still on a cot in the room, and she wakes up crying once in a while. Then Joy rubs her back, sings to her, or quotes Scripture and she goes right back to sleep."

"Sounds much better than sleeping pills. Since she's doing so well, I won't plan to come tomorrow unless you need me. I'll be back Friday to check her out again."

Before Dr. Patterson made it to the door, Daniel ran over, grabbed him around the waist, and squeezed. "Thank you for helping Madison get well!" he mumbled against the older man's coat.

"You are so very welcome, Daniel," said the doctor as he knelt in front of the boy and ruffled his hair. "It's my honor to be a part of this wonderful ministry your family has here."

Daniel grinned. "Can I carry your bag to your car?"

"Of course you can. Anytime you want."

Tatia shut the door behind them and turned around to find Madison just outside the bedroom, leaning against the wall.

"Well, look who's out of bed," she said gently, trying not to scold. "I know it must be lonely in the bedroom by yourself. If you'd like to be out here with the family for a while, I'll bring some pillows and a blanket so you can lie on the sofa."

"No, I was really looking for my clothes. Now that I don't have an IV, I should really go."

"Noooo!" wailed Joy. "You can't go! You're not well yet."

"She's right," agreed Tatia. "You're doing great, but you have a way to go before you're ready to be on your own."

"But you've done so much already, and you don't even know me."

"I know that you saved my daughter, and I know that you need someone to care for you right now – and I can do that. Now come on over to the sofa while I get those pillows."

As Tatia arranged pillows behind her back and Joy tucked a blanket around her legs, Madison asked, "Why do you do it?"

"Do what?" replied Tatia with a smile.

"This. Take care of people."

"It's what God has called me to do – and there was a time when I needed help and someone was there for me."

"I'll bet you didn't need this kind of help."

"Not exactly, but I was in a really bad place. I'll tell you all about it some time. Right now you just relax, and I'll bring you some juice."

"I'll get it," exclaimed Joy, and before anyone could object, she ran for the kitchen.

"You have a great daughter," said Madison wistfully. "In fact, your whole family is wonderful."

"They are, aren't they," replied Tatia, watching her daughter put crushed ice into a glass.

"Well," continued Madison, "if I'm going to stay for a little while longer, at least let me sleep out here so you and Jesse can have your bed back."

Tatia looked at her thoughtfully. "I'll tell you what. That cot I'm sleeping on isn't too bad with an air mattress on it. We'll put you on it in Daniel's room with the kids tonight and see how that works out. Then, when Mama and Papa go home, you can move into Joy's room with her. We'll have to do something about the bed situation since she only has a double, but we'll work it out. How does that sound?"

"It sounds perfect!" said Joy as she handed Madison a glass of apple juice with a straw. "It will be like having a sleepover every night!"

"Except that you really have to sleep!" teased Tatia. "You can't stay up talking and giggling all night if Madison is going to keep getting better."

"We'll be good, won't we, Madison?"

The older girl couldn't suppress a small giggle. "We'll do our best."

Mama G walked in, fresh from the shower, smiling at the scene in front of her. "Isn't this a treat! Our girl is out of bed with no tubes in her arm. How are you feeling?"

"Better, I think. I'm totally overwhelmed by the kindness of all of you, and I don't know how I'll ever be able to repay you."

"Seeing a little color in your cheeks is payment enough, right ladies?" Mother and daughter nodded in agreement as Deborah continued, "Now, our patient looks tired. Let's go fold those clothes that I put in the dryer before my shower so she can have some peace and quiet."

"I am a little tired. Maybe I'll just close my eyes for a few minutes."

"I'll put the rest of your juice in the fridge for when you wake up," said Joy, and the women headed for the laundry room down the hallway toward the children's bedrooms.

"I heard the tail end of your conversation with Madison – the part about doing something about the bed situation in Joy's room. I think Alexander and I can take care of that."

"I had a feeling you'd say that," said Tatia, giving her mother a quick hug. "I can always count on you to bail me out."

Madison fell asleep almost immediately, and Joy settled down in Tatia's favorite overstuffed chair with a book she was reading for school. A report on birds in the Midwest was due in a few days, and she had several chapters to go. She and Daniel were home schooled, and she knew Tatia had cut her and Daniel a little slack this week, but she liked to keep on track.

Daniel came rushing in after seeing Dr. Patterson off and checking the mailbox, but Joy shushed him and pointed to Madison. He screeched to a halt and clapped his hands over his mouth. Tiptoeing dramatically, he went over to his school shelf and pulled out a puzzle. Soon he was settled on the rug between Joy and Madison assembling a picture of a cat that looked a lot like Harley.

A few minutes later, Tatia and Deborah came into the room with stacks of folded linens to be stowed in the kitchen and master bathroom. Tatia let out a soft sigh as she took in the scene: Madison on the sofa, Joy with her legs pulled up in the chair and her head on one of the rolled arms, Daniel lying across his half-finished puzzle with his head resting on his arms, and Harley lying in the middle of Daniel's back. All four were sound asleep. Deborah set her stack of clothes on the floor and slipped her phone out of her pocket. She snapped a picture and whispered to Tatia, "A sweet memory to take home with me."

"And a sweet memory to help me calm down when I want to wring their necks," replied Tatia. "Send me a copy, please."

"How old is Madison," asked Deborah while she put towels and wash cloths onto the proper shelves.

"I'm not sure. At first, she wasn't coherent enough to carry on much of a conversation, and I haven't thought to ask her since she's been more alert. When he was first examining her, Dr. Patterson guessed that she's in her late teens." Tatia chewed on her lower lip silently as she and her mother moved back to the laundry room for more folding. "Do you think she's too old – and maybe too sophisticated – to be in a room with the younger children?" she asked.

Deborah leaned against the dryer thoughtfully for a minute or two before answering. "I don't think so," she said. "From my interactions with her, I think she's close to Joy's age emotionally. And although she knows some of the external trappings like clothes, décor, and food, she's really been very sheltered. Misty rarely let her out of that apartment from what I gather."

"So you think it's okay for her to sleep in the room with them?"

"Yes, I think it's fine. In fact, I think it will be good for both girls." She laughed before she continued, "I'm not so sure how Daniel will feel, but it's only for a few days and then he'll have his room to himself again."

"Oh, I think he'll like it, at least at first. This way, he won't feel so left out."

"Perfect," said Deborah. She put her arm around Tatia's waist and continued, "Now, let's go put clean sheets on your bed and then have a nice quiet cup of tea before everyone wakes up and it's time to start dinner."

"I like the way you think!"

12

Wednesday - 9/27

Nap time ended when Jesse returned from the shop. Tatia and Deborah were still sitting at the table, planning the evening meal. Jesse leaned over and kissed Tatia on the back of the neck.

"What's for dinner, beautiful?"

"Spaghetti, salad, garlic bread, and ice cream."

"Ah, a meal fit for a king at the end of a long, hard day!"

Daniel wandered over sleepily and leaned again his dad's legs. Jesse scooped him up into a hug and added, "And a meal fit for a prince, huh, buddy?"

"Yeah," said Daniel. "Where's Bwush and Johnny?"

"They went home tonight since we already have a house full. Now, why don't we go wash up, and you can tell me about your day."

Madison joined the family for dinner for the first time that evening. The Matthews' dining table was a booth that had been left by the previous owners, and it seated six comfortably. However, the children were happy to scoot closer together on the bench against the wall to make room for their new friend. Madison said she didn't think she was up to eating spaghetti, but she did eat the few noodles Tatia cut up into her chicken broth. And she especially enjoyed the very small dip of ice cream Tatia gave her at the end of the meal. She didn't say much, and after carrying her dishes to the sink with Joy and Daniel, she returned to the sofa and wrapped herself in the blanket that was still lying there.

"Are you okay?" asked Joy.

"Sure. I still feel a little, I don't know, jumpy sometimes – and my head hurts a little – but I'm feeling so much better than I did yesterday. I just feel a little funny sitting around in a hospital gown and pajama bottoms."

"Oh, I wouldn't worry about that. We're very informal around here," said Joy in her best grown-up voice. "Aren't we, Mommy?" she added.

"Yes, we are," replied Tatia. "I washed your clothes and put them in Daniel's room. Tomorrow morning you can take a shower if you feel up to it and put on your jeans and t-shirt. That should make you feel more comfortable."

"That sounds good," said Madison. She sat quietly for a few minutes watching Joy and Daniel work on his puzzle. When Joy invited her to join them, she slipped onto the floor beside Daniel and picked up one of the pieces. "I've never put a puzzle together before."

"It's easy. That piece goes right here," said Daniel pointing to an empty spot at the tip of the cat's tail.

Madison placed the piece where he pointed and sat back, gazing around the room. "Do you have a TV?"

"Sure," responded Daniel. He pointed toward an antique armoire against the wall.

"It's inside the top part," explained Joy. "We don't watch it much, though. It's more fun to play games and talk to each other."

"What do you talk about?"

"Lots of things – what we learned in school, what Daddy did at work, what Mommy wrote about."

"And Daddy always reads to us from the Bible," added Daniel.

"Speaking of our family devotional time, maybe we should go ahead and do that now," said Tatia drying her hands on a dish towel. "Madison has had a big day and will probably want to go to bed early."

As if on cue, Madison yawned. "It seems like I just got up from a nap, but I'm getting pretty tired." She yawned again. "But I've never been in a family devotional time, and I'd like to."

"Come sit with us," said Daniel, patting the floor between him and Joy. "You can be part of our fambly 'votion time."

Bedtime was a little bit raucous, but before the giggling got out of hand, Joy took over. "Daniel, Madison has tired eyes, so it's time to turn out the lights and let her go to sleep."

"But I'm not sleepy!" he pouted.

"If you will be good, I'll use my little flashlight and read you a story."

"Will you come up here so I can hold the light?" Daniel had just graduated to the top bunk, but he sometimes felt isolated in his high perch.

Joy let out a very adult sigh. "Okay. Now, come pick out two stories – quiet ones!"

The adults were very quiet in the living room, listening to the bedtime goings on. There was shuffling as Daniel climbed down the ladder at the head of the bed, and some discussion about which stories were quiet, which definitely did not include an old, old favorite – *The Monster at the End of This Book*. A decision was reached and the ladder creaked indicating that Daniel had returned to his bed.

"Okay," said Joy. "I'm going to turn the light off now, so go ahead and turn on the flashlight so I can see to get to the bed."

"Don't forget to turn on the night light for when we finish the stories."

There was a little more discussion followed by the sounds of Joy ascending the ladder. After a little bit of negotiating for position, Joy began to read.

"That's quite the little mother you've got there," commented Deborah.

"Indeed," agreed Alexander.

Jesse added, "My little girl is growing up too fast."

Tatia dashed away a tear that had slipped down her cheek and jumped up. "How about some decaf and a game of Scrabble!"

The women beat the men soundly, but they managed to contain their celebration enough to avoid waking the children and their new friend. When Jesse did his final house check before following Tatia to bed, he quietly opened the door to Daniel's bedroom. Everyone was in the proper bed, and the only sound was of soft, rhythmic breathing.

Sometime in the night, Tatia thought she heard Madison cry out. She lay still for a couple of minutes, listening intently. Hearing nothing further, she snuggled against Jesse and fell back into a peaceful sleep.

13

Thursday - 9/28

The next morning, Tatia awoke a few minutes before her alarm went off and slipped quietly out of bed. She went into the bathroom where she splashed some warm water on her face and brushed her teeth. Pulling on her robe, she headed for the kitchen, but she stopped when she heard a soft whistle coming from the bed. She turned and smiled at her husband.

"Good morning, beautiful," he said as he sat up and stretched. "It was good to be back in our own bed last night."

"Yes," she agreed. "Separate cots in separate buildings is not what I signed on for."

Jesse rolled out of bed and reached for her. She moved into his embrace and kissed him softly. "Is this what you signed on for?" he asked, kissing her on the ear.

"Absolutely," she whispered, "but not with a houseful of people and more arriving shortly."

He kissed her once more and then allowed her to pull away from him. "Yeah," he sighed. "Reality is a real mood killer. Guess I'll go take a cold shower!"

Tatia laughed and blew him a kiss as she closed the bedroom door. Her first stop was the kitchen where she put food in Harley's bowl. She never knew exactly where the cat spent the night, but he was always at her feet, rubbing against her legs the moment she set foot in the kitchen. Next, she turned on the coffee maker and assembled coffee pods, mugs, creamer, and sweetener. Then she went down the hall to look in on the children. She almost ran into Deborah who was coming out of the bathroom.

"Good morning, Mama," she whispered, offering a hug. "How did you sleep?"

"Very well," said Deborah. "How about you?"

"Me, too. It was good to be back in my own bed with my usual bed partner. I thought I heard Madison cry out once during the night, but then it got quiet." She opened the door as quietly as she could and motioned for her mother to come look.

Madison's cot that had been against the wall was now pushed up against the side of the bottom bunk. Both girls were sleeping on their backs, and they were holding hands. Deborah patted Tatia on the back and said, "It looks like your little mother helped Madison through another rough night."

Brush, the third partner in Fallen Angel Salvage and one of Tatia and Jesse's best friends, pulled into the driveway at 6:30 a.m. on the dot. He used to arrived at 6:00, but since he and Shawna had married, he ate breakfast at home. Now the children slept a half hour later giving Tatia a little more time to herself in the mornings. She often wondered how he managed to be so punctual, given the amount of traffic in the growing Chicago suburb of Heart City. They had chosen the location for their home and business partly for its small town atmosphere but also for its growth potential. So far it had managed to live up to both expectations with new people and businesses moving in regularly without changing the warm community spirit. The increased traffic was one of the few negative side effects, but somehow Brush managed to negotiate his customized Shovelhead with the Screaming Eagle pipes through the morning backup with the timeliness of Old Faithful. And it was the sound of those pipes that made Daniel sit straight up in his bed with a big grin.

"Yay!" he said around a big yawn. "Bwush is here!" He swung his leg over the edge of the bed and shinnied down the ladder, dragging his blanket behind him.

"Is it time to get up?" asked a disoriented Madison. Joy was trying to climb over her cot without stepping on her legs and not doing a very good job of it.

"Sorry. It's hard to sleep late around here. You can go back to sleep if you want, but I have to go get my breakfast and get ready for school."

"No, I'll get up with you. I slept really well last night, especially after we moved the beds together. Thanks for doing that. It helps just knowing someone is there."

"I'm glad it made you feel better. It makes me feel good to be able to help you – you know, kind of like paying back a favor. Wait here. I'll be right back," she said, running out the door. She tapped gently on the door of her room. "Grandma? Grandpa? Are you awake?"

"Come on in. We're up." Alexander opened the door as Deborah pulled the comforter into place.

"Good morning. I'll give hugs later," said Joy, pulling a couple of items out of her closet and dashing out the door.

"Morning comes fast and furious around here," laughed Alexander. "Let's go see if the coffee's on."

Back in Daniel's room, Joy handed Madison a long terrycloth robe. "It's kinda chilly in the kitchen in the morning, so you can wear this. It will be shorter on you than it is on me, but it'll keep you warm - and I'll wear this long sweater. Now, let's go introduce you to Brush. He's amazing!"

Madison followed the children into the dining area but stopped in her tracks when she saw the huge man sitting at the table where she had sat the night before. Daniel ran to him and grabbed him around the waist.

"Good morning, Bwush!"

"Come on up, little buddy," said the man through the huge mustache that covered his upper lip and drooped down beside his mouth almost to his chin. He lifted the boy onto his lap, and Daniel immediately helped himself to the muffin on the plate in front of them. "That's Madison," he said around a mouthful, pointing toward the girl who was slowly coming into the room.

"Hi, Madison," said Brush with a shy grin. "I'd stand up to greet you properly, but something seems to be holding me down."

"Hi," whispered Madison. The uncertainty in her expression faded as she took in the scene in front of her. Deborah and Alexander were waiting for the coffee maker to spew out coffee before taking their seats, Tatia was putting a platter of fresh-cut fruit on the table, and Joy was leaning against Jesse who was sitting on the single bench at the end of the table.

"Daddy, can we get in, please," said Joy.

"It'll cost you a hug and a tickle," he said, sliding one arm around her waist and spider-walking the other hand up the side of her neck.

"Daddy, stop!" Joy screamed with laughter without trying too hard to get away. In one motion, he stood and lifted her onto the bench. She walked around until she was beside Brush. She gave him a hug before sitting down and patting the empty space beside her. "Come on, Madison, there's plenty of room for you to sit here."

"And Joy has already paid your toll, my lady," said Jesse, making a courtly bow.

Madison couldn't keep the smile from her face. "Thank you, kind sir," she replied quietly as she took her place at the table.

14

Thursday - 9/28

Madison was tired after a small breakfast of juice, three slices of banana, and a few bites of a muffin. Tatia encouraged her to lie down on the sofa while the rest of the family prepared for the day and scattered to their various tasks. Madison protested at first, not wanting to take up seating that might be needed by someone else, but Tatia reassured her.

"That won't be a problem this morning. I'll be going to my office for a couple of hours while Mama helps the children with their school work at the table. And I think Papa is going to spend some time in the shop with the guys. So the living room is all yours unless the children bother you with their noise."

"No," said Madison with a slight smile. "I've spent most of my life alone, and I like hearing people around me. When it's quiet, I get a little uneasy. Thinking too much I guess."

"Dr. Patterson said anxiety is normal at this stage of your recovery. Just remember that you're safe here. Now I'm going to get my shower and get dressed. If you need anything or get ready to take a shower, Deborah or Joy can show you where things are."

"Thank you," said Madison, snuggling into the blanket that was still on the sofa from the day before. "I don't know where I'd..." She stopped as the tears that had gathered in her eyes threatened to spill over.

"It is our privilege," said Tatia. She started toward the bedroom but stopped and turned back. "If you'd like to listen to some music, Joy knows how to operate the stereo." But Madison's eyes were closed, and she had already drifted off to sleep.

Later, Madison's eyes fluttered open when Harley decided to cuddle up with her. "Well, hello there," she said, stroking his fur while he purred and pushed his head into her hand.

Daniel looked up from the picture he was drawing and pumped his fist in the air. "Yay! Madison is awake! We can make noise now!"

Madison laughed and sat up. "How long have I been asleep?"

Deborah checked her watch. "A little over an hour. How are you feeling? Can I get you anything?"

"My head hurts a little bit, and I'm pretty thirsty."

"Can I get her some water, Grandma?" asked Joy.

"Yes, it's probably a good time for a break. And I'll get some ibuprofen for that headache."

"I don't really want to take anything..."

"Dr. Patterson recommended you take something for your pain before it gets bad. It's just an over-the-counter pain reliever, and it won't interfere with your recovery."

"Okay. Maybe just one," she said. She took a deep swallow from the bottle of water Joy handed her. Deborah came in with the pill, and Madison swallowed that with another gulp of water. "I think I'd like to take a shower and get dressed now if it's not too much trouble."

"I know where everything is, Grandma," said Joy.

"Okay. I'll take Daniel outside and let him get some of his wiggles out, and you can join us once you get her started."

"I'd rather stay in and read another chapter so I can be here in case Madison needs anything. Is that okay?"

"Of course," replied Deborah. "We'll just be in the back yard if you need us."

Madison's shower was accomplished without incident, and she came back into the living room looking tired but refreshed. Joy was sitting in Tatia's chair and looked up from her book. "You look nice," she said.

Madison touched her hair self-consciously. "Thanks for the brush and all the toiletries. Misty didn't give me time to pack make up or anything. She just pushed me out the door."

"You're welcome. Mommy keeps bags like that in the ministry building - she calls it the Annex because it's connected to the back of her office. Lots of the girls she helps come with nothing when they run away from their...well, you know. Anyway, you look beautiful without makeup."

"Do you really think so? I don't think I'm beautiful even with it. My face and nose are too long, and my hair is too straight."

"I think you're perfectly elegant," said Joy with a sigh. "You look like a princess." Madison let out a sardonic laugh as Joy continued. "What was your life like? That place looked kind of like a palace with the fancy furniture, the huge kitchen, and your own little salon. And those windows looking out over the city were amazing."

"It was a prison regardless of how fancy it was. I almost never left it. Even doctors came to us – and you saw the racks of clothes the stores brought in when Misty wanted to shop. I managed to get out the door and down the elevator once, but they stopped me in the lobby. That's when they put the chip in my arm."

"Didn't you go to school?"

"No. I was home schooled like you and Daniel, except Misty brought in tutors instead of teaching me herself. And she bought lots of books. She didn't read them, but she had to do something to fill the shelves in the library she insisted she needed in the apartment."

"Wow!" said Joy. "It must have been awesome to have a whole library in your house. Were you allowed to go in there?"

"Yes. I think I read every book in there at least once. She subscribed to lots of newspapers and magazines, too. Those were really my favorites, especially the fashion magazines."

"Is that where you learned to fix hair?"

"Yes, and Misty hired someone from one of the top beauty schools to come in and train me after she had the little salon put in next to her bedroom." Madison sighed and her eyes took on a faraway look. "I'd love to have my own salon one day. It would have a little boutique, too, featuring my own clothing designs."

"Would all the clothes be white?" asked Joy.

"What?" replied Madison, surprised by the interruption to her daydream.

"The only clothes I've ever seen you wear are white – except the hospital gown. I just thought maybe that was your favorite color."

Madison laughed. "I never had a choice in what I wore. If you remember, the apartment was all black and white. And since I was part of the furnishings, I had to match – thus, the black hair and white clothes. I don't remember wearing any other color."

"That's so sad!" cried Joy. She sat for a moment and then jumped up. "I have an idea! Come with me," she shouted, grabbing the older girl by the hand and dragging her toward her bedroom. She opened the closet door and pointed to a white box on a shelf above the hanging clothes. "Can you reach that box?"

"Sure," said Madison. "Here ya go."

Joy put the box on the bed and pulled out a deep blue sweater with a simple v-neck. "My friend gave this to me for my birthday, and it's way too big for me. Try it on. I'll wait in the hall. Tell me when you're dressed."

Joy stepped into the hallway and pulled the door closed behind her. She practiced the steps to her latest balance bar routine – minus the tumbles which weren't allowed in the house. She danced down the hall and back, and when she didn't hear anything from inside the room, she tapped gently on the door.

"Can I come in now?"

"Oh, sure," answered Madison. "Come on in." She was staring into the mirror over the dresser with a look of wonder on her face.

"Do you like it?" asked Joy.

"I don't know what to say. I look so different."

"You look beautiful. That color makes your eyes look amazing. You can have the sweater. Let's go show Mommy."

Madison glanced in the mirror one more time before she hurried to catch up. Joy was reaching for the front door when Deborah and Daniel came in the back door.

"Where are they going, Grandma?" asked Daniel. "I wanna go, too!"

Joy stopped so quickly that Madison almost ran into her. Joy grabbed her hand and spun her toward Deborah. "Doesn't she look beautiful in this color, Grandma? Can we go show Mommy real quick? Please!"

"Okay," replied Deborah with a smile. Madison grinned and shrugged as Joy grabbed her hand and dragged her out the door.

"It looks like break time isn't quite over, Daniel. Let's go watch the excitement."

"Yay!" he shouted and was out the front door before she could pull the back door closed. By the time she reached Tatia's office in the other building, Madison was standing shyly in front of Tatia, and Joy was dancing excitedly around the room.

"She's never worn any color but white, Mommy! She loves the sweater, and she looks beautiful in it so I said she could have it. Is that okay? Can we go look at some more clothes for her?"

"Yes, you look beautiful, Madison. And yes, you may help her pick out some more clothes. In fact, one of the women from the church just dropped off a couple of boxes from our clothes drive last week. We can make this a shopping spree and a school lesson all at once."

Daniel groaned and Joy rolled her eyes. "Everything's always a lesson around here," she said. "But usually a fun one," she added quickly, cutting her eyes over at her mother.

Tatia smiled. "Nice save," she said. "Now – assignments. Daniel, you and Grandma unfold a few chairs so we'll have a place to sit down. Joy, you choose a couple of outfits from the closet in – what?" she questioned, looking at Madison. "A size 6?"

"Yes. A 6 or a 4 if it's long enough."

"Good. Joy, bring a couple of each. And be prepared to explain to me why you made the choices you did."

"I don't have to write a report, do I?" Joy asked with a worried look on her face.

"No, you can make an oral report."

"I wanna help," shouted Daniel.

"When you finish with the chairs, you and Grandma can go through the boxes and sort the clothes by size. Lay them out on the table first, and set the 4's and 6's aside. You can start putting the others on hangers if you have time."

"Do they need to be washed first?" asked Deborah.

"No, the ladies at the church took care of that before bringing them over. Now, if there are no other questions, I have a grant application to finish."

With the pleasant sound of excited chatter and giggles as background noise, Tatia was able to complete the application quickly and was doing one last edit when Joy peeked in the door. "Mommy, do you have time to come look?"

"Of course." Tatia saved her work and followed Joy.

"You can come out now," shouted Joy.

Madison stepped hesitantly out of the bathroom and stopped, uncomfortable with all the attention focused on her.

"Remember what I told you," coached Joy. "Head up, shoulders back, three bold steps and strike a pose."

Madison took a deep breath, raised her chin, squared her shoulders, and strode into the room as if she owned it. She did a slow, graceful spin and struck a pose directly from one of her fashion magazines.

"Here we have the lovely Madison," said Joy, holding an imaginary microphone to her mouth. "She's wearing black slim-cut jeans and a scoop-necked tunic top that shows off her slim figure. The purple color brings out the unusual color of our model's eyes, and the green design on the side keeps it from being boring. To finish the outfit, she is wearing black ankle boots that are too small and hurt her feet but were too cute to pass up."

With that, both girls dissolved into laughter, and Madison covered her face in embarrassment. Their audience of three clapped wildly in appreciation until a deep male voice said, "What's going on here?"

Five pairs of startled eyes looked toward the door where Jesse was standing with a big grin on his face. "Whatever it is must be fun. I could hear you all the way over at the shop."

"We're having a fashion show, Daddy. Doesn't Madison look amazing?"

"Yes, she does. But she looks like she might be hungry since it's after noon."

Tatia gasped as she looked at her watch. "How did it get so late?" she cried. "I have sandwich fixings in the fridge. I'll throw something together..."

Jesse scooped her into a hug and silenced her with a quick kiss.

"Oh, gross!" shouted Daniel as Joy giggled.

"Don't worry about it. You've been a bit busy. How about if I order a couple of pizzas while you finish up here. And don't worry about snacks for the men's study tonight. Brush is bringing his air fryer and some frozen wings, and Johnny's picking up some of Tennille's awesome cookies."

"I knew there was a reason I keep you around other than your startling good looks." She hugged him once more and watched him walk out the door before she turned back to the others. "Okay, let's just leave this until later. We need to go turn the classroom back to the dining room, and Madison looks like she could use a little rest before the pizza arrives."

"I am a little tired, but I can't remember ever having so much fun. Except for the boots. They do hurt my feet!"

15

Friday - 9/29

"Grandma and Grandpa have been gone a long time," said Joy the next afternoon as she stirred the pot of Texas-style chili that simmered on the stove. "I hope they get back in time for their special goodbye dinner."

"Don't worry," replied Tatia who was pouring some brownie batter into a baking pan. "Grandma texted me a little while ago and said they're on their way back."

Joy went to the window and looked out at the driveway between the house and the shop. "I wish they didn't have to go home. I'm going to miss them."

"Me, too. I wish they lived closer – Texas is so far away," said Tatia. She put the brownies in the oven and joined Joy at the window. Joy snuggled up close to her mother.

"But look on the bright side. You'll get your room back."

"Yeah, that will be nice." She was quiet for a couple of minutes. "What do you think the secret is?"

"I don't know. It must be pretty big, though, since they took the trailer."

Suddenly the back door burst open, and Daniel rushed in, covered with dried grass clippings and sand. "Daniel Matthews! Get back outside and brush yourself off before you track up my clean kitchen."

The excited five-year-old screeched to a halt, his eyes wide at the use of his first and last names. He backed out the door where he took a couple of half-hearted swipes at his jeans. "Sorry, Mommy!"

Tatia laughed and stepped out the door to help him tidy up. "What have you been doing anyway? Rolling on the ground?"

"I've been practicing 'stop, drop, and roll' like you taught us in class yesterday.'"

"Well," sighed Tatia as she brushed the last of the dust off the back of his jacket. "At least you were listening. Now that you're cleaner, you may come into the house and tell me what was so exciting."

Daniel turned and pointed toward the truck and trailer that had just turned into the driveway. "Grandma and Grandpa are back. I heard them in the alley."

"So they are. And what on earth do they have in the back of that truck? It looks like furniture."

Alexander tapped lightly on the horn, drawing the rest of the family outside to see what was going on. Even Madison, who had been resting on the couch, came to the door with an afghan wrapped around her shoulders to see what was going on.

"Ah," said Jesse. "I see the new beds have arrived. Let me get this grease off my hands and gather the rest of the crew, and we'll get started."

"Get started with what?" questioned Tatia. "Would someone please tell me what's going on!"

Deborah put her hand on Tatia's shoulder and gently turned her toward the house. "I told you we'd take care of your bed situation. Come on, and I'll explain everything while we work. We need to clear a path and take the linens off Joy's bed." They headed into the house, and Deborah continued. "It looks like you'll have a house guest for a while. Now that Alexander and I are leaving, we wanted to help you normalize sleeping arrangements. The most logical place for Madison is with Joy, but we thought twin beds would be more comfortable than a double bed. Besides, it's time Joy had something prettier than this old garage sale brass bed."

"I knew you'd think of something, and as usual you came up with the most logical solution!" replied Tatia, "This will be good when she has friends over, too. Now she switches with Daniel, and that causes all kinds of havoc. But what will we do with the double bed?"

"You have lots of empty space in the Annex. Why don't we set it up there in case God sends you another fallen angel to care for? I think your house is full unless you put someone in Daniel's other bunk bed."

Tatia laughed. "I don't know, Mama. When we bought this place, I thought all that ministry space would be full of girls we rescued from traffickers just like your house was when you first brought me home to The Refuge. Instead, we've become more of a referral service, sending the girls on to other facilities in more remote, and hopefully safer, locations. Maybe God wants me to stick to my speaking and writing."

"I'm sure you've been praying for guidance. Right?"

"Yes. It seems like I've been praying for ages."

The women had cleared the toys out of the walkway to Joy's room and began working on the bed. "I once heard a story of a country church that gathered to pray for relief from a long drought. Many people showed up to pray, but only one brought an umbrella. Let's consider this your umbrella."

"Mama, how did you get so wise?"

###

Joy was thrilled, both with her new beds and her new roommate.

She supervised as the men moved the old bed out and assembled the new ones, keeping up a steady stream of instructions about their exact placement and her reasoning behind her decisions. The work crew had just moved on to the Annex and Joy was struggling to put sheets on the bed when Deborah came in.

"Do you like your new beds, sweetie?"

Joy ran over and grabbed the older woman around the waist. "Oh, Grandma! They're perfect! I love them!" she gushed.

"We looked at some painted ones – white, blue, pink – but I kept coming back to these."

"Those painted ones are for children!" Joy said. "These are more for grownups like me and Madison. And they kind of look like the big bed in your antique bedroom. What's it called again?"

"It's a sleigh bed, and it's a walnut finish. Now, let me help you get them made up. I'm sure Madison is getting tired and needs to lie down before dinner."

Madison appeared from the hallway and leaned against the door jamb. "I hope I'm not intruding," she said quietly. "I've been watching all the activity and wanted to see the results."

Joy ran over and grabbed her hand. "Come in! This is your room, too! Don't you love it! We'll have so much fun together!"

The older girl laughed as she allowed herself to be ushered into the room. "Yes, it's beautiful. I hope you don't mind sharing it with me for a while."

"I think she's looking forward to having an older sister. Joy, why don't you let Madison sit down in your desk chair while we get these sheets on the beds?"

Harley wandered in and jumped on the second bed just as Deborah was spreading out the top sheet. He curled up and purred loudly as the fabric settled over him.

"Daniel," yelled Joy. "Come get Harley! He's getting cat hair all over Madison's bed!"

The cat, startled by the sudden noise, scooted out from between the sheets and hid under Joy's bed. Daniel ran in and yelled at the cat who then darted out and jumped on top of the desk hutch sending a cascade of stuffed animals onto the surface of the desk and into Madison's lap before running out the door with Daniel in hot pursuit. Deborah wiped tears of laughter from her face while Madison sat in stunned silence and Joy frantically threw toys onto the floor.

"Are you okay? Did anything hurt you?"

Madison burst into laughter. "I'm fine! Just a little surprised. I've never been around children – at least not for a long time. I think I'm going to like it."

"Good," said Joy as she returned a stuffed rabbit to its place. Suddenly her hands flew up to her mouth. "The brownies! They'll be burned."

"It's okay," said Deborah in a calming voice. "I took them out before I came in to help with the sheets."

With order restored, the beds linens in place, and Madison settled in for a rest, Deborah and Joy went to check on the progress in the Annex. Under Tatia's supervision, the guys had moved Joy's double bed into a small room in the back.

"Mommy, do you want me to get some clean sheets to put on the bed?" asked Joy.

"I don't think we need to do that right now," answered Tatia. "Nobody will be using this room for a while – if ever." She looked around the bare space and sighed.

"God might surprise you, Mommy. You never know when He's going to send us someone else like Madison to take care of."

"You're right, Joy," responded her grandmother. "I think we need to make this room really pretty, just in case. What do you think we need?"

Tatia laughed. "Okay, while you two have a design consultation

I'm going to bring some bed linens and the vacuum over from the house. What with getting ready for guests and – well, all the other chaos of the last couple of weeks – I've neglected cleaning this place."

By the time she returned with her cleaning equipment, Deborah and Joy were huddled behind the desk in her office with their heads together. Tatia walked quietly to the door to see what was going on. Deborah was sitting in Tatia's chair and Joy was leaning over her shoulder.

"Okay," said Deborah. "We need a night stand, a chair and small table that can double as a desk, and a chest for clothes – or maybe a wardrobe so there will be room for hanging clothes."

"Yes! A wardrobe would be better. And a lamp – in case she likes to read in bed. And a rug in case the floor is cold in the morning."

Tatia smiled and stored another picture in her mental file of precious moments. While she cleaned the dusty floors, the décor consultation continued.

"Got it," said Deborah as she added to her list. "What about bed linens? Should we use your old ones?"

"I don't know. I guess we can start with those, but princesses are a little bit young for most of Mommy's clients. Maybe we can find something more grown up at the thrift store."

Deborah reached over and gave her a quick hug. "You're pretty good at this. What colors do you want to use?"

Joy beamed at the compliment and replied thoughtfully. "We need something kind of soothing – because some of Mommy's clients are really upset. Maybe a soft blue and white?"

"Perfect!" said Deborah, smiling at how much her granddaughter sounded like Tatia. "We'll leave this list on Tatia's desk so you can find it when you're ready to go shopping."

"Great," said Joy, kissing her grandmother on the cheek. "I'm going to miss you when you're gone. Now I have to go stir the chili."

Joy hurried out the door, and Deborah stood and stretched. She wandered into the back where she found her daughter standing beside the idle vacuum cleaner and leaning on the broom she had been using to chase cobwebs out of the corners. She was staring at the large open space between her office and the small, newly furnished bedroom with a very contemplative look on her face. Deborah cleared her throat to avoid startling Tatia and walked over and put her arm around the younger woman's waist. Tatia smiled at Deborah and leaned into her shoulder.

"Where were you?" asked Deborah.

"Daydreaming I guess and maybe praying a little. You know I'm thrilled by the number of girls we've been able to rescue, but it's not exactly what I had planned. But on the advice of a very wise woman who I love more than I can tell her, I've been praying about what to do with all this unused space."

She paused for a moment and hugged her mother. Deborah stroked her hair slowly and asked, "Any answers yet?"

Tatia took a deep breath and stood up straight so she could look Deborah in the eye. "I think so. I haven't even told Jesse this yet, but I have been feeling strongly that God wants me to expand Fallen Angel Salvage to include a crisis pregnancy center. What do you think? Am I crazy?"

Deborah's face lit up, and she threw her head back and laughed. "Crazy? I think you're brilliant! Well, you and God, of course. That's the perfect fit with what you're doing now, and it's exactly what some of the girls you rescue need." She pulled Tatia into another hug. "I'm so excited for you! Alexander and I will pray with you – and you need to tell Jesse so he can pray, too." She glanced at her watch. "I wish we had several hours so you could tell me what you're thinking, but we have a dinner to get ready and a plane to catch. Oh, I wish we could stay longer. When you feel the time is right, create a mission statement and a business plan and send them to me. I'll present them to our Board of Directors to see if they are interested in supporting your expansion."

Now Tatia was laughing. "Mama, if everyone is as excited about the idea as you are…well, maybe that's God's way of giving me the go ahead."

"Amen. Now, let's go see what kind of mess we have in the kitchen."

16

Friday - 9/29

Tatia and Deborah were still having an animated conversation when they reached the front door. As Tatia reached for the knob, Joy yanked the door open from the inside and almost collided with Tatia. Both of them jumped a little before Tatia grabbed her daughter and danced her across the living room toward the kitchen.

"How's that chili coming, Chef Joy?" asked Tatia as she twirled her partner to a stop in front of the stove. Joy snatched the spoon before her mother could reach for it and stirred the simmering concoction of beef, tomatoes, onions, peppers, and mystery spices.

"I was just coming to tell you that it looks ready and smells delicious!" she announced. She laid the spoon down carefully on the spoon rest and continued, "I was going to see what was going on in the Annex, but it's just my old bed. I can wait until after dinner."

"Actually, it can probably wait until tomorrow. We'll visit Shawna's garage sale in the morning to see if we can do some early bird shopping. She just redid her guest bedroom, so she may have some things we can use. Now, turn the burner on the chili down as low as it will go, and I'll pop some cornbread in the oven. Daniel, you and your sister run over to the shop and tell the guys dinner will be ready in about twenty-five minutes."

"Is Grandpa in the shop, too?" asked Joy.

"Yes, he went over with them after they finished their moving chores. Now scoot!"

Daniel looked at his mother doubtfully, but she nodded her head. "Go ahead. It'll be fine."

He sighed and grabbed Joy's hand tight enough that she winced a little. "Sorry," he said. "But I won't let go this time."

Joy hugged him and said, "I know you won't."

"He still blames himself for her kidnapping, doesn't he?" asked Deborah.

"Yes, even though we've told him that they would have taken her even if he hadn't let go of her hand."

"Good thinking – giving him a chance for a do-over."

"I hope so. That's a big burden for such a little guy to carry," replied Tatia. "Oh, I meant to ask Jesse to bring over a small table and several chairs. Would you mind texting him. No need for all nine of us to crowd into the corner."

"Sure. Alexander and I will sit at the table with the children," said Deborah while she typed the message. "How often do Johnny and Brush eat with you?"

Tatia grinned. "Brush comes every morning for coffee. It's a good time for him and Jesse to map out the day's work. Then they both come over for lunch. The three of us take turns in the kitchen so it's no burden – and Brush chips in on groceries and occasionally brings something Shawna has made. If we work out something permanent with Johnny, I'm sure he'll join us for lunch, too. I invited him to eat supper with us tonight because he goes home to an empty house and the temptations of his computer, but I don't know if he'll accept. Brush usually goes home for dinner, but Shawn and Shawna are visiting her sister for the day, so he's staying tonight."

She stopped long enough to pour the cornbread batter into a heated cast iron skillet. She grinned at Deborah. "Just like you taught me."

"Good girl! I haven't seen Brush and Johnny around much this week. I assume that's because of Madison?"

"Yes. I wanted to give her as much privacy and quiet as possible while she recovered. She met Brush yesterday, but she hasn't met Johnny yet."

"I know she has a long way to go," replied Deborah, "but I think she thrives on the energy of the children. Maybe all the coming and going around here will take her mind off herself when she hits the rough patches that are bound to come."

"That's what I'm praying for," said Tatia. She glanced at the clock and continued, "How are we doing for time? Do we need to hurry?"

"At the risk of sounding like an old John Denver song from my childhood: all my bags are packed, I'm ready to go. We're catching the red-eye, so we should have plenty of time. We'll leave shortly after dinner."

Tatia brushed at a tear with the back of her hand. "I'm going to miss you and Papa."

"I know. But you're past the crises with Joy and Madison, and it's time you got back to life as usual."

"Whatever that is," said Tatia with a laugh.

While Tatia stirred sugar into a huge pitcher of tea, also the way she had been taught, and Deborah gathered bowls, napkins, spoons, and glasses, the back door burst open and the two children tumbled in onto the door mat.

Daniel bounced up with his hands in the air. "I won! I won!" he shouted.

"Yes, you did," said Joy in a condescending tone. "And that's a real accomplishment when we were running side-by-side and holding hands!" She grabbed her little brother and began tickling him. He laughed breathlessly, "Okay, okay! We both won!"

"Okay, you two winners," said Tatia. "Don't step on your grand-mother, and don't wake up Madison – if it's not already too late. Go wash your hands for dinner."

"I'm going to miss all this chaos," sighed Deborah. "That big old house is so quiet now that all you girls are grown and gone."

"I used to think a little quiet now and then would be great – but after almost losing Joy, I treasure every noisy moment." Tatia peeked into the oven to check the cornbread and then straightened up with a laugh. "And speaking of noisy moments, here comes one now."

Daniel appeared from the hallway, wiping his damp hands on his dusty pants. "We didn't wake up Madison, Mommy. She was already awake."

"And how did you know she was awake?"

"We opened the door a little bit and asked her."

Madison followed Daniel into the room slowly as if she was intruding. "It's okay, Mrs. Matthews," she said.

Tatia smiled at her, noticing that she was wearing the blue sweater Joy had given her and the black jeans they had found at the ministry closet. She also noticed a slight blush of color in her face that hadn't been there when she arrived. "Remember, Mrs. Matthews was my mother-in-law."

"It's okay, Tatia," corrected Madison. "I was already awake won-dering what smells so good in here."

"It's Mama's famous recipe for Texas-style chili. Are you hungry?"

"Yes. My stomach has been growling, and that hasn't happened for a while."

"That's good news. I made a separate pot the way the kids like it – less spicy. We'll let you try that with some crackers and see how your stomach feels then."

"That sounds good. Is there anything I can do to help?"

"Yes," Deborah broke in. "I see the guys coming over from the shop, so it's time to put ice in the glasses. You can do that while Tatia slices the cornbread and I find the hot sauce for those who never think anything is spicy enough."

"I'll show you where the ice is," shouted Daniel.

"And I'll help you," added Joy.

Tatia looked at her mother and rolled her eyes as she navigated through the crowded kitchen with a hot cast iron skillet held high over her head. "What was that I said about treasuring every noisy moment?"

"I thought I was your treasure," said Jesse, letting in a burst of cool air and a surge of energy. The four men were all talking at once until Joy shouted, "STOP," and pointed an imperious finger at them.

"Oops!" said Jesse. "Back out slowly and wipe your feet before the wrath of Joy descends on us all!"

The men made a show of looking fearful, backing out the door, and carefully wiping their shoes before coming back in. Tears of laughter were rolling down the faces of the women by the time Joy had inspected their boots and hands and allowed them to come in.

Jesse looked at Tatia with a wink and a question in his eyes. She nodded, so he cleared his throat loudly. "Thank you, Madam Inspector of Feet and Hands. You have faithfully discharged your duties and it is now time for the Lord of the Manor to speak – with your permission, of course."

"You may speak," Joy said and snuggled up under her dad's arm.

"This is a very special evening," he said. "We're seeing Mom and Dad G off to Texas after an amazing visit. You are always more important to us than we can express, but we really could not have survived the last few days without the two of you. And I know our two young ladies will think of you every time they see the beautiful new beds and bed linens.."

"And when I see my new superhero blanket," added Daniel.

"Yes," agreed Jesse. "That, too. And tonight we're officially welcoming Madison to our table and our home with a huge debt of gratitude for your part in returning our daughter to us. Madison, you may have seen these two rascals across the driveway, and I know you met Brush briefly yesterday, but I wanted to formally introduce you. Madison, this big guy is Brush, the design wizard and manager of the body shop operation, and the handsome one is Johnny who is now officially adding a computer repair division to Fallen Angel Salvage. Gentlemen, this is Madison."

Both men tipped imaginary hats to her, and Madison murmured a shy hello. She was looking at the floor, unaccustomed to all the attention, so she didn't see the color rise up Johnny's neck and onto his cheeks. But Tatia and Deborah saw and looked at each other with raised eyebrows and suppressed grins.

"Enough with the formalities," said Jesse. "Guys, after I pray let's set up the extra table and chairs – which we wiped off in the shop. Then help yourselves to the food on the counter and enjoy. Now, let's circle up."

Madison looked confused until Daniel took her hand on one side and Tatia took the other one. As Jesse thanked God for their blessings, Tatia thanked Him for that first breakfast at The Refuge when Mama G and a young woman named Ashlie took her hands as they prayed.

17

Friday - 9/29

"What do you mean you haven't found her yet?" said Mr. S in a quiet, steely voice that was more terrifying than his full volume roar. "You have the resources of one of the largest tech organization in existence, and you can't manage to find one naive teenager who has hardly been out of her apartment in the past fifteen years?"

Mr. S was not happy, and he was not a man to be crossed. Born Michael DeSanti on the south side of Chicago in the late 1960s to an unmarried exotic dancer, he had learned to express his unhappiness with his fists and whatever weapon was at hand. Now, as the owner and CEO of Saint International and the rumored boss of various illicit operations, he had all the legal and illegal weapons he needed.

His father was an associate in the Chicago Outfit but was not accepted as a full member because he was not direct family. Although he didn't marry Michael's mother, he spent time with Michael and indoctrinated him into the ways of organized crime until he was killed by a stray bullet in a drive-by shooting. Michael was twelve years old at the time and already had a reputation for doing anything he was asked and doing it well. He became a favorite of those in power, and they continued to school him in the workings of the Outfit. They also paid for a formal education in the new world of electronics.

Michael stayed in the Boss's favor, but like his own father, he was never accepted into upper management because of his heritage. When a new regime came to power, Michael was side-tracked into a dead end position, so he gradually started his own operation and eventually distanced himself from the Outfit altogether. With his knowledge of all things computer, he focused on white-collar crimes like embezzlement and fraudulent stock trading – but he had a weakness for young girls, and part of his operation dealt with very high end and very deep web sex trafficking. The Outfit didn't like his independence but it was not powerful enough to go against him. And he was surrounded by a legal wall so perfect that even the government hadn't been able to touch him.

Michael D. Saint was also surrounded by a facade of respectability and a manufactured lineage that made him one of the beautiful people in Chicago society. His company made the Fortune 500 list several times, and a college graduate scoring a position with Saint International was considered fortunate indeed. However, those who were closest to him knew the real Michael and did everything they could to stay on his good side.

"Apparently she's not as naive as we thought, Mr. S," said Ian with only a slight tremor in his voice. "But I have several experts scouring CCTV in the area of the cab company where we found her tracking chip. They've found several good leads, and I have teams working those as well. We're closing in and should have a location for you soon."

Michael grunted and scowled. "How about Misty. Any word on her?"

"We have a lead there, too. I should have news for you later today. When we find her, do you want to see her?"

"No. Just get what information she has and get back to me."

"And Misty herself? Do you want her back in service?"

"No. She's outlived her usefulness. She's a liability now, so her services are terminated."

"Consider it done. I do have good news. We have some background information on those two kidnappers from the newspaper article – Eric Hall and Victor Ellis. Hall is on parole from Texas for human trafficking, aggravated statutory sexual assault and murder, and Ellis has a record for things like fraud and financial crimes, obscene or offensive content, drug trafficking, and prostitution."

"Real bad boys, huh?" commented Michael.

"Yes, sir," replied Ian. "Our contact at MCC says they're pretty mouthy, spouting off about how much money they have and how easy their time in stir will be because of it."

Michael's anger ebbed a little bit and his interest was piqued. "Is it my money?"

"Possibly. They say all they need is online access."

Michael sat back in his chair, elbows on the arm rests, and fingers steepled against his lower lip. "Keep working that angle, and put out a reward for details like how much, where it came from, where it is now. But make sure they don't get online yet. Make them deal through Vandoren for now. We don't want to get tangled up with them if they're not our guys."

"Yes, sir," said Ian. Before he reached the door, Michael stopped him.

"And Ian," he said with the steel back in his voice. "I want to know where Madison is – soon. Do I make myself clear?"

"Yes, sir. Crystal clear."

18

Saturday - 9/30

Breakfast was a quiet affair around the Matthews house the morning after Grandma and Grandpa G went back to Texas. Shawna needed Brush's help to set up the garage sale, so he wasn't coming to the shop unless there was an emergency, and Johnny had taken his latest computer rebuild home for the weekend. Everyone else sat silently picking at muffins and pushing cereal around in their bowls until Jesse slapped his hand loudly on the table startling the whole bunch.

"Okay, when does the funeral start?"

"What's a funeral?" asked Daniel.

"It's a church service they have when somebody dies, silly," replied Joy. "Who died, Daddy?"

"That's what I want to know. Everybody's sitting around with such sad faces that I thought someone must have died."

Tatia faked a cough to cover a snicker, and Daniel rolled his eyes at Jesse.

"Nobody died, silly Daddy," he said. "But Grandma and Grandpa went home, and Mommy's going shopping." He made a face when he said the last word.

"Well," said Jesse, "We could go with the girls. Wouldn't that be fun?"

"Noooooo!" wailed Daniel. "I hate shopping."

"But they're going to Shawn's house. The two of you could play while the girls shop. And it's a pretty day. How about if we ride the bikes over? All of us!"

"Yeah!"

"But what about Madison," said Joy. "We can't leave her home by herself."

"It's okay," said Madison. "I'll be fine here. I can read or something." Her voice trailed off into a whisper.

"Hmmmm," said Jesse. "I wonder what Johnny's doing today?"

"But don't you have to work, Daddy? And Johnny, too?" asked Joy.

"Got a frog in your throat, Tatia? You're doing a lot of coughing over there," said Jesse with a mischievous grin. She shot him good-natured glare as she choked back a laugh and excused herself to get a glass of water. Jesse turned to Joy. "Honey, none of us has any appointments today, so I was thinking of putting out our "Gone Riding" sign for a few hours. I'll give Johnny a call and see what he's doing."

Daniel had slid off the end of the bench and was dancing from one foot to the other. "I'll get your phone, Daddy," he yelled. Jesse and Tatia usually left their phones on the hallway table when they came in to minimize interruptions of family time. Daniel grabbed Jesse's phone and delivered it with a flourish.

"Thanks, buddy. Now, while I make my call, you finish your breakfast so you'll be ready when it's time to go."

Daniel was back on the bench and shoveling cereal into his mouth before the words were out of Jesse's mouth. Jesse tousled his hair and gave him a thumbs up before he went out the front door to make his call.

He came back inside in a few minutes with a big grin on his face. The children had gone to their rooms to get dressed, but Madison was still sipping her glass of juice. Tatia was putting dishes into the dishwasher, but she looked up when she heard the door open.

"Well?" she asked.

His grin turned into a laugh. "Amazingly he has nothing on his schedule and will be here shortly."

"His bike doesn't have a buddy seat. Do you have one in the shop that will work?"

"Yep. I'll go dig it out now and clean it up."

As soon as he was out the door, Madison spoke up. "Maybe I should stay here."

Tatia had almost forgotten she was sitting there and was surprised to see the apprehensive look on her face. "Madison, I'm so sorry. We didn't even consult you when we started making plans. Aren't you feeling well?"

"I feel fine. It's just that…well…I've never been on a motorcycle."

Tatia went over and sat down at the table. Putting a reassuring hand on Madison's, she said, "I'm sure you haven't, as protected as you were. I think you'll love it, though, and Johnny's a great rider. I tell you what. When he gets here, I'll ask him to ride around the neighborhood with you. If you're too uncomfortable, I'll let Joy ride with Johnny, and you and I will follow them in the car. How does that sound?"

Madison looked at her with watery eyes. "Great, and way too kind as usual. What should I wear?"

"Go put on your black jeans and blue sweater. You may want to add another layer under the sweater. I'll finish up in the kitchen and go see what I have in the way of extra leathers that might fit you?"

"Leathers?"

"Chaps and a leather jacket. They protect you from the weather and flying objects – plus they look cool. I may even have a pair of boots that will fit with an extra pair of socks. And I'm sure we have a helmet in the shop that will work."

Madison's eyes began to shine with excitement instead of tears as she headed for her bedroom. Before she reached the hallway, she ran back and threw her arms around Tatia.

"I love you!"

As she left the room, Tatia was the one with tears in her eyes.

###

Tatia had just finished tying Daniel's boots when they heard Johnny's bike pull into the driveway. "Johnny and Madison are back. I'm gonna go see if she liked it," he yelled as he ran out the door.

"Guess he's not scared of the driveway any more, huh?" said Joy coming in from her bedroom. She was dressed in jeans, a pink sweater, black boots, and pink leather chaps belted around her waist and flapping loose around her legs. She had a pink leather jacket thrown over one arm and was carrying a flowered helmet in the other hand. "Mommy, I need help zipping these legs," she said. "Please."

"I can do that if you'll get your cute little self over here."

While Tatia maneuvered the zippers of the chaps down the sides of Joy's legs, the girl examined the helmet and said, "I think Brush is going to have to paint another helmet for me. This one feels too tight."

"Put it on and let's see." Tatia examined the fit of the helmet and shook her head. "That doesn't look like it would be comfortable for very long. Let's go see what Daddy has in the shop."

Joy took off the helmet and looked longingly at it. "I'm going to miss this one. I've had it since I was a little girl."

Tatia swallowed another laugh and said, "I'm sure Brush will make you an even better one. Now go ask Daddy to see what he's got while I grab the rest of my gear."

Jesse had the bikes lined up and ready to ride by the time Tatia walked out the back door. "Kick stands up in five - last call for the bathroom, water bottles, sunscreen, chapstick, sunglasses, gloves, bandanas, and life savings for garage sale shopping."

She watched her children quickly checking their pockets and finally holding both thumbs up, and she laughed when Daniel shouted, "Madison is ready to go, too! She loves riding!" Tatia thought about what a blessing it was that her children made her laugh a lot. She locked the door and walked over to Madison who was trying to figure out what to do with a loose jacket lapel.

"Can I help you with that," she asked.

"I don't know. It flaps in the wind and hits me in the face sometimes."

"I can fix that. You have two choices." Tatia showed her the two snaps, one that laid the lapel back against her shoulder and one that brought it across her chest to keep the wind from blowing down her neck. She chose the second option, and after she was set, Tatia handed her a small pill holder.

"I know you don't like taking pills, but this is your first outing since you began to detox, and it might be a bit stressful. This has several ibuprofen in case of a headache and a few antacids in case your stomach gets upset. Don't try to be brave if you don't feel well. If these don't help, tell me and I'll borrow Shawna's car and bring you home. We can get my bike later. Okay?"

"Okay," responded Madison, looking down at the pill box. She slid it into an open pocket, zipped it closed, and looked up at Tatia. "Thank you for taking care of me."

Tatia hugged her quickly. "Now, are you comfortable on the bike?"

"So far, but we haven't hit the highway yet."

"Just trust Johnny. He knows what he's doing, and he'll keep you safe. When he leans into a turn, keep your body lined up behind his and you'll be fine."

The guys broke from the huddle where they had been discussing the route, and Jesse yelled, "Circle up so we can bless this ride!"

Jesse grabbed Daniel's hand on one side and Joy's on the other, and Joy took her mother's hand. Tatia slid her hand into Madison's, and Johnny, who had ridden with them enough to be familiar with their pre-ride prayer routine, reached hesitantly for Madison's hand. Tatia watched as Madison looked at him with a shy smile and accepted his hand, and Tatia prayed that God would protect those two vulnerable hearts.

"Amen!" shouted Jesse, "and load up!" Two minutes later, the three bikes pulled out into the alley for a day of fun and what they all hoped would be a new chapter in Madison's life.

Jesse took the long way to Brush and Shawna's home, stretching the fifteen minute trip into a forty-five minute ride. The curb in front of their house was full of customers' cars, but there was a space in front of the neighbor's that was just big enough to accommodate the three bikes. Madison dismounted the way Johnny had told her and was removing her helmet while he put the kickstand down and locked the front wheel.

"Why did you back into the space instead of pulling straight in?" she asked.

"Well, these machines don't have a reverse gear, so we have to propel them with our feet if we want to back up. The road slants down to the curb, and if we headed in, we'd have to back uphill to get out."

"That makes sense," she said, blushing a little. "I hope you don't mind the questions. I know nothing about motorcycles."

"Not at all," he said. "I'm glad you're interested 'cause you've hooked up with a group of real riders...um, not that you're committed or anything…I mean…well, you know." Now it was his turn to blush a little.

Madison drifted over to where Shawna was showing Tatia and Joy what she had in the way of bedding. Joy was almost jumping up and down over a comforter set she had found. Dust ruffle, pillow shams, sheets, and pillow cases were included.

"Mommy," she enthused. "We have to get this one! It's blue and white just like Grandma G and me…I mean Grandma G and I decided we needed. And most of it hasn't even been opened! It's perfect."

"Well, if it's perfect, then you should have it," said Shawna. "And since it's for the ministry, there is no charge."

"Oh, Shawna. I can't let you do that."

"Yes, you can. I insist. In fact, Joy shared the plans she and Mrs. G made for the room, and I think I have some things in the storage that I didn't put out. After we close up this afternoon, I'll have Brush borrow the neighbor's truck and bring them over. I can't take an active part in helping your girls right now, but I can certainly help provide a safe and comfortable space for them."

"Okay. Thank you."

Just then she noticed Madison pulling the pill container out of her pocket. "Are you okay, Madison?"

"Yes. I'm a little tired, and I have a little bit of a headache. Do you think I could get some water?"

"Of course. Shawna, I don't believe you've met Madison."

"Not yet," she said, taking Madison's hand between both of hers. "But I've heard all about what you did for Joy, and I can't tell you how grateful we all are."

Madison mumbled something under her breath that might have been thank you.

"She's a little tired and needs to take some ibuprofen," continued Tatia. "Is it okay if I take her into the house?"

"Absolutely. There are bottles of water in the fridge, and she can lie down on our bed."

"Joy, see if Jesse can fit these into the trunk and saddle bags of the Ultra Glide while I go in and get Madison settled for a rest. Then we can shop some more. Deal?"

"Deal!"

Madison took off her leathers and boots and lay back gratefully onto the bed. "Every time I turn around you do something else that I need to thank you for. I know you say it's what God tells us to do for those who need help, but I still don't understand."

"I tell you what, I wrote a book about my early life. Maybe that will help explain it. It's called 'Groomed for the Streets,' and there's a copy on the book shelf in the living room at home. You can read it any time you want to. Now close your eyes and rest for a little while. Come on out when you feel better, or I'll come get you when we're ready to go."

Madison felt better after her rest and was ready to climb back onto Johnny's bike for the ride home. But first, Joy dragged her over to Jesse's bike so she could show her the rug Shawna gave them to go with the comforter.

"It's a perfect match. Right?"

"It is," agreed Madison enthusiastically, and Joy beamed.

19

Saturday - 9/30

On the way back, the little caravan stopped for burgers, and Madison experienced fast food for the first time. She was almost giddy with the thrill of the day when they arrived at the Fallen Angel complex – far too excited to rest as Tatia suggested.

"I'd rather come to the Annex with you and Joy and help set up the bedroom."

"I'll keep an eye on her, Mommy," said Joy in her little-mother attitude. "I won't let her work too hard."

Tatia suppressed a grin. "Well, come on then. Many hands make light work."

"I'll help carry the stuff you bought!" Johnny hurriedly grabbed the comforter Jesse had just taken out of the trunk of his Ultra Glide.

"Daddy," said Daniel, pointing at Johnny. "His face has that…"

Jesse swept his son up into his arms and interjected quickly. "Hey, buddy. Look who's turning into the driveway. It looks like Brush with a truck full of…furniture? Tatia, do you know what this is about?"

"No," she answered with a puzzled look on her face. "Shawna said something about sending over some things for the new room, but I thought she meant more linens."

An inspection of the truck bed revealed a four-drawer chest, a night stand, a small writing desk, and a desk chair. "Shawna said to tell you that this isn't exactly what Joy had on her floor plan, but maybe it will help for now," explained Brush,

Tatia threw her arms around Brush's neck and kissed him on the cheek. "Tell her it's just what we needed! Daniel, go tell Johnny we need him to help move furniture."

A little while later, Joy spread the rug beside the freshly made up bed and stepped back to admire the newly furnished room. "It's beautiful! All we need is a lamp for the nightstand, and it will be perfect."

"Oh, I forgot," said Brush. "Shawna put a lamp in the cab of the truck so it wouldn't get broken. Johnny, why don't you come with me and get the lamp. I need to get that truck back."

With the lamp in place, Joy pronounced the room just right. "I wish Grandma could see it."

"Why don't we take some pictures to send her," suggested Tatia. Everyone had fun posing for serious and silly pictures. But when the night buzzer on the front door sounded, everyone froze, revealing the tension that still lay below the surface of the recently traumatized group.

"I'll get it," Jesse jumped in before anyone else could speak. "Probably someone at the wrong address or something."

Tatia released the breath she didn't realize she had been holding. "Thanks, hon. Now, let's get this place finished up. Joy, you and Daniel get a trash bag from the cabinet under the sink and pick up all the packaging. Johnny, there's a broom in the utility closet – Joy will show you where it is. Madison, I think there are a couple more pillows in the clothes closet, and we have two empty shams. Let's go see what we can find."

With immediate tasks to perform, faces relaxed, smiles were restored, and the chatter began again.

"I'll get the trash bag."

"Get the big black one. C'mon, Johnny. The broom is over here."

"That's more like it. Now, where did I put those pillows?"

Jesse also relaxed when he saw a small woman in her mid-twenties standing at the door and looking very unsure of herself. He chose a key from the ring he pulled out of his pocket and unlocked the door. He opened it and gave her what he hoped was a reassuring smile.

"Hi! I'm Jesse Matthews. How can I help you this afternoon?"

"I…um…I may be in the wrong place," she said in precise English but with a lilt that spoke of Caribbean nights and palm trees. "It looks like you're closed. I should go," she continued as she began to turn away.

"Wait," said Jesse. Many of the women Tatia helped were hesitant and fearful when they arrived. "Why don't you come in and tell me what you need. If this is the wrong place, maybe I can help you find the right place."

She reluctantly stepped inside and looked around cautiously.

"Have a seat," he said, motioning toward the sofa. She perched on the edge, ramrod straight, until he turned one of the guest chairs around and sat down facing her. Then she seemed to relax a little. "Can I get you something? Water? Tea?"

"No," she said. "I'm fine." It was obvious that she wasn't fine, but Jesse sat quietly, waiting for her to compose herself and find the words she needed. "My name is Lili James," she began. "I am from Antigua, and my parents sent me here to attend college. I am in my second year of medical school so I can go back to my home and help the people in my small town."

Lili fell silent for a few moments and hung her head so that her long, dark spiral curls draped softly around her beautiful coffee and cream face. Jesse spoke quietly. "That's a very noble goal. You sound like a very intelligent young woman."

She looked up and flashed a wide smile that showed off sparkling white teeth, but there was sadness in her brown eyes. "Intelligent, but not very wise. I have no place to stay tonight. I have money, but I have called or visited every hotel and motel in the area, and no one has a vacancy."

"That happens sometimes when there's a big convention in Chicago."

"The cab driver said you might be able to help, and he told me to give you this." Lili handed Jesse a business card.

Jesse looked at the card, but he already knew it was one of Tatia's. He turned it over and smiled when he read the note on the back. *Here's another angel for you, Ted.* When Tatia had first opened her ministry, she hosted an open house and invited the local policemen, hotel owners and staff, cabbies, and anyone else who might come in contact with girls and young women in trouble. She explained the purpose of Fallen Angel Salvage and asked them to refer these people to her. Jesse was nervous about what kind of people might show up at her door, but her presentation had touched her audience deeply, and so far, no one had taken advantage of or abused her kindness.

Jesse glanced up and saw Tatia standing in the doorway from the Annex. "Lili, you have come to exactly the right place, and here is exactly the right person to help you – my wife, Tatia."

###

A couple of hours later, Jesse and the children burst into the room from the backyard. "Whatever you're cooking up over there smells awfully good."

"Yeah," echoed Daniel, "it smells awful good! We've been playing football, and we're starving."

"I can see that," said Tatia. "And judging by the grass stains, I'd guess you were the tackling dummy. Now go wash up. Dinner in five."

Jesse leaned over Tatia's shoulder and inspected the pot while she added a few miscellaneous spices. "I see macaroni and beans in an unidentifiable sauce – but it smells an awful lot like the chili we had last night."

"Bingo," she said, turning around and giving him a quick kiss. "After you wash your hands, you can set the table and put ice in the glasses."

"Yes, ma'am," he said with a grin and a mock salute. Madison moved over a little to allow him access to the sink where she was rinsing a knife and cutting board. "What does the boss have you doing?"

She flashed him a shy grin. "I made a salad and helped stir up some cornbread. I've never cooked before, but I like it."

"That's good! We do a lot of eating around here, so you'll have lots of chances to practice," he said. "Hey, boss! Will Lili be joining us for dinner?"

Tatia straightened up from checking the cornbread. "No, she said she wasn't very hungry, and she looked really tired. I showed her around, and she said she might warm up some soup in the microwave later. She'll be staying the night."

"It's a good thing we got that bed made up. So, what's her story?"

"You heard most of it before you saw me in the doorway. She became involved with a fellow student, and he talked her into moving in with him to save money. They had a fight about something – she wasn't ready to share any details – and he threw her out. Since the lease is still in his name, she has no recourse." Tatia stopped to take the cornbread out of the oven. She turned the cast iron skillet over, caught the bread on her open palm, and flipped it over onto a cooling rack in one smooth, practiced motion.

"That's amazing," said Madison. "How did you know it wouldn't stick to the pan?"

"It's all in the seasoning. I'll show you how that happens after dinner. Right now the food is almost ready. Would you mind rounding up the kids? "

"Not at all!" Madison hurried toward the bathroom she shared with Joy and Daniel.

"So she's homeless. Right?" prompted Jesse.

"Only temporarily. She found an apartment, but the current occupants won't be out until tomorrow. It will take a day or two for cleaning and such, and she has to arrange for some furniture. I told her she could stay as long as she needed to."

"We do run into some interesting people here, don't we?"

"Yes, we do. Now, here comes the rest of the gang, so let's eat."

A flurry of activity filled the next few minutes as serving bowls were passed and plates were filled. Everyone held hands as Jesse blessed the food, and the happy chatter of a loving family began. About halfway through the meal, Daniel looked up from his almost empty plate.

"Is that lady gonna come live with us like Madison?" he asked.

"Not exactly," said Jesse. "Lili is staying in the ministry building for a few days until her apartment is ready."

"Lili," said Joy slowly, testing the name on her tongue. "I like that name. Is she going to church with us tomorrow?"

"No," answered Tatia. "She goes to a church over by the college. She plans to catch a cab, attend the service, and then have lunch with some friends. She'll be back here sometime tomorrow afternoon or evening." She looked at Jesse and responded to the unasked question that was written on his face. "I locked the door to the office and gave her a key to the Annex door. I think we can trust her, but…"

"She seemed honest to me, too, but you did the right thing."

Tatia gave him a look that spoke of the loving bond of trust they shared. The moment was broken when Daniel announced that he was ready for dessert.

"All right, then. Who else is ready for fresh strawberries and whipped cream?"

20

Sunday - 10/1

"Mrs...I mean, Tatia, would you be upset with me if I didn't go to church with you this morning?" asked Madison.

Tatia looked up from the Seven Layer Salad she was preparing. "Of course not. Is anything in particular bothering you, or did we wear you out yesterday?"

"I'm just really tired, and a little achy."

"I'm not surprised. You had quite a day for your first time out since...well, in a long time. Everyone else has finished breakfast, so just have a seat at the table and I'll bring you some coffee and a little something to eat. What sounds good?"

"That oatmeal with the peaches we had the other day was really good. Is that too much trouble?"

"Not at all. A little water and a few seconds in the microwave is all it takes. How about a piece of toast to go with it?"

"That sounds good. Thank you."

Joy came in with her hands behind her neck. "Mommy, the clasp of this necklace is caught in my hair. Help!"

Tatia shook her head and smiled. "Never a dull moment. Madison, can you help her while I finish your breakfast?"

"Sure. Come on over here, Joy."

"You're not dressed!" she said as she turned around in front of Madison. "Are you sick? Do I need to stay home and take care of you?"

"I think she'll be fine by herself for a few hours," said Tatia. "In fact, she will probably enjoy the peace and quiet after the normal chaos around here. Now go check on your brother. It's almost time to go."

Joy thanked Madison for the help with her necklace and skipped away to see if Daniel was ready. "You let me sleep late on purpose, didn't you?" Madison asked Tatia.

"Yes. I could tell last night you were very tired. You're doing great, but you don't need to do too much too soon. I had trouble making up my mind since we have our quarterly potluck after the service today, but there will be plenty of time to introduce you to our church family next week."

"Yes. Meeting Brush's family and all your friends at the garage sale was a little overwhelming for a recluse like me." She stirred the hot cereal Tatia had set in front of her before taking a bite. "This is perfect. Thank you. Is there anything you'd like me to do while you're gone?"

"Just rest. You can watch TV, listen to music, read, or go back to bed. I left you an individual serving of this salad in the fridge and a bowl of the cheesy chicken soup," said Tatia as she zipped the carrier over the slow cooker. "It's hot so I'm leaving it on the counter. It should be fine until you're ready to eat it, but you may want to zap it for a minute or two."

"You mentioned the book you wrote - I think Joy told me it's about what she called your 'before' life. I think I'd like to read that while you're gone if that's okay."

"What a good idea! There's a copy on the top shelf," said Tatia, pointing to the bookcase that held the school supplies. We can discuss it when you finish it if you still have questions."

The next fifteen minutes were hectic as missing shoes were located, errant strands of hair were tamed, the car was loaded, and the Matthews departed for church. The quiet that descended on the house after they had gone was almost scary to Madison, but Tatia had left her cell phone and Jesse's number in case she needed them before they returned. She made up her mind she wasn't going to let her imagination run away with her, so she turned on the sound system to the Southern Gospel station Tatia had introduced her to and busied herself cleaning up her breakfast dishes and tidying the children's rooms. By the time she had showered and dressed in house pants and a sweatshirt she and Joy had found in the box in the Annex, she was feeling much more comfortable.

She located Tatia's book and made another cup of decaf before settling on the couch under the comfy fleece throw that had become her favorite. Harley jumped onto the couch, and after sniffing her thoroughly, he curled up in her lap and began to purr. Feeling warm and safe, she opened the book and was soon engrossed in Tatia's life – and she knew she was going to need tissues.

She was surprised when the back door opened several hours later and Joy and Daniel exploded into the room. Daniel clutched the empty plastic container that had held the salad, and Joy carried the slow cooker in its carrier. Based on the ease with which she handled it, the soup had been a success as well. Tatia followed closely behind them, loaded down with Bibles, Sunday School handouts, jackets, and the miscellaneous detritus that seems to collect around children.

Madison smiled at the unfamiliar domestic scene. "I'm glad you left me some soup and salad. It doesn't look as if you brought home any leftovers."

Tatia grinned. "I never do. Several of our single people don't cook much for themselves and the income of some families doesn't allow many extras. We keep plenty of take-home containers and encourage them to clear out any leftovers. They take home food for a meal or two and we don't have to find a place in the refrigerator for salad that becomes soggy before it's eaten and soup that hides on a bottom shelf until it turns green and furry. A win-win all around."

"I didn't know there were so many kind people in the world," sighed Madison. Her expression turned serious as she looked down at the book in her hands. "I also didn't know there were so many evil people in the world."

"I think you've encountered your share of evil in your short life. Maybe we can talk later if you like, but right now, I need to settle these two wild children down for some quiet time."

"Aw, Mommy," whined Daniel. "I don't wanna take a nap."

"Who said anything about a nap? You two go change out of your church clothes – and hang them up if you didn't spill food on them. If you did – hamper, please. Then come back, choose a book or puzzle, and spend a few quiet minutes in here with Madison."

She looked at Madison, "Jessie's gone to his office for a few minutes. The accountant has been after him for some figures for a couple of weeks now and won't be put off any longer. And I have a little writing to do. Do you mind keeping an eye on them for a little while?"

"I'd love to," said Madison. "Always glad to help."

Joy and Daniel changed more than their clothes while they were in their rooms. Instead of noisy and animated, they moved back into the living room slowly and quietly. Daniel dragged his blanket and rubbed his eyes as he followed Joy to the bookcase, and she stifled a yawn as she pulled a couple of books off the shelf. She handed him a book of illustrated poems, and she carried a well-worn copy of *Anne of Green Gables* to Tatia's chair where she curled up under an afghan.

"I want to sit by you," said Daniel, scrambling up on the sofa beside Madison and snuggling up under her arm.

"Don't bother her, Daniel," said Joy. "She's trying to read."

"It's okay. I can still read, and he'll keep me warm."

Soon the only sound was the occasional turn of a page – and then the soft, regular breathing of children sleeping. Madison had just finished another chapter when Jesse came in the back door. She laid her finger across her lips and pointed at the sleepers. He nodded, closing the door quietly and slipping off his shoes.

"I can take over now if there's anything else you want to do," Jesse whispered

"I would like to go over to the Annex and talk with Tatia for a little while if it's okay."

"Sure. In fact, I may just snuggle down with this little guy and snooze a bit myself." He gently picked up his son so Madison could slip off the sofa. Then he laid down on his side with Daniel spooned up against him. Before Madison made it to the door, Jesse was breathing as evenly and deeply as his children.

Madison was still smiling at the sweet scene when she walked into Tatia's office. The room wasn't big, but it was comfortable and inviting. The front door was offset to the left, and the stained concrete floor was covered with a cream colored Chateau rug with a subtle gray and blue floral design. A damask-covered sofa with a design that picked up the colors of the rug sat against the right-hand wall with a small rosewood coffee table in front of it. Two Queen Anne guest chairs covered in pale gray chenille faced a large rosewood pedestal desk with a gray leather executive chair behind it. The back wall was covered with built-in cabinets and shelves that were filled with books, pamphlets, and small copies of the New Testament. The office radiated the warm feel of the woman who most often occupied it, and the furniture had the well-loved feel of high-end garage sale finds. Tatia had just pushed back from her desk and had her arms stretched above her head.

"Am I bothering you?" asked Madison.

Tatia smiled at her, a smile that went all the way to her eyes and made Madison feel welcome. "Not at all. I was just about to take a break and have some peppermint tea. Would you like some?"

"Yes, please. It's one of my favorites."

She followed Tatia into the large empty space behind the office. They headed toward a small kitchenette that was nestled into the corner formed by the front wall of the bedroom and the side wall of the bathroom. An L-shaped counter held a microwave, a one-cup-at-a-time coffee maker, and a bar-sized sink. A small refrigerator and several feet of storage space filled the area underneath, and storage cabinets hung on the wall above the counter. Tatia pulled a couple of mugs out of one of the cabinets and tea bags out of a drawer beneath the coffee maker. As the tea brewed, Tatia directed her guest to the creamers and sweeteners, and once their tea was mixed to their individual preferences, they returned to the office.

"Let's sit on the couch," invited Tatia. "It's much more comfortable than the desk area and more conducive to a casual chat."

Madison sipped her tea appreciatively, but she had trouble returning Tatia's gaze. She had come in response to Tatia's invitation to talk later, but now that she was here, she didn't know how to begin. But Tatia did.

"I know you have questions about my life, but a lot of those will be answered in the rest of the book. We can talk about me then. But you don't have a book, so why don't you tell me about your life with Misty."

Madison sipped her tea again, and her eyes took on a faraway look, as if she was watching a movie of her past.

"I don't remember much of anything before Misty. I have flashes of memories that I assume are from that time, but it's like photos in an album with no context or meaning. I don't even remember how I ended up with her, and the first couple of years are just a series of disconnected memories. Like being dressed up and photographed the way they did Joy."

Madison made a sound that could have been a laugh, but there was no happiness in it. "That didn't work out the way she intended. One of the first real memories I have is hearing her on the phone talking to a buyer. She was excited by the price he offered but not so much by his terms. I didn't know what it all meant at the time, but I pieced it together later. Apparently, he normally checked out her merchandise personally and then resold them, but this time he wanted to keep me for himself. He wanted her to raise me until he was ready for me."

Madison sipped her tea silently for a few minutes, so Tatia prompted her gently. "Do you know what his intentions were?"

"Yes," continued Madison with a sad smile. "He intended to marry me, or at least use me as a courtesan when he entertained his questionable business associates."

"Was it his business that was questionable or his associates?"

"Both, I think. He always had two men with him that looked like the bodyguards in the movies. They stood outside the door, but sometimes he would call them for some reason and they responded instantly. One of them forgot to button his jacket once, and when he leaned over to hear what Mike was saying, it fell open and exposed a gun in a shoulder holster. Mike yelled at him and I saw a flash of fear or hate in the other man's eyes – maybe both."

"So his name is Mike. Do you know anything else about him?" asked Tatia.

"Not really. He visited maybe once or twice a year when I was younger, but when I approached my teens, he began to visit more regularly – I guess to check on my progress and to see if he was getting his money's worth. He must be a public figure, though. I was allowed to watch TV, but the news channels and updates were blocked. The newspapers and magazines they gave me to read had certain stories cut out. He seemed nice enough. He always brought me gifts, and he seemed interested in what I had to say. But there was something really hard in his eyes that scared me a little bit."

"How was Misty as a surrogate mother?"

"Distant and uninvolved. She hired tutors in every subject you can imagine. I have been trained in all the social graces. I know how to plan and serve a seven-course meal – with a large staff to do the actual work, of course. As Joy can testify, I don't even know how to make a grilled cheese sandwich – or I didn't until I came here." She smiled gratefully at Tatia.

"I've also been trained in how to satisfy a man's physical desires – all those things a good little courtesan knows how to do." Her voice became so soft Tatia had to strain to hear her, and tears began to trickle from the corners of her eyes. Tatia put her hand tentatively on Madison's arm, not sure if her touch would be welcome.

"I'm so sorry you had to go through that."

Madison used her free hand to dash the tears away and then laid it on Tatia's hand. "Oh, it wasn't all that bad. Misty and my tutor showed me explicit movies and illustrated books and described various techniques and positions in detail. The tutor and I even practiced the positions sometimes – everybody was fully clothed, but it was so gross. I learned to kind of disconnect my mind from what my body was doing. I didn't have a happy place to think about, so I just let my mind slide into a void - my own little sensory deprivation tank." She breathed out a heavy sigh. "I'm still technically a virgin, though, so I guess that's something."

Tatia put her other hand on top of Madison's and swallowed hard to push down the anger that rose in her throat. "Sometimes psychological and emotional abuse can be harder to deal with than physical abuse. And, of course, there were the drugs. You told me a little about them when you first came, but tell me about how that started."

A bitter smile twisted Madison's normally beautiful mouth. "That was Misty's doing. Her maternal instincts were weak whenever I woke her up, frightened and crying after having a nightmare. So she gave me valium. A quarter of a tablet at first, but more as I got bigger and developed more of a tolerance. Then when I tried to get away, she started giving me injections to keep me too zoned out to figure out how to operate the elevator even if I managed to get out the door. She eased off a little on the dosage when she knew Mike was coming for a visit."

"I hope you don't mind all the questions."

"Not at all. It's a relief to talk about it after holding it in all these years." She looked at Tatia with gratitude. "And it's a relief not to see shock or revulsion in the way you look at me."

Tatia couldn't stop herself from hugging Madison, and Madison returned the hug. "Oh sweetheart, you've read some of my book. Nothing much shocks me anymore, and you did nothing wrong. As we walk through this with you, it helps to know what you went through. So can I ask another question?"

"Sure. Anything."

"Joy said Victor thought you were Misty's girlfriend. Was that true?"

"No, but not because she didn't want to be. She put me in the guest room at first, but after a few of my nightmares, she took me into her bed." She sat thoughtfully for a moment before she continued. "I guess she was a little bit motherly, after all. Anyway, when I was a little older and wanted to go back to my own bed, she wouldn't let me. Sometimes she'd get a little closer than necessary or drop suggestive hints, but all I had to say was 'What would Mike think about that?' and she'd stop. I guess her fear was stronger than whatever else she had in mind."

"Well, it's a good thing you're out from under Mike's control and Misty's. But enough about him and your old life. Let me shut down my computer and we'll see what kind of trouble the kids have talked Jesse into."

"Sounds good," said Madison, picking up the empty mugs. "I'll go rinse these out while you finish up in here."

"Thanks," replied Tatia. "And thank you for trusting me with your story."

Madison put the clean mugs away and was wiping the counter when she heard the door open behind her. "We're almost done here. We'll be there in a minute."

"I'm sorry," an unfamiliar voice said behind her. "Am I interrupting something?"

"No," said Madison, turning around quickly. "Not at all. I didn't mean to be rude. I thought it was the kids coming over to see if they can have a snack. They're always hungry." She smiled and approached the young woman standing hesitantly in the doorway. She extended her hand and said, "You must be Lili. I'm Madison. Tatia and Jesse are helping me, too."

Lili returned her smile and took her hand. "Hello, Madison. I am pleased to meet you." She relaxed and stepped inside. "I understand about children. I have younger siblings who are also always hungry."

"Good," said Tatia, entering the room and locking the office behind her. "I'm glad you two have introduced yourselves. Now, let's get over to the house before my voracious children come looking for us."

"I do not want to be a bother," said Lili.

Madison laughed, a sound that made Tatia's heart happy after the serious talk they had shared. "You won't be a bother. There are always extra people in this house."

Lili looked at Tatia for confirmation, and seeing her smile she nodded. "Yes. I will come with you. I have missed my family, and it will be good to be around children for a while."

It was Tatia's turn to laugh. "It's decided then," she said as she linked arms with both girls. "But we'll wait and see how good it is until after you've met them."

21

Sunday - 10/1

"I'm hungry," said Daniel before Tatia and Madison were fully into the house. He and Joy were sitting on either side of Jesse while he read them the Sunday comics.

"Of course you are," said Tatia. "You're a five-year-old boy and being hungry is in your job description."

"How about nine-year-old girls?" asked Joy.

"And forty-year-old husbands?"

"Okay, okay! Snacks all around. And while I'm checking to see if there's anything left in this house to eat, put on your best manners and introduce yourselves to our new friend, Lili. And try not to make her regret her decision to come meet you."

Tatia busied herself in the kitchen slicing up a couple of apples, pulling out a variety of cheese sticks, and opening a bag of unsalted almonds. She divided the food onto small plastic plates and lined them up on the counter between the kitchen and the dining area.

"May I take this into the living room and sit with Madison?" asked Joy.

"Sure," replied Tatia. "Take a plate for her, too. Daniel, can you take a plate to Lili?"

"Sure," said Daniel, jumping up from the floor where he had been reading to Harley. He looked at the selection on the plates and said, "Remy's mom gives him cookies and chips for snacks."

"Aren't you blessed that your mommy loves you enough to prepare delicious and healthy snacks?" asked Jesse.

Daniel sighed. "I guess."

"What did you say?" asked Jesse, grabbing the boy and wrestling with him.

"Yes," he said softly with a giggle.

"I can't hear you," said Jesse, pinning him to the floor gently.

"I said yes," yelled Daniel as Jesse rolled over onto his back and let Daniel sit on him..

"That's what I thought you said," said Jesse, sitting up and pulling him into a hug. "Now, serve our guest and eat your delicious and healthy snack. Then we'll go out and throw the football around."

"Yay!" Daniel grabbed two plates and headed for the living room. He stopped and turned back toward the kitchen. "Thank you, Mommy, for the 'licious and healthy snack."

Madison and Lili were watching the interaction from the sofa. "I wish I had a little brother," said Madison.

Joy, who was sitting on the floor in front of them, rolled her eyes. "You can have mine – anytime!"

Tatia and Jesse joined the others in the living room, and Tatia encouraged each person to tell Lili a little about themselves.

Thirty minutes later, snacks were gone, plates were in the dishwasher, and the family was in the back yard having an impromptu punt, pass, and kick contest. Madison, still feeling a little overwhelmed, opted to stay inside and read. Lili, on the other hand, went out to join the fun, but since she was still in her church clothes, she sat on a bench under a tree and shouted encouragement. After being thrown to the grass once too often, Tatia joined her.

"If we could only harness that energy," she said as she sat down.

"Yes," agreed Lili. "Children never do anything slowly."

"Did you work with children in Antigua?"

"No. I did work at the school, but only in the office."

"What kind of things did you do," Tatia said, her interest piqued.

"Anything that needed to be done. My title was Office Manager, but I did everything from keeping the financial records and typing all the correspondence to cleaning the toilets and making the coffee."

Tatia sighed. "If I could only find someone like that."

"You do not have any office help?" asked Lili.

"No. I have volunteers who come in from time to time, but I lost my regular receptionist a couple of months ago when her husband was transferred to the West Coast."

"I do not have classes until late tomorrow afternoon. I would be glad to help in any way I can in return for your kindness."

"Oh, Lili! That would be wonderful."

"Now, if you will not be offended, I will go back to my room. I do not know what has happened to my energy, but I am very tired."

"Everyone will understand. You're going through a lot, and stress is very tiring. We'll probably have sandwiches around 6:00 if you'd like to join us."

"Thank you, but I have leftovers from my lunch, so I will eat that if I get hungry."

"Sounds good. We have breakfast around 6:30. Come on over and join us if you're up by then."

Madison was still in the living room reading Tatia's book, and after finishing a particularly emotional chapter, she leaned over to grab a tissue. Her eyes fell on the front page of the newspaper that was carelessly strewn across the coffee table, and she let out a gasp. Just then, Tatia came in the back door laughing.

"No," she yelled back to the football players. "I'm not coming back to the game. I'm definitely not NFL material." Shaking her head she turned toward the living room. "Those kids are...Madison, what's wrong? You look like you've seen a ghost."

Madison was staring at the newspaper, and what little color she had gained in her face in the last few days was gone. "Come look," she said, pointing to the picture under the banner headline.

Tatia made it across the room in record time and sat next to Madison, sliding her arm around her shoulders and pulling her close. "What is it, sweetheart?"

"Him!" Madison exclaimed. "Read the headline and the caption."

"'Saint under Investigation,'" Tatia read aloud. "'Owner and CEO of tech giant Saint International, Michael D. Saint, is under investigation by the FBI for alleged ties to organized crime, possibly as the boss of a splinter group that broke off from the Outfit in the 90s.' It seems like I read some rumors about him when I was researching trafficking in the Chicago area. But don't let that upset you...wait!" She looked more closely at the photo and then back at Madison. "That's not..."

"Yes," Madison said. "That's Mike – and he's not just a pervert. He's a crime boss."

###

After a light supper of sandwiches, fresh veggies with hummus dip, and peach yogurt Tatia could tell that Madison was fading quickly. She suggested they have their family devotion time before they left the table so Jesse retrieved his Bible. He opened it to the Gospel of Luke and read the parable of the prodigal son. After he had explained the story, with a little extra help from Daniel, he prayed for his family and their new friends, calling them by name and asking a special blessing on each one. When they had finished,

Tatia was pleased to see that the tension had left Madison's face and she wasn't as pale as she had been earlier.

"I'll help clear the table tonight," Madison announced as the children argued over whose turn it was to help. "It's time I began pulling my weight around here instead of just lying around all day."

"Yay! Can we go outside and play football some more?" asked Daniel.

Tatia looked at Jesse, and he gave her a slight nod. "Okay," she said. "But no fussing when Daddy says it's time to come in."

Tatia and Madison made quick work of the dishes. While Tatia wiped out the sink and set out coffee cups for the next morning, Madison wandered over to the windows and stared out the window at Jesse and the children.

"Do you want to go join the game?" asked Tatia.

"No. I think I'll go to bed in a few minutes. I guess I'm not as strong as I thought."

"It's only been a week, and you've done amazingly well, but you need to listen to your body. I think an early bedtime is a good call."

Madison nodded without saying anything, and Tatia could see moisture glistening in her eyes. She crossed to where the girl was standing and asked quietly, "Is anything else bothering you?"

"I was thinking about Mike. That night when they brought Joy to the apartment, I heard Misty on the phone telling somebody about her. I think it was Mike. I think he's the one who bought her."

For a few seconds, Tatia felt like she couldn't breathe, and all the panic of that night returned. She managed to catch her breath, and she forced herself to remain calm. "What did she say that makes you think that?"

"She said something like, 'If you like her, I'll expect my usual finder's fee – but if you buy her, you deal with her. I'm not raising another one.'"

Tatia felt a rush of loathing for the man who had controlled

Madison's life and had tried to do the same thing to her daughter. She crossed her arms in front of her as if trying to hold in the rage that bubbled up, but she couldn't suppress the wordless moan that escaped from her throat.

"Oh, Tatia," exclaimed Madison in alarm. "I didn't mean to upset you."

"No, no!" said Tatia, pulling Madison into a tight embrace. "You did good. I'll call the detectives who are working on Joy's kidnapping. They will probably want to talk with you. In the meantime, you tell me anything you remember that might get that monster off the streets before he ruins more lives."

22

Sunday - 10/1

Eric and Victor were living pretty well in the special housing unit. They were the only two prisoners in a pod consisting of four cells, each with three real walls and one barred wall across the front. They were put at opposites ends of the row, but they were not completely cut off from each other. The cell doors were opened in the morning and left that way until lights out in the evening, and they were allowed free access to a common area in front of the cells. Four reasonably comfortable chairs were lined up against the long wall, and a six-foot table and four chairs sat in the center of the room where they doubled as both work space and dining room.

All their meals, which continued to be acceptable considering the circumstances, were served in the pod, but they were taken to a very small private exercise yard for an hour a day where Victor tossed a basketball at the lone net and Eric paced back and forth like a caged lion. Every other day they were escorted to the roof which featured a large recreational yard surrounded by a thirty-foot concrete wall with fenced openings. With no other inmates to contend with, Victor had plenty of space to dribble from one end to the other and further hone his basketball skills – and Eric had an even larger space in which to pace and wonder how much these special outings were costing them.

Between meals and their occasional outings, Victor spent a good deal of his time studying the Inmate Handbook he had been given during their orientation meeting with the warden their second day at MCC. Each time he found another activity or program that might be available to them, he asked Harris, their daytime guard, about it. After several days, they had developed an odd kind of camaraderie. When Victor asked about reading material, Harris said he couldn't take them to the library on the ninth floor because of their protected status and because there were always other people there – but he did arrange for the library trustee to bring the book cart by a couple of times a week stocked with some computer magazines that Victor wanted and newspapers that Eric wanted.

However, he was unsuccessful in arranging a trip to the recreation center in the basement which the handbook said was stocked with fitness equipment and a selection of board games. He finally resorted to hinting there might be an extra incentive for anyone who could add a twice a week workout to their routine. Harris looked cautiously interested and asked a few general questions. Eric saw this situation as his opportunity to cut Vandoren out of the financial loop.

"At this point," he explained to Harris, "all our requests for special non-commissary items go through our attorney. Of course, he takes his cut which eats into the amount we have to work with. If someone could arrange for Victor to have Internet access, we could make our requests and show our gratitude directly."

Harris nodded his understanding. "I'll look into it," he said with a yawn and went back to the magazine he had been reading.

###

"These guys really don't know how to keep their mouths shut, especially Ellis," said Ian. He was sitting on a sofa in the den of Michael's penthouse one floor above the executive offices of Saint International. Everything around him spoke of luxury and comfort, but he was anything but comfortable, knowing that one wrong word could push a button that would cause an eruption of rage. "Our man on the inside says that Hall is pretty closed-mouthed most of the time, but all it takes to get Ellis to open up is an extra smoke break." He glanced at his notes because Michael demanded accurate as well as speedy reports. "He didn't get a specific account balance, but it's over a million. It came from an underground auction, but he didn't say what was being sold. I guess he's smart enough to know that child traffickers are not viewed kindly in prison."

Michael glared at him so Ian knew he had stepped into sensitive territory and continued quickly. "He also learned that the money is in a numbered Swiss account, and Hall is not computer savvy enough to be able to access it."

"Sounds more and more like our guys – and my money," said Michael with satisfaction.

"Yes, it does. And we got a real break today. Vandoren got a message from our guy that Hall opened up to his guard today. It seems he and Ellis want access to the workout room in the basement, and Hall hinted that he would like to deal direct rather than through Vandoren."

"Okay. Tell them to stall a little longer on computer access but continue to extend credit – for now. Make sure our techs know that locating my money is of critical importance to all concerned. We'll secure our refund and learn whether Hall and his buddy can be of any help in locating Madison before we deal with them permanently."

23

Sunday - 10/1

Later that night, after the children were in bed, Tatia told Jesse what she had learned from Madison. "That's great information," he said. "I'll call Tracy in the morning and let her know. She'll know what to do next."

Tatia snuggled in next to Jesse on the sofa. He was scanning through the newspaper without seeing much, and she had just opened the book she was reading. She was staring at the words but thinking of Detectives Martin and Nelson, the so-called Kiddie Cops who had been so instrumental in tracking down Eric and Victor and rescuing Joy. The quiet moment was shattered when they heard a shriek from the girls' room.

"Another nightmare," exclaimed Tatia. She sat frozen for a moment, waiting to see if Madison quieted on her own. Another terror-filled scream split the air, and Tatia jumped to her feet, dropping her book on the floor. "This sounds like a bad one!"

She made it to the door in seconds and found Madison thrashing against the covers and wailing. "She's on fire! I can't...too hot...my fault... cigarette...Mama!"

Tatia shook her gently by the shoulders and spoke to her softly. "Madison. Wake up, honey. It's just a dream. It's okay. I'm here."

When Madison finally opened her eyes, they were glazed and wild with what they had seen. Tatia continued to sooth with her words while gently rubbing the hysterical girl's arms and shoulders. Gradually, Madison's eyes focused, and she dissolved into tears. She sat up and clutched at Tatia like an exhausted swimmer at a life preserver.

"Oh, Tatia," she whispered. "I remember."

"Mommy," said Joy in a sleepy voice. "Is Madison okay?"

"Yes. We're going into the other room so we can talk. Why don't you close your eyes and pray for her."

"Okay, Mommy," she said with a yawn. Tatia doubted she would get much praying done before sleep drew her back into its embrace.

Madison continued to cling to her as they walked toward the living room. Tatia guided her toward the couch. "Jesse, would you make us some chamomile tea, please?"

While he busied himself in the kitchen, Tatia drew a blanket around herself and Madison, and the girl snuggled even closer. Tatia held her silently until Jesse set a tray with a teapot, two empty mugs, and a small plate of lemon cookies on the coffee table in front of them.

"Good for what ails you, ladies. I'll be in the bedroom if you need anything else." He winked at Tatia and she directed an air kiss toward him before he slipped out of the room. She gently disentangled herself from Madison's grip and began pouring tea. She held a steaming mug of the fragrant liquid out to the girl.

"Here you go, sweetheart. Take a few whiffs of this and see if you can sip a little of it."

Madison stared uncomprehendingly at first, but as the warm steam bathed her face, she took a deep breath. "It does smell nice," she said. She took the mug and cradled it in both hands, taking more deep breaths. She finally took a sip, and Tatia could see some of the tension leave her face and body. Tatia took her own cup and sat back into the sofa.

"Do you think you can tell me what you remembered?"

Madison began to speak in a flat voice as if telling the story of a stranger. "It was in a mobile home – a small, messy one. I woke up on the couch and smelled smoke. I could see flames in the bedroom at the back of the house. That was where Mama slept. I ran back there, but it was too hot. I could see Mama. She looked like..." She choked out a sob and then took a deep breath. She had a faraway look as if seeing the scene play out in front of her. She sipped her tea for a couple of minutes before putting the mug down on the table. When she continued, her voice was a little stronger.

"She looked like the turkey she left in the oven too long at Thanksgiving when she was too busy sampling the wine. My face was getting really hot, and the floor was pretty warm, too. I ran and ran and ran – out of the house, down the driveway between the row of houses, and across the street to the playground in the park. I laid face down across one of the swings and began to spin slowly, winding up the chain. When the chain was tight, I lifted my feet and let it spin me the other way."

Tatia got the feeling Madison had crossed a line somewhere in her narrative between her dream and her memory.

"I kept spinning until I was dizzy and felt a little sick, so I just laid there, not moving. I heard a voice saying, 'Hey, kid, you okay?' I said I was but I didn't look up. I recognized the voice – it was the manager of the mobile home park, and I didn't like him. He came over to our house sometimes, and when he was there, I had to go outside. He stared at me a lot, too, and it gave me the creeps.

"I heard sirens. He said it was the police coming, and he said when they found out my mama was dead, they'd put me in an orphanage. I didn't know what an orphanage was, but he said it was awful. He said he knew a really nice lady who would take care of me – and he said we'd stop for ice cream on the way. Of course, the nice lady was Misty – and we didn't stop for ice cream after all."

After the traumatic return of her early memories, Tatia expected Madison to be agitated or at least troubled. Instead, she was drained and seemed almost relieved to be a giant step closer to the riddle of who she was. Once her narrative ended, she sipped her tea until her eyes began to droop and she yawned again and again. Before the mug was half empty, she set it on the tray and said, "I'm going back to bed now."

"Good idea, Madison. We can talk again in the morning if you like."

"Yes, I'd like that." She leaned over and kissed Tatia lightly on the cheek. "Thank you for being there for me."

24

Monday – 10/2

Tatia didn't hear anything from any of the children until the next morning shortly after Brush arrived. Joy appeared first followed soon by Daniel. Madison came in a few minutes later with no evidence of her nighttime ordeal.

"Madison, come sit by me," said Daniel, a few decibels louder than his inside voice. He stood on the bench and nudged Joy with his foot. "We can scoot over to make room."

Joy scooted, Daniel sidestepped beside her, and Madison slid into the vacant seat. "Good morning, short stuff," she teased. He giggled and then began examining her head closely. Tatia turned to bring Madison a cup of coffee, and her mouth dropped open.

"Daniel Matthews, why are you standing on the bench? Sit down this instant!"

"Wait, Mommy! This is important," he said as ran his finger down the center of Madison's head. "Your black hair is turning brown by your head."

Madison laughed, and Tatia swallowed a gulp of coffee along with her own laughter. "Yes, Daniel," said Madison. "That's my real hair color showing through. Now sit down like Mommy said and I'll tell you something else about me."

Daniel squatted on the bench and cut his eyes over at Tatia to see if she noticed. She shook her head slightly, so he grinned and slid down into a sitting position. He turned his attention on Madison. "I'm sitting. Tell me something else 'bout you."

"Nothing about me is real," said Madison. "Even my name. My mother named me Madelyn, but Misty thought it wasn't sophisticated enough so she changed it."

"I like Madelyn," said Daniel.

"Me, too!" added Joy.

Daniel thought for a minute. "I like Madison, too. Which one should I call you?"

"Well, why don't you call me Maddie."

"Yeah! I like that. What's your last name?"

"I don't even know, Daniel. I never knew my dad. I think Mama told fortunes or something like that, and she called herself Crystal Mystic." There was sadness in her laugh. "Perfect for a tarot card reader, but not so great for a normal person. I guess I'll never be normal."

"Sure you will. You can borrow my last name if you want to. Maddie Matthews. That sounds pretty normal to me." Maddie hugged him and he liked that, but he didn't understand why there were tears in her eyes.

"Maddie," said Joy. "I'll bet Johnny could find out your real name. He knows how to find anything on the computer."

"Joy, that's an excellent idea," said Jesse. "Why don't you ask him about it at lunch?"

"Yeah," added Brush with a grin. "I'm sure he would be willing to spend a little extra time with Madison, I mean Maddie."

Tatia noticed the blush that crept into Maddie's face and spoke up. "Okay, guys. Enough chit-chat. You have a business to run."

"And I have a phone call to make," said Jesse, giving Tatia a meaningful look.

"Speaking of lunch," added Brush, "it's my day in the kitchen. Shawna took pity on us and packed a picnic basket. I looked real cool with that on the back of my bike!"

The family brought their dishes to the kitchen and scattered to their normal Monday activities. Maddie stayed in the kitchen to help Tatia with the cleanup.

"You know, if you want to go back to your natural hair color, I have a stylist who's great with color," said Tatia while they worked.

Maddie smiled. "And let me guess. She volunteers for the ministry and doesn't charge."

"You learn fast, girl!"

"I think I'd like that. I haven't straightened it since I've been here, and it looks like I have a bit of natural wave. Maybe she could trim it up to make use of that - something less severe."

"I think you'd look great with that kind of cut - and nothing lifts the spirits like a new hairstyle! I'll call her this afternoon and get something set up."

Maddie fell silent as she watched Tatia put the last dishes in the dishwasher. "Do you think Johnny could really find out something about my past?" she asked.

"I'm sure of it. He found Joy, didn't he?" answered Tatia.

"Speaking of finding people, where's Lili this morning?"

"She was here earlier. She took a cup of coffee in a go cup and said she wanted to take a walk."

"She doesn't eat much, does she?"

"No, she doesn't. I know she's going through a tough time, but she needs to eat. I plan to talk with her about that later. Now," she said as she wiped out the sink and dried her hands. "I don't know what your plans are for the morning, but Lili offered to help me in the office before her afternoon classes. Joy has an independent project to work on, but would you be willing to help Daniel with his reading and his spelling?"

"I'd love to! As soon as I get dressed, I'll be ready."

Tatia showered and dressed in record time, but Maddie and the children were already seated around the table with their work spread out in front of them when she returned to the dining/classroom. Joy was explaining her project on the history of Texas to Maddie and was proudly displaying her drawings of the six flags that had flown over the Lone Star State.

"I chose this state because Mommy was born there and Grandma and Grandpa live there," she said. "I'm working on maps now. I tried to do the outline by myself, but the Panhandle isn't right and the part down by Mexico looks funny. Daddy said he'd show me how to use math to get the proportions right after he finishes a cover-up tattoo this morning. So now I'm reading about the farming and industry in Texas so I can make an Economic and Resource map. It will show where different crops are grown and where oil, granite, etcetera are found."

"Nice explanation, Joy," said Tatia. "And a good use of one of your vocabulary words. What other types of maps are you creating?"

"A demographic map that will show the areas where people live and a topographic map that shows mountains and deserts and stuff like that."

"It sounds like you know what you're doing – which is a good thing since I didn't learn much geography from my tutors," said Maddie. "And what are you working on, Daniel?"

"I'm reading this," he said, showing her a copy of a book about creation.

"Where's your folder, Daniel?" prompted Tatia.

"Oh, yeah," he said, scooting off the bench and running over to the shelf.

"Get your spelling folder while you're over there." She turned to

Maddie. "He's about halfway through. There's a bookmark. Let him read it out loud to you. Try to let him sound out any unfamiliar words if he can, but you may need to help here and there. There are some vocabulary exercises in his folder – they're pretty self-explanatory – and a word search game as well as a matching game. When he finishes that, move on to spelling. He knows which lesson he's on, and I printed off a sheet that outlines the exercises he needs to go through. They usually take a 15-20 minute break around 10:00. Joy knows what snacks are allowed and where to find them – and no cheating, young lady," she teased.

"Who me?" Joy asked innocently. "I guess you mean no candy or cookies – as if there were any in this house!"

"Good point!" laughed Tatia. "Maddie, do you have any questions?"

"I don't think so. It sounds like a lot of fun. I never thought I'd be a teacher."

"You'll do fine – but if you need me, you know where I am. You two, be good for Maddie. Okay?"

After hugs and kisses all around, Tatia headed out the door leaving school in session. When she reached the Annex, Tatia found Lili dressed and seated at the small desk in the bedroom. She was deeply engrossed in a thick book and flinched slightly when Tatia tapped on the door jamb.

"I'm sorry," said Tatia. "I didn't mean to startle you."

"That is okay," replied Lili. She closed the book and covered it with a notebook, but not before Tatia saw that it was a textbook on embryology. "I was catching up on some of my reading. There's so much of it in med school."

"I can imagine. If you need to study instead of working in the office…"

"No, no! I need a break from bones and muscles."

"Good. I'm going to make a cup of coffee before I begin. Would you like one?"

Lili's face seemed to lose a little color, but after an almost imperceptible hesitation, she responded. "Yes, that would be nice. Thank you."

Tatia chatted as she busied herself with the coffee. "Did you sleep well last night?"

"Yes, the bed is very comfortable and the room is very homelike."

"Joy will be pleased to hear that. She and her grandmother laid out the plans, and she found everything but the bed at a garage sale. The bedding was still in the original packaging." She shut the lid on the coffee pod, and the hot liquid began to spew into the cup. "It's a beautiful morning out there. How was your walk?"

"I enjoyed it very much. You live in a lovely neighborhood, and everyone is so friendly. Everyone I saw nodded, waved, or said good morning."

"Yes. As we say in Texas, they're good folks. Cream and a little stevia, right?"

"Yes, please." Again, a slight hesitation.

Tatia turned and held the steaming cup out to Lili. "It's not gourmet, but..."

As the warm, fragrant steam rose toward Lili's face, she blanched, threw her hand across her mouth, and dashed into the bathroom.

"Well, well, well," mused Tatia softly. She took a sip of the coffee before searching the cabinet for some chamomile tea. When Lili emerged from the bathroom a few minutes later, Tatia was sitting on the couch in her office. Lili kept her head down, avoiding Tatia's gaze.

"I'm so sorry," she said.

"Don't worry about it," said Tatia, patting the sofa beside her. "Have a seat and relax. I made you some tea that might help settle your stomach – but don't force it."

"Thank you," Lili whispered. She settled next to Tatia, clasped her hands in her lap, and stared down at them as if they belonged to someone else. "I must have eaten something bad at lunch yesterday."

Tatia reached over gently and laid her hand on Lili's arm. "How far along are you?"

Lili finally raised her eyes to Tatia's. "About six weeks, I think."

"That's why he threw you out, isn't it?"

"Yes. He said he didn't want any whining brats in his apartment. He said I could come back after I had an abortion."

"How noble of him. Have you seen a doctor yet?"

"No. I don't have insurance, and healthcare is so expensive. I confided in a friend who is studying radiology. She needs a subject for a sonogram, and she has me on the schedule for Thursday. I guess I'll decide what to do next once I find out for sure."

"Dr. Patterson is coming to see Maddie tomorrow. I can ask him to see you if you like."

"Oh," said Lili in surprise. "Is she pregnant as well?"

"No," Tatia said with a smile. "She has a lot of problems, but that's not one of them. And Dr. Patterson isn't an obstetrician. He's an old-fashioned general practitioner who volunteers his time when we need him. I'm sure he'd be glad to at least consult with you."

"I would be grateful." Lili paused and took a few sips of her tea. "I am feeling much better now. I think I am ready to help you with whatever you need to do."

The morning passed quickly and it was soon time to go back to the house for lunch.

"We have accomplished so much in such a short time," said Tatia. "You are amazingly efficient. I need someone like you to tend to ministry business while I work with the children."

"Perhaps I can help on a regular basis if you like. All of my classes are in the afternoon or evening."

"That's a wonderful idea, Lili – if you have time between classes and studying! My ministry budget includes fifteen hours a week for office help, and I'm sure a little extra spending money would be welcome while you're setting up housekeeping."

"I should have plenty of time now that I am not distracted by a relationship,"

"Then it's decided! We'll need to do some paperwork and go over some details, but that can wait until tomorrow. Do you feel like you can eat something?" Tatia asked.

"Yes. The sickness has passed, and I am so hungry I feel as if I can eat anything that is put in front of me."

"Another blessing!" exclaimed Tatia, locking the office door behind her.

Daniel had just lifted his pencil from his spelling test and shouted, "Done!" when Tatia and Lili walked in the front door and Brush walked in the back with a huge basket. Jesse and Johnny followed close behind, and a meal of turkey and cheese wraps, deviled eggs, veggie sticks, dip, and an assortment of fresh fruit was soon in progress. Table conversation was lively as Maddie and the children described their morning in the classroom and Tatia and Lili shared their news about the new ministry secretary.

"That's wonderful, Lili," said Jesse. "You'll take a big load off Tatia."

"It is my pleasure," replied Lili. "Unfortunately, I have to go if I am to catch my bus to my afternoon classes."

"Do you need a ride?" asked Tatia.

"No. I forgot to mention that my friend took me by the bus station yesterday, and I purchased a thirty-day bus pass. It is much less expensive than Uber, and the schedules work out perfectly for my classes."

"That's great! Should we expect you for dinner?"

"No, but thank you. I have a late lab and will eat on campus."

When everyone else was almost finished, Tatia caught Jesse's eye and asked quietly, "Did you make that phone call?"

"Yeah," he responded, "but I had to leave a message." Then he looked at Joy. "Hey, sweetie. Don't you have something you wanted to ask Johnny?"

"Oh, yeah! I almost forgot. Maddie doesn't know her last name or anything like that. Could you look on the computer and find out for her?"

Johnny didn't even try to hide his grin. "I can't promise results, but I'd sure be willing to give it a try."

"I'll bet," said Brush.

Tatia glared at him, and he didn't continue. "Maddie, you'll need to tell him what you do remember. Johnny, you can grab a pen and tablet off the school supply shelf if you need to take notes."

"Thanks, Mrs. M. Maddie, why don't we go out on the front porch where it's quieter," said Johnny, casting a pointed look at Brush.

The table was cleared and the men were getting ready to go back to the shop when Daniel made an observation. "Johnny's eyes get all funny when he looks at Maddie."

"That's because he likes her, silly," replied Joy.

"Likes her? You mean like a girlfriend?" exclaimed Daniel.

"Yes, like a girlfriend!"

"Eww, gross!" groaned Daniel as he threw away his napkin.

Tatia grinned at Jesse and sighed. "Our little boy is learning the facts of life."

###

Maddie and Johnny sat gingerly on the porch swing, both sitting close to an armrest and avoiding eye contact. He started to speak, but his voice cracked. He cleared his throat and began again.

"Okay, let's start with anything you can remember before you started living with Misty. I'm not interested in...I mean, I am interested, but not in a prying way…but I want to know…I mean I need to know…" He stopped and wiped his hand across his red face. "Is it hot out here, or is it just me?"

Maddie tried to hide a small smile. Somehow seeing that he was as nervous as she was helped her loosen up. She turned and looked directly at him. "It is warm. Why don't we swing a little? The movement might stir up a breeze."

Johnny looked relieved and proceeded to push the swing back and forth with his foot. The simple task seemed to relax him a bit, and some of the tension left his shoulders.

Part of Maddie's training had involved how to make a man feel comfortable in her presence, and she knew that a good starting tactic was to get him talking about himself. "Why don't you tell me a little bit about yourself first. Apparently you're very good with computers. Tell me how that fits in with the Matthews' family business."

"We're working on that. I've been into computers as long as I can remember, and I mean really into everything about computers. I can repair, modify, or build anything with a microchip or an integrated circuit. I can use any software on the market, and if it won't do what I want, I can write my own. I'm great at online research, which is how I got into trouble." He stopped and dropped his face down into his hands for a moment. "I can't believe I'm telling you this."

"It's okay," reassured Maddie. "You don't have to tell me anything that makes you uncomfortable."

"No," he continued. "I want to." He turned and looked directly at her, and she noticed that he had very expressive eyes. "I want you to know, and it's how I met Jesse and Tatia."

"Okay then. Tell me – and keep in mind that there's not much I haven't heard in my life."

He nodded and looked off into the distance. "Like I said, I can find anything on the Internet, and I started finding and looking at things I shouldn't. I knew it was wrong, but I couldn't seem to stop. And then I got caught in a sting operation, and I ended up on a child porn site. That wasn't my normal hangout, but it didn't matter. I got arrested and charged. I had a good attorney and an understanding judge, so I got probation on the condition that I attend a recovery program. That's how I ended up in Recovery Ministry, and a guy I met there brought me to Jesse's Bible study. The day Joy was taken, they sent out an email requesting prayer, and I called Jesse to offer my help."

"And you helped in a big way. You helped Joy, and indirectly, you helped me. And I will be forever grateful."

"Even now that you know what I did?"

"Especially now. Knowing that you're recovering and making a better life for yourself gives me hope that I can do the same thing."

"Cool," he said. "So let's try this again. As you said to me, you don't have to tell me anything that makes you uncomfortable, but any details you can remember might be helpful."

Maddie told him what little she remembered about her early life. As she told him about the mobile home park where she lived with her mother, the playground across the street, and the friends she played with, she watched him take notes.

He wasn't exactly handsome, but he wasn't unattractive either. In addition to his expressive eyes, he had blond hair that was cut short to try, unsuccessfully, to control the curls that refused to be tamed. His fair complexion showed some faint scarring from teen-aged acne, and the red undertones gave him the look of someone who had abused alcohol - although she knew that wasn't his addiction. He was a smidgen short of six feet, but his long, thin arms and legs made him seem taller. His hands and feet looked too big for the rest of his body, but she had seen his fingers fly skillfully over the computer keyboard, and there was no trace of awkwardness when he rode his motorcycle. The jeans, boots, and vest he favored were intended to add a rugged air to his appearance, but they did nothing to hide the boy next door beneath the denim and leather.

"And then…" Maddie's voice cracked as she came to the part of her story she had remembered in her dream the night before.

Johnny looked at her with his pen poised over his notebook. "Go on," he encouraged.

"It's not very pretty," she replied.

"Life often isn't."

She smiled at his simple philosophy and told him about the fire and the man who sold her to Misty. To her surprise, instead of being repulsed, he became more animated. "This could be the clue we need."

"I don't understand?"

"A fire, the death of a mother, the disappearance of a child. It should have made the news." So he continued to question her about the weather, recent holidays, anything that would help him narrow down the time. After she had told him everything she could think of, he put down his pen and looked at her, much more at ease than he had been before they began.

"I guess I'd better get back to the shop. They're not going to want me as part of the business if I don't show up!"

They stood up, but neither made a move to leave. "We talked mostly about me," said Maddie. "There's still a lot more I'd like to know about you."

"Like what?"

"Like what your part of the business will look like. You were telling me about it, and then we got sidetracked. But mostly I'd like to know how you found Joy so quickly."

Encouraged by her interest, he grinned. "Do you like ice cream?"

"Oh, yes!" she cried. "Misty almost never let me eat it – she wanted me thin. But I love it."

"Would you like to go for ice cream when I finish work? I'll tell you anything you'd like to know over a double dip of any flavor you want."

"Can we go on the bike?"

"No other way to travel."

"Well, I should probably ask Tatia if she thinks it would be okay, but if she says *yes,* it's a date."

25

Monday - 10/2

Ian and Michael were finally alone in the conference room adjoining Michael's office. The regular Monday meeting was over and the rest of the company executives had returned to their offices to continue their efforts to make Saint International into the number one tech company in North America if not the world. Ian was more relaxed than he was during their Sunday meeting because he was confident that Michel would be pleased with what he had to report.

"What else do you have for me?" asked Michael after taking a sip of the fresh cup of coffee Adrian had left in front of him before she returned to her desk.

Ian opened the one unopened file folder that remained in front of him and began, "Our search team located Misty and debriefed her."

"Outstanding," said Michael. "Go on."

"During her statement, she referred to the two men who brought the girl to her condo as Eric and Victor – so their identification as the two prisoners we've been monitoring is confirmed. She also said that Madison called the girl's mother which is what ultimately led to her rescue before we took possession. When Misty discovered

136

what Madison had done, she lost her temper, slapped her around a bit, and threw her out. Then she realized her fatal error and ran."

"She had failed her one purpose in life – training Madison for me and keeping her safe – so I'd say her reaction was reasonable but futile. She knew I have eyes and ears everywhere so there was no place she could hide. Did she have anything else to say?"

"No. They said after she told them about Madison, she lost it and babbled about mercy and another chance."

"I assume they took appropriate action."

"Yes, sir. They terminated her services as you ordered and left the body with no identification."

"Good." Michael swiveled his chair toward the wall of windows and sipped his coffee thoughtfully. Ian swirled the remains of his own coffee in his cup and waited.

"Madison knew no one outside of our organization, so where would she go after being thrown out on the street? She made some sort of connection with this kid, and she had a phone number. She's smart and she's been taught to be resourceful, so maybe that's where she went. We need to focus on finding the identity of the kid, and when we find her, we find Madison."

"Excellent, sir! I'll direct the search in that direction."

26

Monday - 10/2

"I think that would be fine," said Tatia in response to Maddie's eager request. "There's a really cute, old-fashioned ice cream parlor on the square that has the best salted caramel sundae you ever tasted."

"That sounds wonderful! Is there anything I can do for you this afternoon?"

"Are you sure you don't need to rest for a while? You've had a pretty exciting day."

"No. I'm too excited to rest. I need something to think about besides what Johnny might find out."

Tatia looked over at Joy and Daniel who were reading in the living room. "Okay. How are your multiplication skills?"

"Pretty good as long as you stay in the single digits. After that I need a calculator."

Their laughter was interrupted by Tatia's cell phone. She glanced at it, curious as to why Jesse was calling instead of texting. "Hey, handsome. What's up?"

She paused and glanced at the children again. "She's here with me, and they're reading…uh-huh…okay…be right there." She hit *End Call* and slipped the phone into her pocket. "Class, "she said in her teacher voice, "Maddie and I are going to Daddy's studio for a couple of minutes. Joy, you're in charge of Daniel. Daniel, you're in charge of Harley."

"Okay, Mommy," they said in unison without looking up from their books.

Maddie was wide-eyed as she followed Tatia out the door. "What's going on?"

"I don't know. Jesse just said he needed to talk to both of us without the kids in hearing distance. I'm sure it's nothing serious."

"Hello, ladies," greeted Jesse, brushing a quick kiss across Tatia's lips. "Have a seat." He indicated the two chairs in the tiny reception area as he rolled his stool in from the room where the real work took place.

"Maddie, Tatia and I decided to tell the detectives who are working on Joy's case about your suspicions about Michael Saint." Maddie nodded but didn't speak. "Tracy returned my call a little while ago, and she was pretty excited about this lead. Apparently, they haven't had much luck on the buyer's side of the deal. Anyway, she and her partner would like to interview you to see if they can connect some of the dots. Do you think you're up to that?"

Maddie looked down at her hands and swallowed hard. "Yes, I want to help any way I can."

"Good," he said. "I thought you'd say that. There's something else." Now it was his turn to avert his eyes. "A woman's body was found with no ID except the card of one of their detectives hidden in her bra. He said he had talked with a woman who said she had evidence on Michael Saint and would trade it for protection. She didn't want to give him her number or come to the station, so he gave her his card and told her to call him in a few hours to see if he had a safe house set up. She never called, and the only time he saw her, she was disguised – wig, dark glasses, hoodie, all that, so he wasn't sure the body was her."

Tatia reached over and took Maddie's hand. "Go ahead. Tell us the rest."

"They need Maddie to ID the body. They think it's Misty."

###

"Do I look okay? Do you think he'll remember that I wore the same thing to the garage sale?"

Joy and Daniel were straightening the school shelf and putting away the day's work. "I think you look beautiful," said Joy.

"Me, too!" added Daniel. "Boooooooteeful!"

"Maddie," said Tatia, "he'll get lost in those beautiful violet eyes and he wouldn't notice if you were wearing a trash bag. Besides, you had on all your leathers that day."

"Do you think I need chaps?"

"I don't think so. It's much warmer today, and you won't be riding far. The jacket should be enough."

A light knock on the door brought a shy smile to Maddie's face. "Sounds like your date is here," said Tatia.

"A date," said Maddie. "That sounds so...so normal...like I'm almost a regular person or something."

Tatia hugged her. "You are not regular – you are very special. Now go – and have fun!" She turned to the children and continued, "And you two, go move the laundry from the dryer to the laundry basket while I go to the kitchen and see what's for dinner."

"But I wanna see Johnny," whined Daniel.

"He's not coming to see you, squirt," said Joy, pushing him gently toward the other room.

Johnny had his hand raised to knock again when the door opened, and Maddie giggled nervously. "Hi. I guess I'm ready...unless you want to come in or something."

"No, I'm ready, and your mighty steed awaits, m'lady," extending one arm to her and motioning dramatically toward the bike he had rolled up from the back of the shop. She giggled again, and with a small curtsy, she took his arm.

"Why, thank you, kind sir."

Jesse came in the back door as they walked out the front and found Tatia leaning against the kitchen counter staring toward the front of the house. "You look deep in thought. What's up?"

She turned around, wrapped her arms around his neck, and leaned in for a welcome home kiss. "Oh, I just watched Maddie and Johnny flirt and play around the way we used to do. I hope it's not too much too soon for her. And I hope he's not too old for her."

"I think she'll be fine. She's been confined but not really sheltered, and I gave him a fatherly talk before he left the shop."

"Oh, really! A fatherly talk?"

"Well, what I actually said was that if he hurt her I'd pull his arm off and beat him over the head with it."

"That doesn't sound very nice, Daddy," said Daniel squeezing between Jesse and Tatia.

"You're right, buddy. I wouldn't really do that, but I wanted to be sure he treated Maddie like a lady. You know, like opening the door for her, pulling out her chair, and not licking her ice cream while he's bringing it to the table."

"Daddy, that's gross," said Joy. "And, Daniel, help me carry the laundry basket in here so we can help Mommy fold it."

"Just leave it for now. I think Daddy needs to unwind after work with a game of pitch and catch."

"Yay!" yelled both children as they ran to get their jackets.

Jesse looked at Tatia with a raised eyebrow, and she grinned back at him. "Actually, teacher needs a few minutes of peace and quiet to morph back into Mommy and figure out what to cook."

###

"So many choices!" exclaimed Maddie. "How do I narrow it down to just one?"

"You can have more than one dip, you know," said Johnny. He couldn't take his eyes off Maddie and couldn't keep the grin off his face as she hovered over the array of flavors behind the glass shields. "In fact, you can have as many as you want."

She turned shining eyes on him. "Really? I want to try them all, but I don't want to make myself sick. Maybe just two flavors. You choose for me – your two favorites."

"Oh, such a heavy responsibility," he teased. "How about cookies and cream and salted caramel?"

"Sounds yummy!"

"We'll order it in a cup. That way you can get to both at the same time in case you can't finish it all."

"Perfect! How'd you get so smart?"

The color rose in Johnny's face as he ordered two identical cups from the server who looked both bored and impatient. "Why don't you go get us a table and I'll bring the ice cream when he gets it ready."

The joy on Maddie's face faded a little bit as she chose a table for two by the window. Johnny paid for their treats, asked for cups of water, and hurried to the table. She stared out the window as he emptied the tray onto the table and sat down across from her.

"Is everything okay?" he asked.

She turned toward him with eyes glistening with tears. "I'm sorry if I embarrassed you. I guess in spite of all my training from Misty I still don't know how to act in public."

"No, Maddie!" he exclaimed, reaching over to take her hand. "Is that why you think I asked you to get us a table? No! I didn't like the server's attitude, and I didn't want him to dampen your joy and enthusiasm – and then I ended up doing exactly that. I'm so sorry. Can you forgive me?"

She raised her eyes a little and said with a touch of pleading in her voice, "Really? You weren't ashamed of my excitement over something as silly as ice cream?"

"No! I love your joy over the simple things – going for a ride on the bike, trying a new taste. It's so refreshing after dealing with jaded, cynical people all the time. You are like a new flower peeking out in the sunshine for the first time, and I think it's beautiful!"

She covered a giggle with her free hand. "You're quite the smooth talker Mr…I don't even know your last name."

He dropped her hand and offered his for a handshake. "John Scott Nichols, III at your service, ma'am."

She shook his hand and replied, "I'm pleased to make your acquaintance, Mr. Nichols. I am Madelyn Matthews, at least for now."

With the tension broken, the two began to eat their ice cream. Their conversation was light and comfortable with none of the awkwardness of normal first dates. And then Maddie became a little more serious.

"I'm sorry I was so emotional before. I'm kind of moody lately. You know, up and down from one minute to the next."

"Don't apologize. It's to be expected as your body gets used to life without chemicals. I think you're doing amazingly well. I went through some of the same withdrawal symptoms when I stopped going to the porn sites. I still get antsy now and then, but it gets easier every day."

It was Maddie's turn to put her hand on top of his. "But in a way I'm glad you did. I know it's hard, but if it wasn't for your addiction, you might not have been able to help Tatia and Jesse find Joy, and you and I might not be having ice cream together right now. Last night during our family devotional time Jesse read a verse about how God works everything out for good according to His plans – or something like that. I'm not very good with the Bible yet."

"Me either, but I'm learning a lot from Jesse at our weekly Bible studies and at Recovery Ministry on Wednesday nights."

"Our evening devotionals are pretty simple, but I like learning about God and Jesus. I don't understand it all yet, but I think I want to follow Jesus. I think I'll go to church with the family this Sunday."

"Hey," said Johnny. "Would you like to come to the Recovery meeting with me on Wednesday? They have a chemical dependency group you could sit in on while I'm in my group."

"I don't know, Johnny," replied Maddie pulling her hand back slowly. "Don't misunderstand – I really appreciate the invitation – but I've read about AA meetings and I've seen movies that showed them. I don't think I'm ready to sit around with a bunch of strangers drinking coffee, smoking cigarettes, and talking about their deepest, darkest secrets."

Johnny laughed, but when he saw the stricken look on Maddie's face, he stopped. "Oh, Maddie," he stammered with the color rising in his face. "I'm not laughing at you. It's just the word picture you painted is so different than what it's like. It just struck me as funny. I guess I'm not very good at behaving in public either."

Maddie smiled a little at his discomfort. She took a deep breath and blew it out. "Let's back up to where you asked me if I'd like to come to a meeting with you. I like the idea of going somewhere else with you, but I'm a little nervous about being around a lot of new people and having to talk in front of them. What's it like?"

"Well," he said with a little bit of excitement returning to his expression. "It's really pretty cool. We start with a fellowship meal – something simple like sandwiches or salads. That gets kinda noisy because there's a lot of talking and laughing as we all catch up on what kind of week we're having. Then we have a time of celebration and worship."

"A celebration every week? What do you celebrate?"

"That parts a little bit like AA. They help us celebrate our successes on the road to recovery by giving out chips based on the number of days you've been clean and sober from whatever addiction you're fighting. I'm getting my green chip this week for 60 days."

"That's great, Johnny! I'm proud for you."

"They offer a chip to newcomers, so if you decide to come, you could get a blue one."

Maddie became quiet, and Johnny realized how intimidating the thought of standing up in front of a group would be to her. "But it's up to you," he said quickly. "You don't have to get one if you don't want to."

Maddie relaxed a little bit and encouraged him to tell her more about what to expect. He described the worship time. "And then we break up into our small groups. I think there are only about three or four in the chemical dependency group plus the facilitator. I sometimes wish I could go in that group because they always seem to be laughing and having a lot of fun while they're learning and sharing." He paused and looked deeply into her eyes for a long moment. Then, as if suddenly remembering what they had been talking about he asked, "So, what do you think?"

"I think you make it sound wonderful. And if I don't like it, I don't have to go back. Right?"

"Absolutely!"

"Well, Dr. Patterson is coming tomorrow morning to check me out and see if I'm strong enough to identify Misty's body - or whoever it is - tomorrow afternoon." She stopped and swallowed against a rising tide of emotion. Johnny waited patiently until she calmed herself. "Did Jesse tell you about that?" He nodded, and she continued. "Anyway, while I'm with him, I'll ask if he thinks I'm ready for the group."

"Cool!" said Johnny with enthusiasm.

"If he says yes, can we go on the bike?

27

Tuesday - 10/3

Maddie dressed for the day before going to the kitchen. Dr. Patterson was supposed to come early before he went to his office, and she didn't want to greet him in her pajamas. Jesse and the children were still sitting at the table, but all the other seats were empty.

"Johnny and Bwush already went to work," said Daniel through a spoonful of cereal.

"Don't talk with your mouth full," scolded Joy. She turned her attention to Maddie. "Johnny said hi and he'll see you at lunch, and Mommy said to come to her office when you were dressed. Dr. P is checking Lili now."

Maddie laughed at the barrage of information. "Good morning, everyone." She looked at Jesse with a look of concern. "Why is Dr. P checking out Lili? Is she sick?"

"No," he responded. "I think it's just a checkup."

"Should I wait to be sure he's finished with her?"

"No, I think it's safe to go on over."

"Wow!" Maddie exclaimed with a smile replacing her anxious

expression. "If a girl's late to breakfast around here, she misses a lot! Any other news before I go?"

Jesse returned her smile, happy to see her positive mood in spite of the daunting task she would face later in the day. "No. Just that Tatia left a muffin and a banana on the counter for you, and I think there's a coffee pod over there with your name on it."

"Great. Thanks! I think I'll go on over and have breakfast when I come back."

Maddie went through the front door of the office in case the exam wasn't quite finished. She was surprised to see Tatia seated on the sofa across the coffee table from the other two.

"I'm sorry – I didn't mean to interrupt. I'll go back to the…"

"It's okay," said Dr. P. "We've finished with the exam, and we're just about to discuss it. You can stay if it's okay with Lili."

"Sure," said Lili. "I do not mind at all."

"Come sit with me," said Tatia, patting the empty spot beside her.

"Okay," said the doctor as Maddie settled in beside Tatia. "To answer your first question – yes, Lili, you're going to be a mother."

Maddie gasped. "You're going to be a mother? How exciting!"

"Yes," replied the doctor, grinning at Maddie's reaction. "I detected what I think is a faint heartbeat. It will be much stronger in the next week or so. I'd guess this little one will be here in about 33 to 34 weeks. I'd like you to come by my office to have some lab work done so I can prescribe your prenatal vitamins. And we'll set up an appointment schedule while you're there."

"That will not be necessary," said Lili in a voice so quiet the doctor could barely hear her. "I will be returning to Antigua at the end of the term to have the baby. I will see a doctor there."

"You're not giving up your studies, are you?" asked Tatia in alarm.

"No," said Lili with a sad smile. "I will give my baby to my sister to raise, and I will return to finish my education."

"Oh, no!" exclaimed Maddie. "You're giving away your baby?"

Then her hands flew up to her mouth. "Oh, that sounded really harsh. I didn't mean it that way. I just can't imagine how hard it must be to make that choice."

"No, it did not sound harsh – and it is a very hard decision. But my sister lost a baby last year and cannot have any more. My studies will be very demanding for the next several years, and this will be best for all of us."

"Yes, I understand. You're very brave."

Dr. Patterson cleared his throat to break the tense silence that followed. "I'd still like to keep an eye on you while you're here," he said. "The first trimester is the most crucial for your baby's development, and we want to know right away if there's something we need to do."

"But I do not have insurance, and I cannot pay you myself."

"That's not a problem, Lili. As I'm sure Tatia told you, I offer my services when she needs them. It's part of my contribution to the Fallen Angel Ministry. I can also schedule a sonogram if you like so we can confirm how far along you are."

"Thank you. I will accept your kind offer of care, but a sonogram is unnecessary. A radiology student at the University is using me as a subject on Thursday."

"Good! Here are a couple of my cards. Ask her to send me the results. And then you can call my office to set up an appointment for one day next week. Now, do you have any questions before I move on to my next patient?"

"No. Just how did you get to be such a good man?"

Dr. P smiled at her and then shifted his gaze to Maddie. "You look like you have a question."

"Yes. I don't want to sound dumb, but what's a sonogram?"

"There are no dumb questions when you want to learn something. A sonogram is a procedure where we will use sound waves to create a visual image of what's going on inside Lili's uterus. It's too early to determine the gender, but we should be able to see the throb of the heartbeat."

"It's a moving image?" she asked, her eyes wide.

"Some. There's not much movement at this stage, but we should be able to see the beginnings of arms and legs and maybe some facial features. The real movement usually begins around four or five months along. That's when the baby begins to put on a real show."

"Wow!" breathed Maddie. "I wish I could see that."

"You could go with me if you like," offered Lili.

"Really?"

"Yes. I do not have any classes that morning, and I would enjoy your company."

Maddie looked at Tatia with a question in her eyes. Tatia responded with a smile and a small nod.

"Oh, yes! I'd love to!"

Lili excused herself to go to the house for some breakfast. "This baby is hungry," she said, resting her hand protectively on her stomach.

Maddie let out a big sigh as she watched the door close behind Lili. "To go through all it takes to have a baby and then to give it to someone else. So sad and yet so loving."

Tatia was touched by the depth of understanding Maddie exhibited for one who had been so sheltered. Then the girl made a comment that reminded Tatia that she was more worldly than she sometimes seemed.

"When one of Misty's girls would get pregnant, she'd just send them to the West Coast for a quick D and C. She said that up until about six months it was just a mass of tissue." She stopped and looked at Dr. Patterson. "Lili talked like it was already a baby, and you said it already has arms and legs and a face. There's so much I don't know."

Tatia took her hand. "But you're learning quickly. I can tell that

God has protected you from being hardened by those around you, and I am so thankful He sent you to us."

"Me, too!" said Maddie, sandwiching Tatia's hands between hers. Then she turned a bright smile on the doctor who was typing notes into a small laptop. "And I'm grateful to you Dr. P for all you've done to help me since I got here."

He set his laptop aside and returned her smile. "I'm very pleased with your progress, young lady. You have a little color, and if I'm not mistaken, you've added a pound or two. Come on over and sit in this other chair so I can check your vitals."

For the next few minutes he used a collection of portable equipment to check her temperature, blood pressure, pulse, oxygen saturation, and blood sugar stats. He listened to her heart and lungs; checked her eyes, ears, nose, and throat; and even had her sit on the edge of Tatia's desk so he could check her reflexes. Once they were settled back into their chairs, he opened his laptop and began to ask her about how she was feeling. She admitted to occasional fatigue, mild headaches, and edginess, and then he asked about how she was sleeping.

"Pretty well most of the time, but I do sometimes have night-mares."

"Do you sleep through them, or do they wake you up?"

"Mostly they wake me up along with everybody else in the house. I scream a lot."

"Are you able to go back to sleep afterward?"

"Usually. Sometimes Joy rubs my back and sings me to sleep, and if they're really bad, Tatia makes tea and we talk for a while."

The doctor looked toward Tatia for comment.

"The nightmares don't happen every night. She had a doozy Sunday night shortly after she went to bed, but I don't think she's had one since then. Right?" She looked at Maddie for confirmation.

"That's right. But the one on Sunday was good in a way."

"How's that?" asked the doctor.

"I remembered an event from my childhood, and Johnny thinks it might help him find out my real name."

"That would be good," said Dr. P as he continued to type notes. "Everybody needs at least a birth certificate, if for no other reason than to get a Social Security Number. Right?"

"Yeah. It would make me feel more like a real person."

"Well, Miss Maddie, you are a very real person, with or without a birth certificate – and you are doing better than I ever hoped. If you keep doing what you're doing, I'm going to have to dismiss you."

"Maddie, you have a couple of things to ask about, don't you?"

"Oh, yes I do," replied Maddie, taking a deep breath. "First, the police found the body of a woman they think might be Misty, the woman who raised me and who helped Eric and Victor produce the video of Joy that they used online to sell her. They can't find anyone else who knew her, or at least no one that admits it. So they want me or Joy to come in this afternoon and identify the body. I don't want Joy to have to do that, so is it okay if I do it? Tatia and Jesse will go with me."

"Do you think you're strong enough for that?"

She stared at the floor in front of her for a few minutes without saying anything. Finally, she looked up with tears leaking onto her cheeks. When she spoke, her voice was strong and firm. "I am as strong as I need to be to protect these wonderful people who have taken me into their home and their family."

He looked at Tatia. "What do you think?"

"I think she's right. She is strong, and Jesse and I will be beside her all the way. It has to be done, and I love her for being willing to protect Joy from yet another trauma."

"Okay. Go ahead and do what you have to do. Maddie, I know you are against taking any kind of medication to help you through this, but if this experience brings on the nightmares or any other symptoms, call me. There are some natural remedies we might try if you need them. Okay?"

"Okay. Sounds good."

"Now, what else? You said a couple of things."

"Oh, yeah. Johnny goes to Recovery Ministry every Wednesday night at his church, and he invited me to go with him tomorrow. Do you think I'm ready for a group?"

She had her head down, probably to try and hide the extra color on her face. Dr. P looked at Tatia and, with a question in his eyes, mouthed *Johnny* and pointed toward the shop. She nodded with a small shrug, and he raised his eyebrows.

"I think a group would be an excellent idea if you find people who are supportive and trustworthy. Try it out and see what you think, but don't get too emotionally invested too soon. Do you understand what I'm saying?"

"I think so. When I was four years old I trusted that man who said he would take me for ice cream and take me to a nice lady who would take care of me. I ended up with Misty, and I never got my ice cream. But I showed up at Tatia's door, and she opened not only her home but her heart to me. So I need to wait until I see if they are like the man or like Tatia and her family."

"That's it exactly. And not just groups but individuals, too."

She grinned at him and at Tatia. "You're talking about Johnny now, aren't you?"

He laughed. "Yes, I guess I am. You hide a lot of street smarts behind that innocent facade. Well," he said, beginning to pack his bag, "I'll drop by on Monday to hear how things went. And if you need me before then, you have my number."

28

Tuesday - 10/3

"But I don't wanna wear a jacket, Mommy," whined Daniel. "It's not cold outside."

Tatia knew what he really wanted was to go with her and Jesse when they took Maddie into the city. He didn't really understand what the trip was for, but he knew that road trips for any reason sometimes included a stop for ice cream. Joy on the other hand knew the reason for the trip and was more than happy to accompany Daniel to the neighbors' house where Fran would watch them and they would play with her son Cade. Even though he was the same age as Daniel and an even bigger pain, Joy knew that spending time with them was preferable to what Maddie was being asked to do.

"Tell you what, Daniel," Joy said in her let's-make-a-deal voice, "let's put the jacket in your backpack so you'll have it if it gets cool later. And you'll have room left to take a couple of your favorite toys."

His eyes brightened. "Will you play Dinosaur Escape with us?"

"Yes," she sighed. "I'll play Dinosaur Escape with you."

Tatia grinned at Jesse. "Such a good big sister!"

153

"And quite the negotiator, too. I see diplomatic service in her future."

A few minutes later Daniel dragged his bulging backpack to the door and announced that he was ready to go. Joy followed him with a book and a small blanket under her arm.

"You two look like you're moving out," teased Jesse.

"You probably won't be back before naptime, so I plan to catch up on my reading," explained Joy. "And it's always cold in their house," she went on, pointing to the blanket.

"And we like to play dinosaurs and trucks," added Daniel.

"Well, let's go. Tatia, if you'll check to see if Maddie's ready, I'll walk them next door and then we can head out."

Tatia passed out hugs, kisses, and instructions to be good before turning toward the bedroom Maddie shared with Joy. She found her sitting on the bed with an open Bible in her lap. She smiled at the sight, knowing Maddie had rarely even seen a Bible before coming into their home. She sat quietly beside Maddie and waited for the young woman to speak.

"Jesse read this verse in our devotional time a couple of days ago, and I marked it. It's perfect for today," she said.

"Why don't you read it to me," suggested Tatia.

"It's in Isaiah 41:10. *Fear not, for I am with you; be not dismayed, for I am your God; I will strengthen you, I will help you, I will uphold you with My righteous right hand.* Do you think He will really be with me today?"

"Absolutely! In fact, if you're ready, let's go wait for Jesse in the living room. Before we leave, we'll ask him to pray that very verse over you."

"That would be wonderful!" she exclaimed. "But...you'll both be with me, too, won't you?"

"Of course we will – one on either side of you."

"Good. It's amazing to think that God will be with me, but I have a feeling I'm going to need someone I can physically hold on to."

Once the threesome was in the car and on the way, Maddie began to ask questions. "I know I'm going to identify Misty's body, but where?"

Jesse answered as he maneuvered through traffic. "We're going to the Cook County Morgue. It's about ninety miles southeast of here, close to the southwestern shore of the lake. The GPS estimated almost two hours, but with any luck, it won't take us that long."

"Especially if you keep weaving through microscopic openings between the cars," said Tatia as he edged into an SUV-sized space in front of an 18-wheeler. He grinned at her and continued.

"Adam Nelson and Tracy Martin will meet us there. They're the two detectives who helped track down Joy's kidnappers."

"They're known around their precinct as the Kiddie Kops because they've become the unofficial experts in child abduction and sex trafficking cases," added Tatia.

"On TV it seems like a lot of reporters hang out at places like that," said Maddie. "Will we have people sticking microphones in our face when we go in?"

"I don't think we have to worry about that," said Jesse. "Dead bodies aren't really news around here until they're identified. Besides, Tracy arranged for us to park in the underground garage where all the coroners, technicians, and other staff park. She's instructed the entrance guard to let us in, and Tatia will text her when we get close. She'll meet us at the elevator and escort us up to the viewing area."

Maddie grew quiet after that – so quiet that Tatia glanced back to see if she had fallen asleep. She was awake but was staring sightlessly out the window with her legs drawn up beside her on the seat and her arms crossed protectively in front of her. Tatia whispered a silent prayer that the Lord would strengthen and uphold her as the verse in Isaiah said. Jesse and Tatia continued in the comfortable silence of the happily married until the GPS spoke up.

Turn right in 400 feet. Your destination is on the right. You have reached your destination.

Jesse obediently turned right onto the entrance ramp and stopped beside the guard house. A uniformed officer with a clipboard approached the SUV, and Jesse lowered his window. "We're the Matthews family here to meet Detectives Nelson and Martin."

The officer scribbled a note on his clipboard and walked to the back of the vehicle where he made note of the license number. He returned to Jesse's window, his eyes making a practiced sweep of the interior. "I'll need to see ID for all three of you."

Jesse and Tatia exchanged worried looks as she passed him her driver's license. "Here's my license and my wife's, Officer Williams," said Jesse, reading the name off his name tag. "Maddie doesn't have an ID yet. She's been…"

"Wait here please," said Williams as he spun on his heel and returned to his little hut. He picked up a cell phone from the counter and held it to his ear, speaking into it briefly. "Yes, ma'am," he said, looking toward the vehicle and walking toward the window where Maddie sat. "Miss, lower your window, please."

Maddie fumbled around, looking for the right button until Jesse lowered it from the front seat. Maddie looked up at her own image reflected in the dark sunglasses that covered Officer Williams' eyes. "Yes, ma'am," he said into the phone. "White female, late teens to early twenties, fair complexion, brown hair, dark blue eyes…" He hesitated, removed his glasses, and leaned a little closer to the window. "Yes, ma'am, I guess you could call them violet." He almost cracked a smile. "Never saw anything quite like that."

He listened silently for a moment and then stepped back. He nodded at Maddie and said, "Thank you, miss." Then he looked at Jesse, "If you'll drive straight ahead and turn right on the second row. There's an entrance to the building at the end of the row, and Martin will meet you there." He went back to the guard house where he raised the swing arm that blocked their path. "Have a nice day," he said as he waved them in.

"Well, that was scary," said Maddie.

Tatia let out a deep sigh and reached over the back of her seat to grab Maddie's hand. "Yes, it was. But you handled it beautifully. You're gonna do fine in there."

Maddie exuded confidence when she shook hands with Detective Martin, but when the elevator started down toward the morgue, she grabbed Jesse's arm on one side and clutched Tatia's hand on the other. Her hand was sweaty, and Tatia detected a slight tremor as the elevator doors slid open and they stepped into the hallway. Tatia thought she heard Maddie say something, but when she looked toward her, she realized the girl was reciting the verse from Isaiah under her breath. Tatia squeezed her hand and patted her arm gently.

The threesome was taking up most of the width of the hallway, so Detective Martin walked to the left and slightly ahead of Jesse. Tatia became aware that she actually was speaking to them, so she tuned in and hoped she hadn't missed anything.

"Detective Nelson was detained on another case, but he'll meet us at the restaurant later. I've arranged for us to use the family viewing room so we won't have to go into the autopsy room. There's a window with blinds that will be closed when we go in. Two staffers will be in an adjoining room with the body. It will be on a gurney and will be covered with a sheet. When we're ready, one will open the blind, and the other will lower the sheet to expose the head. Maddie, just say 'okay' when you've seen enough, and they'll close the blinds. Then we can talk. We'll try to make this as painless as possible."

"Thank you," whispered Maddie as she tightened her grip on both Jesse and Tatia.

Martin stopped with her hand on a doorknob and looked at Maddie. "Ready?" she asked.

Maddie recoiled slightly, and Jesse spoke gently to her. "Look at me, Maddie." She turned her face to meet his steady gaze. "We've got you," he said. "You can do this." She continued to look into his eyes for a moment, and then she turned to the detective and nodded.

The room was a small space, painted a pale blue and furnished with an institutional-looking vinyl sofa and two side chairs. Maddie didn't see any of that, though, as she stared at the closed blinds covering the window. "Ready when you are," said a disembodied voice from a speaker in the wall beside the window.

Maddie caught her breath and looked at the speaker. "Can they hear us?" she asked.

"Not until I hit the button. When I opened the door, it signaled our arrival. Just let me know when you're ready."

Tatia shifted Maddie's hand to the other side and put her left arm around the trembling girl. Jesse did the same on the other side until Maddie was sandwiched snugly between them. She took a deep breath and said, "Okay. I'm ready."

"Remember," said Martin. "Just say 'okay' when you've seen enough." Then she pushed the button and said, "Ready."

The blinds opened on a stark, brightly lit room. The two staffers in the room were wearing scrubs, lab coats, shoe covers, head covers, masks, and gloves. Only their eyes gave any indication there was a person inside the protective gear, but even the eyes seemed covered with a shield that protected them from their daily contact with death.

In an effort to avoid looking at the covered form on the gurney, Maddie looked at the person by the blinds. Based on the height and wide shoulders, she guessed it was a man. The other person was much shorter, the hands inside the latex gloves were small and delicate, and what looked like a wedding set was silhouetted on the left hand. Maddie finally let her eyes rest on the body, noting that whoever lay under the sheet was fairly short and heavy set. The staffer grasped the two upper corners of the sheet and gently folded it back to just below the face, a face that had once been well rounded but was now sunken and lifeless. The outstanding feature was the hair which was the texture and color of cotton candy.

Maddie pulled her hand away from Tatia and placed it on the glass. "Bye, Misty," she whispered. She quickly put her hand back into Tatia's and looked at Detective Martin. "Okay," she said, and the woman who had been both captor and caregiver disappeared behind the blinds.

29

Tuesday - 10/3

Maddie took a big bite of her burger and sighed with pleasure.

"Good?" smiled Tatia, pleased to see her really eating instead of nibbling the way she did when she first came to them.

"Yes!" she exclaimed. "I'm so hungry. With all the excitement about Lili, I never went back and ate breakfast." She stopped with a French fry halfway to her mouth and looked at Tatia with stricken eyes. "Oh! I shouldn't be eating when poor Misty is lying all alone in that awful place."

Tatia laid her hand on Maddie's forearm. "You go right ahead and eat. It's normal to be hungry at times of great emotional stress. That's why it's traditional to provide a big meal for the family before or after a funeral."

"It is? I didn't know that," replied Maddie as she put the fry in her mouth. "I've never been to a funeral."

The trio ate quietly until Maddie spoke again. "What will happen to Misty? Will she have a funeral?"

"Probably not," said Jesse. "I'm not sure what will happen if nobody claims her body."

"If the body isn't claimed within a month after the trial is completed," said Detective Martin who had just walked up to the table, "it will be cremated. Cremated remains are held for a while, and twice a year, the unclaimed remains are buried in a city cemetery."

Tatia smiled at the new arrival and Jesse stood and pulled out the empty chair beside him. "Hi, Tracy. I hope you don't mind that we started without you. Maddie was starving after her ordeal." Once she was seated, Jesse took his seat and asked, "Where's Adam?"

"He's waiting to pick up our orders. Food always comes first with him."

"Is he the man at the counter with the really round head?" asked Maddie between bites.

"That's him," replied Tracy with a smile.

Jesse began to laugh. "I never noticed before, but his head is really round – and shiny on top. Kind of like a bowling ball with hair around the edges."

Tatia almost choked on an onion ring, and Maddie stifled a laugh with a hand over her mouth. Tracy continued to smile. "Yeah, you're right. And his belly is the same shape. But don't mention either one to him. He's a little sensitive." In an effort to bring the group under control before Adam arrived at the table, she turned to Maddie and changed the subject. "You did really great this morning. I've seen grown men fall apart when faced with identifying the body of someone they knew."

"Thank you, Detective Martin," said Maddie.

"Call me Tracy."

"Tracy," she repeated tentatively. "I couldn't have done it without Tatia and Jesse."

"Yes, I can see that the three of you have developed quite a bond. But I'm pretty sure you could have done it under any circumstances. You're a pretty tough cookie, and I admire what you did to help us find Joy. We wouldn't have found her, at least not in time, if it hadn't been for your call."

"Yeah, that took a lot of guts, kid," said the man who had caused so much laughter a few minutes before. He set a tray of food down on the table beside Tracy and extended his hand to Maddie. "Adam Nelson, Chicago PD. Pleased to meet you."

Maddie shook his hand and gave him a big smile before returning to the last few bites of her meal. By the time she finished her fries and turned her attention to the milkshake she had saved for last, Adam and Tracy had sorted out their food and settled in to eat. She broke the silence.

"Tracy, you probably think it's strange for me to care about what happens to the body of the woman who sold me to a mobster. But she was the only family I remember – at least until the Matthews."

"It's not strange at all. Have you ever heard of the Stockholm Syndrome?"

"No. It sounds like a disease."

"Not exactly," laughed Tracy. "You can look it up if you want more details, but basically it's a positive emotional response a victim develops toward their abuser or captor. It's pretty common, especially considering the length of time you were with her."

"Yeah, it was weird," said Maddie. "She really was a terrible person in a lot of ways, but it's hard to think of her with nobody to have a funeral for her."

Tatia looked at Jesse with a question in her eyes, and he answered her out loud. "Maddie," he said, "if nobody claims Misty's body, we'll claim her and have a small memorial service. Okay?"

Maddie nodded and lowered her head so no one would see the tears in her eyes. She continued to sip her milkshake in silence while the four adults made small talk. She smiled around her straw as Tracy and Adam bantered back and forth like an old married couple, and she almost laughed out loud at their end-of-the meal routine. Tracy pulled a piece of foil out of her bag, wrapped the uneaten half of her burger and fries, and slid it over to Adam. No words were exchanged, and it was obviously a practice developed during many shared meals. It helped explain the difference between the two, with Tracy being almost too thin and Adam beginning to edge toward too round.

Maddie was fascinated by Tracy. She wasn't exactly pretty, but she wore black-rimmed glasses that magnified her hazel eyes and intensified her penetrating gaze so that she seemed to peer into your brain and read your thoughts. Once she had disposed of her leftovers, she wiped her mouth with a napkin and turned her gaze on Maddie.

"I know you've already had a tough day, but we really need to ask you some questions. Are you up to it?"

"Sure," said Maddie. "Jesse told me you wanted to hear about Michael."

For the next few minutes, Maddie recited the story she had told Tatia about the part Michael Saint had played in her life. When she was finished, the detectives took her back to the night Eric and Victor brought Joy to the condo. She shared her memories of helping Joy in the kitchen.

"She must have thought I was really stupid. I knew how to order sushi, but I didn't even know how to make a grilled cheese sandwich. I do know how to do hair, though, and we had fun fixing her up for her video. She was so pretty and so brave – and so smart. When we went back to the bedroom so she could change back into her street clothes, she gave me Tatia's phone number again. Then she said she was scared, and we cried together."

A heavy silence fell over the table, and more than a few tears were blinked back. Adam finally cleared his throat, looked at his notes, and broke the spell. "You're doing great, kid. We're almost done. Jesse said you believe that Saint was the one who bought Joy. Can you explain?"

Maddie pulled herself away from the memory of holding Joy and repeated what she remembered of Misty's phone call. Adam and Tracy exchanged glances, and Tracy spoke up.

"How long were you with Misty?"

"I don't know exactly, but I was around four when I came to live with her."

"Did anyone else ever live with you – another child maybe?"

"No. It was always just the two of us."

Adam banged his fist on the table causing everyone to jump. "Gotcha, you…"

"Language!" interrupted Tracy just in time.

Jesse stifled a laugh, but Maddie didn't seem to notice. "Are we almost finished? I'm really tired."

"Yes," replied Tracy. "We're finished for now."

"For now?" asked Tatia. "What else do you need from her?"

"Eric and Victor have hired an attorney," explained Tracy. "He's asked to depose both Joy and Maddie. We'll stall as long as possible, but it'll have to be done at some point."

"What about Saint?" asked Jesse. "Will Maddie have to testify against him?"

"It's possible," added Adam, "but he's going to be a hard one to bring down. That could be months or even years down the road."

"We'll want to petition to have the depositions done on video so the girls don't have to face Eric and Victor," said Tatia. "Will that be a problem?"

"Probably not due to both their ages and Maddie's delicate condition."

"But Dr. Patterson said I'm doing great!" protested Maddie.

"I know you are," said Tracy. "You're amazing. But their attorney doesn't need to know that."

Everyone laughed, relieving the tension that had settled over the group. Tatia pushed her chair back and stood.

"Well, if we're finished here, we need to get on the road. Maddie needs to rest, and we have two other children who will be wanting dinner by the time we get home."

30

Wednesday - 10/4

Maddie had been listening to the sound of Joy's soft rhythmic breathing for what seemed like hours, but she was still wide awake. Her bed was a tangled mess, and she still couldn't find a comfortable position or follow her roommate into sleep. Her day had been really good in some ways, but it had been extremely stressful in others, and she felt jittery and anxious. She slid out of bed as quietly as she could, shrugged on the robe that lay across the foot of her bed, and padded into the living room. Unsure of what to do now that she was up, she wandered into the dining area and stared out into the back yard, wondering what was wrong with her.

"Are you okay, sweetheart?"

Maddie turned from the window and saw Tatia coming out of her bedroom tying the belt of her own robe around her. "I'm so sorry I woke you. I tried to be quiet."

Tatia chuckled to herself. "You'll never be so quiet that a mother's ears won't hear you. It's something that happens with the birth of your first child. Suddenly you can hear the sound of the slightest whimper in the middle of a thunderstorm. Come here," she said as she drew Maddie into a hug.

Maddie nestled into the warm embrace and sighed. Then the words began to tumble out. "I don't know what's wrong with me. I was so tired when I went to bed, but I can't seem to settle down. And my skin feels kind of…crawly. Oh, I'm not making any sense."

"You're making perfect sense, my dear. You have experienced more in the last week and a half than many people experience in years, and you had an especially traumatic day. Besides, your body is still getting used to life without drugs." Tatia began to pray quietly, and she felt some of the tension ease in Maddie's shoulders. When she finished her prayer, she guided the girl to a chair at the table. "Now, let's have some chamomile tea and try some aroma therapy."

Tatia disappeared into her bedroom and came back a moment later with a candle which she placed on the table and lit before moving into the kitchen. The small flame dispelled some of the darkness in the room, and Maddie found the gentle spicy orange smell it gave off to be somehow comforting. She was almost hypnotized by the flame, and was surprised when Tatia placed a steaming cup in front of her.

"Give me your hands while the tea steeps for a few minutes," said Tatia. She produced a small bottle of lotion from the pocket of her robe and began to massage it into Maddie's hands and forearms. The smell of lavender mixed with the fragrance of the candle, and Maddie felt wrapped in love and comfort.

"Where did you learn to do this?" she asked.

Tatia smiled wryly. "During my years of recovery, Mama G taught me many soothing techniques, but the most important thing to remember is to always begin with prayer."

###

The men had already had breakfast and gone over to the shop

and Joy was clearing the table by the time Maddie came wandering out of the hallway stretching her arms over her head.

"Good morning," said Tatia. "How did you sleep?"

"Very well after our prayer and tea. Thank you for that."

"Any time. I'm here for you."

Maddie smiled through a yawn. "Guess I missed breakfast, huh?"

"Only the breakfast rush," said Tatia as she put a fresh pod in the coffee maker and hit the button.

"I'll get your juice," said Joy.

"I want to help," whined Daniel, standing on tiptoe to put his plate in the sink.

Tatia leaned over and whispered in his ear, and he immediately brightened and ran over to Maddie who had just slid behind the table. "We have oatmeal, banana bread, and toast on the menu," he announced carefully. "What would you like?"

"What would you suggest, sir?" she asked.

"Banana bread is my favorite!"

"Mine, too! I'll take that and some oatmeal, please. I'm pretty hungry!"

Tatia was already stirring the oats into some boiling water when the young waiter gave her Maddie's order. She handed him a small plate with a slice of banana bread which he delivered with a flourish just after Joy set down a glass of orange juice. Daniel plopped down in the chair across from Maddie because he knew he wouldn't be allowed to carry the hot cereal. He put his elbows on the table and stared at her.

"You need to eat fast," he said. "Johnny wants us to let him know as soon as you get dressed. He said he needs to talk to you and it can't wait until lunch."

Maddie dropped the bite of bread that was halfway to her mouth and stared at Tatia. "Did he find out something?" she almost shouted.

"I don't know, but it will wait until you finish eating. I don't want you to hear something exciting on an empty stomach and pass out," replied Tatia calmly. She couldn't hide her own excitement, though.

"I'll lay out your clothes," offered Joy. "What do you want to wear?"

"You choose. I trust your taste," said Maddie, spooning oatmeal into her mouth as quickly as she could without choking.

A few minutes later she came out of the bedroom dressed in the outfit she had modeled in the Annex, except she was wearing the boots Tatia had given her instead of the ones that hurt her feet.

"Do I look okay," she asked Tatia. "It seems like these boots make my feet look big."

"You look perfect," Tatia assured her. "The way that purple top brings out your eyes, he won't be looking at your feet. Trust me!"

Maddie took a deep breath. "Okay," she said in a trembling voice. "I guess I'm ready."

Tatia texted Johnny and tried to settle her children into their morning school work. Maddie sat down on the sofa and fiddled with the morning paper, but she, along with everyone else in the room, was actually watching for Johnny to come through the door. At the first rattle of the door knob, all four heads popped up, and Maddie shot to her feet. All eyes were on him, but Johnny had eyes only for her.

"Hi, Maddie," he said quietly. "You look really nice."

"Thanks, Johnny," she replied, even more quietly.

Daniel broke the mood by blurting out, "Did you find her name?"

"Hush, Daniel," said Joy. "He'll want to tell her first."

Daniel stuck his tongue out at his sister, but Tatia smiled at her daughter's unusually mature insight. "She's right. There's no private place in this house except the bathrooms. Why don't you two go out on the porch. Maddie, you can grab my jacket. It's on the bench at the foot of my bed."

Maddie looked at Tatia with a look of panic in her eyes as if suddenly she wasn't sure she was ready to hear what Johnny had to say. Tatia smiled and made a shooing motions with her hands - Maddie smiled back and went to get the jacket.

Once they were settled on the porch swing, Maddie and Johnny rocked back and forth slowly for a little while, neither one speaking. She finally broke the silence.

"The wind's a little chilly, but it's a beautiful day."

"Yes, it is."

They rocked a while longer until Johnny looked down at the manila folder in his hand. He stared at it for a minute and then handed it to her.

"I'll keep looking to see what else I can find, but I thought you'd want to see this right away."

"Thank you."

She took it and held it for a minute, looking intently at the blank file that held so much promise. Johnny chewed on a thumbnail for a moment and then spoke again.

"Do you want me to go back to the shop so you can have some privacy?"

"No!" she exclaimed, reaching over and putting her hand on his arm. "No," she repeated more softly. "I want to share this with you, but I guess I'm just a little bit scared."

He covered her hand with his. "Don't be scared. It's all good."

"Okay." She drew her hand back and carefully opened the file. Her hand flew to her mouth, and she looked at him with tear-filled eyes. "Oh, Johnny," she cried, and threw her arms around his neck. The file folder slid off her lap, and an official-looking form with a blue border fluttered across the porch. They both lunged for the paper, and the swing slipped backward, dumping them into a pile on the floor, each with a hand on the precious document. They looked at each other in surprise and burst out laughing.

Johnny relinquished the paper to Maddie, picked up the file folder, and helped her to her feet and back into the swing. She wiped the residual tears from her face and smoothed the paper in her lap. She felt Johnny's gaze on her, and she stared back at him for a moment before beginning to read.

"State of Illinois, Certificate of Live Birth, Child's Name," she stopped and tears began to leak slowly. "Madelyn Jeannette Collier. That's me," she breathed in wonder. "I'm Madelyn Jeannette Collier."

"I'm pleased to meet you, Miss Collier," said Johnny extending his hand. "I'm John Scott Nichols, III, but you can call me Johnny."

Maddie giggled and shook his hand formally. "The pleasure is all mine." Suddenly she jumped up, threw her arms in the air, and let out a shrill screech. The birth certificate went flying again, and Johnny leaped to retrieve it before it hit the floor. The front door flew open and Joy burst through with her eyes wide.

"What's wrong? Are you okay?"

Maddie grabbed both her hands and swung the younger girl around in a circle. "I'm perfect! I have a name!"

Joy squealed almost as loud as Maddie had. "A name?! Who are you?"

"Allow me," said Johnny with a courtly bow. "Miss Matthews, may I present Madelyn Jeannette Collier. Miss Collier, Miss Matthews."

Joy repeated the name several times, testing the sound of it. "I love it! Let's go tell Mommy!" She grabbed Maddie's hand and began dragging her toward the door. Maddie reached for Johnny's hand, and Joy pulled them both into the house.

31

Wednesday - 10/4

Michael Saint and a girl who looked to be in her mid teens were having breakfast on his penthouse balcony overlooking the city when Ian walked through the French doors.

"You know I don't like being disturbed until after breakfast," he growled.

"I know, Mr. S," Ian responded respectfully but firmly. "But you'll want to see this," he continued as he pulled a photograph of Tatia and Jesse out of a leather-covered folder and placed it on the table beside Michael's plate.

Michael glanced at the picture, wiped his hands on a linen napkin, and picked up the photo. "Okay. What am I looking at? And more to the point, who and why?"

Ian looked pointedly at the scantily clad girl on the other side of the table, and Michael seemed surprised that she was still there. Feeling both sets of eyes on her, she looked up hesitantly with her fork halfway to her mouth. "It's time for you to go," said Michael dismissively.

"Go pack your things. I'll call for a car to take you wherever you want to go," said Ian in a gentle but firm tone.

"But," she started to protest, but the look Michael gave her left her speechless and chilled to the bone. She pushed back from the table and left without another word.

Once she was out of earshot, Michael leaned back in his chair and turned slightly to face his second in command. Ian relaxed a little now that he had Michael's full attention. "Facial recognition identified the woman as Tatia Robins Matthews, a woman who was trafficked by Eric Hall when she was a preteen. Her testimony put him in prison. The man is her husband, Jesse Matthews, and they have two children. One is a nine-year-old girl."

Michael looked interested, knowing there was more. "Go on."

"They were caught on CCTV coming out of the Cook County Medical Examiner's Building. Our sources say they brought in a young unknown female to identify a body that was found by the river a few days ago."

"That being Misty's body?"

"Yes, sir."

"Pictures?"

Ian pulled out another picture and handed it to Michael. "This one's a little grainy, but if I'm not mistaken, the young woman with them is your future wife."

"I believe you are correct," said Michael with a triumphant expression that was as close to a smile as he ever came. "So, that's the connection we've been looking for. Mr. Hall, out of revenge, took Mrs. Matthew's daughter. His mistake was in bungling the delivery." He leaned forward suddenly and slapped both hands on the table. "Okay. Cut off his credit, drain his account, and dispose of him and his techie partner. Then go get my fiancée and make arrangements to move to the island. This investigation is getting tiresome, and I think Madison would enjoy a tropical wedding."

"And what about their daughter? Do you want me to dig further to confirm that she is your lost merchandise?"

Michael thought a moment. "We have our money back, and we're going to be busy with other matters for a while. Leave her."

32

Wednesday – 10/4

A few minutes after Maddie and Johnny's dramatic entrance, Jesse and Brush came in the back door for lunch. Instead of finding a meal ready to eat, they found a party atmosphere with lots of hugs and laughter.

"What's going on here?" asked Jesse with a pretend scowl.

"Maddie has a real name!" shouted Daniel, and then he clapped both hands over his mouth and looked at Tatia with eyes wide. "I'm sorry! I was supposed to let Maddie tell."

"It's okay, sweetie," said Maddie, giving him a hug. "It's exciting news whoever tells it."

"Well," said Brush. "Somebody tell us. Who are you?"

"I'm Madelyn Jeannette Collier. Johnny found my birth certificate."

"That's awesome," said Jesse, giving her a hug. "What else did you learn about yourself?"

"Oh!" she gasped. "I was so excited about my name that I forgot to look. Now where did I put it?"

"Here it is," said Johnny, handing her the document.

"Let's see. My mother's name was…," she choked up and couldn't continue. She handed the certificate back to Johnny. "You read it," she managed to get out.

He put his arm around her shoulders and began to read. "Mother's name is Jeanette Renee Collier; by father's name it says *None Given.* It says you were born in Caledonia, Illinois in Boone County. Where's that?"

"It's a little village with a population of about 200," answered Jesse. "It's about ten miles northeast of here. Looks like you've come home, Maddie. What else does it say?"

"Um, there's no hospital listed. Looks like you were born at home with the help of a midwife. That's about it."

"But doesn't it say how old she is?" asked Joy.

"Oh, yeah! That's kinda important, huh?" said Johnny, looking down at Maddie who was glowing in spite of the tears.

"Yeah, kinda," she giggled.

"Okay, it says you will be 18 on October 7. This is the 4th, so you have a birthday coming up on Saturday!"

"Yay!" shouted Daniel. "Let's have a birthday party!"

"That's a great idea, buddy," said Jesse. "But something smells delicious, and I'm starved. Let's have some lunch, and we can make plans while we eat."

Maddie ladled out bowls of chicken and corn chowder that had been simmering on the stove while Tatia put the finishing touches on a large tossed salad and Joy filled glasses with ice and lemonade. Maddie stopped and counted heads and then asked, "Do I need to count Lili for lunch? I haven't seen her today."

"Yes," replied Tatia. "She was here for breakfast, but she had to leave early. I think she said she had a lab today."

"Sounds like a full house," said Jesse. "Good thing we set up the extra table."

"Lili's here," shouted Daniel who was watching for her out the front window. He threw open the door just as she stepped up onto the front porch.

"Why, thank you, young Mr. Matthews," she said with a tired smile.

"You're welcome. Maddie has a name!"

"Of course she does," said Lili. She looked at Maddie in confusion.

Maddie grinned shyly and explained about the discovery of her birth certificate while she ferried bowls of soup to the table. Lili gave her a congratulatory hug and then went to wash up for lunch. She returned and found her place at the table just in time to join hands for grace.

The room was noisy with lunchtime chatter and the sharing of morning activities. When Lili didn't join in the conversation, Tatia asked her if she was okay.

"You look a little tired," she observed.

"I am tired, but I am okay," replied Lili. "My apartment is now ready, and I went by to inspect it and get the key. I guess I am a little distracted. Instead of renting furniture, I have decided to buy the furniture that you put together. My afternoon class was canceled today, so if I place my order before I leave for my evening class, everything should be delivered tomorrow. Then I will have the weekend to assemble the furniture and get settled."

"I helped Grandma design the bedroom in the Annex," said Joy. "I can help you."

"That's not a bad idea, Joy," said Tatia. "If Lili agrees, that is."

"I would love to have any help you can give. Design is not my strength."

"Good! It's a good opportunity to teach Joy to use the interior design program on my computer."

Daniel suddenly interrupted. "I think we should have a weenie roast!"

Lili, who had missed the earlier conversation, looked confused again. "Saturday is Maddie's 18th birthday, and we're going to have a party," explained Joy.

"Maybe you should ask the birthday girl if she likes weenie roasts," suggested Jesse.

"I don't know," said Maddie, looking a little embarrassed. "I've never been to one."

"But you do like hot dogs. Right?" asked Daniel.

"I don't know," repeated Maddie.

"You've never had a hot dog, have you?" said Brush. She shook her head.

"I have never had one either," added Lili.

Brush slapped his hands on the table. "Then it's settled! We'll grill hot dogs and hamburgers."

"We have to have birthday cake and ice cream," added Daniel, bouncing in his seat.

Tatia looked at Jesse. "I think the high on Saturday is supposed to be in the 60s, but it still might be a little chilly for ice cream."

"We can set up that big tent we use when we go to rallies, and we have heaters if we need them."

"Then it sounds like we're having a weenie roast," she declared, and everyone joined in the applause.

"By the way," said Jesse turning to Lili. "If you can get your furniture by Friday, I think we can all come over and help you get it put together and set up."

###

Tatia helped Maddie dress in layers so she would be warm on the bike but not too warm inside. "I may look like a stripper if I take off too many layers," quipped Maddie as she snapped a leather vest over a sweater.

Tatia laughed and Maddie slapped her hand over her mouth, eyes wide in embarrassment. "I shouldn't say something like that about going to church, should I? I'm so sorry."

Tatia hugged her, still smiling broadly. "Don't apologize, sweetheart. I love to see you learning to have fun. I think there are several bikers who attend the recovery group, so you won't be the only one who will be shedding some clothes. Just do it discreetly and you'll be fine."

Just then they heard a knock on the front door and a yell from the living room. "Johnny's here!"

"Go let him in – if Daniel doesn't beat you to it," said Tatia. "I'll get a Bible for you and a notebook in case you want to take notes."

The next few minutes was a flurry of greetings and last minute checks to be sure Maddie had everything she needed. And then the Matthews family stood on the front porch waving goodbye as Johnny and Maddie took off in a roar of pipes.

"Jesse, are we letting her move too fast?" Tatia asked again as the bike disappeared around a corner.

"What do you mean?" asked Jesse.

"She's only been here ten days, and so much has happened. And now we've sent her off to spend an evening with people we don't really know. And this thing with Johnny, whatever it is. It's just all happening so fast."

"Yes, it is. But Dr. Patterson okayed tonight. Right?"

"Uh-huh."

"Okay. Let's all go inside and take it to the Great Physician."

"Yay," shouted Daniel. "Can I pray?"

"Of course, you can. We'll all pray in turn for Johnny to be a safe driver, for Maddie to keep doing well, and for wisdom for us as we guide her."

Tatia looked at him gratefully, and he kissed her on the temple as he slid his arm protectively around her and guided his family toward the door.

###

Maddie experienced a moment of panic as she and Johnny

approached the building. There were lots of cars in the parking lot and even more people heading for the big double doors. Several people were standing outside greeting everyone as they got close and opening a door for them – and they all seemed to know Johnny, calling out a greeting or waving a hello.

"Hey, Johnny," said the man closest to them. He extended his hand and pulled Johnny into a hug. "I was beginning to think you weren't going to make it. You're usually the first one in the food line."

"Hi, Greg. Yeah, I'm a growing boy, but tonight I had to make a stop on the way." He turned toward Maddie who had lagged behind. He took her arm and gently drew her close to him. "This is my friend Maddie. It's her first time."

"Hi Maddie," said Greg, shaking her hand. "Come on in and get something to eat. It's not fancy, but there's plenty of it."

He was right about that. The long food table was filled with large bowls of potato salad and platters piled high with sandwiches. At the end of the table there were bowls of fruit and plates of cookies. Finally, there were several coolers filled with cans of soft drinks and bottles of water beside a small table holding a large coffee urn.

Maddie was almost overwhelmed by the number of choices, but she watched the girl ahead of her and followed her lead – a small scoop of potato salad, a sandwich with a filling she couldn't identify, a small bunch of grapes, a chocolate chip cookie, and a bottle of water. Then she let Johnny take the lead and find them a place to sit. Most of the round tables seated eight, but some people had moved chairs from other tables to squeeze in extra people. She was grateful when he found an empty table along the edge that only had four chairs left, and none of them was taken. He set his plate down and then pulled a chair out for her.

"Thank you," she said as she looked up at him and sat down.

"I thought you might like to watch from the sidelines tonight. I remember how I felt my first time."

"You're very thoughtful, Johnny. I've never been in a room with this many people before."

They chatted easily as they ate. Johnny explained in a little more detail what was going to happen as the program moved on, and he pointed out group leaders, members of the praise band, and others as people finished their food and began to move around the room. When they finished eating, he disposed of their trash and visited the coffee urn.

He returned with two cups of coffee and handed one to her. "I couldn't remember how you take your coffee, so I just added French vanilla creamer. I hope that's okay."

She took a sip and smiled. "Just right. Thank you. Now what?"

"Now we have the chip celebration. You can go up front and get a newcomer's chip if you want to or just sit back and watch."

"Do you have to say anything?"

"Just your first name."

"That doesn't sound too bad, but if you don't mind, I think I'll just watch for now."

"Whatever makes you comfortable."

Their conversation was interrupted when a man stepped to the microphone on the small stage in the front of the room and announced that it was time for the celebration to begin. The crowd responded with applause and cheers that indicated they were ready to celebrate.

"That's the Counseling Pastor," whispered Johnny.

When he called for newcomers or people who were beginning the road to recovery again after a relapse, two people came forward. Each one stepped to the microphone in turn, stated their first name, and accepted a chip and a hug from the pastor.

"That doesn't seem too scary," whispered Maddie.

By the time Johnny went forward to receive his 60-day chip, Maddie had caught the excitement. She stood up and clapped loudly. And at the end of the celebration, when the pastor extended one more invitation to newcomers, Maddie went forward. Her voice was barely audible when she said, "My name is Maddie," but everyone could hear Johnny shouting encouragement as she almost ran back to her seat.

"I can't believe I just did that," she giggled breathlessly.

Before she could sit down, the praise band began to play and everyone stood and began to sing and clap along with the music. She was a bit startled about how lively it was – and how loud – but she loved the energy, and the lyrics touched her deeply even though she didn't understand what a lot of them meant. After the third song, the band members placed their instruments on racks and left the stage, but before she could feel too disappointed, the pastor returned to the microphone. He offered a prayer almost as sweet as the ones Jesse prayed each evening, and he dismissed everyone to their groups. Maddie panicked at the thought that she and Johnny would be separated, but a woman who looked to be about thirty years old walked up and introduced herself.

"Hi, Maddie, and welcome. My name is Sandy. Johnny said you'd be in my group – I'm the facilitator of the substance abuse group. He sometimes gets lost in the hallways around here, so I thought I'd show you the way to our room."

"That's so nice of you. This place is huge!"

An hour later, Sandy walked Maddie back to the double doors where Johnny was waiting. Sandy was talking, and Maddie was listening intently. "You've made a great start, Maddie. I think you're going to do just fine." She grinned and looked up at Johnny. "Especially if this reprobate will bring you back next week."

"You can count on it," said Johnny.

Maddie bubbled and chattered all the way back to the bike where they had stowed their warmer clothes. While they zipped on chaps, snapped vests, and pulled on jackets and gloves, people streamed by, shouting greetings and cautions to be careful. Several included Maddie, and she looked up at Johnny with a sigh. "I can't thank you enough for bringing me here. I just love having friends."

33

Thursday - 10/5

"Why does Joy get to go everywhere and I don't get to go no-where," whined Daniel.

"You don't get to go anywhere," said Tatia automatically in her teacher voice, but the smile on her face was a mommy smile. "Lili checked with her friend who is performing the sonogram to see if Joy and I could come along with Maddie, and she said *yes.* She didn't ask if you could come because we're going to a women's clinic, and some of the women there might be uncomfortable with a curious five-year-old boy running around asking questions. We'll bring you a picture of the sonogram so you can see what the baby looks like inside Lili's tummy. Okay?"

"Okay I guess," said Daniel with his head down.

Tatia hugged him and gave him a kiss on the cheek which he wiped off on his sleeve. "Besides, you get the day off from school because Daddy and Brush have some business at the shop in the city, and you're going with them. Joy, on the other hand, is going on a school field trip and will be taking notes for a science report."

Joy's mouth fell open in surprise, and Daniel did a happy

dance. "You didn't say anything about a science report before," she complained.

"That's because I just thought of it. But I think you'll find this experience so interesting that you'll be able to write a book about it – so a one-page report should be a snap."

Maddie came in from the bedroom carrying her shoes and plopped down on the couch to put them on. "I'm so excited about seeing this that I feel like I could write a book. I'll be glad to help you with your report..." She stopped suddenly and looked at Tatia. "In a strictly advisory way, of course."

Tatia couldn't keep a straight face, and everyone burst out laughing. "Don't worry about it, Joy. I don't want anything formal – just some notes on your thoughts and feelings about the experience, and maybe some thoughts on when life begins."

"That doesn't sound too bad – as long as you don't count off for punctuation – and as long as we can go out to lunch after."

"Sounds like a plan," said Tatia, looking up something on her phone. "There's a bistro near the university that sounds like it might be good – gourmet coffee and snack foods as well as international fusion bowls, salads, wraps, and sandwiches. Would you like to check it out?"

"I don't know," said Joy. "Depends on what fusion food is."

"It says it's food from different cultures and countries like Latin countries, Asian countries, Caribbean, and so forth. What do you think?"

"Yes!" enthused Joy and Maddie in unison.

"Yuck!" shouted Daniel with equal enthusiasm. "I hope we go somewhere with hot dogs and hamburgers and stuff."

"Did I hear someone talking about man food?" said Jesse coming in the door.

"Yeah," said Daniel puffing up his chest. "They're going to some kind of girly place to eat, but I want to go to a man place for lunch."

"You mean someplace where you can burp and spit and do other manly kinds of things?" asked Jesse.

"That's what I'm talkin' about!"

"Where does he get this stuff?" asked Tatia, laughing at her son and his macho act.

"Don't look at me," said Jesse with an innocent expression. "But when we engage in these manly activities, I will be sure to instruct him that, like running around naked, there's nothing wrong with that in certain settings, but in other places it's just not polite."

Jesse delivered this monologue with such seriousness that his audience was laughing hysterically. "Now, if my adoring public will excuse me, I need to get my riding buddy dressed for the road. Brush and I decided it's a great day for a ride, so we're taking the bikes."

"Yay!" shouted Daniel, and he dashed to his room before anyone could say another word.

"I had no idea being part of a family could be so much fun," said Maddie, wiping tears from her eyes.

"I have to agree that this is one of our better days," said Tatia. "Now, last call for bathroom visits, water bottles, jackets, phones, and anything else you can't do without until we get back home. We're supposed to meet Lili in my office in four minutes."

###

"That was the most amazing thing I've ever seen!" said Joy for about the seventh time since they left the clinic. She stared at the picture of the sonogram the tech had given her, ignoring the personal sized veggie pizza she had ordered. "A baby no bigger than the end of my thumb has a heart that's already beating. I wouldn't have believed it if I hadn't seen it with my own eyes."

"Listen to this," said Maddie whose Asian chicken salad had been pushed aside after a couple of bites. "At eight weeks – which will be in about two more weeks for you…right, Lili?"

"That is correct," replied Lili between bites of her Caribbean fusion bowl.

"Okay," continued Maddie. "By then the baby will have all major body parts, all facial features will be developed, hands and feet will be taking shape including fingerprints, and the baby will be moving in its own little exercise routine. Misty always told me that a fetus was just a blob of unformed tissue until just a few weeks before it was born. It sounds to me like it's already a little person."

"Yes, the little person inside me already has its own blood type and its own DNA – that's what gives it a unique identity."

"Joy, we read about DNA in your science lesson last week," interjected Tatia. "You might want to remember that for your report."

"Oh, I remember that. It looks like a long snaky thing called a double something."

"A double helix – very good! Maddie, you look lost in thought. Do you have a question?"

"I was just thinking about what Misty said. When she sent the girls for a D and C, she said it was like getting your tonsils out. But if this is true..." she said, holding up the print-out she had been reading from. "If the fetus is a real little person, then ending the pregnancy is..." She stopped and looked at Tatia with horror in her eyes.

"Yes, Maddie," replied Tatia gently. "Ending a pregnancy is ending a life."

"You mean like murder?" asked Joy around a bite of her pizza.

"Yes," said Lili. "Like murder."

A hush fell over the table, and all four of them busied themselves with their food. After a couple of minutes of silence, Joy looked up and asked, "Can they tell if it's a girl or a boy before it's born?"

The tension around the table broke with an almost audible sigh. "Yes. In about three months my friend wants to do another sonogram, and we may be able to determine the gender at that time. If you would like, you can all come with me, and maybe we can eat here again. This is so good, and I was so hungry!"

Tatia laughed. "That's normal when you're eating for two."

"Yes," said Lili. "And this tastes like home."

"It smells good, but I don't recognize some of the stuff in it," said Joy.

"Well," explained Lili, "this is jerk chicken, this is plantains, and this is couscous. I think you probably recognize everything else. Maybe we could have a special class on island cooking one day and I can teach you how to make it at home."

"Mommy, could we?"

"It sounds like a great idea, but right now, if we can finish our lunch pretty soon, we should have time to visit the thrift store down the street and then go for ice cream before we go home. Anyone interested?"

The positive response was unanimous. Everyone was finishing their ice cream when Lili's phone indicated that she had received a text. "It is from my new landlord. The delivery company has arrived and is unloading my furniture. Would you mind dropping me there on your way home?"

"I'll do better than that. I'll call Jesse and see if they can meet us there. We'll get an early start on putting it together."

34

Thursday - 10/5

"Good news, ladies," whispered Harris as he walked Eric and Victor back to their unit after their daily hour in the small yard. "Ellis now has Internet access, and you both have access to the basement rec room."

"Cool," said Victor under his breath without turning his head back toward the guard. "Shooting baskets is getting boring. When do we get to go – and when do I get a computer?"

"I don't know the details yet, but somebody will come get you tonight after lights out to take you down there. There's a little business to conduct, you know. And then they'll show you around the place a bit. Schedule will be set later. Now shut up and move it. I'm off shift in five minutes."

Once they were back in the unit, Eric immediately resumed his pacing while Victor settled at the table with one of his computer magazines. Eric finally picked up a newspaper and joined Victor at the table as dinnertime approached. He opened the paper and stared at a page until he was sure the guard wasn't watching.

"I don't like this," he whispered to Victor. "We've never seen this guard before, and he keeps glaring at us like he's got something up his sleeve."

"You're just getting paranoid in your old age," Victor replied. "The regular guy probably just took a personal day or something. What could he be up to anyway?"

"I don't know, but I still don't like it."

The food cart rattled in the hallway, and the guard ordered them into their cells where they sat on their beds until the trays were on the table. When the cart was back in the hallway and the guard was back in his position, he called out in a sarcastic voice, "Dinner is served, gentlemen. Enjoy!"

Eric pushed and poked the meatloaf with his spork and pushed the peas around the plate. "How can you eat this slop? The price we're paying, we should be eating steak - with a real knife and fork!"

Victor continued to shovel food into his mouth without looking up. "I've been in jail before, and this is a lot better than what you get in general population."

Eric snorted and pushed his plate away, but not before he snatched up the chocolate chip cookie and bit off half of it. As he expected, Victor cleaned his tray and went to work on his roommate's food.

"You're gonna need to work out if you keep eating like that."

"And you're gonna look like a skeleton."

"Hurry up and finish so we can get the TV turned on." The guards had total control over what television programs were watched, and strict rules regulated the limited times it could be turned on.

"From the look of this guard, you'll be watching a Hallmark movie tonight."

After dinner was finished and the unit was tidied to the guard's satisfaction, he turned the TV on to an old John Wayne movie. Eric decided it was better than nothing so he slouched down in a chair and stared at the screen.

Victor opted to stay in his cell. He had used some of the special commissary funds Vandoren had arranged to buy an MP3 player loaded with some of the old acoustic jazz tunes he favored. He had also purchased a legal pad and a pen. He settled onto his bunk, turned on his music, and began to work on a list of items and services he wanted to purchase once they worked out a direct deal with the inside supplier. He was well into his third page when the lights flashed indicating it was fifteen minutes to lights out.

Victor woke with a start sometime later when the electronic lock on his cell door clicked open and he sensed someone in his cell. He panicked when a hand covered his mouth, and then a strange voice hissed in his ear. "Keep quiet and get dressed. We're going to the rec room."

Moments later Victor and his unknown escort slipped out of his cell. "What about me?" Eric whispered from his cell.

"Shut up! We'll be back for you after the payment is worked out."

By the dimmed lighting in the common area Victor could see that his visitor was dressed in the green uniform of a trustee. The two men walked past the night guard who never looked up from the book he was reading by a clip-on book light. Two very large men dressed in the regular tan prisoner uniforms waited outside the unit, and the party of four hurried silently through the empty hallway and down two flights of stairs to the basement.

Victor was ushered into a large well-lit room furnished on one side with exercise equipment that had seen better days and on the other with several game-sized tables surrounded by four chairs each. A shelf on one wall held a small selection of board games, but the tables were empty except for one that held an open laptop. The trustee shoved Victor toward the laptop and snarled.

"You're on, mister tech guru. Do your stuff."

An angry response bubbled up in Victor's throat, but he did a quick mental check of his situation and swallowed it along with his pride. Besides, he was about to get online for the first time in a couple of weeks, and it felt like coming home. He sat down at the keyboard, and seeing that the computer was already connected, he quickly navigated his way to his numbered account. He grinned as he stared at the seven-digit balance, and without turning his eyes away from the screen he spoke to the trustee.

"Okay, I'm in. I need the account number where...wait! What's going on?"

He sat transfixed as the balance began to drop quickly in a mirror image of the day of Joy's auction when the balance rose from nothing to more than he and Eric could have imagined. He began to pound keys frantically, trying to stop the plundering of his future – but nothing worked. In less than thirty seconds, the balance had fallen to zero. As he stared in disbelief, a message popped up on the screen. It said:

Did you really think you could keep Michael Saint's money after you failed to deliver his merchandise?

After a few seconds, the message disappeared and the screen went black. Victor felt the three men moving into a half circle behind him, and his disbelief turned to terror.

"Wait! We didn't know who the buyer was so we couldn't return his money. Just tell me what I need to do to make this right and I'll do it."

But no one was interested in what he had to say.

"It's about time," yelled Eric as the trustee appeared at the door of his cell.

"Shut up and follow me!" whispered the other inmate urgently. The lock on the cell clicked open and, already dressed in his uniform, Eric moved silently into the common area and followed his guide. The other two men fell in behind Eric, and the four made their way to the rec room.

Eric's eyes adjusted slowly to the brightness of the room after the darkness of the stairwells and the hallways. As his vision cleared, he blinked several times, convinced that his eyes were playing tricks on him. But he couldn't deny what he saw. Victor was lying on a weight bench with a bar supporting five fifty-five-pound plates on each end resting across his chest. His eyes bulged from a face that had a bluish tinge, and the bar was buried in his chest as if it had been dropped from some distance above him.

Eric began to offer large sums of money in exchange for his life, but the trustee held a cell phone in front of his face that showed his account with a balance of $0.00. Then the same message that Victor saw appeared on the screen. As he read it, the reality of his situation settled on him, and Eric began to beg. But the trustee and one of the other inmates each grabbed one of his arms while the third man went to the weight rack and removed one of the empty weight bars. He positioned himself in front of Eric with the bar drawn back over his shoulder like a baseball bat. Then Eric began to scream.

###

Ian was sitting in his office when the call came in from his contact at MCC. As soon as he ended the call, he hit speed dial for Michael's private cell phone. "I hope I didn't wake you, sir...I have news about the late Mr. Hall and the late Mr. Ellis...I'll be right up."

One of Michael's bodyguards met him at the penthouse elevator and escorted him to the balcony outside the living room. Michael was enjoying a snifter of the $20,000 cognac he saved for such occasions and an equally expensive cigar. Ian respectfully turned down his offer to join him, and Michael's face turned serious.

"How did the wrapping up of our business with Mr. Hall and Mr. Ellis go?"

"Perfectly. The keystroke logging software we put on Vandoren's laptop gave us the routing number and account number of their Swiss account. But rather than pull the money immediately, our man set it up so when Ellis logged into the account, the funds automatically transferred to our account. And as an afterthought, he had a message from you pop up when the account was empty. Of course, it disappeared without a trace after a few seconds."

Michael's mouth smiled, but his eyes were those of a predator. "Excellent. And the kidnappers were dealt with appropriately?"

"Let's just say their criminal careers ended rather badly in the basement gym at the prison." He added a few more graphic details and then summed up. "So, the thieves have paid their debt, and you have recovered your money with interest."

"Interest? How so?" asked Michael.

"The fees they took in for the privilege of watching the video, and the entry fees for placing bids in the auction more than covered the amount that they used to pay attorney's fees and miscellaneous expenses while they were inside."

"Speaking of attorneys, will this Vandoren be a problem?"

"No, sir. We showed him pictures of his former clients, and he understands the importance of staying in your good graces. In addition, we gave him a generous tip to cover the lost revenue caused by the untimely demise of his clients. I think he may prove to be a valuable asset in the future."

"Excellent! Is the Gulfstream ready to go?"

"Yes, sir. It's loaded and fueled, and there's a car waiting for you downstairs."

"You're sure this hasty departure is necessary?"

"Yes, sir. Our sources say a raid and an arrest are planned for tomorrow or Sunday."

"Have all the records been moved or destroyed?"

"It's almost done, sir. The records have been transferred, and the techs are doing a final wipe of all electronic traces of Saint

International. Employees have been relocated – the executive staff will be on the island when you arrive. The remainder of the staff will be in a secure location on another island."

"And you will follow as soon as you pick up Madison?"

"Yes, sir. We have the location of the Matthews' home, but we want to confirm that Madison is there before we drop in for a visit."

"Then I will head to the airport and leave you to it. Good work, Ian."

"Thank you, sir."

35

Friday - 10/6

Tatia handed Jesse a second cup of coffee while he and Daniel colored adjoining pages in a coloring book Grandma and Grandpa had brought him when they visited. Daniel leaned into Jesse and looked up at him with the sly look that always meant he was up to something.

"Hey, Daddy, how about you play hooky from work and stay home and play with me all day."

"That sounds like fun, buddy," said Jesse, hugging Daniel close. "But what about your school work? I hear you have a pretty tough teacher."

"Oh, she's not so tough. If you asked her real sweet maybe she'd give me a play day."

"Hey, guys," said Tatia. "I'm right here, you know. I can hear every word."

Jesse and Daniel looked at each other in mock surprise and clapped their hands over their mouths. "Busted!" said Jesse. "It wouldn't work anyway, buddy. I have to mind the shop this morn-ing while Brush and Johnny meet Lili at her apartment to finish

196

setting up and hook up her electronics - TV, WiFi, sound system, all that fun stuff. She should be able to sleep there tonight."

"Maybe," said Tatia to Daniel, "if you and Joy work really hard this morning – and that goes for you, too, buster," she added, giving Jesse the evil eye, "maybe we can take the afternoon to work on party decorations and make the cake."

Joy came in from her bedroom with a hairbrush and a scrunchy in her hand. "Mommy, can you help me with a ponytail, please."

"Sure, sweetie. Come on over."

While she gathered Joy's thick hair in one hand and skillfully secured it with a scrunchy, she asked Jesse a question. "Did I hear Johnny talking to Lili about sub-letting her apartment when she goes back home to have the baby?"

"Yeah, since he's decided to stay on with us permanently, he's been looking for something closer. He doesn't really have the money for all the deposits, and certainly not enough to buy furniture, so this would be a good deal for him, and she could have her place back next fall."

"A win-win all around," said Tatia as she handed the brush back to Joy.

"Thank you, Mommy." She turned her attention to Maddie who had been quietly taking in the morning activity. "You don't seem very excited about your party tomorrow. Are you okay?"

"I'm fine, Joy," she replied. "Just a little slow starting this morning."

"That's okay. You need to rest up because I think I heard something about party decorations and cake this afternoon."

"Yes," said Tatia. "But there are conditions – work hard this morning. So go help your brother get dressed while I finish up the kitchen, and we'll get started."

"Then I guess I'd better get dressed, too," said Maddie.

She followed Joy and Daniel down the hall, listening to them chattering about balloons, streamers, and sugar sprinkles, and Tatia returned to the kitchen. Jesse's phone rang, and the caller I.D. indicated it was Detective Nelson.

"Hey, Adam! What's up?"

Tatia motioned to catch his attention. "Invite him and Tracy to the party."

Jesse nodded while he listened. He slid out from behind the table and stepped out onto the back patio with his phone. Tatia watched him through the window, knowing from his body language that the conversation was serious. Maddie and the children came out of the hallway in a burst of noise and laughter that warmed Tatia's heart in spite of what might be going on outside. She quickly handed out assignments and asked Maddie to supervise for a few minutes while she talked with Jesse.

Her husband was just ending his call when she joined him on the patio. "What's going on, Jesse? You look pretty grim."

He hugged her and kissed her hair. She snuggled against him, giving him time to find the right words. "Yes," he said, pushing her back gently so he could see her face. "It's grim alright, but good news, too." He linked his elbow through hers and grasped her hand. "Let's go over to the shop so we won't be interrupted. We'll need to decide how to tell the kids."

Jesse seated her at the table in the break room and asked if she wanted coffee. "No!" Tatia exclaimed. "You're scaring me, Jesse. Just spit it out!"

"Sorry," he said as he sat down opposite her. "Eric and Victor were found in the basement workout room at the prison this morning. Both had been beaten to death. For now, the media will be told it was an unfortunate accident. Who knows if they'll ever find out who did it, but knowing what Maddie told us about Michael Saint, he probably had a hand in it."

Jesse looked weighed down by the news, but after a moment of silence, he took a breath, straightened up, and smiled. "On the other hand, the girls won't have to give depositions or testimonies about the kidnapping."

"Another reason to celebrate tomorrow," said Tatia. "How shall we break the news to the children? We have to tell them before they hear it on the news or read it in the newspaper."

"I'll tell them after lunch," said Jesse. "I'll give them the media version – an accident in prison – and focus on the good news about not having to testify. Since you've given them the afternoon off, we'll have time to answer questions and deal with emotional repercussions that might come up."

36

Saturday - 10/7

A party atmosphere prevailed in the Matthews' back yard the day of Maddie's birthday. Brush had dragged out the tent and the heater just in case, but the weather was so beautiful they hadn't bothered putting either one up. Daniel and Shawn were playing *Follow the Leader* in the small fenced play yard. Daniel had just executed an awkward flip on the swinging bar, and Shawn was struggling to follow suit. Jesse was grilling burgers and hot dogs while Brush cranked an old-fashioned wooden freezer full of homemade ice cream.

"Where in the world did Tatia find this antique?" asked Brush.

"I'm not sure," Jesse responded, "but it was probably in Mom G's attic."

"Well, this ice cream better be good. This is a lot of work, and the bucket keeps moving around."

"I think you're supposed to get one of the kids to sit on it to hold it down," laughed Jesse. "Hey, Daniel, come over here and sit on this freezer for your Uncle Brush."

"Okay," Daniel shouted as he slid down the small slide at the end of the swing set. He vaulted the low fence, ran over and plopped down on the freezer. "Wow!" he yelled, jumping back up. "Now I know why it's called a freezer! That's too cold to sit on."

Jesse grinned as he flipped a burger. "Go ask your mom to get you an old towel. You can fold it up and use it as a cushion to protect your delicate back side! And tell her I'm about ready for the buns and cheese."

Daniel made a funny face at Joy as he passed the picnic table where she and Maddie were arranging plates, sets of plastic ware wrapped artfully in colorful napkins, and an assortment of condiments. Joy giggled and made a face back at him before turning back to her job.

"You know," said Joy thoughtfully, "I'm sorry about what happened to Eric and Victor but I'm glad we don't have to give depositions or testify about what they did. Do you think that makes me a bad person?"

"I don't think so. It's not like you're glad they got killed or something," said Maddie, standing back to look at their handiwork. "I'm still nervous about testifying about Michael, though. I mean, if he could get to them in prison, how can I expect to be safe from him regardless of where I hide? Sometimes I find myself looking over my shoulder, expecting him to burst through the door and drag me away."

"Do you really think he'd do that? I mean, do you think he's looking for you?"

"Probably. Not that he cared about me or anything. But I belonged to him, and he doesn't like losing things. And if he finds out I'm testifying..."

"Well, Dad and Brush wouldn't let anything happen to you. You should have seen Daddy go off on Eric when they rescued me," bragged Joy. "Speaking of bursting through doors, here comes Daniel!"

Right on cue, the energetic five year old threw the door open and ran to the freezer. After running off Shawn who was trying to prove he could endure the cold seat, Daniel sat down on his towel and let out a theatrical sigh of contentment.

"Just in time," said Brush. "This stuff is beginning to firm up, and the bucket is really twisting. Sit heavy!"

Tatia and Shawna followed Daniel out the still open door carrying potato salad, buns and cheese. "Joy," called Tatia, "Can you and Maddie help us bring out the rest of the food. It's all lined up on the counter. And I think I hear Johnny coming with the ice. As soon as he gets here, we can start filling the glasses."

The rumble of Johnny's bike announced his arrival a few seconds before he turned from the alley into the driveway behind the Fallen Angel Salvage Bike Shop. Tatia noticed how his eyes immediately searched out Maddie and how flushed her cheeks became as she glanced at him. She smiled to herself, pleased that Maddie was able to connect so quickly. It had taken her years to be open to a relationship. Once again, she prayed they weren't moving too fast.

"It's about time you showed up. We've all been dying of thirst, and Brush used up all the ice in the freezer!" shouted Tatia playfully.

"You know me," returned Johnny as he opened the small ice chest bungeed to the luggage rack on the back of his bike. "Always one to arrive fashionably late in order to make a grand entrance," he continued, making a courtly bow with a bag of ice held out like a droopy bouquet of flowers.

"Well, bring it on over and put it in the ice chest before it melts," said Tatia.

Shawn ran over and grabbed Johnny around the waist, almost knocking him off balance. "Hey, buddy," said Johnny. "I'm glad to see you, too. Where's Daniel?" When the two were together, they were rarely more than a few feet apart.

"He's over there sitting on the freezer. He can't get up because his butt's too cold." Shawn laughed nervously and glanced at his mother to see if she would scold him. She was very strict about his language, but she was busy opening chips and hadn't heard him.

Johnny tore open the bag of ice and poured it into the waiting ice chest. "I hope one bag is enough. From the looks of this table, you're planning to feed an army."

"No, it's just the nine of us – or maybe eleven if Tracy and Adam come. It's just my southern roots showing – no one leaves the table hungry!" said Tatia. It felt good to laugh and relax after the tension of the last several weeks.

"I never worry about that!" said Johnny as he returned to his bike. He pulled out a long, thin box that had been secured behind the ice chest. "These are for the birthday girl."

"Oh, Johnny," gasped Maddie as he opened the box to reveal six long-stemmed red roses. "They're beautiful! Thank you!" She kissed him lightly on the cheek, and they both blushed furiously.

"Are you sure about the guest list, honey?" called Jesse. He was looking up and shading his eyes as he pointed up with his long-handled spatula. "That helicopter has been circling here for the last couple of minutes, and it looks like it's coming down across the alley."

"A helicopter! Cool!" shouted Daniel jumping up and racing toward the alley.

"Daniel Matthews, you get back here right now!" yelled Tatia.

"But Mooooommmmm!" he whined.

"Daniel." said Jesse quietly, and the boy stopped with a look of resignation.

The helicopter was continuing to settle, now only about fifteen feet off the ground. "Johnny, can you slide these burgers over to the side to keep warm for a couple of minutes?" said Jesse moving slowly toward the alley. "Brush?"

"On your six, boss," the big man replied. He stood up from the freezer and followed a couple of steps behind Jesse.

Jesse stopped and looked at Brush with one eyebrow raised. "On your six?" he said.

"Sorry," replied Brush. "Shawn and I have been binge watching some old NCIS episodes. But from the look of those guys," he continued, nodding toward the helicopter, "maybe I should have watched a few more."

The helicopter settled to the ground and while the rotors were still whirling, two men stepped out, one on either side. Each man was dressed totally in black and wore black-rimmed sunglasses – and each man held an MP5 fully automatic submachine gun cradled across his left elbow with his right hand resting uncomfortably close to the trigger. Jesse and Brush stared with their mouths open, and Joy pasted herself against Tatia's side while Maddie began to cry softly. Ian finally stepped out of the helicopter wearing a suit that spoke of money. He carried no weapon, but he carried himself with the confidence of a man who is fully armed. The trio strolled across the alley as if no cars would dare hit them and stopped halfway up the driveway.

"I'm sorry to interrupt your little party, but I need to speak with Madison," Ian said.

"And who, may I ask, are you?" asked Jesse, trying hard to sound more confident than he felt.

Ian's mouth twitched in what could have been either a smile or a snarl. "You may ask, but you may not get an answer. My business is with Madison, and I need to speak with her - now."

Out of the corner of his eye Jesse saw movement and turned to see Maddie moving toward the men. Tears were streaming down her face, and her head was moving slowly from side to side. "No, no, no..." she moaned, but her feet kept moving.

Johnny dropped the spatula in the gravel and lunged toward her. "No, Maddie!" he shouted.

Before he reached her, both of the twins shifted their weapons into firing position, and the one on the right fired a short burst into the ground a few inches behind Johnny, spraying the backs of his legs with gravel.

"I wouldn't do that if I were you," said Ian quietly. "My orders are to pick up Madison. Nothing more. But if you try to interfere, I will also take Joy. After all, she has been paid for."

His words were met with a stunned silence, and when no one moved, he continued. "Come now, Madison. Your fiancé is waiting."

Madison's tears had stopped and the emotion on her face had been replaced with a mask of resignation. She gazed at the people standing around her, lingering for a moment on Johnny. "I'm sorry," she said as she turned and walked toward Ian. She stopped halfway and spoke loudly enough for everyone to hear her.

"I won't resist on one condition. Don't hurt my family and leave Joy alone. If you plan to kill them, let me know now and I'll stay and die with them."

"No one has to die, Madison. Mr. S is only interested in you. As for Joy, he has already secured a refund of his money."

Strengthened by his words, Maddie took a deep breath and continued. "And no drugs. I've been clean and sober for two weeks."

"That's not a problem, Madison. The drugs were always Misty's idea. Mr. S prefers you the way you are. Anything else?"

"One more thing. Call me Madelyn – Madelyn Collier. Johnny found my birth records."

Ian laughed. "I see a lot has happened in two weeks, Madelyn. I think we can accommodate the name change. Now come along."

"Wait! Wait!" wailed Joy.

The body guards raised their rifles to their shoulders, but Ian put out his hand and said quietly, "Stand down."

"Please don't shoot me," stammered Joy. "But it's Maddie's birthday, and we didn't get to give her any presents. Can I just give her the special one? Please!"

Ian smiled indulgently. "Okay, but hurry."

Joy wheeled around and sped into the house and returned a moment later carrying a gaily wrapped package. She tore the wrapping off as she ran, revealing a book. She almost threw it into Maddie's hands and threw herself into Maddie's arms.

"It's a Bible," she gasped between sobs. "It has your name on the front – your real name – and we all signed it inside. Don't forget us!"

Maddie squeezed the younger girl and wet her hair with tears. "I'll treasure it always. Now, look at me." Joy leaned her head back and looked into those amazing violet eyes. "I love you – all of you – and I will never forget you."

Then, she released her hold on Joy and clutched the Bible to her chest. Without looking back, she turned and walked toward Ian and took the arm he offered her. The ones she left behind stared in disbelief as Maddie boarded the helicopter followed by Ian and the two body guards. No one moved as the engine roared to life and the rotors began to spin, lifting the four passengers into the air and out of sight.

Joy was the first to break the silence. "Daddy," she screamed. "Do something! You can't let them take Maddie!"

She ran to him and fell into his arms, soaking his shirt with her hysterical sobs. Sudden pandemonium filled the little back yard with screams, shouts, questions, and tears – and then Detectives Nelson and Martin pulled in and parked behind Johnny's bike.

"What in the name of..." Tracy interrupted Adam's question with a slap on his arm and an abrupt exclamation of her own. "Language!"

"Sorry," he said, rubbing his arm. "You don't hit like a girl."

"And don't you forget it! Brush, you seem to be the calmest of the bunch. Can you tell us what's going on?"

Brush found a seat next to Johnny that was opposite two empty chairs and recounted as concisely as possible what had happened in the last few minutes. Both detectives immediately pulled tablets and pens out of their pockets and began taking notes, and when Brush mentioned the helicopter, Adam pulled out his phone. He contacted State Police Aircraft Operations to request a track on the helicopter.

"I'll ask," he said into the phone. "Any identifying marks on the copter?"

"Yeah," said Jesse who had passed Joy to her mother and moved over to listen in on the debriefing. "You remember the other day when Maddie said that Michael Saint was the guy who kept her under lock and key and bought Joy at the auction. That chopper had the Saint International emblem – you know, the orange 'I' inside a blue 'S'."

Adam turned back to the phone, and Brush was about to resume his account when Johnny abruptly stood, almost upsetting the table.

"I can't just sit here," he said. "I'm going to go look for her."

Jesse reached out and grabbed his arm as he started toward his bike. "Johnny," he reasoned, "you don't even know where to start. We don't know which direction they went. They could be out of the country by now."

"But we've got to do something!" he said in defeat.

"What else can we do? Tracy's getting any details we can give her, and Adam is trying to get a track on the chopper. There's not much more to do for now."

Johnny ran his hands through his hair in frustration and plopped back into his chair. "I guess you're right."

Adam turned back toward the table with the phone still at his ear. "Did anyone happen to notice the call sign?"

"What's that?" asked Jesse.

"It's the letters and numbers on the side of the aircraft," replied Brush. Jesse gave him a puzzled look and he shrugged. "What? I took some flying lessons."

"Of course you did. So do you have a license?"

"Yeah, but no, I didn't catch the call sign. It all happened too fast."

"Anybody else see the numbers and letters on the side of the helicopter?"

No one spoke for a moment, and then a small voice came from under the table. "I did," said Daniel.

"Hey," said Adam. "I'll call you back."

Everyone stared down at Daniel, and tears began to slide down his cheeks. "Hey, buddy! What's wrong? Come over here and sit with me," said Jesse.

Daniel scooted out, and Jesse lifted him onto his lap and hugged him close. "I know we're all upset about Maddie leaving, but why the tears now?"

Daniel hid his face against Jesse's chest and, between sobs, began to talk. "They took Joy...now Maddie...he said fiancé...that means getting married...never see her again...and that man almost shot Johnny!" he wailed.

Jesse continued to hold him close, rocking gently back and forth. "Lots of stuff for a little guy, huh?"

Daniel nodded, wiping his nose on Jesse's shirt. "You remember when they took Joy that the police helped find her. Right?" Daniel nodded again. "Well, Adam and Tracy are here right now, and they'll help us find Maddie." More nods. "And I don't think they really meant to hurt Johnny. I think they were just trying to scare him so he would stand still and not try to stop Maddie. What do you think?"

Daniel turned his head toward Johnny and stared at him seriously. "I think yes."

"Now," said Jesse. "If you and I go into the house and get your drawing tablet, do you think you could draw the letters and numbers on the side of the helicopter?"

"Yes," said Daniel as he slid down off Jesse's lap and held out his hand to his dad.

Jesse and Daniel disappeared into the house while Tracy and Adam compared notes. Shawn and Joy sat on the swing set, moving back and forth halfheartedly, and Brush walked over to the grill. He tapped one of the burgers with the spatula, and it emitted a dull clunk.

"These things are useless unless somebody wants to play hockey."

"I forgot about dinner," sighed Tatia, "but we need to eat. If you'll turn off the grill and trash those, I'll order some pizzas."

About ten minutes later, father and son emerged from the house. Daniel joined his sister and Shawn on the swing set, and Jesse handed Adam a crude drawing of a helicopter with a call sign printed in a childish scrawl.

"Good job, Daniel!" exclaimed Adam as he hit redial on his phone. "Hey, Nelson here." He recited the call sign and listened for a few seconds. "Yeah, the kid saw it…5 years old…Whoa – language!" he said and winked at Tracy. "Look, the kid drew a picture of the kidnap vehicle in the Joy Matthews case, and he was spot on. Just run it…No, I'll wait."

He paced for a couple of minutes before he spoke again. "Yeah, whatcha got?…Wait a minute. I'm gonna put you on speaker…Okay, we've got ladies and children present, so watch your language."

"Yeah, whatever. That call sign matches the corporate chopper for Saint International, but we're playing catch up. They landed at a private airfield about ten minutes from your location. They must have hit the ground on the run, because five minutes later one of the two Saint International Gulfstream G700s took off. They filed a flight plan for Montreal, but my guess is they'll fly under the radar and we'll lose them pretty soon. They're probably headed the same place the other jet went yesterday."

"Tell me about that."

"The Feds executed a search and arrest warrant on Saint corporate yesterday, and it was like a ghost town. The whole building was vacant – not a computer, file folder, or janitor in sight. We checked the #1 Gulfstream, and it took off under the same basic flight plan shortly after 1:00 a.m. yesterday morning, but they didn't show up on the radar anywhere."

"Any idea where they went?"

"Scuttlebutt is that Saint owns a private island somewhere in the Caribbean. Look, I gotta go. I'll give you a shout if we learn anything else."

"Okay. Thanks, man."

Since no one had anything to add, Adam and Tracy made their excuses and headed back to their station in the city. They tried not to raise false hopes of finding Maddie, but they promised to do everything they could and to keep in touch.

The detectives had just pulled out of the driveway when the pizza arrived. Tatia and Shawna served the children, and everyone sat around the table eating in silence. Emotional exhaustion had set in, and each one was lost in private grief. After choking down a piece of veggie pizza, Tatia spoke up.

"I don't know about anybody else, but I'm ready for some ice cream and cake."

"Yeah," shouted the kids, relieved to have something fun to focus on.

"Okay! You guys clear the table and box up the leftover pizza. Joy, you come help me in the kitchen. You can get the bowls and toppings, and I'll get the cake."

Joy gathered everything into a basket her mother handed down from the top shelf and stood staring at the cake she and Maddie had decorated the night before.

"Mommy, it doesn't seem right to eat Maddie's birthday cake without her."

"I know, Joy. We're all sad and wish she was here to blow out the candles – but she wouldn't want us to waste the cake. We can all celebrate that God brought her into our lives, even for a short time. And we can all pray that He will bring her back to us, and then we can blow out the candles together."

37

Sunday - 10/8

Michael rattled the ice cubes in a crystal old-fashioned glass as he watched the sun slowly disappear into the ocean. He swallowed the last of the 30-year-old single malt scotch and turned toward his desk where Adrian sat in front of his computer. Instead of her normal tailored suit, she wore loose white trousers and a teal silk blouse that draped perfectly on her tall slender frame.

"Are you having trouble placing the call?" he asked.

"Yes, sir. The plane must be in a dead spot or flying through overcast conditions. The server is searching for a good connection."

"How are your living quarters? Satisfactory I hope."

"More than satisfactory, sir. And the view is spectacular, and my own private workout room is totally unexpected but appreciated."

"And is Bridgette adjusting well?"

"Yes, sir. She has already explored every corner of the guest house, especially the elaborate cat tree you had installed."

"Good," he replied. He didn't really care - his relationship with Adrian had been strictly business for several years now. But he tried to make his staff feel that they were more than office equipment. He thought it made them more loyal.

"It's connecting now, sir. Do you want a refill before I go?"

"Thank you, Adrian, but no. That will be all for now." She lingered for a long moment before leaving his office.

He sat down just as Ian's face appeared on the screen. "Good evening, Mr. S."

"So, how does she look?" Michael asked without preamble.

"Good. Different, but good."

"Different? How?"

"Well, for one thing, her hair is shorter, brown and a bit wavy. And her eyes aren't vacant like they used to be. They're beautiful, at least when she's not crying."

"She cried, huh?"

"Yes, at first. But then she pulled herself together and stood up to me."

"Oh, really. What did she do? Punch you or something?"

"No, but she made demands. She said you had to leave her family alone – that's what she called them – her family. Otherwise she said she'd stay and die with them."

"She did?" said Michael, sounding intrigued. "What else did she say?"

"No drugs. She's apparently been clean since she left Misty two weeks ago."

Michael nodded thoughtfully. "Two weeks, huh? That's a good start. Anything else I should know before I see her?"

"A couple of things. For one thing, she wants to be called Madelyn Collier – Maddie for short. One of her new-found friends looked into her background and found her birth records."

"Hmmm. That spoils one of my surprises. What's the second thing?"

"Well, her bones don't show like they did. She's filled in just enough to soften the edges a bit, and it looks good on her."

Michael laughed. "I may have to buy her another wedding dress! See you in – what – about three hours?"

"Yes, sir. Flight time is estimated at a little under seven hours, and we've been in the air for four."

Not long after Ian completed his call to Michael, Maddie woke up to a sky full of stars outside the window beside her. At first, she didn't remember where she was, but then she remembered – her ruined birthday party, the guns, the tears, the helicopter, the jet. She took in her surroundings, and even though she had never been on an airplane before, she had seen enough movies and magazines to know this wasn't a normal commercial airliner. Even in the subdued lighting everything she saw spoke of luxury. Instead of being stuffed with rows of seats crowded on either side of a narrow aisle, the cabin was appointed like a lavish living room. The recliner where she lay was as comfortable as any bed she had ever slept in, and the throw someone had placed over her was made of some kind of fur that probably cost more than the Matthews' home.

Ian was sitting in a matching recliner a few feet from her, reading a book with the help of the recessed light over his head. Sensing her gaze, he looked over and smiled. "Hello, Madelyn. Can I get you something to drink?"

"Hi, Ian. Yes, some apple juice would be nice." She smiled at his use of her correct name, but she felt as if she had left Madelyn in the Matthews' backyard and that she was once again Madison, courtesan to the biggest gangster in Chicago.

Ian motioned to a stewardess just outside what Maddie assumed was the galley, and she brought Maddie her drink over ice in a crystal tumbler. Maddie thanked her and took a sip of the juice.

"How long did I sleep?" she asked Ian.

"About four hours. We took off around 8:00 p.m. local time, and it's now midnight."

"Where are we, and where are we going?"

"We're over the Caribbean. Our destination is a private island that appears on maps as only an uninhabitable dot."

"But I'm sure Michael has upgraded it a bit," she said with a slight smile.

"Just a bit," Ian agreed. "Would you like something to eat? We don't have a chef on board this trip, but I believe there is a salad and some other snacks in the galley."

"No, thank you. This will be fine. I would like to freshen up, though, before I see Michael."

"Of course. There's a bedroom with a shower through that door. And I believe you'll find a complete supply of toiletries and some clothes in your size if you'd like to change."

By the time they touched down, she had shed as much of Madelyn as she could and resumed her Madison persona. She didn't have the chemicals to dye her hair black, but she straightened it the best she could with the hair dryer that was built into the wall by the sink. She used a pale foundation to cover the evidence of her time in the sun, and she donned a white jumpsuit and white high-heeled sandals. When she stepped off the plane, she floated down the stairs not in a drug-induced haze but in a cloud of grief and hopelessness. Still, she clutched the Bible Joy had given her by her side.

"Hello, Madelyn."

"Hello, Michael."

"You look wonderful – but you must be exhausted."

"Yes, it's been a long day."

"I have a car waiting. I'll take you home and show you to your room. We'll talk tomorrow."

After they were seated in the back of the limo, Maddie gave

Michael a weak smile. "Thank you for using my real name. I assume Ian told you."

"He mentioned it, but I already knew. I was going to surprise you with your family history, but many other surprises are waiting for you."

He allowed her to sit silently for the rest of the ride, so she stared out the window and tried not to think. She knew she was surrounded by moonlit beauty, but she could see none of it through the tears that threatened to spill over and ruin her carefully applied makeup. The car passed through a gate that was guarded on both sides by guards who were dressed and armed like the two men who accompanied Ian on the helicopter. The driveway was lit with small solar lanterns, and the huge house, when it came into view, was bathed in artfully placed lighting that made it look like a castle on a hill. But all she saw was a blur of indistinct shapes and colors.

She fought to maintain her composure as Michael ushered her into the house, up the stairs, and to her suite of rooms that was bigger than the house where she had spent the last two weeks. He walked her through a private sitting room, pointing out the kitchenette hidden behind sliding doors, the balcony overlooking the Caribbean, and a bedroom with a huge en suite bath.

"I trust you'll be comfortable here. Your bed has been turned down and a nightgown has been laid out. If you need anything else, just ring and your personal assistant will be at your service. Sleep as late as you like, and if you'd like breakfast in bed, just ask. But try not to keep me waiting too long. We have plans to make."

She didn't trust herself to speak when he kissed her on the forehead. "Sleep well, my dear," he whispered, and he turned to leave. He stopped and turned back. "By the way, Ian said your hair and other things about you had changed, but I see you recreated your old image tonight. That's not necessary. There are limits, of course, but I want you to be your own person here."

Then he left, closing the door behind him. Maddie began to laugh at the irony of Michael's words. She stumbled to her elegant bedroom, falling across the luxurious bed as the tears began to fall. She wept for the little girl who had just discovered the love of a family only to fall back under the control of the man who considered her just another of his expensive possessions.

38

Sunday - 10/8

Jesse was showing Daniel how to tie his shoes – again – and Tatia was putting the finishing touches on Joy's French braid when they heard a knock on the front door.

"I'll get it," yelled Daniel, streaking across the floor with one shoe lace dangling. He threw open the door and saw Johnny standing there looking awkward and uncomfortable in a long-sleeved button-up shirt and khakis. "Hi, Johnny. You look funny in those clothes. Are you going to church with us?"

"Umm," he stammered. "I thought I would – if that's okay."

"Of course it is," said Jesse, striding across the room to shake Johnny's hand. "We'll be ready to go in a couple of minutes. We can all ride together if you don't mind squeezing in the back seat with the kids."

"Nonsense," said Tatia. "I'll sit with them and he can sit in front with you. Kids, last chance to go to the bathroom – and don't forget your Bibles."

Johnny looked awkward and tugged at his tightly buttoned shirt collar. Tatia walked over and unbuttoned the top button. "There.

Now you don't look so much like a condemned man. You know, our church is pretty casual. You could have worn your regular clothes as long as they were clean."

He relaxed a little and even gave her a slight smile. "I'll remember that for next time. I just didn't want to embarrass you my first time there. I even borrowed my buddy's truck so I wouldn't have helmet hair and bugs on my teeth."

Daniel came back in with his Bible and giggled at the idea of bugs on Johnny's teeth. "I want to sit by Johnny."

"He's going to sit by me in the car, buddy," explained Jesse, "but you can sit by him in church if you're good. Now, let's load up."

Once everybody was seated and belted in, Jesse spoke to Johnny as he backed out of the driveway. "Hey, man, I'm really glad you're going with us. Any particular reason you decided to come today?"

"I've been thinking about it for a while," Johnny replied with a fading smile. "But I was up most of last night praying for Maddie. By the way, I don't guess there's any news this morning."

"I haven't heard from anybody, and I'm sure they'd call if they found anything."

"That's what I thought," replied Johnny. He sat staring out the windshield for a minute and then shook his head and sighed. "Anyway, I was reading the Bible, and I came to that verse in Matthew about when two or three are gathered in His name, He's there. I thought if I prayed with you guys, God might be more likely to hear me."

"We've been praying, too, but there's never too much prayer or too many praying."

"Daddy says God is always with me, 'specially if I believe in Jesus," added Daniel.

"That's right, buddy," said Jesse. "Why don't you practice your Sunday School questions so Johnny can hear what you're learning?"

"Mommy, will you ask me my questions please?" asked Daniel.

"I would be glad to. Who needs to be saved?"

"Everybody," shouted Daniel enthusiastically.

Joy put her hands over her ears and did a big-sister eye roll.

"That's great," laughed Tatia, "but let's use inside voices. Next question. What do we need to be saved from?"

"Sin and death."

"And what is sin?"

"Doing what God says not to do."

"What if I don't sin?"

"All have sinned."

"How can I be saved?"

"Repent and believe."

"What does it mean to repent?

"Turn away from sin and to God."

"How and what do I believe?"

"This is a hard one," said Daniel, scrunching his eyebrows together. "By..."

"Joy, can you help him?"

Joy, who was trying to hide her pride in her little brother, leaned forward so she could see around her mother. "What does Papa Bear say when he sees that Goldilocks has been eating his porridge?"

Daniel looked puzzled. "He says *GRRRR!*"

"Right," said Joy. "Now, you can be saved by grrr..."

The light went on in Daniel's eyes. "By grace alone, through faith alone, in Christ alone!"

Joy high fived him and sat back in her seat with a look of satisfaction.

"One more question. Can you do this by yourself?"

"No. You pray to God for the Holy Spirit to help you."

"Good job, buddy!" said Jesse, holding up his thumb.

"Very good," said Johnny. "Jesse, I need to talk to you about what he just said when you have some time."

"I can always make time for that." He looked at Tatia in the rear-view mirror. "Do we have enough for a guest for lunch?"

"Of course! We're picking up chicken on the way home," she said with a smile.

He held his thumb up again. "So you'll stay for lunch and we'll talk while the kids rest. Deal?"

"Deal," said Johnny. "Especially if we can pray for Maddie when we talk."

39

Sunday - 10/8

Maddie came awake slowly, trying to remember where she was and why her eyes felt sore and swollen. She didn't hear any of the familiar morning sounds of the Matthews' home, and as she stretched out her arms, she realized the bed she was lying on was not the twin bed in the room she shared with Joy. She finally opened her eyes, one at a time, sweeping them slowly around the unfamiliar room, and gradually the events of Saturday came back to her.

She rolled over, still dressed in the jumpsuit and sandals she had worn for her reunion with Michael. She sat up slowly and blinked against the light that shown through the bedroom door. She surveyed the room she had ignored before the flood of emotion overtook her, and she was stunned at the opulence surrounding her. The studies with her many private tutors came to mind as she recognized original oil paintings, antique oriental rugs, hand-carved and gilded furniture – and flowers – vases of fresh flowers on every available surface.

She kicked off her sandals and padded barefoot across the sitting room to the kitchenette. Opening the small refrigerator, she took out a bottle of water and took a deep drink and turned toward the source of the light. The drapes in front of the French doors to the large balcony had been left open, and Maddie gasped at what she saw. When she had looked out in the wee hours of the morning, all she saw was blackness and her own reflection in the glass doors. Now she saw a riot of color – a flower garden filled with every tropical flower she had ever seen and many she had never imagined. A paved walking path wound its way among the flowers down to the white sand beach.

Maddie opened the doors to get a better look and was immediately engulfed by the sea air mixed with the intoxicating scents of the garden and the sound of waves rolling gently onto the sand. From her perch, she saw that the house was located on a bay sheltered on both sides by craggy peninsulas jutting into the sea. The mouth of the bay was protected by a small island that slowed the waves as they crashed against its rocky sides. And just when she thought the sight before her couldn't get any better, two dolphins jumped into the air, side by side, and began to play together in the surf.

Maddie almost forgot her heartache for a moment until she remembered there was no one to share this beauty with. But determined not to wallow in self pity, she went into the bathroom to get ready for her first day in this prison in paradise.

The multiple controls and shower heads confused her at first, but after causing what felt like a rainstorm, Maddie found the adjustment for a simple shower. Revived and refreshed, she began exploring the huge dressing area that was lined on every side with drawers and hanging rods full of more clothes than she could wear in a lifetime. Frustrated in her efforts to find what she was looking for, she pushed the button that Michael told her would summon her personal assistant. A moment later, she heard a gentle knock on her door.

"Come in," she called out.

A large woman wearing a colorful, loose-fitting dress and a smile that was brighter than the morning sunshine stepped into the room. "Good morning, Miss Madelyn. I am Shenice. How can I help you today?"

A small smile crossed Maddie's face at the sound of her real name and an accent that reminded her of Lili. She had an almost irresistible urge to ask for a hug. Instead, she asked for help in finding her way through the overpowering array of clothing and accessories she had found. Shenice let out a contagious belly laugh, and Maddie surprised herself by laughing with her.

"Mr. Michael wanted to be sure you had anything you wanted, but I guess he should have included a map. What do you want to wear this morning, Miss Madelyn?"

"First, call me Maddie, and then help me find a swimsuit and whatever I need to go for a walk on the beach."

After rejecting several more revealing options, Maddie settled on a modest hot pink one-piece with a shirred and twisted front. Shenice found a flowered sarong and showed Maddie how to tie it around her waist so it draped nicely and flowed as she moved. They added beach sandals, sunglasses, and a wide-brimmed hat, and Maddie looked at herself in the mirror. She liked the colors almost as much as she liked the blue sweater Joy gave her.

"I've never been to the beach before, Shenice. What else do I need?"

"I think you're ready, Miss Maddie. Towels, sunscreen, and anything else you need will be in the cabana – unless you want to take something to read."

Maddie suddenly looked stricken. "My Bible! I think I left it in the limo."

"Don't worry, Miss Maddie. Mr. Ian brought it in this morning. It's in the library downstairs."

Maddie couldn't stop herself this time. She threw her arms

around the older woman. "Oh, thank you! It's all I have from my family."

Shenice patted her back maternally. "You're welcome, child. Let's get you a bag to carry it in, and then I'll show you the way to the library and the beach."

Maddie lounged in a cabana positioned perfectly to capture the breeze while sheltering its occupants from the sun's burning rays. Shenice had slathered her with high SPF sunscreen before releasing her to walk on the beach, and had summoned her back into the shade after about thirty minutes.

"Miss Maddie, that is enough exposure for your first day on the beach. We don't want to burn that beautiful fair skin. Besides, I have brought you some breakfast."

Maddie came reluctantly with a small collection of shells gathered into the edge of her sarong. But when she saw the tempting array of fresh fruit and dainty pastries laid out on the table, her protests died in her throat. "You're going to spoil me, Shenice."

"That is my job, Miss Maddie. To make sure you are content in your new home. Now, let me have your shells. I will clean them so they will not smell while you sit and enjoy your breakfast. This carafe contains decaffeinated coffee, this pitcher contains French vanilla creamer, and this carafe is fresh pineapple juice. If you want anything else, I will get it for you when I return."

"Thank you. You're very good at your job."

Shenice shook with laughter and disappeared with the seashells wrapped in a linen napkin. She returned in a few minutes with Maddie's shells cleaned and beautifully arranged in a small handmade basket. A piece of each kind of fruit was missing from the platter, crumbs from two miniature muffins were scattered on a small plate on the table beside Maddie's lounge, and she was sipping a glass of juice. Shenice nodded her approval as she placed the basket in the center of the table.

"Did you enjoy your breakfast, Miss Maddie?"

"Very much," she said. "Everything was delicious, but it was too quiet." When Shenice looked confused, Maddie continued. "Oh, the sound of the waves and the calls of the birds are amazing, but it's not like the chaos at home…I mean, at the Matthews' home."

"I would love to hear about the Matthews family," said Shenice, still standing by the table.

A little bit of the sadness in Maddie's eyes was replaced by a hint of mischief. "It would make me very happy if you would pour yourself a cup of coffee or a glass of juice and pull up a lounge beside me while I tell you about the wonderful people I have met the last couple of weeks."

That laugh again! With a glass of juice in hand, Shenice sat next to her new mistress and listened to Maddie describe her adopted family. When she got to the part about Recovery Ministry, she stopped talking and stared into the surf with a faraway look in her eyes. Shenice took her hand and turned it palm up so the fading scars in the crook of her elbow were visible.

"You miss your new family. No?"

"Yes. More than I knew was possible. They are at church this morning – and I was going to go with them for the first time."

Shenice touched one of the scars gently. "And I am sure they are praying for you right now. But it still hurts, and you are thinking how easy it would be to just numb the pain with a pill or a shot."

"Yes," Maddie whispered, and the tears spilled over.

Shenice stood suddenly and clapped her hands, startling Maddie. "Enough!" she said gently but firmly. "I want you to get that Bible out of your bag and open it to the book of Proverbs. I want you to read out loud Chapter 20, verse 1 and Chapter 23, verses 29 through 35. I will be back in a moment."

Maddie wiped her eyes and did as Shenice had instructed. "*Wine is a mocker, strong drink a brawler, and whoever is led astray by it is not wise.*" She was just finishing the last verse when Shenice returned. "*'They struck me,' you will say, 'but I was not hurt; they beat me, but I did not feel it. When shall I awake? I must have another drink.'*" She looked up from the book and sighed. "That's exactly what it's like with the drugs, isn't it?"

"Yes, child, it is. Is that what you want?"

"No," she whispered, covering her face with her hands.

Shenice sat down beside her. "I have something for you that will help."

Maddie lowered her hands, not sure what to expect. When she saw the small spiral notebook and pen in her new friend's hand, she looked at her with a question in her eyes.

"I want you to take this and promise yourself you will write nine things in it every day – three bad things about drugs, three good things about being sober, and three things you are thankful for."

Maddie took the notebook and pen. "I will – thank you. Can I write other things in it, too? I mean, Tatia suggested I keep a journal, but I hadn't started it yet."

"Yes, child. You can write anything you want to. We have plenty of notebooks and lots of pens. Now why don't you begin working on today's nine things while I clear away breakfast. Then I'll tell you a little more about your new home."

When Shenice returned, she found a more relaxed young woman than she had left. Maddie had set her journal aside and was standing in front of the cabana watching the clouds that were gathering above her head. Without turning away from the sky, she asked,

"Does it rain here a lot?"

"It rains almost every afternoon during the hurricane season.

Then around the end of the year, the rains end and it is dry until May or June."

"I used to watch the clouds out the window of Misty's condo and wish I could ride away on one of them."

"Sometimes journeys of the imagination are as effective as real ones. How did the writing go?"

"Very well." Maddie finally looked away from the clouds and returned to the shelter of the cabana. "Once I got started, I had no trouble thinking of nine things – and you are the first thing on my thankful list."

"I am pleased that you feel that way. Now, Mr. Michael would like to have lunch with you at noon in the sun room. We have a couple of hours before then, so if you like I can show you a few more rooms in the house before you return to your suite to get ready for lunch."

"Yes, I'd like that," said Maddie, smiling to cover the nervousness she felt about seeing Michael in such an intimate setting. "But what about my feet? I don't really want to put them into my sandals, and I don't want to track sand through the house."

"That is not a problem. There is a small fountain in front of the beach house where you may rinse your feet."

Maddie was amazed by the small amenities that had been provided throughout the house that seemed to anticipate every possible need or want of the occupants. After drying her feet with a small towel and placing it in a basket provided for the used linens, she followed Shenice on a guided tour that included a lap pool, a diving pool, and an inside/outside general use pool as well as a huge hot tub. They visited the greenhouse where the flowers that graced her suite were grown, the sun room where she would lunch with her future husband, a music room furnished with a grand piano and other musical instruments, the library they had visited earlier, an enormous dining room, and a matching great room featuring fire-places on either end.

"Does it get cold enough here to need a fire?" asked Maddie.

"Not really, but we light them for effect from time to time and turn down the air conditioning to keep the guests, the few we have, comfortable." After laughing at her own reply, she ended the tour. "It is time to prepare yourself for lunch. Can you find your way back to your suite?"

"I think so, but would you come with me and help me pick out something to wear? I'm a little nervous, and I want to make sure I'm acceptable."

Shenice linked her arm through Maddie's and patted her hand. "Of course, child. We cannot possibly make you more beautiful, but I will try to make you feel more confident."

40

Sunday - 10/8

Johnny was uncharacteristically quiet in the van after church. No one seemed to notice because of the constant chatter of Joy about her Sunday School class and Daniel about the KIDZ Church lesson. They even sang one of the songs the children were learning for the Christmas musical in a couple of months. Jesse pulled into their Sunday afternoon lunch stop, a small restaurant that carried an odd mixture of fried chicken with Southern side dishes as well as a few Asian dishes. The kids piled out of the back seat and dashed through the door ahead of Tatia. The owner always gave them each a small bag with a couple of chicken nuggets and a fortune cookie, so there was never a question about whether they would go in or wait in the car with Jesse.

The silence was a relief, but Jesse turned to Johnny and broke it. "Tell me what you're thinking, man."

It was obvious Johnny was having trouble putting his thoughts into words, so Jesse encouraged. "Don't worry about how it comes out. Just say what's on your heart."

"Well," he began, still staring down at his hands. "After our

Thursday night Bible studies, the teachings, my own reading, and today's sermon, I know I need Jesus. I mean, with my background, I can't deny that I'm a sinner, and I know I can't do anything about it on my own." Then he fell silent.

Jesse waited a minute or two and then asked, "Okay, that's great – but I sense a 'but...' in there somewhere."

Johnny's face was beet red by this point, and when he finally looked up at Jesse, his eyes were flashing with anger. "But I'm really angry at God right now," he blurted out. "Why did He let those men take Maddie, and why can't we find her?"

"We always have to approach God with reverence and respect, but it's okay to express honest feelings to Him, even anger. Jonah was angry when God was lenient with Nineveh, and Job was angry when he felt he was being tormented unjustly. And in 1 Chronicles 13 it says that David was angry when the Lord broke out against Uzzah. It's not the anger that's the problem, it's the way we react to God in our anger."

When Johnny didn't respond, Jesse put his hand on his shoulder and said, "Let me pray for you." He asked God to take the bitterness and anger out of Johnny's heart and replace it with faith and trust. He prayed for a changed heart, and before he finished, Johnny began to pray.

"God, I don't really know how to do this, but if You listened to lepers and beggars, I guess You will listen to me, too. I want to turn away from my sins, but I know I can't really do that without Your help. Please fill me with Your Spirit so I can learn what it means to be a Your child. Like the man said to Jesus in the chapter I read last night, *I believe, help my unbelief.* And God, even if You don't bring Maddie back to us, please send someone to tell her about You."

When Jesse opened his eyes, he saw Daniel outside Johnny's window jumping up and down and making faces. He laughed and made a face back at him and motioned for Tatia to get in. She opened the door and climbed over Daniel's car seat to her place in the middle. The noise of children and the smell of lunch filled the van, and the sadness that had filled Johnny's eyes since Maddie had been taken was tempered with peace and hope.

41

Sunday - 10/8

With the help of her new mentor, Maddie chose a jumpsuit with an impressionistic palm-leaf print in shades of aqua and coral. The strapless neckline emphasized her creamy, sun-kissed shoulders, and the wide pants flowed gracefully around her long legs. The sun had brought out some of the subtle golden reddish highlights in her chestnut hair, and the humidity of the ocean air had relaxed it into natural waves that softened the lines of the face she thought was too long and thin. With the help of Shenice, she applied a fresh coat of coral nail polish to fingers and toes and just enough makeup to highlight the blush of a morning spent on the beach. She completed her look with simple shell earrings, a hand-made beaded necklace, and bangle bracelets on each wrist.

Shenice took a step back to assess the results of their choices. "You look amazing! You will take away Mr. Michael's breath."

"Thank you, but I'm still nervous." Her eyes began to move around the room restlessly, and she avoided looking at Shenice. "I just wish…"

Taking both her delicate hands in her larger ones, Shenice said,

"Hush, child. That is the enemy talking. We must ask the Lord for protection."

Without waiting for Maddie's approval, she bowed her head and began to pray. "Father, I pray Your protection over this child. Help her to take every thought captive, especially when the substances we will not even name call her back into their grip. And now as she goes to meet her future husband in a new setting, I pray that You will calm her spirit and help her to feel Your presence. Make her pleasing to Mr. Michael as Queen Esther was to King Ahasuerus. In the name of Christ our Savior, Amen."

Maddie's smile was much more relaxed when she opened her eyes. "I've heard Jesse talk about taking every thought captive. Is that in the Bible?"

"Yes, and so is the story of Queen Esther."

"How do you know so much about the Bible?"

"My husband is a minister, and I study with him when I can."

"Oh! I made you miss church today!"

"You did not make me miss church today, Miss Maddie. Everyone works when Mr. Michael has plans, and I will always be here when you need me. Now, I will show you where to find the passage about captive thoughts and also the story of Esther later, but we must not keep Mr. Michael waiting any longer."

Maddie could tell by the appreciative look on Michael's face that Shenice had prepared her well – but his look was the same one she imagined he had when viewing a fine painting or a new sports car for his collection. He held out both his hands to her, and she placed hers in his. He kissed her chastely on both cheeks and then twirled her around as if they were on a dance floor.

"Sea air agrees with you. You are more beautiful than ever."

"Thanks to you, Michael. You've provided a beautiful wardrobe and everything I need to look my best. And thank you for Shenice. She's amazing."

"I'm glad you're pleased," he said, offering his arm and escorting her to a table by the open windows. The staff served a lovely lunch that reminded Maddie of the Caribbean bowl Lili ordered after her sonogram. The conversation was interesting and informative as Michael explained the water collection cisterns, the desalination plant, and the solar farm and storage batteries that made this formerly uninhabitable island the self-sufficient haven he had constructed. He told her that the staff had been recruited from one of the larger islands and was housed in a village he had constructed for them.

"The village is complete with a school and a few stores."

"Company stores?" she asked.

"No. Company built but now individually-owned and operated. And I believe they have built a church on their own – with the help of some company-owned equipment."

"Your employees must be very happy. You treat them well."

"I try."

Maddie took a sip of her mango-infused sparkling water. "I appreciate this instead of what you're enjoying," she said, nodding toward his wine glass.

He smiled at her and covered one of her hands with his. "I will honor your request that you not be compelled in any way to take drugs or even alcohol. And I will not hurt the Matthews family or your friends in Heart City."

"And I will be the best wife I can be, using everything I've learned to be the companion, hostess, and lover a man like you needs by his side."

"What more could I ask?" He stood up and held out his hand toward her. "Let's go for a stroll on the beach."

Maddie took his hand and let him lead her down a path between beds of roses. "I didn't know roses grew in the tropics," she exclaimed.

"Some don't, but I found a gardener who specializes in warm climate roses. He has found some that flower year round."

She stopped at the end of the path to slip off her sandals and noticed that two men were following them. She had seen a guard at each of the doors in the sunroom, so she wasn't surprised to see that they wouldn't be alone on the beach.

"Do they follow you everywhere?" she said with a slight nod of her head in their direction.

He let out a humorless laugh. "Pretty much. One of the benefits of my business. I have assigned a couple of men to escort you any time you venture far from the house, especially if you go outside the fence."

"Are there limits to where I can go?"

"Very few. My personal suite and the executive suites are off limits. Outside the house, it's best to stay away from the utility areas for safety reasons. Other than that, just stay on the island unless I okay a boat excursion. By the way, do you drive?"

"No, Jesse was going to teach me after I was a little further along in my rehab."

"Yes, I guess there are some areas of your education that have been neglected. Well, I provide utility vehicles for the staff to get from the village and back and for any other transportation needs they might have. I'll have my vehicle manager get one ready for you, and Shenice can teach you to drive it."

"That sounds like fun. Thank you." They walked in silence for a few minutes. Then, Maddie broke the silence. "Can I ask you something?"

"Of course. There are some questions I can't or won't answer, but I'll try to explain why if I can."

"Why are your personal rooms off limits?" He laughed – a real one this time. She blushed and stammered, "I mean, if we're going to be married and everything..."

He pulled her into a big hug. "Oh, my sweet, innocent Madelyn. Mostly because I'm a grumpy old man who is set in my ways. In addition, I sometimes do business there, and I don't want to have to worry about you or anyone else seeing something you shouldn't. Do you understand?"

"I think so," she replied. Encouraged by his laughter, she continued with an impish grin. "Like, if I saw something I shouldn't, you'd have to kill me?"

He laughed even harder this time. "Maddie, you are a light in the dark world I inhabit. I'm glad Misty didn't extinguish it."

"She almost did, but the last two weeks have rekindled it."

"I'm glad to hear that. Any other questions?"

"Well, yes," she said, blushing again. "Will we share my bedroom at night?"

"We can do that if you will not feel like your privacy is being invaded – or we can share a separate marriage suite if you prefer."

"No, I would enjoy having you visit me," she said, stroking his ego as she had been trained. "I have no secrets."

Michael didn't speak for a moment. Finally he nodded and said, "I chose well." He reached into his pocket and pulled out a small jeweler's box. "I'm not a romantic man, and I'm too old to get down on one knee, but I want to make this official." He opened the box to reveal a four carat radiant-cut diamond in a platinum band with four small diamonds on each side. "Madelyn Collier, will you do me the honor of becoming my wife."

"Oh, Michael, it's beautiful," she cried with what she hoped was an adequate amount of enthusiasm. "It would be my honor to be your wife."

He slid the ring onto her finger and swept her into an amorous embrace and a kiss that was far from chaste. As Maddie returned his kiss, the weight of the ring on her finger felt like a shackle, and she thought she heard the sound of a cell door slamming closed.

42

Monday – 10/9

Maddie sat straight up in bed, soaked in sweat and trembling violently. The nightmare about her mother had returned, but this time the burning house was the one in Heart City she had called home the last two weeks – and the charred body in the bed was Tatia. She jumped up as if the bed itself had caused her dream and fled to the living area where she fell into one of the overstuffed chairs. She pulled her knees up to her chest, dragged an afghan up to her neck, and cried herself to sleep, longing for Joy to sing to her or for Tatia to make her a cup of tea.

A light tap on the door woke her some time later. She squeezed her eyelids together tightly to shut out the bright light that flooded the room and pulled the afghan up over her face when she heard the door open slightly. A soft voice called out.

"Miss Maddie, it's Shenice. May I come in?"

Remembering where she was, Maddie lowered the afghan a few inches and replied. "Come on in, Shenice."

"I'm sorry to disturb you, but it's almost ten o'clock, and I was worried." When she saw her new mistress wedged into the corner of the chair and tangled in the afghan, her maternal instincts kicked in.. "Oh, Miss Maddie! What are you doing over here? Your eyes are red and swollen and your face is puffy! Are you ill?"

"Not really," replied Maddie, moving slowly out of her cramped position. "I just had a nightmare."

"I'm so sorry, child. Come on over and stretch out on the sofa. I'll make you a cup of tea and you can tell me all about it."

Maddie obeyed docilely and lay quietly while Shenice busied herself in the little kitchenette in the corner. The light floral fragrance of jasmine tea filled the room, and Maddie sat up and took the steaming cup Shenice offered her.

"Sit with me while I drink it?" she asked, sitting up and patting the cushion next to her.

"Of course," Shenice replied, settling next to Maddie with a cup of her own. After a few sips, she broke the silence. "Do you often have nightmares?"

"Yes, several times a week."

"Is it always the same?"

"Usually, but last night was different." She took a sip and stared off into space for a while before continuing. "When I was four or five my mother set her bed on fire with a cigarette in the middle of the night. When I woke up and found her, she wasn't much more than a skeleton. I didn't remember that until I began to detox, and the scene came back in the night."

"But last night was different?" prompted Shenice.

"Yes. It was the Matthews' house that was on fire, and it was Tatia in the bed. I woke up in a cold sweat, and all I could think of was getting away from that dream. I ran over here and cried for a long time before I fell asleep." She ignored the tears that wet her face and the front of her pajamas as she focused on the images in her mind.

Shenice encouraged Maddie to keep talking. "Tell me about what you and Tatia talked about after your nightmares."

Maddie described their conversations, and when she became quiet again, Shenice asked another question. "What songs did Joy sing to you when you couldn't sleep?"

"Always the same one – *Jesus Loves Me*," said Maddie with her first smile since Shenice had come in. "And sometimes she quoted Psalm 23."

"Excellent choices," said Shenice. "Now, if you have finished your tea, let's see if we can relax you a bit."

Within a few minutes, Maddie was settled into a tub of warm water with gentle jets massaging her tense muscles. Shenice placed a cool cloth over her eyes, and the throbbing in her head began to subside.

"Will you be okay if I leave you briefly? I want to go see the IT manager for a few minutes."

"I'll be fine, Shenice. Thank you is not enough, but it's all I have."

Thirty minutes later Shenice found Maddie sitting at her dressing table wrapped in a fluffy terry cloth robe. Her wet hair and the steamy room indicated that she had ended her bath with a shampoo and shower. She smiled at Shenice in the mirror as she spread moisturizer on her face.

"I'm much better now," she said. "Are you teaching me to drive today?"

Shenice laughed her contagious laugh. "Ah, the resilience of youth! Yes! Your new vehicle is waiting in the motor pool. We'll stop by IT on the way there to see if we can at least pick up your phone. I want you to be able to reach me anytime you need me - night or day. Also, Mr. Michael is tied up for the day, so we will drive to the village for lunch, and you might want to take some pictures on our outing. Now, do you know what you want to wear, or should I choose something?"

Shenice and Maddie worked together to pick out a short set with colorful hibiscus blooms and leaves on a black background. They added a pair of cute flip flops that would survive a sandy walk on the beach and more island jewelry. Maddie placed a pair of sunglasses in her hair like a headband and filled her bag with a sun hat, a couple of bottles of water, sunscreen, and her Bible which she carried everywhere except when she was with Michael. Shenice threw in a banana and a small cup of pineapple chunks since Maddie had declined her offer of breakfast.

"I feel guilty leaving the bathroom in a mess and my bed unmade," said Maddie as Shenice urged her toward the door.

"Don't, Miss Maddie. Mr. Michael has hired a complete staff to keep the house clean and neat, and if you don't leave them enough to do, he may send some of them back to the island we came from. No one wants to go back unless we are all sent home together."

"Okay. If you're sure."

Shenice showed Maddie another unfamiliar wing of the house which seemed to be the operating center of the island. It looked like a suite of regular offices, but all the doors had keypads and required a pass code except the one they entered. Maddie felt as if she had stepped into a small electronics store, or at least what she imagined one would look like since she had never been in one. There were phones, laptops, tablets, and all kinds of communications equipment in racks along one wall, and across the back was a counter where several technicians worked on a variety of devices.

The man in the middle looked up and smiled broadly when he saw Shenice. "Hello again, my friend!" he said with a hug. Then he turned to Maddie and extended his hand. She took it and he enclosed it between both of his. This kind of greeting seemed to be common on the island, and she liked the warmth of it. "And you must be Miss Madelyn. I am Sam. Welcome to our island. I believe we have everything ready for you except the laptop. We are still loading the software and all the reference material Shenice requested."

His deep rolling voice reminded her of the actor who played a voodoo priest in one of the old James Bond movies Misty used to watch. She smiled and thanked him for his welcome. "There's no hurry. Shenice is going to teach me how to drive today so I won't need anything except the phone until later. I want to take some pictures this morning."

"Perfect!" he replied. "I will personally deliver the computer and the tablet to your suite when they are ready. Now, I understand this is your first phone, so I will give you a quick lesson."

Thirty minutes later Maddie and Shenice were on their way to the motor pool, and her nightmare was a fading memory. She clapped her hands in excitement when she saw her new wheels. It was more of a golf cart than a four-wheeler, and it was painted a turquoise blue that perfectly matched the water surrounding the island. The four seats, two of which faced the rear, as well as the fringed canopy, were covered in a blue and white striped fabric.

"I was afraid it would be one of those big black things I've seen on TV racing up and down hills at ninety miles an hour."

Shenice laughed and climbed into the driver's seat. "Mr. Michael ordered this especially for you. He didn't want one of the high-powered vehicles to get away from you and throw you into the ocean before the wedding."

Maddie nodded toward the two men seated in one of those high-powered vehicles several yards behind them. "Did he order them, too?"

"Yes, child. I am required to submit a 'travel plan' any time we leave the grounds, and you must have protection. But just ignore them. They are trained not to get in the way except in the event of trouble – and we will have none of that. Now, let me show you how this thing works, and then you can give it a try."

43

Monday - 10/9

Breakfast was unusually quiet in the Matthews' kitchen. Joy was pushing spoonfuls of cold oatmeal into a mound in the center of her bowl, and Daniel was drawing a picture of a helicopter flanked by two men dressed in black and carrying black rifles. Tatia was staring out the window above the sink while she continued to wipe the same cup again and again long after all traces of moisture were gone, and the three men sat silently drinking coffee, lost in their own thoughts.

The sound of an old car horn erupted from Jesse's phone, splitting the silence and animating everyone in the room. Jesse jerked his phone against one ear as questions bombarded him from every direction.

"Is it…"

"Have they found…"

"Do they know…"

"Where is…"

"Just a minute," he said, covering his other ear with his free hand. "Let me go outside where I can hear you."

He stepped out onto the back patio and continued his conversation with five pairs of eyes staring at him in anticipation. His responses were short and few, and Tatia could tell by the slump of the shoulders and the fact that he turned his back to the windows that there was no good news. After two or three minutes he ended the call and turned toward the house, shaking his head.

"Sorry, guys," he said as he stepped through the door. "They've got nothing. As they expected, the plane disappeared from the radar a few miles north of Chicago and they've seen no sign of it since. Either they're flying really low or Saint International has cracked the secret of stealth flying. Tracy said they'd call us with an update later in the week – or sooner if there's a break. She did say there are rumblings in the crime underground that there's a contract out on Saint. I didn't ask for details, but apparently he left some people high and dry when he took off like he did, and they want to get even."

The group, all of whom had risen from their seats when Jesse went outside, stood in silence until Tatia spoke up. "Well, standing around here won't help anything. Children, go get dressed. As soon as we're all ready we'll take a nature walk to the park and talk about the changing seasons."

Joy challenged Daniel to a getting-dressed-the-quickest race, and they ran toward their bedrooms. "And they're off!" Tatia chuckled. She kissed Jesse lightly and waved at Brush and Johnny. "See y'all at lunch," she said and disappeared into the other side of the house.

"There's got to be something we can do," Johnny blurted out. "Brush, you said yesterday you have a pilot's license. We could rent a plane and search the smaller islands for signs of life. I mean, it's gotta be hard to hide a runway that's long enough for even a small jet – and how many islands can there be?"

"About 700 over a million square miles – give or take," said Brush who had sat back down and picked up his coffee.

"And you would know that because…" said Jesse with a grin.

"So I read a lot," shrugged Brush. "And do you have any idea how expensive it would be to rent a plane?"

"No, but I'm sure you'll tell us," quipped Jesse.

"Around $200 give or take."

"That's not bad," said Johnny. "We probably wouldn't need it for more than a day or two."

"That's per hour," said Brush. "Plus, you've got the cost of getting from here to there. How much have you got to devote to this search?"

Johnny stood with his hands in his pockets and his head down. "Well, can we at least pray together before we go open the shop?"

44

Monday - 10/9

Maddie hit the accelerator too hard – again – and almost threw Shenice over the back of the seat – again. "Sorry!" she laughed. "Are you okay?"

Shenice laughed along with her, delighted to see a smile on her face. "I'm fine, child. I taught my own daughter to drive, so I know how to hold on tight."

Maddie's driving improved quickly as she steered her new vehicle along the graveled path that overlooked the Caribbean on one side and groves of palmettos on the other. The sea breeze and the joy of a newfound freedom had chased the memory of her nightmare out of her mind and brought a blush of color back to her cheeks and a sparkle to her eyes.

"Oh!" she said suddenly but being careful to stop gently. "I haven't taken any pictures yet." She pulled her phone out of her bag and snapped a photo of the ocean. She looked at the results, but the smile on her face dimmed a little bit. "It's pretty, but it would be much better if you went over there and posed against that rock."

"Oh, no!" Shenice protested. "You don't want to break your new phone on the first day with my old face."

Maddie touched the side of her face and said, "You have no idea how beautiful you are. Now go!"

With her characteristic laugh, Shenice crossed the path and sat casually on the rock. Maddie snapped the shutter and pronounced the results perfect. She joined her friend by the rock to show off her first photographs.

"I guess anybody looks pretty good in this setting – but it would look better with you in it, too. Let me show you how to take a selfie."

Maddie had a knack for choosing subjects and composing pictures, and she captured image after image. Finally she moved back to her cart and put her phone away, but before she touched the key, she became serious and turned to Shenice.

"Thank you for helping me find Esther's story and the verse about taking thoughts captive yesterday afternoon. I'm using one of the notebooks you gave me to make notes about favorite verses so I can find them again."

"That's very good, child. But you look as if you have questions."

"Yes. After I read Esther I started reading John like you suggested. It's really beautiful, especially the first few verses about the Word, but chapter three is a little confusing. It says we should believe in Jesus – and Jesse talked about that during devotional times with the family. I want what they have and what you seem to have, but I'm not sure what it all means."

"It sounds like you may have a divine appointment in the village today."

"What do you mean?"

"I believe that God has prepared your heart to meet and talk with my husband. He loves nothing more than explaining how to become a believer in Jesus."

Maddie smiled with both relief and anticipation as she fired up the golf cart. Each turn brought another breathtaking view, and just when she thought nothing could be more beautiful, she rounded a curve and caught her first sight of the village. She took her foot off the accelerator and coasted to a stop as she stared at the painting-like scene before her. A row of pastel-colored houses with wrap-around porches and white shutters lined the right side of the path. At the end of the row stood a white building with a cross on top and large double doors that were open and inviting. The left side of the road sloped down to the beach in a riot of color that, although it was not nearly as organized as Michael's gardens, was even more amazing.

"This is where you live," whispered Maddie with a longing in her voice that tugged at Shenice's heart.

"Yes. Our home is the one next to the church."

"Michael said there is a school and stores."

"Those are around the next curve beyond the church. We'll see those later, but first let's go to the church and I will introduce you to my husband."

Before Maddie could move the cart, they were surrounded and overrun by children, all of whom seemed to be under five years old. "Mama Shenice!" they shouted as they climbed into her lap, hugged her neck, and stared at Maddie with shy curiosity.

Maddie was amazed at the joy and love that flowed between her new friend and these little ones. "Do they all belong to you?"

Shenice laughed as one of the little girls reached out and touched Maddie's arm with a tentative pat. "In our village, we all belong to each other, but some of these are my grandchildren. The older ones are in class right now." She began gently lifting little bodies off her lap and onto the ground. "We are going to see Papa Jaden, so you must move out of the way."

They obeyed her reluctantly, but Maddie didn't move for a

moment. She sighed wistfully, "I don't remember ever belonging to anyone but Michael."

Shenice reached over and lifted Maddie's chin, turning her face gently so she could look into her eyes. "Mr. Michael may have temporary custody of you, but you belong to the Lord. Now, let's go to the church."

Maddie felt like she was leading a parade as she carefully pressed the accelerator to avoid losing any of the children who had managed to keep their places on the back seats in spite of Shenice's attempts to clear the cart. The rest of the little ones ran beside the cart or followed behind, and their squeals and laughter brought the smile back to her face. When they reached the church, Shenice directed her to park next to the four steps that led up to the wide porch across the front of the building. Then she began to shoo the children away.

"Now, go play. We must visit with Papa for a while. I will see you again at lunch."

Maddie suddenly felt shy and continued to sit in the cart. "I've never been in a church or talked to a minister before."

"Miss Maddie, it is a building like any other, and he is just a man. It is the Spirit of God using the building and working through the people that makes them all special – and that Spirit is with us everywhere." She held out her hand in invitation. "Now come."

The inside of the church was as simple as the outside. The whitewashed walls were adorned with local artwork, some obviously created by the children she had met outside. The furnishings consisted of folding chairs and a simple lectern on a slightly raised platform at the front of the room. Several pendant lights hung from the ceiling, and although Maddie saw a few air conditioning vents, the cool breeze she felt came from the air that was drawn through the open windows by four ceiling fans turning lazily overhead. On either side of the platform were doors she assumed led to classrooms, restrooms, and possibly the minister's office. In front of the door on the left was a man wielding a dustpan and broom with the ease of experience.

He must have heard the tap of their shoes on the wooden floor because he straightened up as they approached. He was taller than Shenice and sturdy but not fat. His smile was full of a love that only comes with years of sharing, and he welcomed his wife with a one-armed embrace and a whisper of a kiss.

"What a lovely surprise," he said in a soft, gentle voice that had an underlying richness that promised power when he proclaimed the Gospel. "And you must be Miss Maddie," he continued, taking her hand between his in the way she had come to expect. "Shenice has told me so much about you since you arrived. I am very pleased to meet you." He looked at her with dark brown eyes that seemed to read her thoughts, but she felt accepted rather than invaded.

"Maddie has some questions about the third chapter of John. I was hoping you could visit with her while I help Gabrielle with lunch – if she'll let me!"

"Gabrielle is our oldest daughter," Jaden explained, "and she is very possessive of her kitchen. As for me, I enjoy nothing more than answering questions about God's Word. Would you like to take a walk down toward the beach?" he asked Maddie, offering his arm.

The uneasiness she was feeling melted away. "I'd like that very much," she said as she slipped her hand into the crook of his elbow.

There was a peace about Papa Jaden that was inviting and made Maddie look forward to spending time with him. He led her down the sloping path, pointing out various flowers and birds, and even a few odd insects she had never seen. Several children tagged along for a while adding a sound track of laughter and chatter to their walk. But when they were halfway down to the beach, they came to a bench in a small bower under several palm trees. Jaden seated Maddie and turned to the children.

"Papa and Miss Maddie need some time alone with Jesus, so run on back to the village for now. We will be back in time for lunch."

The children gathered around him for hugs, and a few of the bolder ones asked Maddie for a hug, too. She felt warmed and accepted as she watched them scamper back up the path.

"I wish I lived here instead of the other side of the island in the big house. There is so much life and light here that is missing from Michael's house. Why is that?" she asked Jaden who had joined her on the bench.

"Why do you think, Miss Maddie? What is missing from Mr. Michael's house?"

Maddie thought seriously about his question before answering. "For the two weeks before I came here, I lived with the Matthews family - Jesse and Tatia and their two children, Joy and Daniel. Your village reminds me of their home, and your children remind me of theirs. Their house was small and always seemed crowded - first with grandparents who came from Texas to help when Joy was taken, then Lili, a young woman who needed a place to stay, and Brush and Johnny who work with them in their business but are treated like family.

"If I had to choose one thing that makes a difference between the two happy places and Michael's house, I'd have to say 'love.' Not the kind of love you see in the movies or in novels. It seems to come from somewhere deep inside. Most of the people I've known until I met Tatia and Shenice have seemed empty inside." She looked at Jaden with hope in her eyes. "I don't want to be empty. Do you think I could learn to love like that - even being married to a man who is empty and living in a house without love?"

"Let's see what God has to say about love. Shenice says you always carry your Bible with you. Do you have it in your bag now?"

Maddie had almost forgotten the bag she had slung over her

shoulder when she got out of the cart. She reached over, pulled the bag into her lap, took out her Bible, and offered it to Jaden.

"You keep it for now. Do you know where the book of First John is?"

She looked confused. "Is that the same as the Gospel of John after Luke?"

"No, First John is a very short epistle or letter just before Revelation."

"Revelation is at the end. Right?"

"That is correct. Find the beginning of Revelation and turn back one page at a time until you find 1 John 4."

She turned past Jude, 3rd John, and 2nd John - and when she found the chapter she was looking for, she turned to him with a triumphant smile. "Here it is! Just like you said."

"Now, read verses 7 through 14."

"Out loud?" she asked, looking a little uncomfortable.

"Silently is fine."

She read through it quickly and looked at him nervously. Realizing he was not watching her but was leaning back with his eyes closed, she relaxed a little bit and turned back to the book in her lap. "Give me a minute. I want to read it again more carefully." She read it once and then one more time, following the words slowly with her finger. "That is so beautiful," she breathed.

"Yes, it is," he agreed without opening his eyes. "What is it talking about?"

"Love."

"And where does it say love is from?"

"From God."

"What is the relationship between God and love?"

"It says that God is love."

"How was the love of God revealed?"

"He sent His only Son - it's talking about Jesus, right?"

"Yes."

"And it says He paid for our sins - for my sins. Why would He die that horrible death for someone like me? I've never done anything good in my whole life."

"The first part of verse 11 tells you why."

"It says 'Beloved, if God so loved us.' That's like the verse Joy was teaching to Daniel. 'For God so loved the world, that He gave His only Son, so that everyone who believes in Him will not perish, but have eternal life.' I don't understand it all, and I sure don't understand why He would love me that much, but I do believe that Jesus is the Son of God and that He died for my sins."

Jaden had his eyes open now and was staring straight into hers. "Jesus' first sermon was 'Repent...' and throughout His ministry He told people again and again to repent and believe. You say you believe, and you seem to understand that you are a sinner. Do you understand what it means to repent?"

"I think it means to turn away from myself and my sin and to turn to God. I do repent, I do turn to God, I do believe, I want Him to fill my heart with His love."

The light that shone in Maddie's eyes brought joy to Jaden's heart. He took both her hands in his and said, "Let us pray."

Jaden and Maddie prayed together for a few minutes, and the moment they said *Amen*, two of the children that had followed them a few minutes before peeked shyly around the palmetto where they had been hiding. They stared at Maddie with wide eyes, and the little girl asked, "Is Jesus in your heart now?"

"Yes," laughed Maddie, "I believe He is! Isn't that wonderful?"

"Yes, it is wonderful!" echoed Jaden. "Now run back to the village and tell Mama Shenice that lunch must be a celebration. We must have a spiritual birthday party."

"Yay! A party!" shouted the children as they raced up the path.

Maddie grew quiet and seemed to stare at something Jaden couldn't see. "Miss Maddie," he asked, "what are you thinking?"

She turned a teary but joyful smile on him. "I was thinking about parties. We were in the middle of my first birthday party - or the first one I can remember - when Michael's men showed up. Isn't it wonderful that God arranged another one for me so soon?"

Jaden chuckled. "In the Old Testament book of Joel we read that God will restore the years the locusts have eaten. He was, of course, talking about the nation of Israel, but I think the principle applies here. I think God loves parties."

They sat and talked about what her new life in Christ would look like until a bell began to clang in the village. In answer to Maddie's unspoken question, Jaden stood and offered his hand. "That is the signal to the teachers to release the children for lunch and to any-one who is in the garden or elsewhere to come and eat. Are you hungry?"

She took his hand with the smile that hadn't left her face. "I'm starved. I can't wait to see how they put together a party in such a short time."

More children met them on the path, grabbing at her hands, each one wanting to be the one to escort the guest of honor to lunch. She was laughing like one of the children when they reached the top of the path. Then she stopped in her tracks and stared in amazement at the transformation that had taken place in the street. Tables covered with colorful cloths were set up end to end stretch-ing from the church past at least half the houses. Chairs of every description were set up on either side of the table, and the tables were loaded with bowls and platters of food to rival the church pot-lucks Tatia had described to her. Arrangements of cut flowers and seashells accented the fruit, vegetables, bread, meat, and desserts that reminded Maddie of how hungry she really was.

"How did you put all this together so quickly?" she asked Shenice who hugged her tightly and then pushed her away just far enough that she could look into her face.

"Welcome to the family of God," she said with tears of joy in her eyes. "When everyone heard what was going on, they just moved their lunch outdoors. We love to celebrate when another lamb is brought into the fold. Now, Papa, bless the food so we can eat!"

The next couple of hours was a kaleidoscope of tastes, smells, faces, hugs, and sounds. The children were more interested in playing than eating, and impromptu singing groups serenaded the diners from time to time.

Finally, when Maddie couldn't eat another bite or accept another hug, Shenice leaned over and whispered. "You look tired, child. Come with me and you can rest a bit before we go back to the big house."

Maddie hadn't realized how tired she was until she stood up, then she leaned against Shenice gratefully as they walked to the home she shared with Jaden. Maddie breathed in the cool quietness gratefully after the unfamiliar excitement of a crowd of people. Shenice took her to a screened lanai on the back of the house and settled her onto a daybed covered with a pile of pillows of all colors and sizes. Maddie sighed with pleasure as Shenice pulled a light afghan over her, a perfect weight under the cool breeze of the ceiling fan.

Before her eyes closed completely, she mumbled in a voice almost too quiet for Shenice to hear, "We have to plan the wedding."

Shenice stopped short. "I thought Mr. Michael had everything arranged."

"He did, but he could tell I wasn't thrilled with the formal dress he had designed for me and the stiff, formal ceremony he had planned. He wants it to be on Saturday in the late morning with lunch afterward, but other than that, he said we could plan whatever we want."

"And do you know what you want?"

"Something like today," she yawned. "On the beach, in a dress like what one of you would wear - and a big party like we had today with all of you there." Her eyes had almost drifted shut when she added. "And I want you and Papa Jaden to walk me down the aisle and him to perform the ceremony."

Shenice smiled at her lovingly as her breathing settled in the regular rhythm of sleep. "You have had so much unhappiness, child," she whispered. "We will try to bring you as much joy as possible on your wedding day."

45

Tuesday - 10/10

Maddie was already dressed, had finished breakfast, and was writing in her journal when Shenice arrived carrying a tablet. She was accompanied by Gabrielle who was carrying a zippered garment bag and what looked like a small tool box.

"Good morning, Miss Maddie," she said with a huge smile. "You look more beautiful than ever this morning. You remember my daughter Gabrielle? She came to help me with…well, I don't want to spoil the surprise which we will save for later."

She paused to take a breath, and Maddie took the opportunity to interject. "Good morning to you, too." She hugged both women and continued, "Of course, I remember Gabrielle. You put together that amazing fruit bouquet. If it's not too much trouble, maybe you could do another one for Saturday."

"It is in the plans." Gabrielle smiled modestly in response to the compliment. "In fact, with time to plan, it will be even more elaborate."

"Wonderful! Can I get either of you something to drink?

Coffee, tea, juice? And I have some pastries and fruit left from my breakfast."

"Yes, tea would be lovely. For both of us?" replied Shenice, looking toward Gabrielle for confirmation. Once she received a nod, she continued. "We have been running at top speed since yesterday afternoon. I think we need a few minutes to sit down with you and go over where we are with wedding plans and make sure you approve."

"I trust you," smiled Maddie. "I'm sure whatever you have in mind will be lovely." She busied herself making tea and preparing a small plate for each of her guests. Once everyone had food and a cup of tea, she sat and looked at both ladies brightly. "Now, tell me what you've planned."

Shenice put a hand over Maddie's. "Before I begin," she said, "let me say again that you look amazing today. You look rested and, well, you look happy."

"I am happy," she replied. "I am still very sad about being away from my family, but I no longer feel alone." She waved toward the open balcony doors and continued, "God has blessed me with a view beyond anything I've ever imagined and with amazing new friends. And I slept through the night without a single nightmare!"

"That is wonderful news indeed!" Shenice squeezed her hand and picked up her tablet. For the next hour, the three women discussed the menu, who was making which dish, decorations, and table set up.

"We will have a non-alcoholic fruit punch and a full bar for those who want to indulge. We need to discuss the cake. Do you want a traditional American cake or a traditional Caribbean black cake?"

"Black cake!" exclaimed Maddie. "That sounds very strange."

"It's a dark spiced fruit cake. I'll let Gabrielle explain it to you because she's the one who will be making it."

After a more detailed description, including the rum-soaked

fruit and the rum drizzle in place of frosting, Maddie asked, "That sounds delicious. But can you make a non-alcoholic version?"

More discussion followed, and Maddie decided on a three-layer traditional rum cake and a single layer with rum flavoring for her and anyone else who might prefer it.

"You are very wise," said Shenice. "I believe Mr. Michael will be pleased."

"I hope so. This is so different from what he originally planned."

"I stopped by his office this morning, mainly to check on what he's planning to wear. I told him about our plans, and he was fine with everything. He even allowed me to order this for him." She tapped on her tablet screen a few times and turned it so Maddie could see a picture of a white long-sleeved linen shirt with two rows of blue embroidery in a wave pattern down the front.

"I love that!" enthused Maddie. "That will look so good on him with his olive complexion. What about the slacks? The tan ones the model has on look great."

"I'm so glad you approve," said Shenice. "I agree about the slacks, and so did Mr. Michael. What he did not agree to was bare feet, but he will wear sandals."

Maddie laughed at the thought of the Michael who she had never seen in anything more casual than slacks and a sport coat walking barefoot in the sand. "You two have done a wonderful job of planning. It will definitely be a day to remember." She stared wistfully at the rolling waves, thinking about Heart City and what might have been. Shenice and Gabrielle exchanged sympathetic looks, and Shenice nodded toward the garment bag.

"There's one more thing, Miss Maddie," said Gabrielle. "We haven't shown you what you will wear."

"I guess that is an important detail," quipped Maddie, trying to sound enthusiastic.

Gabrielle laid the garment bag across the table and unzipped it revealing a white cotton satin dress that was hand-embroidered in vertical rows with hibiscus blossoms and leaves in a cream color. Maddie gasped and her hands flew up to cover her gaping mouth. Gabrielle smiled with pleasure and pulled the dress out of the bag to reveal the small ruffles that edged the straight neckline and the off-the-shoulder cap sleeves. Small darts drew the bodice into a loose empire waistline and then loosened to free the skirt to flare to the floor.

"Where did you find something so simple and beautiful so quickly?" asked Maddie as she felt the fabric almost reverently.

"It is the dress I was married in," said Gabrielle shyly.

"Oh, Gabrielle!" she was about to protest when Shenice caught her eye and shook her head slightly. "I am so honored that you would allow me to wear your dress. I will be extra careful with it so it will look new for your daughter."

Gabrielle beamed. "It is my honor, and it will be hers. Now, you need to try it on. I believe you are slimmer than I am, so I will need to tuck in the darts a little bit."

Maddie stood on a low stool in her dressing room while Gabrielle pinned the darts and measured the hem which they had decided to raise a couple of inches to protect it from the sand. Shenice and Gabrielle discussed the wreath of flowers they would make for her hair and the bouquet she would carry, but Maddie was lost in thought. When Gabrielle had finished her measurements, she slipped the dress back into the bag and excused herself.

"I need to get back home and prepare lunch for my family," she explained.

"Thank you again for all you're doing to make the wedding as special as it can be."

Shenice hugged her daughter. "Let me know if there are any questions about the preparations, and I will be home later."

Then she turned to Maddie who was back in her own clothes.

"Let's go sit on the balcony. I sense you have something on your mind."

Maddie grabbed a couple of bottles of water and followed her outside. "You're so perceptive - I have been wrestling with something. I was reading 2 Corinthians this morning, and I came across the part about not being unequally matched with unbelievers. Do you know the part I'm talking about?"

"I do. You constantly surprise me with how much of the Bible you have read in a short time."

"Well, I don't have a lot to do, and after yesterday, I want to know everything I can about my new Savior. But sometimes what I read scares me a little bit. If I'm not to be mismatched with unbelievers, will God be angry with me for marrying a man like Michael?"

"It is very good that you want to know about and to please your heavenly Father, but remember the story of Esther. What did her uncle tell her when she had to do something difficult to save her people?"

"Something like maybe she was brought to the place where she was just for that purpose."

"Yes. She had no choice about marrying a pagan king, but God used her situation for His purposes. You had no choice about this marriage, but it is no surprise to God, and He will use it and you for His purposes."

46

Friday - 10/13

Johnny dragged in to breakfast thirty minutes later than usual. He declined the muffin Tatia offered him, stifling a yawn and opting for coffee only.

"You look tired," observed Joy. "Did you have trouble sleeping?"

Johnny rubbed his hands over his face and yawned again. "I didn't ever go to bed," he admitted. "I was on the computer all night."

The heads of all the adults immediately turned to look at him, and Jesse voiced their concern. "You weren't visiting the sites you used to frequent, were you?"

"Oh, no!" he exclaimed. "Nothing like that - I promise! I was on Google Earth again looking for signs of an airstrip or other buildings on supposedly uninhabited islands. I think I've looked at all 700 islands, inhabited and not, at least once with no luck. I don't know what else to do." He took a big gulp of his coffee and then rested his head in his hands.

"Maybe you need a nap," offered Daniel. "Mommy says I think better after a nap."

Johnny gave Daniel a high five. "That's good advice, buddy, but when I lie down and close my eyes, I keep seeing the look on Maddie's face when she turned back and looked at me. She said she was sorry, like it was her fault or something. Why did she say that?"

Tatia sat down across the table from him and waited until he felt her gaze and looked up at her. "She was expressing her sorrow at all the things that could have been. She was saying goodbye for what she felt like would be the last time, but we don't know what God has planned. It seems strange that He would have brought her into our lives and allowed us all to become so attached for such a short time. But then, His thoughts are not ours, and His ways are not ours."

"Yeah," agreed Johnny. "I don't get it either."

"Speaking of God, we missed you at Bible study last night," said Jesse. "Did you make it to Recovery on Wednesday?"

"No. I guess I've been hibernating, feeling sorry for myself."

"Not a good idea," said Jesse, putting his hand on his friend's back. "You've done all you can on a human level to find Maddie. Now the best thing you can do is strengthen your relationship with the Lord by getting into the Word and spending time on your knees - and spending time with other believers. And you need to get some sleep. You're no good to anybody in this condition."

Brush pushed back from the table. "I need to open the shop. Johnny, we've still got that cot in the back if you want to grab a couple of hours before you get started."

Tatia and Joy began clearing the table. "Joy, I'm going to run over to my office and get Lili started on that new filing system. You two get dressed and continue reading your books for your reports. I'll be back in fifteen minutes or less."

47

Friday - 10/13

Maddie spent most of Wednesday and Thursday walking on the beach alone or sitting in her room reading her Bible. She had read through the four Gospels and then had turned to the Psalms. She related to the chapters where David cried out to God in his times of trouble, but she had fallen in love with the twenty-third Psalm. She had read it so many times that she could quote it from memory.

But this morning, the morning before her wedding, she sat on her balcony and stared at the Bible in her lap without seeing the words. The reality that she was really to be married to a man she barely knew and who was a major criminal sat heavily on her spirit. She had sent Shenice away earlier, but now she was lonely and regretted her decision. She was thinking about calling her back, but she knew final wedding preparations were demanding all her attention, so she continued to sit. After a few minutes, she began to nod off.

She was dreaming of sitting across the table from Johnny with a new flavor of ice cream in front of her when voices brought her back to the balcony. She opened her eyes and saw a man and a woman on the path between her flower garden and the beach. She yawned and rubbed her eyes, and then she recognized the pair as Michael and his assistant Adrian who she had met the day before. She felt like an intruder, but it was impossible not to see them, and their words were drifting toward her on the wind.

"I don't understand how you can prefer her to me!" she cried. "She's just a child!"

"You were just a child when you came to me, Adrian," he responded quietly.

"But I learned and matured into the woman who is the perfect fit for the man you are," she countered, raising her voice a notch or two.

"Adrian," he said with a warning in his voice. "If you can't keep your voice down, this conversation is over. I will not have our past relationship discussed by the entire staff."

"I'm sorry, Michael, but you know how I feel about you. I always knew you had other women, but I thought you had at least some affection for me." There were tears in her voice.

"I never lied to you about my feelings, and you knew from the beginning that I am a man who requires variety. I told you that you had ten years max, and you exceeded that by several years. Maddie comes to me young and schooled to meet all my needs – including some you have not been able to meet. You are fortunate to still be employed by my company, but that can change if you are unhappy. Do I make myself clear?" There was steel in his voice.

"Yes, Michael."

"Good. Now let's get back to the office. It's almost time for my conference call."

Maddie was wide awake now, stunned by the callous way Michael had spoken to the woman who had been so much more than an employee to him. And by this time tomorrow she would be, not the cherished wife every girl dreams of becoming, but little more than Esther - the only one with a ring, but still a member of the harem. She buried her face in her hands and wept.

48

Saturday - 10/14

Maddie's sleep was troubled with new nightmares, but she didn't remember the details when the rays of the rising sun woke her. What she did remember was that today was her wedding day, the day she would become legally bound to Michael forever. She buried her face in the pillow and prayed that God would help her be like Esther, fulfilling whatever purpose He had for her.

She finally rolled over with a sigh and rolled out of bed. She knew Shenice would be arriving soon with a whole crew to prepare her for the day, so she headed for the shower. But when she caught a glimpse of herself in the mirror, she grabbed her phone and dashed off a text.

You'd better bring some magic with you this morning. Rough night. Face and eyes are puffy and red again!

Shenice replied immediately with an affirmation and several hearts. When she arrived about half an hour later, Maddie was dressed in her bathrobe and was reading Psalm 23 over and over. She couldn't help but smile at the parade of women who marched into her suite carrying baskets of fresh flowers and ribbons which would soon become her headpiece and her bouquet, the garment bag that held her altered dress, and several trays of food for an impromptu bachelorette party.

Shenice had brought a cooling compress and a masque as well as other spa treatments made of fragrant herbs and mysterious ingredients Maddie didn't recognize. The women chattered and giggled as they tended to the bride's face, hands, and feet and gave her a relaxing massage. Their labors were accompanied by the noise of the preparations that were being made on the beach outside her window. The festive mood was contagious and the darkness of the night soon disappeared.

By mid-morning Maddie was relaxed and her face was glowing with the feeling of being loved by this new family. Shenice also reminded her more than once that she was loved by her Creator who knew exactly where she was and what was happening to her. She was surprised that, when everyone took a brunch break, she was hungry, and she thoroughly enjoyed every bite. All too soon, though, Shenice stood and clapped her hands.

"The ceremony is set for noon, so we have a little less than two hours to dress the bride and ourselves. Time to get back to work!"

The noise level rose another notch along with the excitement as each woman turned to the task she had been assigned. Several cleared the remains of the food, and one began to braid Maddie's hair into an intricate crown interspersed with gold and silver beads that would sparkle in the sunlight. A final sealer coat was applied to her nails, and a tray holding an array of brushes and cosmetics was laid out in readiness. Those who were not otherwise engaged began donning colorful dresses and lots of beaded jewelry.

Finally, Shenice nodded her approval and announced it was time for the dress. Gabrielle unzipped the bag which she had hung in a place of honor, and held it for the bride to step into. She zipped it up and glowed with pride at the perfect fit. Shenice placed a wreath of multi-colored roses on Maddie's head, fastening it securely and arranging the multi-colored ribbons so they flowed down her back past her waist. Then she presented Maddie with a small box wrapped in white and tied with a gold ribbon.

"This is Mr. Michael's wedding gift to you."

"Oh no! I didn't think about a gift for him!"

"It is not necessary. He has everything he wants or needs except you as his wife. And that is your gift to him today."

Maddie smiled sadly as a little of the heaviness returned to her heart. She opened the box that contained a strand of perfect pearls with a diamond clasp and a pair of perfect pearl drop earrings. Shenice fastened the necklace around the bride's neck, put the earrings in place, and stepped back to survey the effect.

"Perfect," she pronounced. "Except for one thing," she added.

One of the younger girls who had been helping with the flowers stepped forward shyly and handed Maddie a colorful bouquet of flowers and ribbons that added just the right touch of color without detracting from the bride herself.

Shenice hugged her and kissed her gently on the cheek so as not to mess up her makeup. "Now you may look," she said as she led her to the mirror to the cheers and clapping of her ladies-in-waiting.

Maddie smiled at her reflection in spite of herself. All traces of her nighttime turmoil had been erased, and she would have been ecstatic if only she were presenting herself to a different groom. But she trusted in the divine plan that had brought her to this place at this time and was determined to show a joyful countenance to her new family who had worked so hard to please her.

A quiet knock interrupted the chatter, and Jaden's voice sounded through the door. "Is the bride ready?"

Maddie took a deep breath and smiled at Shenice. "Yes, the bride is ready."

The group gathered around her, laying hands on her gently,

being careful not to muss her, and Jaden prayed a blessing over her. As the wedding procession formed in the hallway, Shenice hugged her one last time and then held her at arm's length for one last look. A worried look suddenly replaced Maddie's smile.

"What is it, child?"

"This room! It's a mess! I didn't have time to prepare it for tonight!"

Shenice laughed and linked her arm through Maddie's. "Don't worry your pretty head about that. The girls will come up during the party and make this room suitable for Solomon and his bride."

"How would I ever make it through this without you?"

Maddie left the room she would next enter as a married woman and took her place between Shenice and Jaden at the end of the procession. As they moved down the stairs toward the garden, the women began to sing a joyful island song, and Maddie prayed for strength.

Each bridal attendant was met by a groomsman as she stepped out the door onto the path to the beach. The men and the crowd below joined in singing, and the sound of their voices rang out with such a pure, sweet harmony that Maddie was swept into the joy of the moment. The couples ahead of her began to sway and twirl with the music, and her escorts broke into a simple rhythmic step that Maddie easily followed. Her formal march to the altar became a celebration of the new life she had found with these beautiful people.

Just before Maddie reached the sand, the attendants split into two lines in front of her, and two young boys rolled out a red carpet that led to the white canopy that had been set up a hundred yards away. For the first time she caught sight of Michael, waiting for her. He looked rather handsome in his casual wedding attire and seemed more comfortable than she expected. But the look on his face was the same cool expression he wore when he saw her at their first lunch, not the enraptured look of a man catching his first glimpse of the woman he loves on their wedding day.

Just when the dark truth was about to close in, a group of giggling children carrying baskets of flower petals closed in around her. They began scattering their flowers on the carpet in front of her and throwing them into the air until she was enveloped in a shower of fragrant color and childish excitement. When she and her escorts finally waded through the crowd of small bodies and took their places under the canopy, her face was aglow and she felt the strength she had prayed for. The ceremony was short but meaningful as Papa Jaden emphasized the biblical significance of marriage. And suddenly she was Mrs. Michael D. Saint.

The rest of the day was a blur of music, dancing, food, laughter, and love. Maddie and Michael shared the traditional first dance, but after two or three minutes, Shenice and Jaden assumed the role of her parents and cut in. The two couples grew to four, and soon the dance floor was full. Michael retired to a comfortable chair in a relatively quiet corner where he sipped rum punch while Maddie danced gracefully with the older men, pranced playfully with the children, and learned some line dances from the teens that were more Gulf Coast than Caribbean Island.

The celebration continued through the afternoon, and when the setting sun began to send streaks of color through the sky, torches were lit and small fires were kindled in fire pits that had been dug in the sand around the perimeter of the party. Tired children fell asleep on the shoulders of parents who were gathered in groups quietly rehashing the highlights of the day and discussing plans for the following day. Maddie looked for Shenice and saw her talking to her daughter by the remains of the wedding cakes. She began walking in that direction, and when Shenice saw her, she excused herself and met Maddie halfway.

"I'm very tired," said Maddie. "Is it too soon for the bride to leave?"

"Not at all," said Shenice. "I think everyone is tired, and your leaving will give them permission to go as well. Why don't I get everyone's attention so you can thank them for coming. After that, we'll go to your room and you can refresh yourself. How long do you think you will need before you are ready to receive your husband?"

"Is an hour too long?"

"I do not think it is long enough. Mr. Michael has been speaking with Mr. Ian a lot in the last hour and looking at his phone. I think he would appreciate some time to check on his business responsibilities. And you need time to rest. Express your appreciation, and then go invite your husband to visit you around ten o'clock."

For the next several hours, Maddie took a relaxing bath and a nap. Shenice and Gabrielle helped take the flowers from her hair and modify her style to something that would still look beautiful in the morning. At 9:30, Gabrielle went back to the garment bag that had held the dress and took out a white peignoir set that was both demure and enticing. The bed sported new linens, candles had been placed strategically around the room, and a bottle of non-alcoholic champagne that Michael had sent up was chilling in a silver bucket beside a huge bouquet of flowers, also compliments of Michael.

Gabrielle began to light the candles while Shenice opened the balcony door to let in the light of the rising moon and the sounds of the surf. "Perfect," said Maddie. Then she asked the virtual assistant to play the collection of music she had chosen earlier in the week. Strains of *Moonlight Sonata* drifted into the air, joining the surf sounds in a soft duet. She moved around the room making last-minute adjustments to pillows, flowers, and the champagne flutes, and Shenice knew she had shifted from the carefree girl who danced with the children to the special young woman who had been groomed for this night since she was taken to Misty's condo.

She hugged Maddie gently and kissed her cheek. "May the Lord bless your union," she whispered.

"Thank you," replied Maddie. "Leave the door slightly ajar as you leave."

Shenice and Gabrielle picked up baskets of flower petals from the closet where they had been waiting and scattered them across the bed. As they backed out of the room, they left a trail of petals across the floor and down the hallway.

Alone in the room, Maddie turned to face the balcony, arranging her peignoir so the shadows worked together with the moonlight and the candles to accentuate the curves of her body perfectly. She heard Michael's footsteps approaching her door, and her mind slipped into that place of safety that had protected her from the lessons that were too much for her. But this time, instead of an empty black void she found green pastures, quiet waters, and her Shepherd waiting with outstretched arms.

49

Sunday - 10/15

Maddie woke up sometime before sunrise and realized that she was alone in the bed. Michael had turned off the music, blown out the candles, and left a note on his pillow that said: *Mrs. Saint, would you do me the honor of meeting me for breakfast at 10:30 in the sun room. Affectionately, Michael*

She was relieved that he was gone, and she drifted back to sleep after setting an alarm for 8:30. She was still tired after the festivities and the stress of the day before, but she knew Shenice would be at church. However, she was learning her way around her wardrobe, and she managed to dress in a way that made her new husband smile when he saw her.

"You are lovely as always, my dear," he greeted her.

"You are too kind, Michael."

He kissed her lightly on the cheek and held her chair for her. She was relieved that he chose to maintain the same public decorum in spite of the intimacy of the previous night. A member of the kitchen staff appeared with two cups and two silver carafes on a silver tray - black coffee for him and decaf with French vanilla creamer for her. Michael requested a full breakfast, but she asked for fruit and a croissant, still feeling the heaviness of the rich food from the wedding. They sipped their coffee and chatted easily about the beautiful morning and the wedding.

"You were right to veto my formal plans in favor of a more casual ceremony and reception," he said. "I actually enjoyed it."

She felt a twinge of sympathy for this man who had brought so much misery to so many lives. "You haven't had much fun in your life, have you?"

Michael gave her a quizzical look, not sure exactly how to respond to such a casual yet personal remark. "No, I haven't," he said, slapping a hand gently on the table. "And it's time I remedied that. Since we already live in an island paradise, I didn't plan a trip, but how would you like to spend a couple of days on the yacht."

She was genuinely surprised and pleased. "That would be wonderful! I've never been on a boat."

He picked up his phone and buzzed Adrian. "Yes, Michael," she answered in a flat voice.

"Adrian, clear my calendar for the next three days and prepare the yacht. Mrs. Saint and I are going on a honeymoon cruise around the islands."

"Do you want the big one?"

"No, the Amel 50 will do. It will just be the two of us and a skeleton crew."

Maddie took to sea life the same way she had to every new experience since leaving Misty's condo. She loved the motion and the sea breeze in her face, even when Michael had to apply a sea sickness patch. She squealed with delight when a small pod of dolphins appeared, racing alongside them and darting back and forth in front of the bow. When they anchored in a beautiful cove with a white sand beach, Michael had the crew prepare the dinghy, and he took her ashore where she ran in the sand, splashed in the surf, and collected shells with the freedom of the child she had been before her world went up in smoke with her mother's bed.

Michael watched his new wife with a mixture of pride and envy. During the day he envied the joy she found in the simple things of life, and at night he felt pride that his investment had produced a wife who was the perfect combination of innocence and sensuality. But all too soon, reality intruded and Ian called him home to handle an emergency. He ordered the captain to weigh anchor immediately and soothed Maddie's disappointment by promising her sailing lessons on one of his smaller vessels.

After their brief respite, the couple settled into a routine. Michael worked in his office, and she spent time in the village. Under the watchful eye of Shenice, she learned to sail, swim, and snorkel, and she used her new skills to explore the colorful world under the waves. She spent hours each day reading her Bible, listening to the sermons and podcasts Sam had loaded onto her tablet, and discussing what she was learning with Shenice and Jaden.

She and Michael shared meals and small talk several times a week, and he came to her suite every two or three days. His visits were surprisingly reserved, and she was relieved that he was always gone when she woke up the next morning. She was aware that, between visits, he spent many nights on the yacht with women who had been brought from other islands, but instead of jealousy, she felt a further sense of relief that, because of these visitors, she wasn't required to use many of the techniques Misty had taught her.

50

Wednesday - 11/15

The light-hearted breakfast atmosphere of pre-Maddie days was still lacking at the Matthews' home. Johnny and Brush still came for coffee and pastry before the shop opened for the day, and Lili usually arrived early enough from her apartment to join them before she opened the office - but the smiles were not as bright and the laughter not as contagious. With Thanksgiving a little over a week away, Tatia was determined to get everyone in a holiday mood.

"Do you know what this family needs?" she announced. Everyone looked at her as if they expected her to tell a bad joke. "We need a little Christmas!"

"You mean like in that musical we watched on TV a couple of months ago?" asked Joy.

"Yes, just like that! Joy, you can ask Grace and Sadie to come over Friday for a sleepover, and Daniel can ask Cade and Shawn. We'll make decorations and put them up, and on Saturday, we'll have all the adults join us for a cookie exchange. What do you think?"

"Yay! I get to have a sleepover!" yelled Daniel, jumping up and doing a little dance around the table.

"I don't really feel like a sleepover. Can I just invite my friends for Saturday?" asked Joy. Tatia knew by the way Joy avoided looking at her that there was more to her request than she let on, so she did a little motherly probing.

"That's fine if that's what you want. Are you worried about three girls and only two beds?"

"Well, kind of." Joy was still looking at the floor. Tatia waited quietly until Joy let out a sigh and looked up at her mother. "It's just that - I don't want anyone else sleeping in Maddie's bed."

"I can understand that." Tatia reached across the table and took her daughter's hand. "I miss her, too. What if you had your friends bring sleeping bags and you can camp out in the living room?"

Joy's eyes brightened up a bit. "That would work. It would be like a slumber party."

"No fair!" whined Daniel. "I wanna have a slumber party!"

Tatia rolled her eyes and looked at Jesse. "We need a bigger house!"

Lili was wiping the counters and listening to the plans. "If I'm not interfering, I may have a solution."

"Please interfere!" said Jesse. "We can't afford a new house, at least not right now.'

"Besides," added Tatia. "You're part of the family. Your input is always welcome."

"Well, there's plenty of room in the Annex. The girls could have their slumber party there. I would be glad to sleep over and supervise."

"Lili, that's a wonderful idea, but are you sure it wouldn't be an imposition?" asked Tatia.

"Not at all," said Lili, warming to the idea. "I would enjoy the company - and I need the practice if I'm going to baby-sit for my niece," she smiled, patting her growing baby bump. "We have a couple of room-sized rugs from that last load of donations. We could spread them out and put the sleeping bags on them. We could have popcorn and hot chocolate and even watch a video on my laptop."

Joy jumped up and ran over to give Lili a hug. "That sounds super fun! Thank you!"

Jesse saw that Daniel's face had fallen even further, so he jumped in. "Hey, buddy! How about if the guys camp out in the meeting room over the shop?"

Daniel immediately brightened at that suggestion. "Yeah! And maybe Johnny could come, too!"

"Johnny might have other plans already, buddy."

"No, it's okay," said Johnny. "I have nothing planned except to spend more hours staring at Google Earth pictures of deserted islands. I'd love to come, Daniel."

"Hey," said Brush who had quietly watched the Friday night party take shape. "Can I come? I like sleepovers, too."

Jesse almost spit out his coffee and tried to cover his laughter with a fake cough - and Tatia experienced a feeling of accomplishment looking at the smiles around the table.

51

Saturday - 12/9

Saturdays were often lonely times for Maddie. Although she regularly went to the village for church on Sunday, she tried not to schedule any Saturday activities that required supervision so Shenice could spend time with her family. On this Saturday morning she woke up with the empty feeling of not knowing what she would do with her day. Michael was away until some time the following week, and the house was empty except for the few staff members who were required to maintain security and minimal operation of the various island systems.

She had a small breakfast of coffee, yogurt, and granola from the supplies she kept in her kitchenette. After a quick shower, she dressed and went downstairs to the library to look for a book that would hold her attention all day. She found a Christian cozy mystery and smiled, knowing that it had definitely not been added to the library for Michael's reading pleasure. She took it with her, hoping it might take her mind off the long hours that stretched ahead of her.

She left the library and wandered through some of the rooms

that were seldom used. She went into the music room and walked her fingers across some of the piano keys, wondering if anyone in the village could teach her to play. She walked through the great room and slowly inspected the art hung on the walls and strategically placed on pedestals around the room. She wondered how many sonogram machines she could buy for Tatia if she sold all this art that no one ever saw or appreciated. The dining room was across the hall, and Maddie went in and sat in a chair at one end of the long table. She put her hands to her mouth like a megaphone and called out to an imaginary person at the other end.

"Michael, can you please pass me the salt."

She smiled at her own joke and then stopped. "Wait!" she said to the empty room. "What's the date?" She pulled her phone out of her bag and checked. "The 9th! Our two-month anniversary is Thursday!"

Maddie had experienced a little disappointment that she had not been able to utilize the hostess skills she had learned under Misty's tutelage. Shenice had mentioned visitors, but she wasn't sure who they had been or if Michael would want to let anyone else know where he was under the present circumstances. After all his elaborate preparations, he wouldn't want to take any chances on leading the FBI to the island. But there was no reason she and Michael couldn't have a fancy dinner to celebrate their mini-anniversary. She could wear the long black dress that looked so out of place among all the casual clothes in her dressing room.

She thought again of the story of Esther. The reader is not told whether Esther loved her husband or not, but she worked hard to be the best queen she could be. Maddie pulled her tablet out of her bag and began making notes. When she finished, she headed for the kitchen hoping Skipper was on duty today. The chef Michael had brought in from Italy was very aloof and didn't like anyone but his staff in his kitchen. Skipper, on the other hand, was from the village and was in training. He was glad to explain what he was doing and even let her help if she wanted. And unlike his boss, he would do his best to provide any special requests if the ingredients were on hand.

"Well," said Skipper with a smile. "If it isn't Mrs. Maddie. Do you want something special for lunch today?"

"No, Skipper. Anything you have on hand is fine. But I do want to ask for a very special dinner on Thursday night. Do you have a few minutes to talk about it?"

"You're in luck. I was about to take a break. Do you want some coffee or juice? I've been experimenting with several juice combinations. You could be my taster."

Once they were seated at the small table in the back of the kitchen, Maddie complimented his latest invention and told him about the anniversary dinner. "I know it's less than a week away, but here's what I'd like to serve, or as close as you can get." She handed him her tablet, and he read the suggested menu aloud.

"Crab claws sauteed in butter, garlic, and white wine. Nice! Hearts of palm with bibb lettuce, plum tomatoes, and a lime vinaigrette. I may have to substitute another lettuce, but I can get close. Veal sauteed in a butter and cream sauce with fresh apples and Calvados. Calvados, huh? It's a good thing Mr. Saint has an extensive liquor collection. Minced potatoes baked with Swiss cheese, cream, and a pinch of nutmeg. Simple. And raspberry sorbet with chocolate and pistachio biscotti. Got it!"

"Could you choose the appropriate wines to go with the appetizers and the main course. I've not visited the wine cellar, so I don't know what's available."

"Happy to. And I assume you'll want your regular sparkling water, maybe infused with a little bit of fruit."

"Yes, thank you! You always remember. And we'll have coffee and cognac on the patio - with tea for me."

He grinned at her. "Mrs. Maddie, if he wasn't already married to you, he'd definitely propose after this meal."

She blushed with pleasure at the compliment. "Thank you, Skipper. If you have any questions, I'll be in my room. I'm tired for some reason. I think I'll go snuggle in with the book I picked out in the library and take it easy."

"Don't worry about a thing, Mrs. Maddie. Shall I send up a shrimp salad for lunch?"

"That sounds good. I'll leave the door ajar in case I fall asleep."

52

Monday - 12/11

Maddie just barely made it to the village in time for the worship service Sunday morning. The greeter at the door escorted her down to the seat Shenice always saved for her on the front row. They exchanged a quick hug and Maddie apologized for missing Bible Study.

"Don't worry about it. Are you okay?"

"Yes, I just overslept. I don't know why - I napped most of the afternoon yesterday."

She enjoyed the singing, praise and prayer time, and the meet and greet time, but she had trouble keeping her eyes open during Papa Jaden's message. When the final *Amen* was said, Shenice began to talk about lunch, but Maddie begged off, saying she was just too tired.

Now it was Monday morning, and the direction of the rays of sunshine coming through her windows told her it was almost 8:00. She wanted to roll over and sleep some more, but she had asked Shenice and Gabrielle to come over this morning and help with her dress for Thursday. She made herself get up and had just finished her shower when her friends tapped on the door.

"Come on in," she called. She explained her plans for Thursday night and pulled the black dress off the rod. "This is what I want to wear. It's my size but when I tried it on, it didn't seem to fit right. It feels a little tight across the top, and it wrinkles a little across my hips and belly."

Shenice and Gabrielle exchanged knowing glances but didn't say anything. "Let me take a look," said Gabrielle. She examined the seams and found enough extra fabric to loosen the fit just enough to make the dress drape perfectly.

"Do you think I'm getting fat?" asked Maddie.

"Not at all," reassured Shenice. "You are just developing a woman's body instead of a girl's, and you are more beautiful than ever."

While Gabrielle sewed, Shenice and Maddie went downstairs and surveyed the dining room. They enlisted the help of Maddie's bodyguards to remove enough leaves from the table to make it the perfect length for two with a low centerpiece between. However, the smaller table was dwarfed by the size of the room, so they scouted some of the unoccupied guest rooms for privacy screens. With the help of some strategically placed potted palms and creative lighting, they designed a beautifully intimate setting. With the last of the large plants in place, the greenhouse manager suggested a few touches of color including a centerpiece of orchids.

"This is going to look stunning," said Maddie. "Can we do the same thing with the patio?"

French doors with leaded glass insets opened onto a large patio. Maddie loved the three-tiered water feature with the subtle underwater lighting and the firepit. "But it's so big!" she exclaimed.

"That will not be a problem," said the master gardener. 'Some of these planters are movable, and we can bring in more greenery and color to create a continuation of the dining room."

"Yes! That's exactly what I had in mind."

The manager went back to the greenhouse and the bodyguards faded into the background. "Shall we go see how Gabrielle is coming with the dress?"

"Sounds good," said Maddie. "Let's stop by the kitchen and see if they can throw some chicken and veggies in a bowl of rice for lunch. We can eat on the balcony."

"You do remember that you can text your request to the kitchen, don't you?"

"I know, but after so many years of being in that condo with Misty, I like talking to people face to face."

Skipper greeted her with his ever-present smile. "Of course, Mrs. Maddie," he said after she told him what she wanted. "And how about some fresh fruit for dessert."

"Yes, please."

"Consider it done. We have everything we need for Thursday except the guest of honor. He hasn't told us when he plans to return."

"Oh," said Maddie. "I was thinking he said mid-week so I just assumed..."

It hurt Shenice to see the crestfallen look on Maddie's face. "You will just have to send him a special invitation. I'm sure he won't be able to refuse his lovely wife. Now, let's go check on that dress."

The dress fit perfectly, and lunch was delicious. Maddie filled Gabrielle in on the preparations that were being made, and Gabrielle showed Maddie a program on her computer that would produce a document that looked like a formal invitation hand-written in fancy calligraphy.

After Maddie yawned for the third time in a few minutes, Shenice stood and began to gather the dishes onto the delivery cart.

"Gabrielle, I think it's time you and I left our young charge to rest a bit after her exciting morning. We'll take these dishes down with us so you won't have to call the kitchen. I'll be downstairs if you need me."

"No, you go on home with Gabrielle. I don't plan to do anything more strenuous this afternoon than reading on the beach." She hugged both women and said, "Thank you both for all your help.

53

Thursday - 12/14

Maddie received a reply from Michael early Tuesday morning that he would be honored to attend a celebratory dinner on their two-month anniversary. She was so relieved that her plans were working out that she and Shenice went snorkeling to celebrate. The rest of the week was spent meeting with the greenhouse manager and Skipper, tweaking details and making sure nothing had been overlooked, and fighting the fatigue that continued to plague her.

Thursday morning she heard the jet coming in for a landing so she knew Michael had made it home. He apparently went straight to his office because she didn't see him when she and Shenice made one final sweep through the kitchen, dining room, and patio. After lunch she slept for a while and then began her final preparations for the evening. Shenice brought several of the women from the village to help with her hair and makeup, and they made almost as big a fuss over her as they did before the wedding.

After they worked their magic, Maddie swept down the stairwell and into the great room with the confidence and poise of a much older and much more experienced woman of the world. Michael, dressed in a black tux and pleated white shirt, stood and greeted her with a gallant bow and a kiss of her hand.

"I was instructed by Skipper, who is apparently acting as butler tonight, to wait for Madam in here," he said with a smile. "Evidently the entire staff has taken ownership of this event. I'm looking forward to seeing what you've created for us."

She smiled a little mysteriously and replied, "I feel as if this is my practicum after my doctoral studies. And I'm excited to do something very special for you. Would you like a drink before dinner?"

"No, let's skip the drink if that's okay."

"Of course," she said as she took his arm. "Skipper, you may serve now."

Skipper was decked out in a white dress shirt, black slacks, and a wide smile. He took hold of the door handles, swung them open with a flourish, and bowed them into the dining room.

"Wow!" said Michael under his breath as he seated her. Before he took his seat he stood beside his wife and slowly looked around the room. "I've always thought this room was a bit cold, but I'll never feel that way about it again."

He sat and cocked his head slightly, listening to the soft music that seemed to float through the air from no specific source. "This is from the Miles Davis 'Kind of Blue' album, isn't it."

"Yes, I thought you'd like it."

"One of my favorites. Did you know that this album birthed what was called the cool jazz movement when it was recorded in 1959?"

"Really?" she said, although Misty had told her about the movement when she gave her his top ten list. "I wish I could have heard him live."

"He was amazing. I was about your age the first time I heard him. I've been a fan ever since"

Skipper began to serve while the chef stood at the door and watched with a critical eye, and they proceeded through dinner exchanging small talk and comments on the food. Michael praised each course and each wine choice, but Maddie noticed he took only a bite or two and a sip or two. When the sorbet and biscotti had been sampled and the napkins placed on the table, Maddie caught Skipper's eye.

"Coffee and cognac on the patio." She gave him a mischievous half-smile. "We'll see ourselves out."

Michael was as complimentary about the outdoor ambience as he was about the dining room, but Maddie could tell he had something on his mind. She took his hand and led him to a two-seat glider by the fire pit. They sat, and he covered her hand with his free hand.

"It was a lovely dinner, Mrs. Saint. Probably the nicest evening of my life," he said with something like resignation in his voice.

"You didn't eat much."

Skipper appeared with coffee and cognac for him and tea for her. He placed them on the tables on either end of the glider and pulled the doors discreetly closed as he went back inside. Michael released her hand and stared into the fire as he sipped his cognac. Finally, he replaced his snifter on the table and took her hand again.

"Maddie, I'm not well," he said. "My time is short and the predators are circling. The doctors have given up on me, but I have enemies that won't give up. It's time I prepare you for what is to come."

She didn't understand what he was saying, so she remained silent and waited for him to continue.

"I've been poking the sleeping bear, so to speak, in an effort to find out if any are loyal to me. There are none. What I'm doing is dangerous, but I don't want to hang around until I'm an invalid wearing diapers anyway, so I'm willing to take the risk. But I don't want you to share that risk. I have taken too much of your life already, and you have much more to live."

Maddie began to tremble as the reality of what he was saying sank in. Her eyes began to glisten with unshed tears, and she looked pale in the firelight. Michael saw her distress and patted her hand.

"It's admirable that you're upset over the fate of a diabolical man like me, but don't be." When she began to protest, he held up his other hand and continued. "I've done things that would make you feel nothing but revulsion for me. I've done them knowingly and willingly. The situation I'm in is the result of choices on my part, and I'm willing to accept the consequences. But as always, I want to control those consequences and share some of those consequences with others. But not with you.

"When you go back to your room, you'll find a leather bag in the back of the bottom drawer in your dressing room. It's what you might call a go bag. I want you to keep it hidden but readily accessible. When Ian or Adrian comes to you or texts you and says 'It's time,' I want you to grab it and go with them immediately."

She dabbed at the outside corners of her eyes. "What's in it - and where will we be going?"

"It contains your passport, a copy of our marriage certificate - which you might want to keep secret unless absolutely necessary..."

"Passport?" she interrupted. "How can I have a passport when I don't have any official form of identification?"

"Oh, but you do. I have a certified copy of your birth certificate that I secured shortly after you came to live with Misty. I was going to present it to you as a wedding gift, but you already had that information. I used it to apply for a Social Security number for you and various other documents."

"Are they, you know, legal?"

He laughed. "You mean, are they forged? No, they are completely legitimate. There are some other legal papers that might be of use to you, and there is some cash to help you get settled. As to where you'll go, my instructions are to take you back to Chicago. They'll probably not be able to take you all the way home, but the cash will take care of that."

She felt dazed and sat quietly for a few minutes. "When?" she finally asked, avoiding his eyes.

"Hard to predict. It could be months, or it could be days." He stared into the fire again for a moment and then said, "One more thing." He reached into his pocket, pulled out a flash drive, and handed it to her. "Keep this very safe - in your go bag or hidden nearby. Be certain you take this with you when you go. Don't look at it, but when you get back to the U.S., get the best lawyer you can find and give this to him. He'll know what to do."

"A lawyer?" Maddie was confused. "Am I in trouble?"

"No, my dear," he said with a slight smile at the absurdity of his innocent young wife being in trouble. "But I want to be sure no one takes advantage of you." He raised her hand to his lips in a genteel kiss. "Now, I have enjoyed our celebration, but I'm afraid I have to say good night."

"Don't you want to come upstairs with me?"

"I would like nothing more, but we'll probably have to confine our visits to lunch or dinner now and then."

He kissed her on the cheek and left her sitting by the fire, staring at the flash drive in her hand and pondering what it meant for her future.

54

Friday - 12/15

"Hey, Adam," said Jesse into his phone. "What's up?"

He instantly had the attention of everyone in the room, each body unconsciously leaning toward him as if those extra few inches might enable them to hear the voice on the other end of the call. Jesse continued to listen, making appropriate noises now and then to indicate that he was still there. The call lasted a few more minutes.

"Thanks for the update. Keep me posted," said Jesse. He ended the connection and looked around the room.

"The rumblings in the underground are getting louder. The fear is that Saint took records with him that could gut most of the families if they get into the wrong hands - or the right ones, depending on which side you're on. An uneasy bond has formed - a kind of the enemy of my enemy is my friend kind of thing - and they've got a worldwide search going. The rumors about a Caribbean island are getting stronger. The search seems to be centering around the Lesser Antilles."

"Where's that?" asked Tatia. She and Lili were rearranging the pantry to hold some items Lili had brought from her apartment as she prepared to move back home.

"Did you say Lesser Antilles?" asked Lili. When Jesse nodded, she said, "That's where I live." All eyes were on her as she continued. "If you have a globe, I will show you."

Joy retrieved a globe from the school shelf and set it in the middle of the table. Lili spun it around to the Caribbean and pointed. "Here is Cuba and east of there is the Dominican Republic and Puerto Rico. That and a few other islands make up the Greater Antilles. This string of islands that curves southward toward Venezuela is the Lesser Antilles. And right here is Antigua." She pointed to a small island at the north end of the chain. Every eye stared at the globe as if they might be able to see Maddie there.

Johnny jumped up, almost upsetting his chair. "I'm going back to Google Earth and search that area again."

"Wait up," said Jesse. "If Saint is in danger, Maddie's in danger, too. Let's pray for her safety before you go."

55

Friday - 12/15

Maddie and Shenice had made a date to meet for breakfast and then go for a swim in the pool. Shenice had complained good-naturedly that cramming her old body into a swimsuit was not part of her job description, but Maddie, conscious of her apparent weight gain, wanted to get some exercise.

When Shenice tapped on the door of Maddie's suite, she got no response, so she opened the door a few inches and called out. When Maddie still didn't answer, she assumed she was in the shower and stepped into the room just in time to hear an unpleasant but familiar sound coming from the bathroom. She found her young charge kneeling beside the toilet bowl wiping her mouth with tissue.

"Oh, child!" she exclaimed. "You should have called me!" She helped Maddie to her feet and led her to a vanity stool in front of the mirror where she wiped her face with a cool, damp cloth.

"I didn't have time," said Maddie. "It hit me all of a sudden. It's probably all the rich food from last night."

"Probably," agreed Shenice, but she looked skeptical. "Get yourself cleaned up, and we will see if you feel like eating breakfast."

"Strangely, I'm starving. Why don't you call down to the kitchen and order breakfast for us. I want an old-fashioned American breakfast - scrambled eggs, bacon, hash browns, and toast."

"If you are sure," said Shenice. "In the cabana in thirty minutes?"

"That will work!"

Maddie finished every bite of her breakfast as well as a cup of coffee and a small bowl of mixed fruit. Shenice watched her closely as she ate her own breakfast, on guard for a return of her earlier distress, but all she saw was the healthy color that replaced the previous pallor. While they ate, Maddie recounted the details of her evening with Michael, but she stopped short when she came to their time on the patio. Shenice started to ask her a question about it, but Maddie stopped her with an almost imperceptible shake of her head. Shenice place her napkin on the table and stood up.

"I do not think we should go for a swim right after eating such a big meal. You said last week you wanted to practice driving more. Do you want to take a spin around the island?"

"Sounds good to me. I'll call the motor pool and alert the men in black," said Maddie with a grin.

A few minutes later the two women were traveling down the cart path at a good clip with Maddie's body guards - the men in black - following behind. When they were halfway between the house and the village, she pulled over to the side.

"Let's go walk on the beach," she suggested.

"The water is beautiful today," said Shenice. "We can take some pictures."

"Sure," said Maddie, but halfway down the slope, she took Shenice's phone and dropped it along with her own into her beach bag. She casually dropped the bag on the ocean side of a large dune and continued walking toward the water. They took off their shoes and walked in the surf until they reached a pile of rocks. They climbed up out of the reach of the spray where they sat down and Maddie began to tell Shenice what Michael had told her on the patio.

"I don't know exactly what it means, but I don't want all of you to get caught in the crossfire of a gang war if it comes to that. I want you and Jaden to come up with an evacuation plan. If anyone challenges you, tell them you are simply preparing for some storms that are in the forecasts. If you get a text or voice mail from me that says *GO*, get everyone to the boats and leave as fast as you can."

"And you will fly off to America and I will never see you again," said Shenice in a tone of resignation.

"Oh, I will find you," Maddie said, taking her hand. "There can't be that many Shenices on Montserrat. It's a forty square mile island - no place to go, no place to hide."

The two friends sat in silence, staring off into an unknown future, and tears began to trail silently down Maddie's cheeks. "I'm pregnant, aren't I? I'm going to be an 18-year-old widow carrying the child of a major crime boss. I don't think I can do this."

56

Saturday - 12/16

In spite of Lili's protestations, Tatia insisted on hosting a combination bon voyage party and baby shower as she prepared to return to Antigua the following Tuesday. Shawna, Fran, and their families pitched in to help with the food, and they were in the process of turning the Annex into a party room. Brush and Jesse were hanging streamers while Johnny made a run to the store for ice. Joy and her two best friends, under the supervision of Shawna, were carefully piping lop-sided frosting flowers around the edges of cupcakes and arranging them on a platter while Daniel, Shawn, and Cade placed baby-bottle-shaped glitter on the tables one piece at a time.

Fran stood with her arms crossed, behind several bowls of assorted chips and dips. She watched the boys with a perplexed look on her face. "Isn't that glitter supposed to be sprinkled randomly?"

"Probably," said Tatia as she filled a vegetable tray. "But then they'd be through in thirty seconds. Do you really want them fighting with the girls over the frosting?"

"Hm. Good point," replied Fran, swiping an olive off Tatia's tray and popping it into her mouth.

"Now look what you've done," whined Tatia in mock distress. "You've disrupted the feng shui and thrown off the energy of the entire tray!"

"How's that for feng shui," said Fran, nodding toward Lili. She was putting the finishing touches on a charcuterie board featuring several salami roses.

"Oh, her," said Tatia, munching on a stick of celery. "She's just showing off!"

"And she can hear every word you are saying," said Lili without raising her head from her work. She placed one last bouquet of fresh rosemary decorated with several tiny grape tomatoes. "Finished," she announced with a satisfied look.

"It's beautiful!" said Tatia, pulling her into a hug.

"Thank you," replied Lili, much more comfortable with the light-hearted banter and the shows of affection than she had been a few short months before. "And thank you for allowing me to help with the preparations. I haven't had this much fun since my sister's bridal shower."

The next fifteen minutes was a flurry of activity. Johnny arrived with the ice, Brush and Jesse moved the ladder into the storeroom, and Fran's husband Brad came in after closing up his shop for the day. The children were sent outside to play and to watch for guests while the ladies finished setting up the tables. Instead of being fashionably late, the guests arrived right on time - friends of Lili's from church and school and a few of the neighbors who had met her since her arrival.

Tatia had made up a list of four simple questions and passed out copies to everyone. The object was for each guest to partner up with someone they didn't know, take ten minutes to interview each other, and then introduce each other to the group. Names and connections to Lili were shared along with funny stories about baby care and tidbits of supposedly wise advice, and any social anxieties melted away in the laughter.

Next came food, and while everyone enjoyed the goodies, Lili opened gifts. The invitations suggested that gifts be ordered from an online baby shopping store in Antigua with delivery scheduled after Lili arrived home. Pictures of the gifts had been printed and enclosed in cards offering best wishes and congratulations. Lili's excitement and expressions of thanks were tinged with sadness as she looked at items that would be used by her sister after Lili returned to the States to continue her studies.

As soon as all the cards had been opened, the guests began to say their goodbyes and leave. The three boys who had lost interest after their plates were empty were asleep in the bedroom, and the host families cleaned up with little to no conversation. Joy stayed close to Lili while they worked, and she watched closely when Lili began to gather her cards and the few serving pieces she had brought with her. Finally, Joy spoke.

"When will you be back?" she asked without looking at Lili.

"I will be back in late August - two weeks before the fall semester begins."

"That's a long time. Why do you have to stay gone so long."

Lili scooted two chairs together and motioned for Joy to join her. "Come sit with me before someone comes to put these chairs away." When Joy was seated, she slipped her arm around the girl's shoulders, and Joy leaned against her.

"The baby is due on May 30. The spring semester ends on May 24. If I stayed that long, I would be, as you Americans say, cutting it close. The baby might come early."

"What will you do until the baby comes?"

"I will take some classes by Internet, and I have a job at the hospital as a medical assistant. By the time I return I will be certified and will be able to get a job here which will help with expenses. I don't want to be a burden to my sister since she and her husband will be raising the baby."

"What if you change your mind?" Tears began to roll down her cheeks. "Maddie went away, and she didn't come back."

Lili wrapped both arms tightly around her young friend. "I will not change my mind. I will return in August. I promise!"

57

Monday - 12/18

Jesse's phone rang again during breakfast, and he recognized a familiar number. He looked around the table and said, "It's Adam," before he hit the speaker phone icon and answered the call.

"Morning, Adam. The troops are gathered, and I've got you on speaker."

"Thanks for the heads up! I'll try to keep it clean," Adam chuckled. "and straight to the point. An informant claims to have seen Michael at the large cancer treatment center in Houston on Wednesday of last week. An alert went out to all the airports in the area, and one of his jets took off from a private field near Houston very early Thursday morning. It headed north and then disappeared, but it showed up above some storm clouds on a heading toward the Lesser Antilles before it disappeared again. We're scanning that area again for signs of life on anything that is supposed to be deserted."

"Yeah," interrupted Jesse. "Johnny's been doing the same thing."

"And I may have found something last night," added Johnny.

"Okay, you have my email?" asked Adam.

"Yeah."

"Send me the coordinates and any other pertinent info. I'll pass it on - and anything else you come up with. The informant said the word is that the delicate balance has tipped away from Saint - violently away. We need to move ASAP."

58

Tuesday - 12/19

Maddie didn't see Michael much over the weekend, and when she did, he was usually on his phone. He seemed pale and drawn, and Maddie asked Shenice about the situation.

"I know he's an evil man, but I still find myself praying for him. Is that bad?"

"No, it is not bad. We are to love our neighbors as ourselves, and if I were sick, I would want people to pray for me. While you are praying, you should pray that God will change his heart."

Maddie smiled. "You're right, of course. I'm not to judge who deserves my prayers. And I did promise Michael to be the very best wife I could be. That probably includes praying for him."

"You are growing into a wise woman very quickly!"

"I think I'll invite him to lunch. He's probably not eating well."

She texted Michael asking if he was available, and he said he could get way around 1:30. They agreed to meet in the sun room, and when she asked what he wanted to eat, he replied *Surprise me!*

Maddie shared their exchange with Shenice and said, "Let's go to the kitchen and see what kind of surprise Skipper can come up with today."

The final menu consisted of conch fritters with a spicy dipping sauce, jerk chicken with rice and black beans, and spiced plantains. Skipper served it himself with his characteristic grin and a light-hearted flare that made Maddie giggle. Even Michael shed his serious demeanor, and though he still did little more than taste each course, he seemed to enjoy himself immensely. When the table had been cleared and he was sipping a glass of wine, he watched Maddie with that look of appreciative ownership that she found both flattering and disconcerting at the same time.

"Do you feel up to a walk on the beach," she asked, as much to break the tension as from a desire for an after-lunch stroll.

"Certainly," he said, rising slowly from his seat and offering his arm.

She kicked off her sandals and linked her elbow in his, making small talk about the beautiful weather and the dolphins she had seen that morning. They had walked only a few minutes when one of the bodyguards called out to him.

"Mr. Saint, we have a code red security alert."

Michael immediately dropped her arm. "Wait here, Madelyn," in a calm tone that belied the urgent look on his face. He turned and strode back to the guard with more energy than she had seen him exhibit in several weeks. Even though they turned their backs to her and kept their heads together, their words were carried to her on the sea breeze.

"Radar has detected several incoming aircraft, probably drones and probably armed. ETA ten to fifteen minutes."

"Prepare the jet for Mrs. Saint. Have the limo brought around to the front door to take her to the air strip, and order emergency conditions."

Without waiting for a response, he pivoted and motioned to her. "Come now! Hurry!"

She ran to him and took his extended hand, allowing him to pull her toward the house.

"The time has come. Get your go bag and meet me at the front door in two minutes. Don't bring your phone or anything electronic that might be tracked." When they reached the back door, he dropped her hand and headed toward his office. She stretched out her long legs, taking the stairs two at a time. She slammed into her room, not bothering to close the door. She grabbed her phone and the tote bag containing her Bible and her journal off the coffee table. As she ran to her closet, she pulled up Shenice's number and sent her a brief message: *GO NOW!* She took the go bag out of the bottom drawer and threw it into her tote with her books. Remembering Michael's instructions about the phone, she dropped it on the floor of the closet and flew down the stairs.

Michael met her in the entry hall and practically dragged her out the door toward the waiting limo. Ian was standing by the open back door, and Maddie could see Adrian sitting in the front seat on the passenger side. Michael handed her into the back seat and kissed her quickly.

"Live well, my dear," and started to close the door.

She put out her hand to stop the door. "Aren't you coming?"

"Not this time." He closed the door and stepped back. Ian had slipped into the driver's seat and was looking back at his boss. "Go, go, go!" Michael shouted.

Maddie turned so she could watch him out the back window, and she saw a ball of fire rise into the air somewhere near the power plant. She saw a second explosion, and the house went dark. She could still see Michael silhouetted against the fire that seemed to be spreading toward the house. Just before the limo took the curve that would take them out of sight of the house, a third explosion hit in front of the house, and her husband disintegrated in a ball of flames.

Maddie continued to stare out the back window in disbelief, too stunned to even pray. She was faintly aware of Ian talking on his radio to the pilot and of Adrian screaming and crying. She could hear explosions going off , but she felt only a numb disconnect to everything around her. When Ian took one curve so fast she was thrown into the door, she turned around to face the front. She could see the air strip just ahead, so she didn't bother with her seat belt. The jet rolled to the end of the runway and turned into take-off position - and then, like Michael, it disappeared in a flash of light and sound. Ian slammed on the brakes, and Maddie grabbed her bag, hugging it to her chest. Suddenly, the limo shook violently, and she was surrounded by a blinding flash and a deafening roar. She felt herself flying through the air - and then the world went black.

59

Wednesday - 12/20

Jesse had started placing his phone in the middle of the table any time he was in the kitchen area, and the rest of the family - nuclear and extended - spent a great deal of time sitting there. They sat with a cup of coffee or tea and a book in front of them, but they paid more attention to the phone than the book as if willing it to ring. When it finally rang during breakfast, everyone jumped, and spoons and forks clattered into bowls and plates. All eyes were on Jesse as he hit the speaker button and accepted the call.

"Hey, Adam! We're all here. Go ahead!"

"Right. The Feds have been monitoring the area - the one Johnny zeroed in on - by satellite. Yesterday they detected what looked like smoke or something, so they sent a drone to do some surveillance. The place looked like a war zone. It looked like somebody had set up a really nice hideaway there, but there wasn't much left."

"Did you find Maddie?" asked Joy, voicing the question in every-one's mind.

"Well..."

"Go ahead," said Jesse. "Tell us everything."

"Okay," replied Adam, drawing in a deep breath. "They sent in a recon crew early this morning. On the air strip they found the remains of a Gulfstream. The part of the tail with the call sign survived, and it was Saint's."

He stopped, and Jesse prompted him again. "And what else?"

Daniel had scooted into Johnny's lap, and Tatia pulled Joy tightly against her. "Please, God! Noooo!" Joy moaned quietly, and tears dripped off her chin onto Tatia's shirt.

"Near the air strip they found the remains of a limo. It contained two bodies - one man and one woman. They were burned beyond recognition, but the woman was tall and slender."

"Like Maddie," breathed Tatia.

Adam hurried on. "No positive identification has been made. They're running some DNA tests. Do you have anything of Maddie's that might have traces of DNA - toothbrush, hairbrush, anything like that?"

Tatia nodded, and Jesse answered for her. "Not positive, but we'll check. And I'll call Dr. Patterson. I know he drew blood when she first came. I don't know if he still has samples and, if so, if they're still viable."

"Great! Collect what you can. Tracy and I will stop by later to pick them up."

After Jesse ended the call, the family sat in silence until Daniel spoke up. "Is Maddie dead now?" he asked in a shaky voice.

Johnny, who was still holding Daniel in his lap, responded. "We don't know for sure. The police think maybe yes, but I think no. What do you think?"

Daniel thought hard for a minute and then said, "I think no."

Brush, who had not spoken during the conversation said, "May God make it so." And they all said, "Amen!"

60

Saturday - 12/23

Although the sleepovers and the cookie exchange of several weeks earlier had been a great success, the mood at Fallen Angel Salvage was anything but Christmasy. Jesse was tuning his bike in the shop, the kids were playing a game of Yahtzee, but nobody was keeping score, and Tatia was going through her recipe file trying to plan holiday meals that nobody would feel like eating. Suddenly the back door slammed open, and Jesse burst in waving his phone in the air.

"It isn't Maddie!" he yelled. "It isn't Maddie!"

Joy was the first to react. She jumped up and ran to him. "Really! Daddy, how do you know?"

Joy's question roused Tatia and Daniel, and Jesse was surrounded by bodies and questions. He raised his hands for quiet. "I got a text from Adam. Short version is they were able to get a blood type from the pelvic bone which was fairly well preserved. It doesn't match Maddie's blood type."

"Praise the Lord!" said Tatia, and the family melted into a group hug.

61

Saturday - 12/23

Maddie heard sounds that she somehow knew were not in a dream. She fought her way toward consciousness, and she tried to sort through the sounds - muffled footsteps, voices in the distance, mechanical sounds that seemed closer. She caught a whiff of soap and something almost familiar that she couldn't quite identify. The closer she came to the surface, the more aware she was of her body - and of the pain. Her left leg hurt - a lot - and it felt heavy. Her chest felt like it was trapped inside something that was too tight, and it ached when she breathed. The skin on her face and arms felt hot and tingly. Her head was pounding. And she felt tired - so very tired.

She was sinking back into the darkness when she heard a different sound. It was soft and beautiful, calm and soothing. She wanted to open her eyes, but her eyelids felt so heavy. And then she recognized the sound - music. Someone was humming, and they were close to her. Maddie tried to hum a few notes, and the sound stopped.

"Don't stop," she whispered.

"Maddie?"

She knew that voice. She forced her eyelids up, but she closed them quickly. "Shenice?"

"Yes, child. I'm here." Maddie felt a hand touch hers, ever so gently. "Can you open your eyes?"

"The light. It hurts."

"Oh, I am so sorry. I was doing needlework." The hand disappeared for a few seconds and then returned. "There, I turned it off."

Maddie raised one eyelid a tiny bit. When that didn't hurt, she opened both her eyes slowly. The room was dim, but she could see Shenice standing over her. "You're blurry."

"That is the ointment. It is to keep your eyes from drying out. I am going to tell the doctor you are awake."

"Don't leave."

"Oh, child, I have not left you since we got here. I will call the nurse." She pressed the call button that was pinned to the sheet beside Maddie's pillow.

"How may I help you?" asked a disembodied voice Maddie couldn't quite locate.

"Miss Maddie is awake," replied Shenice.

"Wonderful! I'll call the doctor."

"Where? How long?" asked Maddie, struggling to speak through a dry throat.

"All in good time." Shenice wet a cloth from a pitcher of water on the bedside table. She gently wet Maddie's lips and squeezed a few drops of water into her mouth.

The curtain opened and a doctor and nurse came in along with a blaze of light. Maddie closed her eyes, and for the next few minutes she endured the disruption of the peace she felt with Shenice. When the intruders finally left, her friend moved her chair to her bedside, took her hand, and began to hum again until Maddie fell asleep.

62

Sunday - 12/24

The next time Maddie woke up, consciousness came more gently, and when she opened her eyes a crack, the dim light didn't seem like an assault. Her eyesight was less blurred, and her headache was a dull ache instead of a throb, so she opened her eyes all the way. She saw that the bottom part of her bed was raised so hip to knee was at a gentle angle and knee down was flat. A large bandage covered the outside of her left thigh and a complicated device of metal rods and velcro straps supported the leg. It still hurt, but the pain was more focused in the area around the bandage, and it wasn't as intense.

She rubbed her hands gently along her forearms and her face. The heat was gone, but everything felt slick with lotion of some kind - and she felt an IV needle inside her right elbow. She detected a slight herbal smell that reminded her of something Shenice had rubbed on her when she fell asleep in the sun and suffered a sunburn. Her chest was still tight, so she slipped one hand under the blanket and sheet that covered her and touched the sore area. She felt a wide elastic band wrapped around her and guessed she had some broken ribs.

She visually toured the room and found the IV bag that was dripping through the needle and the heart monitor that made the noise she heard as she came out of the darkness. She knew she was in a hospital, but she didn't know how she got there or how long she had been there. She closed her eyes and searched her mind for the last thing she remembered. She had just found herself sitting with her husband having lunch in the sun room when she heard Shenice's voice.

"Maddie," she whispered as she slipped through the opening in the curtain. "Are you awake?"

Maddie opened her eyes with a smile and said, "Shenice, you were here before. I was afraid I dreamed you."

"No, I have been with you almost non-stop. I slipped out to go to the service in the chapel."

"What day is it?"

"Sunday. Christmas Eve."

Maddie thought a minute. "So I've been here five days?"

"Yes, do you remember what happened?"

"It's coming back in pieces."

"Before we get into that, are you thirsty?"

"Dry as a bone!"

"You have not had anything by mouth in a long time. We will try some ice chips first and see how you do before we try liquids. I will be right back."

The nurse came in to check on Maddie and pronounced her much better. "The doctor isn't in today, but I'll let him know how you're doing. If you keep this up, you'll be in a regular room in no time."

She left, and Shenice gave the improving patient several ice chips. Maddie declared them to be the best thing she had ever had in her mouth. After half a dozen chips, she indicated that was enough for now. Shenice sat down carefully on the side of the bed and took Maddie's hand.

"Do you feel like talking a little bit?" Maddie nodded and she continued. "What is the last thing you remember?"

"Just before you came in I was picturing lunch with Michael in the sun room - jerk chicken, I think. Was that real?"

"Yes, child. That was Tuesday afternoon around 1:30. What happened after you ate?"

"I think we took a walk on the beach."

Step by step Shenice helped her move from memory to memory until she finally said with unshed tears glistening in her eyes, "Then I was thrown up out of the car, and it felt like I was flying through the air - and then everything went black - until yesterday."

"That is wonderful. I know it is hard to remember, but the doctor was afraid since you were out for so long that you might have some permanent memory loss. You should rest for a while now."

"No. I want to know what happened, how I got here, everything you know. But first, could we try some water?"

After a few sips, she settled back into her pillows with the appre-hensive anticipation of a child who has asked for a scary story and is rethinking her choice. Shenice had thought about this moment for five days, so she tried to tell the story as gently but accurately as possible.

"A bomb went off in front of the limo. The blast took the roof off the car and you were thrown pretty far behind it. We had prepared according to your warning, and when you texted me, we ran for the boats. Jaden and some of the elders were waiting in the village to be sure everyone got out safely when they saw a huge explosion in the direction of the airstrip. Jaden ran over to check and found you unconscious and with a bone sticking out of your leg."

Maddie pointed at the bandage on her leg. "Right here, I assume?"

Shenice chuckled at her strength in the face of what she had endured. "Yes, right there. He called the other men to come help. They applied a tourniquet and splinted the leg the best they could. They fashioned a stretcher out of a blanket and carried you to the last boat where I was waiting. We brought you directly to the hospital on Antigua because our little island does not have the medical facilities to care for your injuries."

"I know about the broken leg. What else?"

"A concussion, some cracked ribs, and some superficial second degree burns on your face, upper chest, arms, and hands . You had surgery to realign the bone in your leg and insert a metal rod. The doctor says it will take four to six months for your leg to heal completely. I do not think we have to worry about the concussion since you are awake and your memory seems to be intact. The burns were superficial, so there should be little to no scarring."

"What about..." Maddie looked down toward her belly.

Shenice smiled. "The doctor confirmed that you are about six weeks pregnant, and the baby is fine."

Maddie didn't share Shenice's smile. She turned her face away and said, "Maybe it would have been better if it had died - if both of us had died."

"I once heard a famous preacher from America say that no child is ever conceived by a man and woman that was not first conceived in the mind of God. He has special plans for this child. Now, I am going to go sit quietly in my chair and let you get some rest."

She stood up from the side of the bed where she had been sitting and sat down with her Bible that had a small reading lamp attached to it. Maddie spoke without turning her head toward Shenice.

"Did they find my bag?"

"Yes. When they found you, you were clutching it to your belly as if using it to shield your child."

63

Monday - 12/25

When Maddie opened her eyes, light was filtering through the shades on the window, and she realized she had slept through the night. She took a quick inventory and, since she found no unbearable pain, she decided the day was off to a good start. She found the bed control and raised herself into a semi-sitting position. She pushed buttons until she turned on enough light to supplement the diffused light from the window and looked around the room. She saw that the guest chair was empty, but a small gift bag sat on the overbed table that had been left within her reach. She peeked inside and found her Bible and prayer journal along with a small tube of her favorite hand cream and a card. On the front of the card was a beautiful nativity scene, and inside was a hand-written note:

Jaden came to get me after you went to sleep last night.

The children are asking for Mama Shenice.

I will be back after lunch.

Merry Christmas!

Love,

Shenice

Maddie sighed at the thought of spending her first Christmas out of Michael's control alone in a hospital bed. But it was also her first Christmas as a believer, so she felt a deep sense of joy and gratitude. She propped Shenice's card on the table where she could see it and rubbed some of the cream into her hands. Then she pulled the Bible into her lap and opened it. She was wondering where she could find the story of Jesus' birth when she noticed two bookmarks peeking out from between the pages. The one on her right was decorated with angels and led her to Luke 2 where two small sticky strips bracketed verses one through twenty. A smile lit her face as she began to read the original Christmas story.

She had just finished reading when the curtain was drawn back a few inches and an aide she didn't recognize peeked in. "I thought I heard you rustling around in here," she said, pushing the curtain further back and stepping in. "My name is Annie." She kept up a constant stream of chatter as she opened the shades, fluffed Maddie's pillows, and straightened her covers. "It is good to see you awake. We have monitored your vitals from the desk, and your numbers are good. How are you feeling this morning?"

"Much better, I think. My headache is gone, and everything else is bearable."

"That sounds like progress," she said. "I see on your chart that you had ice chips and water last night. The doctor said you can try juice and broth this morning. How does that sound?"

"Wonderful!"

"Good! I will go get it. A student medical assistant will be in soon to change your bandages and administer your meds."

"Meds?" asked Maddie in alarm. "You're not giving me any narcotics, are you?"

"I do not believe so, but the MA can confirm that when she comes in."

Maddie thoroughly enjoyed her liquid breakfast. The chicken

broth warmed her all the way down, and the apple juice was the best she had ever tasted. She managed about half of each but was ready for a rest by the time she finished. She had just dozed when she heard someone enter her room.

"Good morning! I am student MA Lili James, and you are," she looked down at her chart. "Madelyn Collier…"

Her voice trailed off and she looked up at the same moment Maddie opened her eyes. "Lili, is that really you?"

"Madelyn! I cannot believe it."

Lili made her way through the wires and wheels to Maddie's side and grasped her hands with both of hers. "We were not sure if you were dead or alive. What a wonderful Christmas gift!"

The two young women enjoyed their reunion for a few minutes, but duty called. "I would love to spend the day with you," said Lili, "but I have work to do."

She checked Maddie's vital signs, explaining that she preferred a hands-on approach rather than relying on machine printouts. She removed the bandage on Maddie's leg, nodded her approval on the healing, and replaced it with a smaller bandage that just barely covered the incision. When she saw the wrapping around Maddie's ribs, she shook her head in disapproval.

"We have some old-fashioned doctors here. We are no longer taught to wrap broken ribs, because the patient cannot take a deep breath. This can lead to pneumonia or a collapsed lung, and the ribs will heal on their own in a few weeks. Thankfully, the doctor said we can get you out of that corset!"

Lili's gentle and caring bedside manner made Maddie smile. "You are such a good doctor, Lili."

It was hard to tell because of the mask she wore, but she thought Lili blushed. "Oh, I have much to learn before I become a doctor, but I love the work." She examined Maddie's burns and said there were no blisters, so there should be no scarring.

"Now, I will inject a little cocktail into your IV bag, and you can go back to your nap."

"Wait!" said Maddie, putting a restraining hand on Lili's arm. "You're not giving me any narcotics, are you?"

"No, Madelyn. Your friend told us that you are recovering, so we are giving you an antibiotic to fight any infection, acetaminophen, and a vitamin complex to hopefully prevent morning sickness." She looked up from the chart and smiled. "I am sure you have been told that your baby is fine. A sonogram will be scheduled in a few weeks. But why do you look so sad?"

"Lili, I'm not sure it's the right thing to have this baby."

"But why? I remember how excited you were when you saw the pictures of my little one - who, by the way, is moving quite a bit now."

"I know. It's just that...the father of your baby is a jerk, and he treated you badly. But Michael was a criminal, a drug lord, a trafficker, a murderer. How can I inflict his baby on the world?"

"Madelyn, it is your baby, too - half its genes are from you. And if this Bible and prayer journal on your table are any indication, I would guess that you have come to be a believer since I last saw you."

"Yes, Shenice and her husband Jaden introduced me to Jesus."

Lili picked up Maddie's Bible. She opened it to Psalm 139 and found a bookmark with a picture of the Baby Jesus on it. "I see someone has already marked this passage." She handed the Bible to Maddie and pointed to verses thirteen through sixteen that had been bracketed by little sticky strips. "The whole chapter is good," she said, "but especially these verses. Read them several times and then tell me what God thinks about the baby in your womb.

"Now, one more doctor thing before I move on to my next patient. If you feel nauseous, ask one of the nurses to bring you some tea - ginger, raspberry leaf, peppermint, or anise - all are good to calm morning sickness. And dry crackers are good, too.

"I will see you tomorrow. I will recommend that the doctor move you out of ICU and into a regular room - and we will see what we can do about getting you a shower."

She was almost out the door when she stopped and turned back to Maddie. "It is so good to see you again, Madelyn. I cannot wait to tell Tatia and her family that you are here."

"Please don't do that yet, Lili. I don't understand it all, but before he died, Michael told me to be careful because I might be in danger. Contact Johnny only and make it as vague and short as possible. Ask him to set up an encrypted conversation with the family, and then we'll tell them."

Maddie read the passage from Psalm 139 twice before the nap that was interrupted by Lili's visit overtook her. As she drifted into sleep, a dreamlike voice repeated the words she had just read:

For you formed my inward parts;

you knitted me together in my mother's womb.

I praise you, for I am fearfully and wonderfully made.

Wonderful are your works;

my soul knows it very well.

My frame was not hidden from you,

when I was being made in secret,

intricately woven in the depths of the earth.

Your eyes saw my unformed substance;

in your book were written, every one of them,

the days that were formed for me,

when as yet there was none of them.

Maddie saw herself lying on a bed while a pair of hands worked inside her belly with a pair of knitting needles and a skein of yarn shaped like the double helix her tutor had made her copy out of a textbook. The needles flew, and a baby's head took shape followed by shoulders, arms, and hands. As soon as one hand was complete, the tiny thumb went into the baby's mouth. The body continued to take shape, and it became obvious that the child was a boy with chubby little legs and ten perfect toes. Then the picture changed, and a photo album appeared. The hands that wielded the knitting needles turned the pages quickly, and Maddie watched the child grow from an infant to a toddler to a little boy with wavy auburn hair, big brown eyes, and a missing front tooth. The pages stopped turning and the boy moved, grinning and holding the tooth out for Maddie to see. But before she could respond, the image began to fade leaving only a picture of an empty grassy lawn. Maddie cried out, "Wait! Scottie, don't go..."

She felt a hand on her arm. "Maddie, you are dreaming, child. I am here. Shenice is here."

Maddie opened her eyes and looked around in confusion. "Where did he go? He was just..." Her voice drifted off as she came fully awake. "Oh, I must have fallen asleep and had a dream."

"Yes," replied Shenice as she patted Maddie's hand and brushed some stray hair out of her face. "It must have been a vivid one. Who were you reaching for?"

Maddie avoided Shenice's eyes. "You know how dreams are - vivid and hazy at the same time."

"Yes, I know. Maybe you will remember later. How has your Christmas been so far?"

"It has been very nice. Thank you for the beautiful and thought-ful gift!" She gave her friend a one-armed hug. Then she brought her up to date on her breakfast, her reunion with Lili, and the results of her brief examination. "She thinks I may be moved to a regular room in the next day or two and may be able to get up and take a shower."

"That is wonderful. Have you had lunch?"

"Not yet, and I'm beginning to get a little bit hungry."

As if on cue, the aide from earlier brought in a tray with more broth and juice and several packages of saltines. "Would you like anything else? Some herb tea maybe?"

Maddie opted to try what she had first and save the tea for later. After the nurse left, Shenice pulled a couple of small plastic containers and a plastic spoon out of her bag. "You will never get your strength back on broth and juice. I brought you a little bit of macaroni and cheese as well as some sweet potato pudding - Caribbean style, of course."

After sampling a little of everything, Maddie pronounced it all delicious. "And I don't feel the least bit nauseous. I'm sure the ginger in the sweet potatoes helped! I'm sorry you're missing Christmas with your family."

"Not at all! I attended the Christmas Eve service last night in the village and watched my grandchildren open their gifts this morning. We had a festive brunch, and I left everyone else to do the cleanup!"

Maddie chuckled and then rubbed her ribs. "It feels good to laugh, but it hurts a little, too."

"I will try not to make you laugh, but I cannot promise what your friends from the village will do."

Maddie heard a commotion outside her room, and Annie pulled the curtain back. "Do you feel up to a field trip?" she asked.

"Sounds good, but how is that going to work?" replied Maddie.

"Come on in," said Annie, and a couple of orderlies came in and began unhooking machines and hooking a small IV pole onto the head of the bed. Once everything was secure, they began to roll the bed out of the room and into the waiting area outside the ICU where Maddie was greeted by the smiling faces of thirty or more men, women, and children from Shenice's village in Montserrat.

She recognized some of them from Michael's island, but some were new faces. All of them had two things in common, though - all of them wore huge smiles, and all of them carried a small gift. Since flowers were not allowed in ICU, many of the children had made paper flowers or drawn pictures. Some brought various ointments and lotions made from island ingredients; small bags with cookies, muffins, or homemade candy; and some small baby toys and hand-made clothes. Papa Jaden stood at the foot of Maddie's bed holding a handmade basket, and each person filed by, placing their gift in the basket and saying *Merry Christmas* or *Thank you*. Maddie managed to hold her emotions in check until the last little boy - who looked strangely like the child in her dream - hopped to her bed, pulled a bag of crumbled cookies out of his pocket, and dropped it in the basket. He climbed onto the lower rail at the foot of the hospital bed and, holding onto the top rail, he stared into Maddie's eyes. "Thank you for saving Papa Jaden and Mama Shenice!" he shouted, and that's when Maddie lost it.

She managed to pull herself together while Jaden read the Christmas Story and everyone sang carols. She thanked them all for making her Christmas the best she had ever had, then she gave Shenice a look that all the mothers in the room understood.

"Thank you all so much for taking your Christmas afternoon to visit our special friend, but now I think it is time to say goodbye. You have a ninety-minute ferry ride back to Montserrat, and our patient needs to rest."

Once she was back in her room, Maddie insisted that Shenice go home with Jaden. "I am so tired I will probably sleep straight through until morning. I'm doing very well, and you need some time at home. You can come back tomorrow, or you can just call me." She pointed at the phone on her table and said, "I know it's old school, but it works."

Shenice finally agreed, and Maddie settled back in her bed and began to review the day. Jaden had set the basket on a table within her reach, and she tried to remember each face as she looked at the individual gifts. When she came to the bag of crumbled cookies, she remembered the energetic little boy who gave them to her and the little boy in her dream. Both were adorable, and she could imagine how it would feel to hold them in her arms, but she still wasn't convinced that having the baby was the right thing to do.

64

Tuesday - 12/26

Annie's cheerful morning greeting and the delightful smells from the tray she was carrying convinced Maddie to finally open her eyes. She wasn't looking forward to another long day in bed, so she had tried to pass some of it by going back to sleep. It wasn't working, though, and she was glad to see the aide's cheerful face.

"Annie, don't you ever go home?" she asked playfully.

"Oh, yes Miss Maddie," she chuckled. "I left right after your party last night. My shift ended two hours earlier, but I did not want to miss the excitement. And I only arrived this morning about thirty minutes ago. Did you sleep well?"

"Pretty well. I dreamed quite a bit." She thought of the recurring image of the toddler raising his arms to her and begging *Hold you, Mommy. Hold you.* "Maybe it's because I'm so tired of this bed, and my brain was trying to entertain me through the night."

"Well," replied Annie. "I have good news for you." She set the tray down on the overbed table and moved it in front of Maddie who was raising herself into a sitting position. Annie removed the plate cover with a flourish to reveal a small serving of soft scrambled eggs, a half cup of oatmeal, and a piece of dry toast. There was also a covered cup of what smelled like ginger tea. "Since you handled liquids - and the soft food your friend smuggled in - the doctor said you may have a soft diet today. If all goes well, tomorrow you will receive the regular diet."

Maddie laughed. "Shenice didn't fool you for a minute, did she? This looks delicious, and I don't think I'll have any problems this morning. Those vitamins you're giving me must be working!"

"Excellent," said Annie. "Now I will leave you to your breakfast - but prepare yourself. The doctor also ordered you out of ICU, so in about an hour, someone will come to move you."

As predicted, Maddie thoroughly enjoyed her breakfast and had just finished the last bite of toast when a man she didn't recognize came in with a strange looking contraption with lots of velcro straps.

"I am from orthopedics, and since your incision is healing well and you are going to be moving a bit more, the doctor has ordered this femoral cast-brace that will be less awkward than this monster you have now but will provide plenty of support. I am going to make sure it fits properly, and then I will show you how to take it off and put it on."

"Will I finally be able to take a shower?"

"A modified one. Someone will be in later today or tomorrow to help you with that. You will not be able to put any weight on the leg for about seven more weeks, so you will need a bit of training. I think a wheelchair with a leg support has been ordered."

He worked while he talked and soon had her leg strapped into a device that covered her thigh from hip to knee. An extra strap connected the brace to a belt he had slipped around her waist to help hold everything in place.

"How does that feel?" he asked.

"Kind of weird," she answered. "But it doesn't hurt or anything."

"Good! I will check back this afternoon after you have moved around some to make sure it is not chafing anywhere."

"Thanks!" she said, but he was already gone to take care of his next patient.

For the next few minutes, a steady stream of people came into her room. Annie came in to pick up her tray and congratulate her on how well she ate. The doctor checked her over and seemed pleased with what he saw, and Maddie could see him talking with the nurse after he left her room. The nurse came in and removed the IV, explaining that the danger of infection had passed, and since she was handling liquids well enough to keep her hydrated, the acetaminophen and vitamins could be taken by mouth. Once the IV was gone, a physical therapist and her assistant came in with a wheelchair and helped Maddie into it, and Annie came back with a cart and began loading her personal items onto it.

The transfer to the wheelchair was made with a minimum of pain, mostly in her ribs, but she was so happy to be out of bed she hardly noticed it. During the ride to her new room, her obvious joy at the progress she was making brought many cheerful greetings, but when they wheeled her into her new room, her smile faded a bit.

"I really don't want to get back in bed right away. I saw what looked like a sunny waiting room at the end of the hall. Could I sit there for a while?"

"Good idea!" replied the therapist. "In fact, there is a small patio outside if you would like to sit in the sun for a little while."

"You are my favorite person right now!"

A few minutes later she was basking in the warmth of the sun, the smell of the ocean breeze, and the sound of random birds serenading her. Annie had set her Bible and prayer journal along with water, juice, and crackers on the table beside her, but all she wanted to do was breathe in the beautiful morning. After a few minutes, she released the brake on the wheelchair and practiced a few of the moves the therapist has shown her to reposition herself. She was just about to return to her original spot when she saw Shenice and Lili walking down the hall toward where she was sitting.

Maddie waved and shouted, "Here I am!"

Shenice hurried to her and leaned over to plant a kiss on her cheek. "It is wonderful to see you out of bed! I met your friend, Lili, and she helped me find you."

"Thank you, Lili," said Maddie, holding out her arms for a hug.

"I see you are now wireless," quipped Shenice.

"Yes, I am unplugged except for one more tube. And once the therapist comes back and teaches me to get to the bathroom on my own, that will be gone, too!"

Lili had a laptop under her arm and kept looking at her watch and then at Shenice. "Lili, do you have time to visit with us a bit, or do you have something else you need to do?" asked Maddie diplomatically.

"No, Maddie. It is just that…" She looked at Shenice uncomfortably. "The call…"

"Oh! The call. Did you get Johnny to set it up?"

"Yes, but you said…private." She lowered her voice on the last word.

Maddie laughed. "Shenice is part of private. She has been through everything I've been through since I was taken. In fact, I want our family to meet her."

Lili smiled shyly at the implication that she was part of the Matthews' extended family. "Wonderful! The call is scheduled in about fifteen minutes, so we have time to get set up."

"Will there be too much glare on the screen out here?" Maddie asked. "We can go to my room if that would be better."

"I think it will work fine out here if we move to the shade on the other side of the table. And it is less likely we will be interrupted out here."

Maddie brought Shenice up to date while Lili booted up the computer and logged into the call site. "You said to be vague, so I did not tell him who would be on the call. Let me speak to them alone first to prepare the way."

"Okay," agreed Maddie. "But let's keep this as short as possible, just in case."

Maddie sat in the middle with Lili on one side of her and Shenice on the other. When the tone sounded indicating that the call was coming through, Lili moved the laptop so only she would be on camera.

"Ready?" she asked, and when Maddie nodded her head, she clicked *GO*. A small picture appeared in the center, and Lili clicked again so the picture filled the whole screen. In the center sat Tatia and Jesse with Joy on one side and Daniel on the other. Brush and Johnny hovered in the background. Maddie covered her mouth with her hands to stifle the sob that was trying to escape. Tears trickled down her cheeks, and Shenice pressed a tissue into her hand.

"Hi, Lili," said Jesse. "Good to see you. Johnny said you were very mysterious about this - so, what's going on?"

"I did not want to give any details on an open line, because what we have to talk about could be dangerous in the wrong hands. You will understand why when you see who is sitting next to me." With that, she shifted the laptop so Maddie was center screen.

"You all look so wonderful!" she cried. "Except that your mouths are all hanging open," she giggled through her tears.

"Maddie!" Joy was the first to recover her voice. "I didn't think I'd ever see you again. The police said you died in an explosion."

"Yeah," said Johnny in a shaky voice and a red face, "but I didn't believe them."

"I know! And I know you all have a hundred questions, but

we need to keep this short for now. But first, I want you to meet Shenice." Her friend leaned into the picture and waved.

"We all love Miss Maddie!"

"So do we," said Tatia. "So tell us what we need to know and what we need to do."

"First, I'm doing very well - I was moved out of ICU to a regular room today. My concussion is gone - no more headaches - and all I have left of the burns is some dry, flaky skin. I have three cracked ribs, but I'm fine if I don't laugh - so no jokes, Daniel!" He giggled and snuggled closer to Jesse. "I have a compound fracture of my thigh, but they put in a pin and it's healing nicely. I can't put any weight on it for about seven more weeks, and I should be completely healed in four to six months. Now, to back up.

"Michael and I were married a week after I arrived, and he treated me well, all things considered. A few days before the attack - which he did not survive - he told me something bad might happen. He gave me some papers and a flash drive and instructions for getting away if something happened. He said the first thing I should do was get a very good lawyer. He said I'm not in trouble, but he didn't want anyone to take advantage of me. I don't know what to do, so I need your help."

"Of course we'll help you," said Jesse. "Tatia, your mom will probably know someone."

"I'm sure she will," she said with a wry smile. "If not, she'll meet someone. Maddie, I'll talk with Mama and get back in touch with you."

"When are you coming home?" asked Joy.

"I don't know yet, sweetie. I want to come now, but not until it's safe for all of us."

"I'll come there," said Johnny. "I can help you better from there than from here."

"Johnny, that's sweet, but if you come before we get safeguards set up, you might lead someone to me - or even worse, back to all of you. Let's just see what the attorney has to say."

"Okay. But you let me know what you need me to do - anything at all."

"I will." She paused for a moment and took a deep breath. "Before I go, I have a couple more things to tell you. First, Shenice and her husband Jaden lead a church on a small island near here. Shenice was my constant companion on Michael's island, and I am eternally grateful to her because she and Jaden introduced me to Jesus,"

She waited while everyone expressed their joy and congratulations before continuing. "Second..." Maddie hesitated, and then shook her head. "Just pray for me. I have an important decision to make."

65

Tuesday - 12/26

Before Maddie could say more, the therapist appeared with a pair of crutches and announced it was time for her next lesson. "I have to go. I love you all," she said, looking into each face and lingering a few seconds longer on Johnny. Then she ended the call.

The group gathered around the Matthews' table sat in silence for a few seconds before bursting into excited chatter, exchanging high fives, and pulling each other into celebratory hugs. Tatia was the first to recover and move into action.

"Johnny," she asked, "how long will it take to set up another encrypted call to Mama and Papa G?"

"Just a few minutes since I have everything in place."

"Let me call Mama on her cell phone to be sure they're home, and then we'll call her."

"I want to tell them about Maddie," said Joy.

"And I want to show them my new truck," added Daniel.

The Grochowskys were taking it easy after hosting their Home Group Bible study for Christmas dinner. They were almost as excited about the news about Maddie as they were to see their grandchildren. They listened carefully to the details of Maddie's situation, and Deborah nodded when Tatia asked if she could help locate a suitable attorney.

"Of course!" she replied. "I'll begin with Elizabeth. She certainly came through when we needed help for Joy. I'll call her as soon as we finish here."

Elizabeth Delaney was the District Attorney who tried Eric Hall's case in Texas. When Joy was taken, she contacted the human trafficking specialist at the Cook County State Attorney's Office and the Deputy Director of the Cook County Youth Services Department to assist in the search and rescue operation. Within an hour after they ended the call to Texas, Tatia's ministry phone, which she had transferred to their home landline for a few days, rang.

"Fallen Angel Ministry," Tatia answered. "This is Tatia. How may I help you today?"

"Ah, just the person I needed to talk to," replied a business-like voice. "I'm calling at the request of Deborah about a mutual friend who might require my assistance."

"Yes!" exclaimed Tatia. "Thank you for calling so quickly. What our friend has requested is that we set up a secure call between the two of you as soon as possible."

"Based on the little I know, that sounds like the best approach to take. Where are you located?"

"We're about an hour and a half northwest of Chicago, but we'll meet you wherever you say."

"That will work out well. I'm visiting family in the area. I can meet you at the ice cream parlor on the square in about forty-five minutes if that works for you."

"That's perfect! You'll recognize us. There's a herd of us, and we'll have a couple of biker types with us."

The professional demeanor softened as the woman on the phone let out a laugh. "Sounds like a perfect cover. See you shortly."

The meeting went very well. Brush and his family met the Matthews there, so there was lots of noise to cover the brief conversation between Jesse, Johnny, and McKenna Hartel. Dressed in casual clothes and eating a double-dip ice cream cone, she didn't look very impressive, but after a few minutes, Jesse could tell she had a brilliant mind that immediately grasped the gravity of the situation. Satisfied that she would care as intensely about Maddie as she did about her entire client base, Jesse left her and Johnny to work out the details, and he returned to his family.

McKenna informed Johnny that she had the equipment and expertise to set up the call from her office. All she required from him was Maddie's contact information and that he notify Lili to be ready to accept her call Wednesday morning at 10:30 Antigua time.

66

Wednesday - 12/27

Maddie was chewing on a saltine and drinking ginger tea when Lili entered her room around 7:30 a.m. "Are you having trouble with nausea this morning?"

"A little," she said, taking a small sip. "This is helping, though."

"Good. Your body is adjusting to being off the IV fluids. Just let me know if you need additional help to keep it under control." She motioned toward the crutches that were leaning against the side of her bed. "How are you doing with those?"

"Okay, I guess. I was a little unsteady yesterday, so the therapist told me not to try to use them without her help for now. She's going to come in this morning and see if I can manage a shower."

"I know you will enjoy that."

"Yes, I will. Bed baths just aren't the same."

Lili smiled at that and looked at her watch. "I have other duties to attend to. If possible, be on the patio at 10:30. We have a call scheduled."

Maddie worked hard during her therapy session. She learned to move from the bed to her wheelchair using her crutches. She also learned how to remove her brace before a shower and how to safely enter and exit the shower using the grab bars and her crutches. By the time she worked her way through all of that, took a brief shower, and dressed in a loose dress Shenice had brought her, she was ready for a rest. Annie, who had helped with the shower and with dressing, was still in her room, and Maddie asked if she would wheel her out to the patio.

She was enjoying the warmth of the sun on her face when Shenice joined her. "You look happy this morning," said her friend.

"I am! The bandage is gone from my leg, I took a shower, and my last tube is gone!"

"And you are wearing real clothes instead of a hospital gown. Next thing you know, I will be taking you home with me."

Maddie reached out and took her hand. "It can't be a moment too soon."

"I hope I am not interrupting anything important," said Lili, walking in with her laptop. "But we are expecting a call in ten minutes. If I read Johnny's cryptic message correctly, it is an attorney who will be calling."

"That was quick," said Maddie with a smile.

"If I am not mistaken, he will do anything it takes to get you home quickly."

Shenice looked at Maddie with raised eyebrows. "Oh, really? Is there something - or someone - you haven't told me about?"

Maddie reddened a bit. "It's not a big deal. I think I told you that Johnny is working on adding a computer repair element to the Fallen Angel family. He used his computer skills to help find Joy, and they have kind of adopted him. He found my birth certificate, and we went for ice cream and to Recovery Ministry a couple of times. That's all."

"I see," said Shenice, exchanging an understanding look with Lili.

Lili ducked her head to hide the smile on her face. "We need to get you in place now. We have two minutes."

The call came right on time, and Lili clicked to join. The image of a woman with a rather plain, square face appeared.

"Hello," she said. "I am McKenna Hartel, and may I assume you are Madelyn Collier?" Her wide mouth turned up slightly in what could have been a smile, but it did little to soften the serious expression on her face.

"Yes, I'm Madelyn, but you can call me Maddie."

"Very well, Maddie. I met with your family last night, and they asked that I contact you. Our business is confidential, so I suggest we keep our conversation between the two of us."

"Oh, it's okay if Lili and Shenice stay. Lili is part of our Fallen Angel family, who just came back to her other family to have her baby. And Shenice has been with me since I was taken, so she knows everything anyway."

"As you wish. Before we begin, do you have any objection to my recording our conversation?"

"No. That's fine."

"Very good. And do you want me to act as your attorney in the matters of settling your husband's estate and any legal issues that may arise along the way?"

"Yes, very much!"

"Last night Mr. Matthews gave me one dollar on your behalf, and based on that and your wish that I represent you, we now have an attorney/client relationship, so anything we discuss is confidential."

McKenna began to ask questions and gradually drew out everything Maddie knew about Michael's business. When she realized that Maddie knew very little about the inner workings of Saint International, she switched to asking about the information Michael gave her. After about twenty minutes, McKenna put down her pen and closed the file in front of her.

"Wow!" she said with a small break in her professional demeanor. "The feds are going to jump all over this. But first, I want to see the files and the flash drive."

"Do you want me to send them to you?" asked Maddie.

"No. I don't trust any of the carriers. I will come there. It may take me a few days to tie up some loose ends here and make travel arrangements."

"I may be released from the hospital in the next day or two," interrupted Maddie.

"And where will you go then?"

Shenice spoke for the first time. "She will come home with me to Montserrat."

"And where is that?"

"It's about ninety minutes from here by ferry."

McKenna made a note. "Good. I will be in touch to let you know when to expect me." Without further communication, she ended the call.

67

Thursday - 12/28

The physical therapist came in early to watch Maddie walk to the bathroom on her crutches and take a shower on her own. Thirty minutes later Maddie hobbled back to her bed wearing clean shorts, a t-shirt, and a ponytail that was clean but still wet.

"I did pretty good, didn't I?" she said with a grin.

"You did very well," replied the therapist. "But don't sit down yet. Let me adjust your brace a little." She tightened a couple of straps and took Maddie's crutches once she was settled in her wheelchair. "I will recommend that you be released today. The final decision will be up to the doctor."

Maddie thanked her for all the help, and she left as Annie brought in her breakfast tray. Before she finished eating, the obstetrician came in to check her one more time.

"Do you need me to move to the bed?" she asked.

"No, I will save that for next week. My office will call you to set up an appointment for a sonogram, and I will do a full exam then. Today I will make sure you are ready to travel."

He asked her a few questions to see if she was having any

issues, then he listened to her heart and lungs. Finally, he moved the stethoscope to her belly. He smiled and straightened up. "I'm not sure if I'm hearing your breakfast or your little one's heartbeat, but everything looks and sounds great. I will leave a sheet of instructions in your release papers, and I will see you next week."

Maddie was just finishing her tea when Shenice came in with a big bag to carry all the gifts she had accumulated during her hospital stay. "I am believing that you will be released today," she said. Like everyone else this morning, she wore a big smile as she hugged Maddie.

Her belief was well founded, and an hour later she was walking beside the nurse who was pushing Maddie's wheelchair toward the door. She struggled with the weight of the bag that was stuffed to overflowing, even after Maddie gave many of the gifts to nurses and staff members. Even without the gifts, Maddie was a favorite with those who worked with her, and there were more than a few tears when they said goodbye. But Maddie's tears had dried, and her smile grew brighter the closer she came to the door. Then a shadow of worry crossed her face.

"How are we going to get to the ferry?" she asked. "I'm not sure I can get on a bus."

"I have reserved a van with a wheelchair lift for this end. There is a ramp onto the Ferry, and Jaden will meet us at the other end with the van and several church members to help get you aboard and get you to the village."

"It sounds as if you've thought of everything. I don't know how I'll ever repay you."

Shenice laughed her rolling belly laugh that Maddie had grown to love. "Child, you - or rather Michael - have paid for everything. Your husband provided for you very well. There was a very large amount of cash in the bag he gave you. It was enough to pay all your medical bills that weren't covered by the government plus any extra expenses. And there is still plenty left over for you and your little one."

Maddie didn't have time to respond as the nurse rolled her onto the lift and the driver hit the "UP" button. She had seen nothing of Antigua except the hospital grounds outside her window and the little bit she could see between the trees and shrubbery surrounding the patio. Once the van began to move, she became fascinated with the wildly colored red-roofed buildings set close together in a haphazard manner. They seemed to stretch all the way to the water's edge and beyond.

"Are they floating?" she asked.

"No," explained Shenice. "They are built on stilts, and so are the wooden boardwalks on the outside."

When they reached the edge of the city and neared the sea, the landscape became a mixture of green and rocky hills. The shoreline was broken up by coves filled with clear blue water and populated with sailboats at anchor. Maddie was so absorbed with the sights that she was surprised when the van stopped. She was even more surprised when she saw the size of the ferry.

Shenice laughed again. "Did you think it would be a raft like some of those western movies you like to watch?"

Maddie laughed with her. "Maybe not that small, but I pictured something more like one of Michael's yachts. This looks like a baby ocean liner."

The driver lowered Maddie's chair and offered to push her up the ramp to the terminal. When Shenice started to object, he insisted. "You have enough to deal with, getting that bag you are carrying to the boat. It looks like the next ferry is boarding now. You buy your tickets, and I will meet you at the boarding ramp."

With his help, they found the section in the seating area set aside for wheelchairs. He secured her wheels and wished them a safe trip.

Before he left, Maddie dug through the bag and found a beaded necklace that she had received for Christmas.

"I received more jewelry than I will ever wear. Do you think your wife would like this?"

His face brightened, and he accepted the gift with a grin and a slight bow. After he left, Maddie sighed and leaned back heavily against the pillow the nurse had tucked behind her. "I was a little disappointed when I saw that I had to sit inside, but now I'm glad. I'm very tired after all the excitement. I think I'll just close my eyes for a few minutes."

"Yes, you rest," said Shenice, settling in on the bench beside her and pulling a book out of the bag. The next time she looked at Maddie, she was sound asleep, and she didn't open her eyes again until they were approaching the terminal in Montserrat.

68

Saturday - 12/30

After the warm welcome the villagers gave her and Shenice when they arrived, Maddie slept most of Friday afternoon. And as much as she wanted to take in the scenic beauty of Montserrat, from the volcanic mountains to the black sand beaches, she slept most of Saturday, too. But Shenice had received a text from Lili saying McKenna Hartel would arrive that afternoon, so she made herself get out of bed, shower, and dress in something other than her pajamas. Shenice had served her a late breakfast on the lanai that offered a beautiful view of Fox Bay Beach and Isle's Bay Beach. After she had cleaned her plate, Shenice cleared her dishes and brought back two steaming cups of tea. Maddie breathed in the warm fragrance of spices and ginger and settled back with a sigh of contentment.

"Tell me about your little island home," she said.

"Little is the operative word!" chuckled Shenice. "Montserrat is a volcanic island that is about ten miles long and seven miles wide with almost twenty-five miles of coastline. You can see the Soufriere Hills Volcano behind us. The last major eruption was near the turn of the century, and it wiped out most of the southern end of the island. You can see the ruins of two towns to the north and south of us."

"Isn't it dangerous to live in this area?"

Shenice smiled. "Probably. Most of the island population is very wealthy, and they cater to extremely rich tourists. They need us to cook, clean, and garden, but they don't want us to be highly visible. The government lets us live in this area for free because no one else wants it. We love the natural setting, we're on the leeward side of the island away from the ocean storms, and we overlook two of the most beautiful beaches on the island. Besides, the volcano hasn't had even a small eruption since 2003."

They sipped their tea in companionable silence for a few minutes. Then Maddie's face darkened a little. "Did you lose much in the raid on the island?"

Shenice shrugged and made a rocking motion with her hand. "Some. Thanks to your warning, we had bags packed with our cherished items and essentials. Most of us lived a minimalist lifestyle there, knowing we wouldn't be there permanently."

"Now that you mention it, the furnishings there were far from elaborate. But the setting was so beautiful that I didn't really notice."

"Mr. Michael paid us very well, he charged us nothing for rent or utilities, and he even furnished us with basic groceries. Most of us put aside a large portion of what he paid us, so we have enough to replace what we lost."

"No one was killed, were they?"

"No, and very few injuries. There were a few cuts and bruises, and one boy tripped on the way to the boat and broke his arm, but nothing else. God was watching out for us."

"Indeed, He was."

"Do you remember when you asked me if God would be mad at you for marrying a man like Michael?"

"Yes, and you told me that God had a purpose even for something like that."

"Exactly. Do you think that maybe part of His purpose was to save me and my people from the bombs?" She watched Maddie's face as she thought about what Shenice had said. "That's the smile I love to see! Now, if you will be okay on your own for a little while, I need to be sure Ms. Hartel's cottage is ready. Jaden will be leaving in about thirty minutes to pick her up from the ferry."

Jaden arrived back at the village with Maddie's attorney around 5:00 p.m. She wanted to sit down with her client immediately, but Shenice hustled her over to her cottage with instructions to change into something more comfortable before dinner. After dinner, she and Maddie spent about an hour together on the lanai before Maddie's eyes began to droop.

"That's enough for tonight," announced Shenice. She set a cup of tea in front of both Maddie and McKenna. "Maddie is still fragile, and she needs her rest if she's going to make it to church tomorrow morning."

"Church?" said McKenna in surprise. "But tomorrow is New Year's Eve. Don't you take the holiday off?"

"Oh," said Shenice, "there is never a holiday from the worship of God."

"And I especially want to go tomorrow since I missed the Christmas service," added Maddie. "You can come with us, McKenna. You'll love it."

McKenna took a sudden interest in the papers in the file in front of her. "I'm not much of a church person. I'll just stay in my room and go over these files until…"

"Nonsense!" exclaimed Shenice. "You look as if you could use a break yourself. You can study your files tonight before you go to bed. The service begins at 8:00 a.m. because many of our villagers must go to work in the city. We will have a nice brunch, and then Maddie can answer more of your questions if you need her."

McKenna, who was accustomed to being the one in charge, was not sure how to respond. "Well…okay," she finally managed. "When in Rome…"

Maddie faked a cough to cover a giggle while McKenna returned Michael's files and her notebook to her briefcase. "Thank you for dinner, and I will see you in the morning around 7:30."

69

Sunday - 12/31

McKenna stepped onto the lanai at 7:30 sharp dressed in black slacks and a light gray tailored shirt. She had dark circles under her eyes, but she was flushed with excitement. Maddie looked up from the tea she was sipping and smiled.

"You don't look as if you slept much, but you look wide awake." She pointed to the tray holding a teapot and several extra cups. "Help yourself to ginger tea."

McKenna frowned slightly before pouring herself half a cup. "I'm more of a coffee person myself, but I'll give it a try." She took a small sip, made a face, and set the cup back on the table.

"Shenice probably has coffee in the kitchen. She makes the tea for me to keep the morning sickness at bay."

McKenna rose but sat back down when Maddie mentioned her morning sickness. "Oh," she said, picking up the cup again. "So you're pregnant?"

"Yes. Michael and I were married on the island on October 14. I'm about six weeks along…well, probably seven now. Is that important?"

"It might be. We might be able to claim spousal privilege if there are things you'd rather not talk about." She was silent for a minute, absently sipping the tea without tasting it. "Did he leave a will?"

"I don't know. He mentioned a passport and a marriage certificate, but I don't remember anything about a will."

"I'll check this afternoon. I spent most of the evening - in fact, most of the night, going through the information on the flash drive. The feds are going to have a field day with that. But even if there is a will, they will probably contest it and try to confiscate all the funds in all his accounts."

"That's okay. I don't really want any of the money. It wouldn't seem right."

McKenna regarded her curiously. "You are an interesting young lady. Most people would be drooling and wanting to know how much they were going to get. Regardless, you are legally entitled to some reimbursements for damages suffered all the years he held you captive, not to mention the trauma of being taken at gunpoint." As she talked, she noticed that Maddie's expression changed. "Do I see a hint of interest?"

"I was just thinking about damages and suffering. I was thinking about Joy, the girl I told you about last night."

"Yes, Joy Matthews. I read about the case on the flight from Chicago."

"The men who kidnapped her are dead, probably killed by Michael. I believe he is the one who bought her. Would she be entitled to anything?"

"Very possibly." She pulled out her phone and began to type. "I'll make a note to look into it."

"Good morning, McKenna," said Shenice from the door. "I'll take the tea things to the kitchen and we'll be on our way."

"How far is it to the church?" asked Maddie. "I'm not sure I'm up to a long walk on crutches this morning."

"Neither am I," grinned Shenice as the screen door banged shut behind her. "Our ride should be here any minute," she shouted from inside.

McKenna was checking messages on her phone and Maddie was enjoying the breeze on her face when a four-wheeler appeared on the path that ran in front of the house. It was driven by a man with a familiar smile that was shockingly white against his coffee-colored skin. Maddie's eyes opened wide, and her smile was as wide as his.

"Sam!" she exclaimed. "I didn't know if you made it out or not. I was afraid you were trapped in the IT room when the raid came."

He stopped the cart in front of the porch and stepped out. He was almost as tall as Brush, but with a wiry build. "I am safe, Miss Madelyn, thanks to your warning," he said, taking her hand in both of his. "When Mama Shenice sent out her text, I grabbed my bag and ran out the door. I did not stop until I reached the beach. Skipper made it home safely, too. He should be at church today."

"That's wonderful! I can't wait to see him." Maddie looked toward the door. "Shenice will bring my wheelchair. I hope there's room for it."

"Do not worry about it, Miss Madelyn. I will be your wheels today." With that, he scooped her up in his arms and carried her down the steps, placing her gently into the seat behind the driver.

Maddie was taken by surprise by his sudden move, and she let out a laugh. "Wow, Sam! You're really strong."

"And he's a handy man to have around," said Shenice, coming out the door and taking a seat beside Sam.

McKenna slipped her phone into her briefcase. "Don't you want to lock up before we leave?" she asked.

Shenice laughed. "No one locks their doors around here. We are such a small, close-knit community that if anyone showed up with something that did not belong to them, someone would notice and report it. Now, time for church, island style."

###

It was mid-morning when the group returned to the house, and even McKenna was smiling and chatting. "The spirit of joy in your church is almost palpable - so very unlike the stiff, formal church where I was raised."

Shenice laughed. "Give us a few weeks and we will turn you into an island girl! Now, everyone get comfortable while I get the meal on the table."

"These are the most casual clothes I brought," replied McKenna, "so I'll sit on the lanai unless I can help in the kitchen."

Shenice just laughed again and went inside. "Nobody helps in Mama's kitchen except under very special circumstances," explained Maddie. "Sam, if you would give me one more ride, I'll sit with McKenna."

Sam swept her up and settled her onto a chaise lounge where she could elevate her injured leg. "If you do not need nothing else, I will go home to my own meal. I will be back this evening to drive you to the New Year's worship and celebration."

Maddie blew him a kiss and sank back into the cushions with a sigh of contentment. McKenna looked over her shoulder to make sure Shenice wasn't hovering before she shifted into full attorney mode.

"I know you will want to rest after we eat, but I want to let you know my plan of attack if that's okay," she said with an uncharacteristic lack of command in her voice.

"Sure," replied Maddie. "Shenice means well, but she does tend to be overprotective."

"Good. The material you have about Saint International and the rest of the Outfit is astounding - enough to put them all out of business if it's handled correctly. While you're resting, I plan to reach out to my contact at the FBI, and I'm sure he and others will want to do in-person interviews with you and some of the islanders who worked for Saint."

Maddie was silent for a moment as she considered McKenna's plan. "I don't want to do anything that might lead those criminals to Shenice and her people. I don't want the FBI coming here. Is there any way to meet somewhere else?"

"Understandable," replied McKenna. "I believe the feds are still combing Saint's island for human remains and information. If I can arrange a meeting there, would that be acceptable?"

Maddie cringed at the mention of human remains, wondering if there was anything left of Michael to find. "If you think we can do it discreetly enough that no one is endangered, that would be okay. But I can't go until Wednesday or later. I have an appointment on the big island for a sonogram on Tuesday."

70

Tuesday - 1/2

Between New Year's visits and celebrations, McKenna spent most of her time on the phone and computer, working out a plan that was acceptable to everyone. As she had predicted, the feds wanted to interview some of the islanders in addition to Maddie, so they granted permission for a limited number of them to visit the island. The village had not sustained as much damage as originally thought, so the visit would also allow them to sift through the ruins for any additional belongings that had survived. Jaden and Shenice would go as well as Sam, the IT tech; Skipper, the chef trainee; and several others who had close contact with Michael and his staff.

Maddie was not looking forward to returning to the island, especially since she would have to stay below deck during the trip, but she was willing to do whatever was necessary to protect those she loved. But first, she had her sonogram to deal with. While Shenice cleaned up from breakfast, Maddie practiced using her crutches by making her way to the lanai. She settled onto the chaise and let her mind drift back to the only other sonogram she had been a part of. She remembered how excited she was when she saw the scans

353

of Lili's baby, but she was not at all excited about seeing Michael's child. She tried to pray for wisdom, but she couldn't find the words.

She gave up when Jaden pulled up in front of the steps and greeted her with his characteristic smile. "Are you ready for your trip to the big island?"

Maddie returned his smile the best she could. "As ready as I'm going to get," she replied, pulling herself awkwardly to her feet with the help of her crutches. She declined his offer to carry her but allowed him to steady her as she descended the three steps. Once she was seated, he took her crutches and went inside to get her wheelchair and let Shenice know it was time to leave for the ferry terminal.

Shenice found two chairs on deck and helped Maddie into one of them before taking the wheelchair inside. After she settled beside her to enjoy the sea breeze, Maddie finally broke the silence with the question that had plagued her since she realized she was pregnant. "Shenice, I know that God creates life, but when do you think it begins?"

"I am not a scientist or a theologian, but I am a mother. People sometimes laugh when I say this, but with all my children, I knew from the moment of conception that new life was growing inside of me."

Maddie didn't respond, but her hand drifted over to rest on her still flat belly as if trying to sense the life within her. She was still lost in thought when the ferry whistle signaled their approach to the dock. The transfer from the ferry to a waiting taxi went smoothly, and before she had time to worry further, Maddie was lying on an exam table with Shenice holding her hand while a radiology technician spread a cold, slick gel on her belly.

Maddie closed her eyes, determined not to look at this reminder of her marriage to a crime boss. But when she heard a fast thumping sound, her eyes flew open. It sounded almost mechanical, and she wondered if something was wrong with the equipment.

"What's that?" she asked.

The tech chuckled. "That is your baby's heartbeat."

Maddie squeezed Shenice's hand and turned her face toward the screen. "Is that him?"

"It is your baby, but we will not know if it is a boy for several more weeks. Let me give you a closeup." The image grew in size, and the tech pointed to the small irregularly shaped oval inside the uterus. "The heartbeat sounds healthy, and the fetus is about an inch long from head to bottom. These little bumps on the sides are arm and leg buds, the head is closed, and the little pulsing spot in the middle is the heart."

Maddie reached her hand out toward the screen. "My son's heart," she whispered.

The tech smiled indulgently. "As I said, we won't be able to determine the gender for certain until twenty weeks, but you may want to schedule a genetic screening at twelve to thirteen weeks. At that point we can check for abnormalities to see if you want to continue or terminate the pregnancy, and we can attempt to determine gender then."

"Neither one will be necessary," replied Maddie. "I know it's a boy. He's already visited me in a dream." Now it was Shenice's turn to squeeze Maddie's hand. "And termination is not an option. Regardless of what a sonogram reveals - or who his father is - God is creating him, and he's perfect just the way he is."

Shenice treated Maddie to a special lunch before they boarded the afternoon ferry. "You are, after all, eating for two," she quipped. She had not stopped smiling since Maddie had made her declaration about her baby, but Maddie's smile was being replaced by fatigue. She dozed off and on in her deck chair, and when they reached Shenice's home, she barely made it to the chaise on the lanai before she was sound asleep. When she woke up an hour later, she found Shenice in the guest room packing all the baby gifts Maddie had received from the islanders and her few clothes.

"What are you doing?" she asked in alarm. "Are you kicking me out?" she continued in a failed attempt at humor.

Shenice looked up from the small pajamas in her hand and smiled sadly. "No, child. What I am doing is one of the hardest things I have ever done. After you meet with the FBI, they will most likely take you back to the United States. That is where you belong - back with the Matthews family and your other friends there. But saying goodbye will leave a big hole in my heart."

Tears began to flow down both their faces as Maddie dropped her crutches and held out her arms. Shenice caught her just before she toppled, and they sobbed out of a sorrow that was beyond words.

71

Wednesday - 1/3

The boat left Montserrat shortly after dawn, outfitted like an excursion boat taking a group of fun seekers out for a day of fishing and snorkeling. McKenna looked uncomfortable in shorts, a flowered camp shirt, and a brimmed sun hat, and she was overly anxious about the rolling suitcase she dragged behind her that held her computer, sat phone, and files. The rest of her luggage and everything Shenice was sending home with Maddie had been distributed to other passengers in picnic hampers, coolers, and tackle boxes.

Maddie and McKenna began the trip in the cabin. McKenna was content to sit at the table where she could open her laptop, spread out her files, and continue her work. But a few miles from shore, Maddie suffered an attack of cabin fever. She begged and pleaded and finally convinced everyone that, dressed as she was in a floppy hat and a long, flowered dress, she could pass as just another party girl.

"If even a blip shows up on the radar, you can hide me in the cargo hold!"

No one else was sighted except a pod of dolphins that Maddie swore were the same ones that visited her on her trips around what they had begun to refer to as Saint Island. She laughed and clapped, and the big creatures responded with arching jumps and flips, and one even rolled onto its back and waved its flipper at her.

As they neared the island, she became quiet and pensive. Shenice came and sat by her, taking her hand and sitting quietly. Finally, Maddie spoke.

"Everything will be different when I get back."

"Yes, it will. But none of it is a surprise to Jesus who is now Lord of your life. If you pray and follow His Word, everything will work out as it should."

Maddie turned and looked at her. "It sounds so simple when you say it."

"It is simple, but it isn't always easy," replied Shenice. The boat came alongside the dock and two men jumped onto it to tie up the lines. "Now it is time to go ashore and see what He has planned for the rest of your day."

A young man wearing an FBI hat stood at the end of the dock in front of a four-wheeler. As soon as the boat was secure, McKenna climbed to the dock, stretched out her short legs, and hurried to meet him. Extending her hand, she introduced herself.

"McKenna Hartel, attorney for Madelyn Collier-Saint. It will take a few minutes to get her ashore. In the meantime, I can answer any preliminary questions you might have."

The young man shook her hand and smiled wryly. "That's a fine offer, ma'am," he drawled, "but I'm fresh out of Quantico, and I'm just here to observe and run errands."

McKenna's professional exterior cracked a little, letting the island version of her personality show through. "And I'd guess fresh out of Texas based on that accent."

"Yes, ma'am," he grinned, touching the bill of his cap. "Born and raised. Most people just call me Tex. Now, if you'll be okay for a minute, I'll go see if I can help move Mrs. Saint from ship to shore."

The transfer was accomplished with no problems, and Shenice walked beside Maddie's wheelchair until they reached the end of the dock. Tex helped her into one of the back seats, but when Shenice started to climb in beside her, McKenna laid a hand gently on her arm.

"Why don't you stay with your husband for now. Someone will want to interview you both later, but for now, they would probably make you stay outside. I promise to take good care of her."

Shenice looked doubtful, but she finally nodded. "Don't let her get too tired. I brought food for lunch and will set up a buffet in the village street around noon. Make them give her a break and both of you come to share our meal."

McKenna reiterated her promise to look after Maddie and took a seat beside Tex. He kept up a constant stream of chatter about the difference in the weather from Chicago where he was currently stationed and the islands and how different the surroundings were from the dusty landscape in West Texas. When he paused to take a breath, McKenna jumped in.

"Where are we going, Tex?"

"To the air strip. Some of the big shots flew in on a Gulfstream yesterday for an inspection tour - and to talk with Mrs. Saint - and the plane is set up as the on-site headquarters."

"My client will not be able to negotiate the stairs. I hope some accommodation has been made for her."

"Yes, ma'am. They also brought in a C-130 earlier to carry the heavy equipment for going through the wreckage and everything. If they decided to use that we could just drive right up the ramp in back. But they brought a big tent and lots of wireless equipment, so it's all outside and on ground level. The weather is so nice they even raised the sides so they could enjoy the sea breeze. You and Mrs. Saint should be very comfortable."

When the air strip came into sight, Maddie wanted to look away from the wreckage, but her eyes were drawn to the twisted, blackened remains of Michael's two planes that had been pushed aside by heavy equipment to make room for the incoming aircraft. Tears came to her eyes when she spotted what was left of the limo, and she wondered if there was enough left of Ian and Adrian to bury. Her thoughts were interrupted by Tex announcing their arrival.

"Would you like me to get your wheelchair, ma'am, or would you like me to carry you to the tent?"

Maddie couldn't help but smile at his solicitous offer, but she declined both suggestions. "Thank you, Tex, but I think I'll try my crutches. I need to learn to be more independent. And, Tex, please call me Maddie."

"Yes, ma'am," he said with a grin.

Tex stayed right beside her, just in case, but she made it to a chair on her own. He found an empty chair to support her leg, and a bottle of water when she declined coffee or tea. Two agents took the flash drive and the files into the Gulfstream, and two more agents pulled up chairs in front of Maddie and McKenna.

Both men looked to be in their late forties or early fifties, but one was much slimmer than the other. He was the first to speak, holding out his hand.

"I'm Benjamin Sedano, Special Agent in Charge of the Chicago region." He shook hands with both Maddie and McKenna and then introduced the larger man as FBI Director Noah Dickerson. "Do you have any questions before we begin?" he asked.

"Yes," replied McKenna. "Before Maddie says anything, I want a guarantee in writing that nothing she says will be used against her."

"I anticipated that," said Sedano, pulling a file out of the briefcase that lay open on the table to his right. He handed McKenna two pieces of paper. "This is a letter of immunity signed by the Cook County Prosecutor. There is an extra copy for your records. If you and Mrs. Saint will sign both copies, we'll proceed."

"Please call me Maddie," she said with a quavering voice.

McKenna looked at her, and in a rare moment of sensitivity, noticed the look of fear in her eyes and put what she hoped was a comforting hand on her arm. "What's wrong, Maddie?"

"Am I in trouble?" she almost whispered. "I mean - the FBI Director, a letter of immunity - it sounds really bad."

The Director chuckled. "No, Maddie. You're not in trouble at all. I just wanted to come along for the ride."

The smile he gave her didn't reach his eyes, so Maddie wasn't convinced, but McKenna said, "Don't worry. I'm here to make sure that no one tries to accuse you of anything. Just wait a few seconds after each question, and I'll let you know whether to proceed or not. Okay?"

"Okay," replied Maddie, reassured by McKenna's softer side.

For the next two hours, Maddie told the story of her life as Michael's bride-to-be, of her escape from Misty, her time with the Matthews, her abduction, her time on the island, the raid, and her recovery since then.

"Then McKenna arrived on Saturday, and you know the rest."

The men had sat mostly silent during her recitation, with only a few questions for clarification here and there. When she finished, Agent Sedano turned off the recorder they had used with McKenna's permission.

"Wow!" he said, shaking his head slightly.

"Yes," added Director Dickerson, leaning back and folding his hands across his prominent belly. With one eyebrow raised skeptically, he said, "That's quite a tale, Mrs. Saint."

McKenna scowled at his tone and decided it was a good time to take a break. She made a show of looking at her watch and said,

"Shenice has prepared lunch, and I promised to have Maddie back by noon. It's almost that time now, so we will take a break and be back around 2:00."

Dickerson was not pleased at losing the opportunity to question Maddie when she was emotionally and physically tired and possibly vulnerable to revealing more than she intended. But he still had the upper hand.

"Good idea. Most of the task force will remain a few more days, but Agent Sedona and I have to be back in Chicago tonight. You two will return with us on the Gulfstream. We can continue our talk during the flight." He stood quickly, putting an end to further discussion. "Don't be late. Wheels up at 2:15."

Lunch was a somber meal with more food being pushed around the plates than eaten. Jaden finally stood and shouted "Enough!" He used his preacher voice, startling everyone around the table and focusing every eye on him. "We all knew this day was coming. We all know that Madelyn's place is in Heart City in the United States with Mr. and Mrs. Matthews, their two children, all their friends, and especially with Mr. Johnny."

Everyone around the table nodded knowingly and grinned, and Maddie looked startled that so many knew about Johnny. She smiled shyly, and a slight blush rose in her cheeks. "I guess I must have talked about him more than I realized," she laughed and everyone joined her.

Sam, who had been silently working on his laptop, looked up and said, "I may be able to lighten the mood a bit, Ms. Maddie. I have some people here who would like to speak with you." He moved the computer so it was in front of her and clicked *Join Conversation* in the middle of the screen. There in front of her were Tatia, Jesse, Joy, Daniel, Brush, and Johnny.

"Surprise!" they said in a ragged chorus. "And happy New Year!" added Joy.

"Oh!" Maddie cried, reaching out toward the screen. "You all look wonderful. I miss you so much."

"Us, too!" said Jesse. "Sam said you have something to tell us and that you only have a minute or two. What's your big surprise."

Maddie looked at McKenna with a question in her eyes. The attorney smiled and nodded. "It's okay," she said.

"Well," Maddie took a deep breath, "apparently I'm coming home."

"What? When?" The group in Heart City all spoke at once.

"We take off from here in about thirty minutes. Flight time is almost seven hours."

"Where will you land?" asked Jesse. "We'll pick you up."

"No," interrupted McKenna. "I'll bring her to you. We want to keep you as safe as possible. I have a plan that hopefully will minimize the possibility of your location being compromised."

Tatia laughed nervously. "You make it sound like the mob might be after us or something."

"Exactly." replied McKenna. "I don't mean to be abrupt, but we have to go. We should be at your home between 9:30 and 10:00 your time. I'll explain more then."

She stood and left Maddie to say goodbye. Maddie laughed at Daniel who was celebrating with a football touchdown dance he had invented while she was still with them, and Joy was already trying to negotiate a later bedtime with Tatia. "You all can work out the details on your end. I'll see you in a few hours, so have my bed ready. I love you all. Bye!"

Her island friends were thrilled to see the love between Maddie and her American family, and they cheered and clapped when the call ended.

"That's better!" declared Jaden. "Now, several of you men go bring the ladies' luggage. The rest of you bring all the four-wheelers. We're all going to escort Maddie and McKenna to the plane."

"But the Director is sending Tex to pick us up," protested McKenna.

"If he arrives before we leave," replied Jaden, "he can join the parade. But Maddie is one of our own, so we will give her an island sendoff."

When Tex drove up fifteen minutes later, he was shocked to see a miniature version of the Rose Parade lined up on the path to the air strip. Half a dozen four-wheelers were decked with palmetto branches and bunches of flowers. All the women had flowers in their hair and a few of the men wore leis that had been hastily put together by twining a few flowers into braided vines. Even Maddie's crutches were decorated with flowers, and most of them remained in place as she hobbled toward the first cart in the line. All the other carts were packed - all seats taken and extra passengers standing on the running boards.

"Welcome back, Tex," said Jaden. "Perfect timing. We need one more cart to carry the luggage."

"Wow!" said Tex with a wide grin. "I don't know what Director Dickerson will think of all this, but I like it! Can I have one of those necklaces, too?"

The luggage was loaded, and an extra lei was produced for Tex. Someone began singing a joyful native song, and everyone was soon singing along. Maddie didn't understand all the words, but she recognized the word for *home* and hummed along, getting more excited as the procession began to move. The excitement flagged, though, when the jet came into sight, and she grabbed Shenice's hand and squeezed.

As soon as their cart stopped, Jaden stood and took charge. He appointed two men to help Tex load the luggage and then told everyone else to gather around. "We don't have much time, but if you have a special memory of our time with Madelyn that you would like to share and can do it in a few words, now is the time."

All eyes were on Maddie as, one after the other, they began to speak.

"I remember how beautiful you looked on your wedding day."

"I remember how excited you were when we raised the sails on your first outing on the yacht."

"And when you caught your first fish."

"And saw your first pod of dolphins."

"I will never forget the shine in your eyes the day you met Jesus."

"My little girl will never forget how you picked her up when she skinned her knee."

The memories and tributes went on until SAC Sedona appeared and cleared his throat. "I really hate to end this, but Director Dickerson says we are already late and wheels will be up in five minutes. Mrs. Saint - Maddie - two of my men will carry you on board."

Sam stepped forward. "It would be my honor to be your wheels one last time, Maddie."

She looked imploring at Sedona. "Please?"

He sighed and nodded.

Jaden raised his hand high and shouted, "Circle up!" All Maddie's island friends gathered close around her, either touching her or touching someone who was near her. When all heads were bowed and silence had fallen, Jaden pronounced a blessing from the Book of Numbers over her. "May the Lord bless you and keep you; may the Lord make his face to shine upon you and be gracious to you; may the Lord lift up his countenance upon you and give you peace. Father, thank you for bringing Maddie into our lives and for what she has meant to all of us. Now go with her and go before her. Bring her safely to her home in America, and may we see her again, either in this world or the next. Amen."

Maddie clung to Shenice while people quickly passed by to say one last goodbye. Finally, the older woman gently extricated herself from Maddie's grasp and lifted her chin until they were eye to eye.

"You can do this. You are not alone. Like Paul, you have learned to be content in all circumstances, and also like him, you can do all things through Him who gives you strength. I am just a phone call or an email away, and if the Lord wills it, we will see each other again before too long. After all, we need to meet your little one before he is a grown man."

Maddie smiled through her tears at the mention of her son, and kissed Shenice on the cheek. "Thank you for everything." Then she turned and hugged Jaden. "And thank you for introducing me to Jesus." Without another word, she turned to Sam and allowed herself to be swept up into his arms and carried into the plane.

Seated and belted in, Maddie watched out the window as her friends waved and blew kisses, growing smaller as the Gulfstream raced down the runway and into the air. When she could no longer see them, she collapsed back into her seat and closed her eyes. Even Director Dickerson could see that she was emotionally and physically wrung out. When McKenna suggested that he and Agent Sedona go through the files with her for a couple of hours while Maddie rested, he agreed.

McKenna carefully laid out what she had gleaned from the files which contained detailed financial records and names, dates, and details of crimes. There were also recordings of meetings that incriminated men the FBI had been seeking to prosecute for decades. Beside this information, she laid out what they had learned from questioning Maddie, pointing out that she had absolutely no contact with anyone other than Michael Saint, his second-in-command, Ian Childress, and a few nameless bodyguards.

"Maddie is more than willing to tell you anything she knows," stated McKenna when they took a brief break from their work. "But I am convinced that she has no information that will be of value to you. I must insist on total discretion and anonymity for her safety and the safety of her unborn child."

"Are you asking for witness protection?"

"No, I just want you to leave her out of your public reports and anything that might leak to the public. These crime families are like the old Roman emperors, wanting to wipe out any trace of their predecessors' families. No one needs to know that Saint had a wife and a child."

When Maddie woke from her nap, the agents asked her a few more questions, but she was able to spend most of the flight reading and writing in her journal. When the lights of Chicago appeared below, she really began to believe that she would see her family soon. McKenna could see the excitement and anticipation in her face and it warmed her. She wondered, not for the first time, how this young woman and her friends had so easily broken through her tough, professional exterior to a soft side she thought no longer existed.

When the Gulfstream finally touched down on a private airstrip outside the city, the Uber van McKenna had ordered was waiting at the small office building. The driver earned a good rating and a better tip by loading all the luggage and by moving the van to the foot of the steps of the plane to make Maddie's transfer easier. She refused to give Dickerson Maddie's contact information, insisting that any communication come through her.

"Where to, ma'am?" asked the driver when they reached the exit gate. McKenna gave him the address of a hotel about ten miles away where an agent from a rental company was waiting in the parking lot with a van. Again, the transfer of vehicles was accomplished quickly and easily, and more money changed hands.

"Why did you tip them so much," asked Maddie once they were on the road.

"So that if anyone asked, they would remember only me."

Maddie thought she would sleep on the way to Heart City, but she was too excited to close her eyes. When they pulled into the driveway, the door of the house burst open before the engine was turned off and the entire Fallen Angel Family including all four Matthews, Brush and his wife and son, and Johnny came tumbling out. Maddie was home!

72

Thursday - 1/4

Maddie woke the next morning to the familiar sound of Brush's motorcycle pulling into the driveway at 6:30 a.m. She smiled and stretched, feeling refreshed in spite of her late night. But Joy was still sleeping, so she lay quietly and thought about her homecoming the night before.

Brush carried her into the house with the whole family trailing behind, everyone talking at the same time. Brush set her gently in Tatia's chair so she could rest her leg on the ottoman. Joy and Daniel hung over the big rolled arms of the chair, and Shawn, who didn't know her very well, settled into Shawna's lap and soon fell asleep. Tatia offered herb tea and decaf coffee all around, and then an awkward silence fell. So much had happened that no one knew where to start.

Maddie finally broke the silence by asking Daniel what he got for Christmas. He showed her the latest addition to his toy truck collection and a new football since his old one rolled in the street and got "runned over" by a passing truck. Joy modeled her new pajamas and pointed to a stack of new books on the table.

"I got some neat new clothes, too, but I'll show you those tomorrow. You were in the hospital on Christmas. Did you get anything?"

"Oh, yes! Many of the villagers rode the ferry to Antigua and brought me gifts of food and pretty sea shells and lots of…well, if someone will bring that blue bag, I'll show you."

When she had the bag in her lap, she stared at it for a minute, trying to find the words. "On our first video call I asked you to pray for a decision I had to make. I made it, and I brought someone home with me."

"A puppy?" asked a wide-eyed Daniel.

"No," chuckled Maddie. "Not a puppy." She pulled out a small frame that held a copy of her ultrasound. She handed it to Joy and asked, "What does that look like?"

Joy stared at it for a few seconds before her mouth fell open and her eyes widened. "It looks like Lili's baby! You're going to have a baby?"

Maddie held up a bib with a teddy bear on it. "I got a lot of things like this for Christmas. What do you think?"

"I think yay!" shouted Joy, and then she clapped her hand over her mouth when Shawn mumbled and shifted. "I think that's amazing!" she said more quietly. She leaned further across the armrest and gave Maddie an awkward hug.

"I think yay, too!" echoed Daniel. He leaned over with his mouth close to Maddie's belly. "Hello, baby. Come out and play soon!"

The adults all laughed, but Maddie noticed some less than excited expressions. Johnny wouldn't look at her as a fiery red color crept up his face. Shawna nodded with a look of understanding, and Tatia unconsciously leaned toward her with compassion in her eyes.

"And you weren't sure whether you could handle this after being abducted, married, and widowed in the space of a few months."

"Yes, and I wasn't sure I wanted to have Michael's baby,"

answered Maddie, drawn by her concerned look. "But God let me see him in a dream - by the way, I'm sure it's a boy." At this, Johnny seemed to get his initial reaction under control, and he raised his head and grinned a little bit. "Shenice showed me Psalm 139, and then I saw his little heart beating. After that, there was no decision to make."

The next morning, memories of her warm homecoming made her smile all over again. She stretched and realized that the pressure her enlarged uterus was putting on her bladder couldn't be ignored any longer. She couldn't imagine how stressful this would be when the baby really began to grow. She sat up, pulled on her robe, and grabbed the crutches that were leaned against the wall next to the headboard. She stood without making any noise, but she had only taken a step or two when she heard Joy's sleepy voice.

"Wait! Wait! I'll open the door for you."

Joy escorted her to the bathroom, and after making sure the toilet seat was in the proper position, she closed the door behind her. Maddie smiled at Joy's hovering, and thinking about how much she had missed her American family eased some of the pain of leaving so many behind on the island. When Maddie had washed her hands and called for the door to be opened, Joy escorted her into the kitchen where the rest of the family was gathered around the table drinking coffee and eating warm blueberry muffins. Johnny, who was sitting in the chair at the end of the table, jumped up and pulled out his chair.

"Here," he said, "sit here. It'll be easier to get in and out." She sat and he took her crutches and leaned them against the wall. "Just let me know when you want to get up, and I'll get those for you. Do you want me to bring the ottoman over here so you can elevate your leg."

"No, thank you, Johnny," she said, trying not to let her smile break into a laugh. She appreciated his thoughtfulness, but she had some work to do to convince him she wasn't made of porcelain.

"We've contacted Dr. Patterson, and he's going to stop by later today to check you out and see what we need to do for you," said Jesse once Johnny was settled again. "Is there anything you can think of that you will need?"

"Yes," she replied. "I'll need a shower chair. I can take my brace off to take a shower, but I won't be able to put any weight on my leg for several more weeks. Other than that, I think I'm good."

After the men left to open the shop, Tatia sent the children to their rooms to get dressed while she took a shower, and Maddie followed Joy to their room to see what she could get into with her brace. Tatia had just finished drying her hair when Joy appeared at her door with a distressed look on her face.

"Mommy, we can't get Maddie's jeans on, and I think she's about to cry."

"Tell her to just relax, and I'll be right there."

Tatia found both girls lying back on Maddie's bed. Joy was telling her knock-knock jokes, and Maddie was laughing through her tears. Tatia sat down on the edge of the bed.

"Okay, tell me the problem."

"The problem," answered Maddie, "is that it's much easier to pull on a loose dress for warm weather around this stupid brace than it is to put on jeans for cold weather. I have to have something under the brace or it chafes my skin - but if I try to put the jeans on first, it hurts. And if I put on shorts and then the brace - which is what I have been doing - the jeans won't fit over the brace. And I'm so tired of being helpless!"

Tatia laid down beside her and pulled her into a hug. "I know. You've been through so much, and that little one inside you is making your hormones crazy. Sometimes you just gotta scream. Let's all scream!"

All three of them let out a scream that would put any banshee to shame, and Daniel came running in with wide eyes. "Mommy, what's wrong! Do I need to go get Daddy?"

They looked at him and burst out laughing. Tatia reached out and pulled him onto the bed with her. "No, son. We're just letting off a little steam. Do you want to do it with us? Let's all scream again!" And they did.

"Now that we have that out of our systems," she said, standing up and setting Daniel on his feet, "I think I have a solution to your problem. Be right back."

Two minutes later she appeared with a pair of navy blue sweat pants in one hand and a pair of tan suede boots with an off-white fleece lining in the other. She held out the pants and said, "See if you can slip these on over your brace."

With a minimum of contortion, Maddie was able to get the sweat pants on. "The waist is a little big," she said, "but I can cinch them up with the drawstring. And I'm sure I'll grow into them."

"Yes, you will. Now, let's try the boots."

"Shouldn't I put on socks first?"

"Honey, these are UGG boots from a decade ago. You wear them however you can, and when you're finished with them, we can throw them in the trash if we need to."

Maddie slipped right into them with a little help from Joy when she couldn't push her heel down. "These feel great - soft and warm! Thank you so much! Now I'm ready to help with school or just stay out of the way."

"Come on!" invited Tatia. "You can quiz Daniel on his spelling words."

The morning flew by, and the lunch table had just been cleared when Dr. Patterson tapped on the door. He checked Maddie's vitals, and after a general exam, declared her healthy. "So how are you doing on the drugs with your injuries and all?"

"Good," she said. "Mama Shenice, the personal assistant Michael hired for me, watched me like a mother hen. When I was in the hospital, she wouldn't let them give me anything stronger than acetaminophen, and she prayed for me a lot. In fact, she and her husband led me to Jesus, and He filled a lot of the empty spots the drugs used to fill."

"Excellent medicine! Now, your ribs seem to have healed nicely, and I see no lasting effects from your concussion or your burns. You will need to see an orthopedist about your leg and physical therapy. I have a colleague who owes me a favor and will see you here."

"Dr. P., how do you know so much about my injuries?"

"Oh, didn't I mention? Your attorney came by my office this morning and dropped off a flash drive with your medical records from Antigua including x-rays and MRI images. She is definitely worth every penny you're paying her."

"That would be nothing so far. Michael put some cash in my go bag, but I think most of that has already been spent for medical bills. I don't know how I'll pay an orthopedist."

"Ms. Hartel said if you mentioned money to tell you not to worry about it. She has it handled. And she said that she will come by one day next week and bring you up to date. Back to your healthcare, what about your pregnancy? Do you want a regular OB-GYN or a midwife?"

"Do you deliver babies?"

"I have delivered my share over the years."

"I'd like you to continue to care for me and my son if that works for you."

"Of course, although I can't guarantee a boy. Do you have any questions for me before I go?"

"Yes! I was taking some vitamins to help fight nausea. Do my records show what they were?"

"Of course. I'm glad you reminded me." He reached into his bag and pulled out a plastic bag stuffed full of vitamin samples.

"Oh, no!" objected Maddie. "That's too many. What about your other patients?"

"My dear," he said with a laugh, "most of my patients are asking for cures for hot flashes. I'm glad to put these to good use before they go out of date."

He brought in a bath stool and walker he had left on the porch. "I'll leave these for you to use until you can stand on your own. If you need me, call any time. Otherwise, I'll see you in two weeks."

Dr. Patterson let himself out, and Tatia brought the children back inside from the break they had taken to give her some privacy. They were just settling down to some free reading time when there was another tap on the door.

"The good doctor must have forgotten something," said Tatia. She was surprised when she opened the door to Johnny. "Hi, Johnny. What's up?"

"Um," he said hesitantly, "could I talk with Maddie for a couple of minutes?"

"Sure. Come on in. Hey, kids, grab your coats. I think I saw some unusual birds flying toward the park. Joy, you get the binoculars and Daniel, you get the drawing tablet and colored pencils. Let's go do some bird watching!" She looked at Johnny and said, "This will last about fifteen minutes at most."

"Okay," he said with a red face. The door closed behind Tatia and the kids, and Johnny stood in front of Maddie staring at the floor.

"Johnny, why don't you sit…"

"Maddie, let me say this before I lose my nerve." He dropped to one knee and took her hand in both of his. He finally raised his head and looked into her eyes and said, "Madelyn Jeanette Collier…I mean Saint…uh…would you do me the honor…"

Maddie quickly laid the index finger of her free hand against his lips. "Johnny, hush," she said softly. "I know what you want to say, and I'm very touched, but not now." She smiled warmly at him, hoping to take some of the hurt from his eyes. "Johnny, get up off the floor and come sit by me."

He stood and sat down beside her, but he didn't let go of her hand. She didn't object. In fact, she covered his hand with her free hand. "Johnny, I am so thrilled to see you. Before I was taken, I hoped we might have a future together, and I thought about you every day while I was gone. But it's too soon. In a little over three months I have escaped from the woman who held me captive most of my life, I have gone through withdrawal and detox, I identified a dead body, I remembered how my mother died and learned my true identity, I had - or almost had - my first birthday party, I was abducted, married, almost blown up, and discovered I'm going to be a mother. I need some time to catch my breath. But in the midst of that, I met Jesus, and if it's His will that we be together, He will make it happen in His timing. Do you understand what I'm saying?"

"Yes, I do. I didn't get a chance to tell you, but while you were gone, I met Jesus, too, so I understand about His timing."

"That's wonderful," she cried, throwing her arms around his neck and kissing his cheek. "Now we are brother and sister in Christ." Then she realized what she had done and sat back.

"But I don't want to be your brother. I want you to know that, when the time is right, I want to be your husband and the father of your son."

"Even though he's the son of a major crime boss?"

"Even then. He is your son, too, and I know how wonderful you are."

"You are a very special man, Johnny, and my son would be very blessed to have you for a dad. But for now, let's just spend some time getting to know each other better. Deal?"

"Deal."

73

Friday - 1/6

Friday morning Maddie crutched to the bathroom and into the kitchen without Joy's assistance, but before she could join the family at the table, she felt a small pat on her hand.

"Hey, Maddie," said Daniel who was standing beside her and holding out a phone. "The day the helicopter came, you dropped this under the table. I put it in my toy box to keep it safe until you came home."

"Oh, Daniel!" she cried. "Thank you so much! Can you bring it to the table for me, and then I want to give you a great big hug!"

He grinned and strutted to the table where he proudly placed the phone at the seat where she normally sat now. While Maddie sat down and gave Daniel the promised hug, Johnny picked up the phone and looked it over.

"It's dead," he announced, "but that's to be expected. I'll take it to the shop and charge it up for you. I'll check it over and bring it back at lunchtime."

"Great! I wish I had my phone from the island. I had lots of pictures on it. But I was told not to take it when we ran because

377

someone might track me through it. I don't know how. It wasn't much more than a two-way radio with a camera. Michael didn't want me to get on-line or contact anyone off the island." She saw a flash of anger in Johnny's eyes, but it passed quickly.

"Not cool," he said under his breath. Then to her he said, "Do you have any contacts you want me to add?"

"Add McKenna, also Lili and Shenice if we have their information. And be sure your number is in there if it isn't already," she said with a hint of flirtation in her eyes.

Once the guys had gone to work, Joy asked Maddie if she needed help getting dressed this morning. "With the sweat pants, I think I can handle it myself. But I want to take a shower first." She directed a questioning look toward Tatia.

"Everything's ready for you in our room - the step-in shower should be easier for you. I set up the shower chair, my dressing stool, and the walker Dr. P left. There's also a drying rack with a towel, wash cloth, and fresh clothes. Why don't you leave the door open in case you need something."

Maddie accomplished her shower successfully, and as she tidied up before returning to the living room, she couldn't help but compare the simple surroundings with her luxurious suite in Michael's house. She wasn't surprised that she was much more content here than she was there.

Once back in the living room, she collapsed on the sofa with a sigh. Daniel, who had been lying on the floor copying his spelling words in large block letters, climbed onto the sofa and snuggled against her. He held his paper in front of her face and asked. "Do you want to quiz me again?"

"Daniel..." began Tatia.

Maddie held up her hand. "It's okay. As long as I can do it sitting down, I'm good."

After they finished his spelling words, he brought his reading book to Maddie. "Want me to read to you?"

Tatia looked at Maddie questioningly, and Maddie smiled. "It's okay. I'd love to listen to you read." Daniel entertained her with a very dramatic reading of *The Monster at the End of This Book*. The more she laughed, the more dramatic he became.

Finally, he handed her the book and said, "You do the turning the pages part and I'll do the Grover parts."

They were so into the story, they didn't notice that Joy had stopped to watch and Tatia was making a video with her phone. When Jesse and crew came in the back door expecting lunch to be on the table, Joy shushed them and pointed to the performance in progress. When the last page was finished, the small audience broke into applause. Maddie and Daniel looked at each other in surprise, and Daniel took a deep bow. She pulled him close, carefully avoiding her damaged leg, gave him a squeeze, and kissed the top of his head. Then she motioned Joy over and dragged her into the hug.

"Oh, how I missed you two! I was afraid you'd be all grown up by the time I saw you again." Her voice broke, and a heavy silence fell.

Tatia was the first to regain her composure. "I know we're all glad to have you back, but right now, I know some guys who would also be glad to have lunch on the table. Whose turn is it in the kitchen with me?"

"That would be me, ma'am," said Jesse with a mock salute. "Awaiting orders."

In just a few minutes hands were washed, the table was set, and everyone was seated in front of bowls of beef stew, plates of salad, and lots of crackers. Conversation was lively, but Johnny spent most of the meal watching Maddie in case she needed anything. When the meal was finished and Jesse and Tatia were cleaning up, Johnny handed Maddie her phone.

"I put it on the supercharger, so it's up to 100%. I think I added all the pertinent contacts. I also added some safety apps which should keep you from being hacked or tracked. If you find something I forgot, just let me know and I'll take care of it. Oh, and I emailed Shenice. I gave her this number and asked her to send any pictures she has of your time with her."

Tatia watched out of the corner of her eye and thought he reminded her of a puppy eager to please - and Maddie seemed very pleased. Jesse closed the dishwasher and started it, and Tatia dried her hands and announced, "Okay, everybody! It's quiet time around here and time for you working types to get back to earning a living. Joy and Daniel, choose a book and get comfortable on the floor. Let's leave the sofa for Maddie. And Maddie, I need to go over to my office for a little while. Can I ask you to be sure they are at least quiet if not sleeping?"

"Of course! My pleasure."

Tatia stood in the doorway for a few minutes watching the three settle down and Harley trying to decide who to grace with his company. "Thank you, Lord," she whispered, "for keeping all my family safe."

When Tatia returned about an hour later, both Maddie's legs were resting on the ottoman and the broken leg was also resting on a pillow. One child was snuggled up under each arm and all three of them were sound asleep. Tatia tried to move about very quietly, but when Harley saw her, he meowed a very loud welcome, and Daniel stirred and rubbed his eyes.

"Is it snack time yet?" he asked.

Tatia put a finger to her lips, so he repeated his question in a very loud, emphatic whisper.

Maddie and Joy both yawned and opened their eyes. "Nice job, buddy," smiled Tatia.

"Yeah," said Daniel proudly. "I whisper real good!"

"Well, it's not quite time for snacks yet, so why don't you get out your math notebook and do the next sheet of addition problems."

Joy yawned again and stretched. "Math for me, too?"

"Yes, ma'am," replied Tatia, going into the kitchen to put together spaghetti sauce for dinner.

To add to the activity, Maddie's phone rang. "Perfect timing," she laughed. "Hi, McKenna. I didn't know you had this number?"

McKenna explained that Johnny had texted it to her earlier in the day when he was working on her phone. She went on to give Maddie the name of the orthopedist Dr. Patterson had chosen. She had called his office on Maddie's behalf to be sure he was taking new patients and had emailed Maddie's medical records and contact information to his office. Anticipating Maddie's concern about payment, McKenna continued.

"As for payment, I explained your situation, and they are content to wait for a resolution. And concerning that, I am working on some new information that has arisen and will call you with details early next week." With that, she ended that call abruptly, leaving Maddie holding a silent phone.

"Who was that?" asked Daniel. "You said 'uh-huh' a lot."

"That was her lawyer," interjected Joy. "Lawyers talk really fast." She stopped with a puzzled look on her face. "But they get paid by the minute, so you'd think they would talk slower."

Maddie was still laughing when her phone rang again. "This must be the doctor's office," she said, answering the call. They agreed on Monday at 1:00 p.m., and since McKenna had sent all the necessary information, the call lasted less than two minutes. She had just laid the phone down and reached for her crutches when the phone rang a third time.

"Hi, Johnny. It's a good thing you fixed my phone this morning. I've had three calls in the last ten minutes.

"No other gentlemen callers, I hope," he joked.

"No, just my lawyer and the doctor's office. That seems to be the story of my life these days."

"How about I take you away from all that? Do you want to go for a burger and some ice cream when I finish work?"

"I'd love that! I've been craving a salted caramel sundae for weeks! But how will we get there? I don't think I can swing a leg over the bike!"

"No worries. Brush bought a big SUV and sold me his hybrid."

"We're all set then!"

Tatia assured her that a sweat suit was acceptable for a casual date, especially under the circumstances, so Maddie spent the afternoon reading quietly. When Johnny picked her up, he showed just the right mixture of being helpful and allowing her to move independently.

Maddie really enjoyed the fries, because Michael's chef would never lower himself to preparing anything so common. But she especially enjoyed getting reacquainted with Johnny in their new circumstances and exchanging stories about their new relationship with Jesus. On the way to the ice cream parlor, they talked about the challenges of life on one leg. And then, once they were settled at their favorite table with their ice cream in front of them, Johnny asked her to tell him about her life on the island.

"Do you want to know about Michael?" she asked hesitantly.

"Only if you feel a need to tell me about him. What I really want to know is who all the people are in the pictures Shenice sent."

Her face brightened, and she spent the next hour introducing him to Jaden, Shenice, and their family and friends. Before they knew it, the evening was almost gone. He cleared the table and helped her back to the car.

"By the way," he asked when they were almost back to Fallen Angel. "Do you want to go back to Recovery Ministry next Wednesday?"

"Absolutely! I've had Shenice watching me like a mother hen for any sign of going back to the drugs, but I need to strengthen my own will power and resolve."

"Great! I'll bring the car to work and we can go from there."

Tatia had just finished cleaning the kitchen when they arrived, and she invited Johnny to stay for coffee. "No, but thanks. I need to do some laundry, and you need some family time."

"Okay, but I have a favor to ask."

"Anything."

"Maddie would like to go to church Sunday, but she's afraid she's not ready to handle all morning. Would you mind skipping Bible study and bringing her to church?"

His grin said the answer was obvious, but he answered anyway. "It would be my honor," he said with a slight bow.

"My knight in shining armor," Maddie said, giving him a kiss on the cheek. He turned bright red and said good night.

74

Monday - 1/8

Maddie woke up when she heard what she considered her week-day alarm clock - the sound of Brush's motorcycle arriving at 6:30 on the dot. Joy's bed was already empty, but Maddie stayed in bed for a while, reliving her first church service with her U.S. family. It was very different than what she had experienced on Montserrat, but she felt the strong presence of the Lord and loved how the Pastor preached directly from the Word. What she kept coming back to, though, was the look Johnny gave her when he picked her up. It wasn't the look Michael gave her, as if she was a piece of artwork. It was a look from his heart. It warmed her, and it scared her a little.

Her thoughts were interrupted when the door opened quietly and Tatia looked in. When she saw that Maddie was awake but still in bed, she said, "I can come back later if you want to sleep in for a while. I can get these sheets later."

"No, come on in. I was just about to get up." She sat up and stretched. "I slept most of the afternoon yesterday, and I slept really well last night. But I still feel tired. Why is that?"

"It's hard work learning to live without drugs, it's hard work mending a leg bone, and it's hard work growing a baby. You're doing all three!"

By the time Maddie pulled herself together a little and made her way to the kitchen, Tatia was already there with coffee, fruit, and a muffin waiting for her.

"Thank you," she said, smiling a little sheepishly. "I may need a bowl of cereal, too. This baby is starving this morning."

"That's a good sign," said Jesse. "When Tatia started eating everything in sight, it meant the morning sickness was over."

The morning went quickly. The children had finished their first segment of lessons and were playing outside before Maddie finished her quiet time and her shower. Then Johnny surprised her with a video call to Jaden and Shenice. She almost cried when she saw their smiling faces, but the tears dried quickly as they talked and laughed together. Lunch came and went, and she had just settled onto the sofa to read for a few minutes when the doorbell rang. Tatia opened the door and was surprised to see a woman who looked to be in her mid-forties standing there and holding a large case.

"Dr. Riley Bourland," said the woman, extending her free hand.

"Oh," said Tatia, shaking the woman's hand. "I was…"

"I know. You were expecting a man. My mother was determined to name her first child after her father. You must be Mrs. Matthews."

"Yes, of course," said Tatia, stepping back so the doctor could enter. She indicated Maddie on the sofa. "And this is your new patient, Madelyn Collier." Maddie had stored her married name in a drawer along with her wedding rings as soon as she arrived in the States.

For the next half hour, Dr. Bourland checked out Maddie's leg, her use of the crutches, and her shower situation, and she showed Maddie the x-rays that had been included in her digital files.

"Everything looks good," she announced. "Your Caribbean doctors did a good job, and you're getting around very well on your crutches. Just continue to keep that foot off the floor for now. I'll set up a physical therapist to come in twice a week to prevent muscle loss and to be sure you maintain your range of motion. I'll see you in two weeks, and we'll plan to do an x-ray and an MRI in about six weeks to see if you can begin to put some weight on that leg. Do you have any questions for me?"

Maddie had no questions, so the doctor packed her bag and took her leave - and then Maddie took a long nap. When she emerged from her room later in the afternoon, Tatia said she had received two phone calls while she was asleep.

"I didn't want to disturb you, so I answered them. One was the physical therapist. He wants to come on Tuesday and Thursday, so he'll be here tomorrow morning around 11:00. And your attorney called. She wants to come by tomorrow afternoon. She says she has some really good news to share."

Maddie wondered what kind of news McKenna had, but she didn't have time to think much about it. Daniel and Joy wanted her to play a board game with them, and then it was time for dinner. After dinner, she managed to stay awake for half a movie, but then she excused herself and went to bed.

75

Tuesday - 1/9

Tuesday morning, Maddie's first priority was to get ready for physical therapy. Her session went well, although some of the movements were a bit painful.

"I know," the therapist said when she grimaced as he carefully moved her leg. "You won't like me much now, but when you're back on your feet, you'll be making me pies."

Her favorite part was at the end when he put a cold pack he had brought in a small cooler on her leg. She enjoyed it so much that he left it with her.

Lunch came and went in a rush, and McKenna came during quiet time. Everyone including Daniel was awake when she arrived, excited to hear the good news. McKenna wasn't used to working with an audience, though.

"Is there somewhere private we can meet?" she asked.

"That won't be necessary," replied Maddie. "I have no secrets from my family. In fact, I texted Jesse and asked him to join us so we don't have to repeat everything."

On cue, Jesse walked in the back door, and they all gathered in the dining area. McKenna pulled two files out of her briefcase and put them on the table.

Opening the first file, she began, "I have been in contact with the FBI. After reviewing the files Michael gave you and information you provided during your interview with them, they have decided to proceed without further involvement from you - for now."

There were smiles and high fives all around the table. "What about the islanders?" Maddie asked.

"They aren't needed either, for now, but the FBI is extending its nets to include those Michael named in his files. Since the staff was on the island before you came, they may have pertinent information that will need to be investigated later."

"Will the FBI go there, or will they bring them here?" asked Jesse.

"I hope they come here so we can meet them in person," added Tatia.

"And if they come around mid-August, they can meet the baby," said Maddie.

McKenna didn't smile often, but she made an exception when she heard their comments. "I may not be involved in the plans, but if I have any input, I will try to steer the conversation in that direction."

She made a note in the file. "If there are no other questions, we'll move to the next matter." When no one spoke, she opened the second file. "After her death, the FBI made a thorough search of Misty Love's condo, and she kept detailed records. Her files not only confirmed a lot of what you told them about her relationship with Mr. Saint and yours, it also revealed some very interesting financial information concerning you.

"Mr. Saint not only paid a large sum of money for you, but he also sent Ms. Love a large monthly stipend for your care and education. The money came from Saint International, Mr. Saint's legitimate company, and the money was transferred directly into a trust account for your benefit. Ms. Love submitted invoices to the trustee for payment, and at the end of the month, any excess funds were moved into a high yield money market account. The current balance is just over $339,000."

Maddie gasped. "That's wonderful! I know doctor and lawyer fees are very high, but at least I'll be able to make a dent."

"Let's not worry about lawyer fees for now, and hopefully there may be more to come. I'm working on several other angles, but I won't go into detail until I know more. There is one catch to the trust fund. You will not have direct access to the money until you're twenty-one. The former trustee is under investigation in the Saint International cases, so the court has appointed me as temporary trustee. However, finance is not my forte, so you need to think about a permanent trustee. Do you have any suggestions?"

Maddie looked at Jesse. "Is that something you would do for me?"

Jesse looked please, but he shook his head. "I'm honored that you would put that kind of trust in me, but I'm an artist and a mechanic apprentice. I'm not an investor. You need a professional."

Maddie shrugged in confusion, "Then I have no idea."

"I thought that might be your answer, so I took the liberty of contacting Mrs. Grochowsky for her advice."

Tatia laughed. "And, of course, Mama knew the perfect person for the job."

McKenna smiled for the second time in one afternoon. "As a matter of fact, she did."

76

Monday - 4/3

With a medical regimen set up and financial worries temporarily on hold, Maddie's life settled into a fairly simple routine. Continuing the habit she had developed during her time with Michael, she spent time in prayer and Bible study immediately after breakfast. With lots of practice, she became quite mobile on her crutches, and she faithfully followed the exercise routine her therapist had given her. She wasn't much help with the housework, but she helped the children with their schoolwork and took care of some of the ministry's clerical work that had piled up in Lili's absence. And she spent a lot of time with Johnny.

They saw each other every day at breakfast and lunch, and he usually picked her up on Sundays for church which by now included Bible study before the service. Wednesday night became one of her favorite times as she finally began her journey through Recovery Ministry. The friendships she made and the lessons she learned deepened her faith, and sharing the experience with Johnny deepened her feelings for him. At least once a week Johnny took her somewhere, always keeping a low profile and staying in Heart

City. They went out for ice cream or visited garage sales and the few antique shops in town. One Saturday he took her to the Winnebago County Public Library where she signed up for her first library card, and one week they took in an afternoon movie - her first movie in a theater.

In mid-February, Dr. Bourland set up appointments for x-rays and an MRI. "This is one procedure I can't bring to you," she told Maddie. "I'm sending you to the medical school because they have the closest MRI equipment that's safe with the pin in your leg."

The results of the tests showed that she was healing well in spite of the little one leaching calcium out of her system. She had to continue to wear the brace for a while, but the therapist began teaching her to safely put weight on her leg and how to use a cane instead of crutches.

A few weeks later, everyone was gathered around the table making plans for the day. Suddenly, Maddie's eyes opened wide and she put her hand on her belly that was beginning to swell a bit. Johnny, who rarely took his eyes off her, almost jumped out of his seat.

"What's wrong?" he cried.

"Nothing!" she laughed. "Sit down. I think this kid just kicked me."

Everyone began to talk at once. "What did it feel like?" Did it hurt?" "Is that the first movement you've felt?"

"One at a time!" she continued to laugh. "No, it doesn't hurt. It just surprised me. I've been feeling some little flutters for the last couple of weeks, but it's hard to tell. This was definite, though - little rhythmic taps as if he's wanting to come out and join us."

"It's probably hiccups," explained Tatia. "Both of mine had those, before and after birth."

At her next check-up, Dr. P confirmed that the baby was having bouts of hiccups and that he was progressing nicely. Even he deferred to Maddie's insistence on the gender of the baby and referred to him as a boy.

The Monday after April Fool's Day, a day when everyone in the Fallen Angel family fell victim to one of Daniel's pranks, Jesse opened the morning newspaper to a huge headline: **FBI MAKES MASSIVE RAIDS!**

"Hey, listen to this," he called out to whoever was in earshot. *Early this morning the FBI and cooperating agencies carried out simultaneous raids on every crime family in Chicago netting more arrests in one day than were made in the past two decades.* Maddie, it looks like they finally moved on the information you gave them."

His announcement was met with shouts of approval and applause just as Maddie's phone began to ring.

"It's McKenna," she said as she accepted the call. "Good morning, McKenna."

Without preamble, her attorney almost shouted, "Have you seen the morning paper?"

"Jesse was just reading it to us. Great news!"

"Yes, in lots of ways. They think they got everyone with no loss of life. Their intention is to deny bail to everyone, but we'll see if that happens. Anyway, for now, you should be safe, and I don't believe you'll have to testify, either. These guys are climbing over each other to make a deal and rat each other out."

In her excitement, she didn't pause or take a breath, so Maddie just listened and tried not to laugh at the vernacular that had replaced the more formal way she usually spoke. When she finally did take a breath, Maddie asked the question that was pressing on her mind.

"Will Shenice and Jaden still need to testify?"

"It's too soon to know, but I have your note to try and get them here around your due date. I won't forget."

77

Tuesday - 4/30

By the end of April, Maddie had developed a definite baby bump, and her clothes were becoming uncomfortably tight. One morning she was late coming to breakfast, and Tatia asked Joy to go check on her. Joy came back shortly with a concerned look on her face.

"Mommy," she said, "I think Maddie needs you. She's lying on her bed crying and she has clothes spread all over the place."

Johnny immediately jumped to his feet. "Is she okay?"

"She's fine." Tatia chuckled. "Sounds like a mid-pregnancy hormonal crisis to me. Jesse, in the storage closet in the back of the meeting room over the shop there's a box on the top shelf marked *Maternity Clothes.* Would you go get that please." She stood up from the table and followed Joy.

"Should I go check on her?" Johnny asked Jesse.

"Believe me," said Jesse. "The last place you want to be is in the middle of a pregnancy meltdown. Why don't you come with me. I think there's more than one box."

Brush gulped down the last of the coffee. "I'm coming, too. You're not leaving me here alone!"

Jesse and Johnny returned a few minutes later with two boxes which they dropped in the hallway and returned to the shop as quickly as possible. By the time they returned for lunch a few hours later, Maddie was wearing a pair of jeans that Daniel explained had a special baby-bump panel in front, a cute tunic top that flared below an empire waistline, and a big smile.

"We can go shopping this weekend for some clothes of your own if you like," suggested Tatia, but Maddie shook her head.

"No, I like the idea of wearing things you wore. It's like getting hand-me-downs from a big sister. Besides, I want to save my money to spoil my son!"

The following week, Maddie and Johnny walked to the park as she worked to strengthen her leg. Instead of carrying her cane, she agreed to Johnny's suggestion that she hold onto his arm. As they strolled along slowly, enjoying the spring weather, Johnny brought up Lili.

"She's going to be back in a little over three months, so I need to find a place to live. I've been thinking,.." His voice quavered a little bit, and he stopped and turned to face her.

"Thinking what?" Maddie said, trying not to giggle.

He took a deep breath and blurted out what was on his mind all in one breath. "Thinking that I should look for a two bedroom place." His face was bright red as he began to stammer. "Uh, you know, an extra room for, uh, you know."

"No, I don't know," she looked him straight in the eye. "Tell me."

He tried to look away, but those violet eyes gripped him. "For a nursery, you know, just in case."

"Just in case, huh?" she smiled. "Okay. Two bedrooms. What else?"

Encouraged, he turned back toward the park and they began to stroll again. "Well, hypothetically, of course."

"Of course," she agreed.

"I'd like to get something in this neighborhood so I can be close to work and can come home for lunch. A house instead of an apartment so the baby will have a yard to play in." He cut his eyes over at Maddie. "Hypothetically, of course."

"Understood. Go on."

They reached the park and sat down on a shaded bench. "I'd like to have a little space somewhere," Johnny continued. "It doesn't have to be another room, but somewhere I can work at home sometimes so I can be there to help you with the baby."

"That would be good," said Maddie, getting caught up in his dreams. "I would eventually need some time to go to beauty school and get my license. Of course, I would need another room, or better yet, a small she shed out back where I could set up my salon when the baby is a little older."

Johnny nodded. "You'd be good at that. I've seen what you do with Joy's hair sometimes. You're amazing. One problem with all this - money."

"I have the money in my trust fund, and I'm sure Tatia and Jesse would help us get a loan. Anyway, it's all hypothetical - isn't it?"

Johnny grinned, blushed, and helped her to her feet. "I'd better get you back home before they send out a search party."

After that, the two of them had many hypothetical conversations during which they fine-tuned their dreams even to the point of discussing colors and furniture styles. Johnny continued to work on building up his computer business and putting as much of his income as possible into savings. On weekends, he and Maddie cruised around the neighborhood in his little hybrid looking for houses for lease or sale.

78

Tuesday - 5/9

Lili was less than a month away from her expected delivery, and her video calls to Maddie during which they compared pregnancies and shared experiences became more frequent. They also discussed Lili's return to the States to continue her studies.

"Has Johnny been looking for a place to live after I return?" she asked Maddie one morning about three weeks before her due date.

"Yes, he…well…we have been looking for a place with at least two bedrooms, you know for a nursery. Of course, this is all hypothetical at this point."

"Maddie! The time for hypotheticals has passed. You will be a mother in three months, and you need to be ready. If Johnny is the one you want to help you raise your child, you need to begin talking for real."

"You're right. It just seems so far away and kind of unreal. Do you know what I mean?"

"Yes, but when you go to birthing classes, it will become very real."

"Birthing classes? Dr. P mentioned them at our last appointment, but I didn't really know what he was talking about and didn't ask him any questions."

"Birthing classes will teach you what to expect during labor and delivery and afterward. And you need a partner, someone you love, so you won't have your baby surrounded only by professionals you barely know. And you need to get started now. There are usually twelve sessions, so you may have to double up and go twice a week as it is."

After she and Lili said goodbye, Maddie immediately called Dr. P's office and asked his assistant about classes.

"Yes," she said. "In fact, you are next on my list of calls this morning. A new twelve-week session begins next week with classes on Tuesday nights from 7:00 to 8:00. Would that work for you?"

"That sounds great!" replied Maddie. "Where are they held."

"They're at the birthing center adjacent to the hospital. I'll get you enrolled and email you the information. Have you chosen a birthing partner?"

"Not exactly. I have one in mind, but I haven't asked yet."

Promising to get back to her the next day, Maddie ended the call and bowed her head. "Father," she said out loud, "I know we're not supposed to test You by asking for a sign, but I'm about to take a really big step. If You want Johnny and me - and this little boy - to be a family, please help me to be sure. And if not, please let me know how to let him down easy. Thank you. Amen."

When she opened her eyes, she was surprised to see Tatia standing in the entry hall. "I'm so sorry to intrude on a private moment," she said quickly. "I opened the door quietly in case you were napping and couldn't help but hear your prayer. At the risk of being presumptuous, God may have sent me in at just this moment to be your sign. May I put in my two cents worth?"

"Absolutely!" cried Maddie. "There's no one I trust more than you."

Tatia sat down on the sofa next to Maddie. "I saw the look on Johnny's face back in September when he first laid eyes on you. He has been head over heels in love with you from that moment. I saw the friendship that blossomed in those few days before you were taken, and I saw the look of sorrow in your eyes as you looked at him before you walked to the helicopter. I saw how you looked at each other on the video calls to Antigua, and all the looks since you came home. I have watched you grow closer at church as you come to know the Lord together, and I've seen you sharing your lives in simple ways that many couples never do even after years of marriage. I think God brought you together, and I think He means for you to spend your lives together."

"Thank you," whispered Maddie, and Tatia wasn't sure if she was talking to her or praying again. Tatia drew her into a hug and felt her tears soaking into the shoulder of her shirt. After a minute or two, Maddie drew back and grinned and wiped the tears from her face.

"I guess I have a phone call to make," she said.

"And I have snacks to deliver to two hungry kids."

"Hi, Johnny," Maddie said when he answered on the first ring.

"Is everything okay?" He was concerned because she rarely called him while he was at work.

"Yes, everything's fine. It's just that…" She took a deep breath and plunged ahead. "You remember that question you tried to ask me when I first came back?"

"You…you mean THE question?" he stammered.

"Yes, that's the one."

"Of course, I remember."

"Well, I think I'm ready."

There was silence on the other end of the call for a minute. "Maddie, you don't know how long I've waited to hear those words."

Maddie laughed. "I think I do - a little over four months."

Johnny laughed, too. "Oh, yeah. You were there, weren't you? Uh, okay. Let's see, it's four o'clock now. I'll pick you up at six. Will that work for you?"

"That's perfect. See you then."

"So," she asked as Tatia walked toward the door with bottles of water, apples, and cheese sticks. "What does a six-month pregnant woman wear to her own engagement?"

"How about one of your island dresses?" suggested Tatia. "I'll be right back, and we'll see if anything fits."

When Johnny rang the bell at 6:00 p.m. on the dot, Maddie answered the door wearing a long flowered muumuu Shenice had given her while she was in the hospital. Since the evenings were still a little cool, she also wore a light-weight mid-length green cape from one of Tatia's maternity boxes. Joy had done an excellent job of painting her fingernails and toenails, and a pair of seashell earrings brought it all together.

Johnny looked moonstruck all over again. "You look amazing," he breathed.

He was wearing his usual jeans and boots, but the boots were highly polished. And instead of a leather vest, he had on a pale blue button down shirt, a navy blazer, and a sky-blue tie that perfectly matched his eyes. "You look pretty good yourself," she returned.

Jesse was helping Tatia in the kitchen. "Don't forget," he called out. "Pregnant women get hangry if you don't feed them regularly."

"Daddy!" exclaimed Joy, and Maddie laughed.

"Don't worry," said Johnny. "That's on the schedule, but we have a stop to make first. Are you ready, m'lady?" he asked, offering his arm.

"Where are we going?" she asked after he helped her into the car.

"Just up the road a little way."

She recognized the route as one they often took on their morning walks, especially since they had been looking at houses. In fact, the street he turned on next was one of their favorites because there was a house that looked exactly like the one they had mapped out as perfect. It was a ranch style, probably built in the sixties or seventies, but it had been kept up nicely. It was white, trimmed in slate blue, with a gray composition roof. She particularly loved the narrow porch across the front of the house and the picture window flanked by faux shutters. The problem was, it wasn't for sale. That's why she was so surprised when he pulled to the curb in front of their house and parked. Lights shone through the mini blinds on the windows, and the house looked more lived in than it did in the mornings. She wanted to ask why they were stopping, but she decided to let Johnny do this his own way. He came around, helped her out of the car, and walked her toward the front door. When he reached for the doorknob, she put her hand on his arm.

"Shouldn't we ring the bell?"

He grinned like the Cheshire Cat and said, "There's no one home." He swung the door open, and she could see it was completely empty. "Let me show you around, ma'am. This is the living/dining room. If you don't need a formal dining room, this end could be screened off to be used as a work area."

She immediately caught his mood. "Nice, but where would we have dinner?"

"I'm glad you asked." He ushered her through a wide arched opening into the kitchen. "You'll notice the large kitchen which features this lovely breakfast nook that overlooks the back yard. And you'll notice the original stylish almond appliances, which by the way are much better than avocado green."

"I agree!" she giggled.

He took her into the hallway and pointed out a small bathroom with a tub/shower combination. "The guest bathroom, ma'am. And the water is on in case you and the little one need to make a visit while we're here."

She laughed out loud. "I may have to if you keep making me laugh."

He showed her through a small guest bedroom and the master bedroom that featured a huge bathroom with his and her walk-in closets, double sinks set in a marble vanity, a walk-in shower, and a separate whirlpool tub. An outside door opened from the bedroom onto a large cement patio facing a wide grassy lawn.

"No pool," Johnny commented, "but plenty of room for a she shed."

"It's beautiful," sighed Maddie, "but probably way over our budget."

"Maybe not. It just went on the market which explains why there was no sign. It's part of an estate that has been tied up in probate. Neither of the surviving children wants it, and both are well-off in their own right. All they want is to dispose of it quickly, so the listing agent thinks they may be willing to deal."

"Very exciting," she said, holding his arm closely for support and also because she liked it. "But now, I think the little one and I need to visit the toilet."

When she came out, she was shaking her wet hands. "Thankfully, they left toilet paper, but there was no hand towel." She rubbed her hand together to dry them faster. "What about that room at the end of the hall. I don't think we went in there."

"I saved the best for last," said Johnny with a nervous smile. He escorted her down the hall and opened the door with a flourish. Maddie put her hands over her mouth and her eyes filled with tears. A rocking chair they had seen at a garage sale a few weeks before sat in the corner, and next to it was a changing table they had seen at the same sale. On the table was a vase holding a dozen long-stemmed red roses. He took her hand and led her to the chair where she sat and cradled her growing belly.

"You and I will spend a lot of time in this chair together," she said quietly.

Johnny gazed at the scene, imprinting it on his mind as one of the most beautiful things he had ever seen. He sank to one knee and pulled a small velvet box out of his jacket pocket. When he had her full attention, he opened the box to reveal a white gold ring with a round cut half carat diamond solitaire. "As I was saying, Madelyn Jeanette Collier, would you do me the honor of taking me as your husband and allowing me to be the father of your child."

Her face glowed with happiness. "Yes!" she said, and then, with a mischievous twinkle in her eye, she added, "on one condition. You have to be my birthing partner at childbirth classes beginning next week."

He took her left hand in his and slid the ring onto her finger where it fit perfectly. "Anything you want, now and forever." He stood and pulled her to her feet. Drawing her close, he looked into her amazing violet eyes and said, "I love you, Madelyn," and he kissed her for the first time. As she returned his kiss, the ring on her finger felt like a promise, and she heard the sound of prison doors being thrown open.

79

Mid to Late May

The next morning Maddie placed a video call to Shenice so she could share her news and show off her ring. "It is about time you stopped playing with that boy's heart, child. I can see from thousands of miles away that he is mad about you. Have you set a date?"

"Johnny wants to get married as soon as we can get a license, but I want to wait until July 27. Lili should be back by then, and maybe we can figure out a way for you and Jaden to come, too."

"That is possible. Ms. Hartel said the defense lawyers are asking for depositions. She has told them they will have to pay for our flight and all our expenses while we are there, and they are willing. They seem to believe that we will be able to help their case in some way, but I cannot imagine how. I would love to see you married, though - happily this time!"

Maddie shared that she and Johnny would be starting birthing classes the following week, and Shenice shared that Lili had been having false labor pains. "I believe the baby will come any day."

The next six days passed in a blur, and Maddie found herself preparing for her first birthing class. Johnny picked her up right on time, and they chatted excitedly about the coming experience. At one point, Maddie looked a little worried.

"The class description says they may show videos of actual births. Do you think that will bother you, you know, with your recovery and everything?"

He took her hand as he stopped for a red light and turned to look at her. "Maddie, I have thought of nothing but you since I first met you, and I can't even remember why I thought those pictures were so important. If they show pictures or videos, I will be watching to see what the man is doing to help make the process as easy as possible for his wife." He blushed and grinned when he said that last word. "I am extremely grateful to be a part of your life and a part of this process, and I want to learn enough about it that I can deliver the baby myself if I have to!"

Maddie couldn't help but laugh at the seriousness of his expression. The light turned green and he turned his attention back to his driving, but he held onto her hand. She squeezed his hand and said, "That's beautiful, Johnny. I would say 'I love you,' but I'm afraid you'd drive off the road, so I'll save that for later."

He was so attentive in class that Maddie wasn't sure he was even aware of her presence. He took notes, asked questions, and stared intensely at the screen as if trying to memorize every word and movement. On the way to the ice cream shop afterward, he asked what method of childbirth she was leaning toward.

"I think I'd like to go as natural as I can. I'm a little scared of the pain, but I want to be fully present during as much of the process as possible. I want to remember every minute clearly, not through a medicated fog - if I'm brave enough, that is." She laughed at herself.

He laughed with her. "I may be the one who needs some relief. Some of that stuff looked pretty tough."

"Yes, but look at the results. I'd hate to miss those first moments because I was drugged up. Besides, I don't want to mess up my record - I'll have been ten months clean by then!"

###

A little over a week later, Maddie received a call from Lili telling her that she had delivered a healthy baby girl the day before. "The midwife allowed my sister to catch the baby, and her husband cut the cord," she explained. "I was sad not to be the first to hold her, but I know it was the best way. They have already bonded so closely - it is as if she birthed the baby herself. I am so grateful I could be the means God used to answer her prayers for a child. Now I can re-focus on returning to the States for your wedding and the next semester of my studies."

The two young women chatted and planned for the next few minutes before Maddie said she had to go. "My physical therapist wants me to walk at least half a mile a day, and Johnny shows up about this time like clockwork to walk with me."

"You are blessed to have a man like that in your life."

"Amen to that!" They had just said goodbye when Johnny tapped on the door. She greeted him with a hug, but he seemed distracted as they started toward the park at a steady clip. When they reached the bench where they usually took a break she asked about it.

"You're unusually quiet today. Is everything okay at the shop?"

"Huh?" he said as if he had been somewhere else. "Oh, yeah. Everything's fine."

"Then what is it?"

He blew out his breath and then cut his eyes over at her and grinned. "You give a girl a ring and she thinks you gotta tell her stuff."

"Absolutely!" she said, snuggling up to him. "I'm listening."

"I checked the Winnebago County website last night about marriage licenses. There's a four day waiting period after you apply and then the license is good for sixty days. It's sixty-five days until July

27, so I was thinking - if we go to the courthouse next Tuesday, it would be good until the wedding day. What do you think?"

"I think that sounds really exciting - but why don't we wait a couple of weeks, just in case."

"Just in case what?" he exclaimed with a worried look on his face. "You're not having second thoughts, are you?"

"Of course not, silly. But what if the 60th day is on July 27. And what if the baby comes early or Lili's arrival is delayed - something that causes us to have to change the wedding date. Then we'd have to start all over again."

"Okay, I'll buy that. How about three weeks from Friday?"

"It's a date. Is there anything else before we walk back so you can go back to work and earn enough money to support me and this kid?"

"Just one more thing," he said, sliding his arm around her shoulders and drawing her close. "Last week when we were driving to class, you said you had something to tell me but you thought it might distract me from my driving. Well, we got involved talking about class and you never told me. But I'm not driving now, and I'm listening."

"Hm," she teased. "What was it I was going to say? Oh yes, I remember." She leaned into him with her lips almost touching his. "Are you sure I didn't say this already? In fact, I'm pretty sure I said it several times."

"Probably, but I've got a short memory."

"Okay. One more time. John Scott Nichols, III, I love you, and I'm looking forward to raising our son together and growing old with you."

"Wow!" he breathed, and then he closed the distance between them - one more time.

80

June and July

Johnny and Maddie came out of the courthouse holding hands and laughing like children. Johnny was clutching their marriage license in his free hand, and the joy on his face made everyone around them smile - or almost everyone. One prim older woman stopped and scowled at them.

"It's about time you made an honest woman out of her, son," she admonished.

"Oh," said Maddie with a straight face. "It's not his."

The shocked look on her face sent them into another uncontrollable fit of laughter as they continued down the wide steps. Suddenly Maddie stopped, let out a surprised gasp, and slowly sat down on one of the steps. Johnny knelt in front of her, the joy on his face replaced by worry.

"What's wrong, sweetheart? Is it the baby? Do I need to take you to the hospital?"

"No, no," she laughed. "I'm fine. Do you remember what we talked about in class last week?"

"You mean the false contractions? What was it they called them?"

"Braxton Hicks contractions. I think I just had one."

"Wow!" said Johnny, and what was about to happen became a little more real. "What did it feel like? Did it hurt?"

"No, it didn't hurt. It's like they said - kinda like my belly just tightened up all over. It made me feel a little dizzy, though."

"Are you okay now, or do we need to go home?"

"Not on your life, buddy! You promised me ice cream, and after this, I may get an extra dip."

"Anything you want, my love."

Maddie made good on her speculation by ordering a scoop of salted caramel, one of cookies and cream, and another of strawberries and cream. She compromised by having it in a dish instead of a waffle cone, but Johnny watched her with a grin as she devoured every bite.

"Are you still going to love me when I'm big and fat from all the ice cream?" she teased.

"I will love you if you break out in pink and purple polka dots and grow a third arm out of the top of your head!" he proclaimed loudly enough to draw the attention of the other customers. "But as active as you've been, even with a broken leg, I predict that you'll shed your baby weight before he's sitting up by himself."

"I hope so!" she replied, squeezing his hand. "Now, let's go show our license to the family. Besides, I don't want to be late for dinner," she added with a wink.

The display of the license caused an excited celebration that included hugs and even a few tears. And it brought this comment from Tatia, "July 27th, right? We'd better get busy! We have six weeks to plan a wedding."

Maddie looked at Johnny and took his hand. "We've talked about that, and we want to keep it small and very simple. More like a completion of the backyard birthday party that was so rudely interrupted last year. If that's okay with you."

"Of course it's okay!" agreed Tatia, and you could almost see the ideas running around in her head. "Is it okay if I invite Mama and Papa? I know they'd love to be here, and maybe hang around for the birth."

"Yes! We'd love to see them again. I'm also hoping Jaden and Shenice will be here. I wouldn't tell anyone they couldn't come if they hear about it, but I don't want to broadcast it or send out invitations."

During the next several weeks, Maddie and Johnny continued their birthing classes, and with help and advice from his business partners, Johnny made an offer on the house. The seller accepted the offer, and in order to avoid using any of her trust money, Maddie sold the wedding rings and the other jewelry Michael had given her to make a sizeable down payment. With so much going on, the couple didn't want any showers, but at the insistence of Tatia and several friends, they registered for baby equipment and household items on an online shopping site. Fallen Angel Salvage became a regular stop for delivery trucks, and the Annex was soon filled with boxes.

"I wish we could have this stuff delivered directly to our house," said Johnny as he added a box containing a highchair to a stack that was threatening to topple.

"That's a great idea!" exclaimed Maddie. "I'll call the realtor and see if we can work it out."

The sellers had taken an instant liking to Johnny and Maddie, and since the loan approval seemed to be just a formality, they agreed immediately. That afternoon after the shop was closed, the guys loaded up the trailer and transferred the accumulated items to the house. Maddie, Tatia, and Shawna met them there. Shawna wiped out kitchen cabinets and papered shelves, and Tatia opened boxes while Maddie decided where the items should be placed. She also filled a large box with baby clothes, bed linens, and towels.

"I should have separated these out first," she said. "I'll have to take them back home so I can wash them before we use them."

"Why don't you hold off on that," she said. "Hey, everybody! Come in here for a minute."

"Let me guess," said Jesse. "You've changed the arrangement and we get to move everything around."

"Don't give us any ideas!" grinned Tatia. "No, we haven't made any changes - yet. But Maddie needs to wash the baby's things before they're used."

Johnny looked confused. "Why wash them when they're brand new?"

Jesse elbowed him playfully and stage whispered, "Just say 'Yes, dear,' and don't interrupt."

When the laughter died down, Tatia continued. "I'll let Maddie explain that to you. What I wanted to do was reveal a surprise a little early. Maddie, you can leave your laundry here. Brush, Shawna, Jesse, and I pitched in and bought the two of you a washer and dryer. It should be delivered early next week."

Maddie burst into tears, and Johnny looked terrified. "It's okay," Jesse reassured him. "You know what this is. You've seen it before."

"Oh, yeah. Pregnancy hormones, right?'

"Yeah, that. And a lot of women cry when they're happy."

"Man! You're gonna need to write all this stuff down for me."

81

The Wedding Week

Maddie was crying again, this time as if her heart would break. "I..I..It's two days till the w..w..wedding," she sniffled, "and nothing fits. I'm gonna get married in a sweat suit!"

Tatia stood holding the flowered muumuu Maddie had worn the night Johnny proposed. She was right - it just didn't fit any more. Tatia wracked her brain, thinking of where they could find a dress in two days. Her phone rang, and she absently answered it.

"Hi, Shawna. We're in the middle of a wedding crisis. The dress Maddie was going to wear doesn't fit any more...Really!...Where?...Yes, I know where it is. Ten minutes!"

She dropped the dress on the bed and headed into the hall. "Go wash your face and put on some shoes," she called to Maddie. "Shawna found a dress."

Maddie's breath was still coming in small spasms, but the sobs had subsided. She slipped into a pair of flip-flops, splashed some cold water on her face, pulled a few tissues from the box, and followed Tatia to the car. She stared at her hands in her lap and only raised her head when the car stopped in front of the Good

411

Samaritans Thrift Store and Food Bank. Tatia and Maddie shopped here often for clothes for the whole family, toys, books, and other treasures that generous patrons had donated. They had looked for a suitable wedding dress several times in recent weeks, but their lack of success made her less than hopeful on this trip.

They walked in the door and heard Shawna calling them from the back of the store. Her head was sticking out from the curtain across the small recess in the corner that served as a fitting room.

"Hurry," she called. "I've already had three people try to take this dress away from me."

"Why?" asked Maddie, apparently regaining a little of her humor. "Is there a plague of pregnant brides?"

Shawna grabbed her by the arm and shoved her into the fitting room. "Get in there, girl. Try that dress on before I have to whack somebody with my purse."

Maddie undressed awkwardly in the cramped space and slipped into the dress without paying much attention to it. It felt comfortable as the soft fabric fell loosely around her large belly, but there was no mirror, so she couldn't see how it looked. She stepped out and tried to smile.

"So, how do I look? Like a white elephant?" she quipped.

"You look gorgeous," whispered Shawna.

"Oh, Maddie," echoed Tatia, "it's perfect! Come and look."

She led the bride-to-be to a free-standing mirror next to the tiny fitting booth. Maddie stood for a moment with her head down before raising her eyes and looking at her reflection. The white dotted swiss dress had a gently scooped neckline and butterfly sleeves. The empire waistline was accented with a braided cord tied in a small bow in front. The skirt draped perfectly over the baby and fell gracefully to the scalloped hem that brushed her ankles. A broad smile lit her face.

"You're right. I love it!"

Tatia threw her arms in the air and exclaimed, "And we have a YES to the dress!" Everyone in the store turned to look, and even those who had fought Shawna for the dress were caught up in the joyful celebration of the small group.

The next forty-eight hours flew by in a flurry of activity. Johnny had worked hard to finish jobs for his growing client list and had put a message on his phone that he would be unavailable for the next two weeks. He planned to take his new bride to a luxury spa resort after the wedding where she could be pampered for a couple of days before her motherhood duties began. He helped the men when they needed an extra hand, but most of the time he spent by Maddie's side, watching her every move in case she wanted or needed anything.

Maddie and Johnny finally closed on their house, Johnny moved in, and Lili's apartment was prepared for her return. Maddie helped Johnny get settled and began moving her clothes and other personal items, but mostly she watched from the comfort of the sofa. She kept waiting for the burst of nesting energy other women talked about, but she felt tired and worn out, both from the excitement and from the contractions. They were occurring more and more frequently, and they didn't feel exactly like Braxton Hicks anymore.

Mama and Papa G arrived from Texas and were settled into the Annex that served nicely as a guest room. McKenna rented a van and made an airport run to pick up not only Lili but also Jaden, Shenice, Sam, and Skipper. She dropped Lili at her apartment before taking the others to the small hotel in Heart City where they planned to stay until they moved into Chicago where they were scheduled to give depositions. McKenna had maintained a small suite there since she had taken Maddie's case and had cleared her calendar so she could join the festivities.

Tatia's kitchen became the center of activity as she prepared for the wedding reception and meals for the guests. Shawna, Mama G,

Lili, Shenice, and Skipper pitched in to help, and the result was an interesting mix of Chicago, Texas, and Caribbean cuisine with lots of love and laughter thrown in. McKenna, not being much of a cook, continued to provide shuttle services for those without their own transportation, and she ran to the store for last minute and forgotten items.

Thursday night before the Bible study, the men set up the canopy and brought tables and chairs from the meeting room and set them up around the patio. The grill, ice cream freezer, and ice chests were cleaned and readied for the party, and a few simple decorations were gathered to be put up at the last minute. When their chores were done, the rest of the men's meeting turned into an impromptu bachelor party, so the ladies decided to go out for Mexican food. Maddie almost begged off, but when they added a stop at the ice cream parlor, she couldn't resist.

Friday morning Maddie woke to sniffling coming from the bed on the other side of the room. She opened her eyes and saw Joy wiping hers. "Are you crying, little sis?" she asked.

"No," said Joy in a quavering voice that ended in a sob.

"Come over here," invited Maddie, holding up the covers.

Joy scooted across the room and into Maddie's arms where she cried as Maddie comforted her. "I know that change is hard. I'm a little sad and scared, too. I'm about to become a wife and mother, and you're going back to being the big sister. We will both have new responsibilities, and life will be different in some ways, but we will always have each other. I will be within walking distance, and I'll always be a phone call away."

"Will you love Johnny and the new baby more than me?" mumbled Joy.

"Absolutely not! It's true that I will love them, but that love won't be taken away from the love I have for you. God will give me more love to give them. Do you understand?"

Joy nodded and snuggled closer. "Good," said Maddie as she kissed Joy's hair. "Now, I love snuggling with you, but this kid is stomping on my bladder…"

"…and if I don't let you up, we're both gonna be wet." Joy laughed, jumped up, and helped Maddie out of bed.

The sun was shining, and the temperature was pleasant. Maddie enjoyed her shower and felt more energetic than she had in several days. She had a couple of contractions while she was getting ready, and they were a little harder and a little lower than before, but she kept that to herself. She knew everyone would hover over her all day anyway, and she didn't want to add another reason. Shortly after breakfast, the hovering began when Tatia asked to do her hair and Joy asked to do her nails.

"The creative things you do with Joy's hair have inspired me," explained Tatia. "I found a style I like on-line, and I've been practicing it on Joy. I'd like to try it on you if that's okay. It's still a little over two hours until noon, so we have time to do it over if you don't like it."

"I'm sure I'll love it - I'm in your hands. And in yours, sister. I'd love to have you do my nails."

Tatia began by brushing through Maddie's still slightly damp hair and explaining what she was going to do. "I'll leave a little bit loose around your face and then pull the sides up to begin the braid. I'll weave them together in the back to form a kind of crown, leaving the hair below it loose. We can put just a little curl back here if you like."

"That sounds wonderful."

"And I think Shenice wants to add some flowers."

"Beautiful!"

Joy had finished her prep work and asked what color Maddie wanted. "You choose, sweetie. Anything goes with white." Joy chose a barely there pink and had just finished her final top coat when

Tatia announced she was finished and Shenice walked in with a handful of white daisies. Mama G was with her and said they had come so the first shift could get dressed while they put the finishing touches on the bride.

"Perfect timing!" exclaimed Tatia. "I need to make sure the rest of the wedding party is decent. Joy, you know what you're wearing, right?"

"Yes, ma'am. My green sundress and matching stuff."

At ten minutes before noon, Maddie was standing in front of Shenice and Mama G who declared her the most beautiful of brides. A soft tap on the door signaled that Maddie's escort had arrived and it was time for the ladies to take their seats. Mama G opened the door to Brush who was awkwardly holding a bouquet of white roses surrounded by violets and baby's breath. He stood in the hallway and stared at Maddie.

"You are a beautiful bride, Maddie," he said in his soft voice.

"Thank you. Are those for me?" she asked, pointing at the flowers.

"Oh, yeah!" He handed her the bouquet and explained. "Johnny brought them and said to tell you that the violets are beautiful but are nothing compared to your eyes." He offered his arm. "Are you ready?"

He escorted her down the hallway but stopped just short of the living room so she could see what was going on without being seen. The men had taken the chairs from around the tables and set them up facing away from the house. They were divided into two sections with a center aisle, and off to the left Greg from Recovery was sitting on a stool with a guitar strapped around his neck. The clock in the living room began to strike twelve, and he began to sing *There Is Love*. Jaden and Johnny who had been sitting on the front row stood and took their places at the front.

"The Pastor had a last minute emergency," Brush whispered to Maddie, "so Jaden stepped in. I hope that's okay."

"Yes, more than okay," she assured him.

The rest of the wedding party, the Matthews family, was standing just inside the back door. Joy took Daniel's hand, and the two of them walked slowly to the front where Daniel walked to Johnny and took his hand and Joy walked to the opposite side. They watched their parents walk arm in arm to the front and take their places beside their children. Then it was the bride's turn.

"Are you ready?" asked Brush gently.

She stared at the scene in front of her. Jaden was in the white linen pants and white island shirt he always wore when he preached. The other men, including Daniel, were dressed in sharply pressed jeans and crisp white dress shirts. Joy was wearing her green sundress, and Tatia wore a similar one that matched her blue eyes. Maddie hoped someone was taking pictures, but regardless, she knew she would always carry what she was seeing in her heart. She looked at Brush with shining eyes and a radiant smile that answered his question without words.

The wedding was beautiful. The guests gasped when they saw Maddie, and Johnny's face was wet with tears. There were tears from everyone when they exchanged their vows, and there was joy when Johnny kissed his bride. Then there was chaos as everyone wanted to pat Johnny on the back and kiss the bride. Chairs were moved back around the tables, food was brought from the kitchen, grace was said, and lunch was served.

Finally, it was time for the cutting of the wedding cake and serving the homemade ice cream. Jesse carried out a three-tiered masterpiece that Shawna had baked and placed it in the center of the table. The bride and groom placed their hands on the knife and pressed down. Maddie gasped, her eyes wide, and she stared at Johnny.

"I think someone else will have to serve the cake," she said as she looked down.

Johnny followed her gaze and saw the puddle widening at her feet and began to laugh. "Folks, I think we have a party crasher," he announced. "Maddie's water just broke."

82

The Birth

Dr. Patterson, who was one of the guests, stepped to the table and began to question Maddie quietly. "Have you been having contractions?"

"Yes, for a couple of months."

"Yes, I know about those. Have they changed recently?"

"About two days ago, they shifted from an overall tightening to more like a pain - and lower."

"Why didn't you tell me?" asked Johnny.

"I didn't want to mess up the wedding plans."

Suddenly she leaned over, clasped her belly, and moaned softly.

"I think we should head for the birthing center," said Dr. Patterson.

"I'm not sure there's time," said Maddie. "They said in class I'd know when it was time to push, and it feels like now's the time."

Dr. Patterson was all business now. "Tatia, do you have any of those plastic tablecloths that haven't been opened?"

"Yes. I'll get one and spread it on our bed. Joy, bring her a towel!"

"Good. Jesse, get my bag from my car, and Johnny, get your wife to the bed while I go wash up."

Johnny held Maddie while Tatia threw everything except the bottom sheet off her bed and onto the floor and then spread the sheet of plastic across it.

"My wife. I love that. I love you."

"I love you…oh, it's happening again."

He could feel her belly tightening against his, and he could feel her whole body tightening up. "Don't fight it, babe. Ride it out, Breathe with me. Pant-2-3-4-5-Blow-Pant-2-3-4-5-Blow." When he felt her belly begin to soften, he rubbed the small of her back and continued to whisper in her ear. "You did good, baby. Real good."

"Don't leave me. I can't do this if you leave."

"I'm not going anywhere."

"Even if I yell and scream?"

"Even then."

"Even when it gets bloody and gross?

"Well, I might throw up on you, but I won't leave." He felt her smile against his chest. "Made ya' smile."

She leaned her head back and looked up at him. "You always do."

Dr. P walked in pulling on a pair of gloves. "If you two are through making out over there, I need to examine my patient before another contraction hits."

"The bed's ready," said Tatia as she brought in a stack of towels from the bathroom. "What else do you need?"

"If we end up doing the delivery here, we may need two more people - you know, for stirrups."

Tatia rolled her eyes playfully. "Whatever happened to squatting in the field? Any preferences as to who holds your legs, kiddo?"

"Maybe Mama Shenice and Mama G?"

"Good choices. A girl can never have too many mamas."

When Tatia came back with the rest of the labor team, Dr. P

was just finishing his examination. "Well, she's 100% effaced and dilated to ten centimeters. It looks like we're having a coming out party right here."

"Here comes another one, Doc," panted Maddie. "Can I push now?"

"Doc, is it? Aren't you the saucy one when you're in labor? Ride this one out while we get in position, and I promise you can push on the next one."

Once the contraction let up, Doc placed the labor team. "This bed isn't ideal - too wide - but we'll make do. Maddie, scoot down toward the foot of the bed. Tatia, kneel on the bed beside her right shoulder, and Johnny, take the left. Hold her hands, and when she's ready to push, slide your free hand under her shoulders and lift her at about a forty-five degree angle. Mamas, each of you support a leg..."

"...and when she begins to push lean into her so she has something to push against," finished Shenice.

"Done this before, have you?"

"What will you be doing?" asked Johnny.

"Playing catcher."

"It's starting."

"Okay, when you're ready to push, just say NOW."

By the second push, Doc announced that he could see the head. "Hey, Johnny. Do you want to do this?"

"You mean catch the baby? What do you think, Maddie?"

"I think it would be wonderful for the first hands the baby feels to be his daddy's."

Doc looked at Tatia. "Has Jesse done this before?" When she nodded, he bellowed, "Jesse, get in here!" In no more than five seconds, he appeared at the door. "Take Johnny's place. He's gonna catch."

"Got it," Jesse said and climbed onto the bed as Johnny kissed

Maddie's sweaty forehead and moved to the foot of the bed beside Dr. P.

After the next two contractions, Maddie cracked up laughing. Thinking she was hysterical from the pain, Johnny jumped up and grabbed her hand. "It's okay, baby! We're almost there. I know it's hard but you can do it!"

"No, no," she said, wiping tears of laughter from her eyes. "I'm laughing at all of you! I'm the one with a complete human being trying to push his way out of my body, and y'all are screaming like fans at the Super Bowl!"

"So," asked Johnny looking relieved, "what you're saying is we should shut up and let you work?"

Maddie's face softened and she stroked Johnny's face with her hand. "No, I'm saying I've never felt so supported and loved. Here comes another one! Come on, team! Let's get this kid out this time!"

Everyone let out a yell, and Maddie began to push. "It's working!" shouted Johnny. "Push! Push!"

"As the top of the head clears the birth canal," instructed Dr. P, "cup your hand under it and continue to support it as it pushes further out without applying any pressure. Good! I'm assisting with the shoulders. Now, you put your other hand under the rear end. And we have a boy! Hold him steady while I make sure his airway is clear."

The baby let out a wail, and the new father grinned. "Sounds clear to me."

"Yep. Now, we'll lift him onto Mommy's tummy so they can say hello. Tatia, you stay and help me finish up here. The rest of you can go share the news."

Within a few minutes the new family was clean and comfortably snuggled alone in the bed. Johnny and Maddie watched in wonder as their little boy found his way to her breast and begin to suckle.

"I think he's going to be a big eater," whispered Maddie. "You're going to have to work more nights to pay the food bills."

"Whatever it takes. What are we going to call him? We never talked about names."

"I thought we'd name him after his father."

"You mean - Michael." She could hear the hurt in his voice.

"No, silly. He was just the sperm donor. Yours were the first hands that touched him. You cut his cord. You are his father. His name is John Scott Nichols, IV, and we'll call him Scottie - if that's okay with you." And she knew by the look on his face and the tears in his eyes that it was.

Friday - 8/26

Jesse almost missed the phone ringing because of all the noise and laughter on the patio. When he noticed it, he answered quickly. "Hey, McKenna! Are you still there?...You're not interrupting. We're just having a small celebration of the one month anniversary of Scottie's birth and his parents wedding...No, come on by. The more the merrier... Business, huh? Look, you were at the wedding, so you know what we've shared. We literally have no secrets in this group."

Tatia looked at him quizzically. "What was that all about?"

"I don't really know. McKenna is in town on business and wants to stop by - says she has news for us and for the Nichols family. She wanted to come later when she could meet with us individually, but I told her we'd probably tell each other anyway so come on. I hope that's okay."

"Sure," agreed Johnny and Maddie who were cuddling Scottie while the older children looked on, reaching out occasionally to pat or offer a finger to hold.

"Do you lovebirds agree about everything?" asked Brush.

Johnny grinned. "A wise man once told me there are three secret phrases to a happy marriage: You're right, I'm wrong, and I'm sorry. It's working so far."

Shawna looked a little unsure. "Brush, maybe we should go. This sounds like family business."

"Don't go. You're family, too. Besides, she just pulled into the driveway. It would be awkward if you left now."

McKenna shed her professional demeanor and joined the party. She even had a little of the cake and ice cream Maddie had requested since they had missed it at the wedding. When Maddie asked if she'd like to hold Scottie, she hesitated a little but finally took the little bundle in her arms. He was awake and looked at her curiously with his big brown eyes. Her face softened in a way none of them had ever witnessed before.

"Little man," she said, "you could be dangerous to a woman's career. Just holding you could start my biological clock ticking like mad."

"If he poops or throws up on you, that clock will slow down in a hurry!" said Brush.

As if on cue, Scottie began to whimper and fuss. McKenna gladly relinquished him to Maddie who explained, "It's been over three hours, so he probably needs to be changed and fed."

Johnny followed his family inside, and Jesse suggested they all go in so McKenna could share her news while Maddie fed the baby.

"Shouldn't we wait until she's finished?" objected McKenna. "I wouldn't want to invade her privacy."

"It's okay," interjected Joy. "She nurses in front of us all the time. She has a nursing cover. It's very discreet."

"I'll stay outside with the children," offered Shawna. "I probably wouldn't understand the business talk anyway, and the children would be bored."

The children immediately began a rousing game of *Keep Away,* and the adults gathered around the kitchen table. While McKenna organized her files in front of her, Tatia offered coffee all around. When everyone was settled and Scottie was discreetly nursing, McKenna began, every bit the serious lawyer.

"It's just as well that you are all together, because this first matter concerns both Miss Matthews and Mrs. Nichols." She paused and relaxed a bit. "I know the formality seems strange after all we've been through, but that's the way my files are set up. No offense is intended."

"None taken," said Jesse, and everyone agreed with him.

"Good. I'll make this as simple as possible. Some years ago the United Nations set up some international guidelines for dealing with human trafficking, some binding and some not. One guideline of particular interest in your situations called for the States, meaning government entities of various kinds throughout the world, to set up victim funds to compensate victims of trafficking for all types of losses ranging from loss of wages to physical, psychological, and emotional and also punitive damages. This fund was to protect the victims from further victimization by complex public legal procedures and long delays.

"Before I go any further, I'll remind you, Mr. and Mrs. Matthews, that when you enlisted my services on behalf of Mrs. Nichols, you also asked me to represent your family if the need arose in the course of this situation. When I told Mrs. Nichols that I intended to pursue compensation for her from this victim fund, she asked that I do the same for Miss Matthews. I should have discussed it with you before I began the research, but given the chaos of the last few months, I trust you will overlook my lack of formality."

"Sure," said Jesse, giving Tatia a confused look.

"Alright, then. I was able to verify from Ms. Love's and Mr. Saint's records that he was the purchaser of Miss Matthews. His payment was traced to a numbered Swiss account connected to Mr.

Hall and Mr. Ellis. There are also records of a transaction reversing that payment the day Hall and Ellis were killed. This means that the money that paid for Miss Matthews is part of the funds that were recovered from Mr. Saint's estate.

"Since both Miss Matthews and Mrs. Nichols were involved in and injured by the kidnapping of Miss Matthews and the aftermath, I filed a joint claim in connection with that incident, and I requested special consideration based on all the assistance both of you provided to law enforcement. I received a response late yesterday, and I need your signatures and instructions on the distribution of the funds." She placed paperwork in front of both couples. "Do any of you have questions?" she asked.

Jesse glanced at the top sheet and then did a double take. "Is this amount correct?"

"Indeed it is," replied McKenna, enjoying their reactions.

Jesse held the paperwork so Tatia could see. "Wow!" she exclaimed. Joy will certainly be able to go to any college she chooses."

"Let me see," said a little voice behind them.

"Oh, Joy," said Tatia. She put her arm around the girl and pulled her close. "I didn't hear you come in. It's some papers saying you are getting some money to compensate - do you remember that vocabulary word?"

"Yes, it's to pay back."

"You are being given some money to pay you back, or to make up for, the trauma of being kidnapped. Of course, it will be in trust for you until you're older."

"Where does the money come from?"

"From the estate of the man who bought you."

"That seems fair. I want to go to a college that has a good gymnastics program. Can Daniel go to college, too?"

"It looks like there's enough if you want to share."

"Okay. I know we had ice cream, but it's really hot. Can...I mean, may we have popsicles?"

"Yes, you may."

"Thank you!" Joy retrieved the treats from the freezer and hurried back outside.

"You have such a wonderful family," sighed McKenna, and Tatia was surprised to see the wistful look in her eyes. The attorney turned her attention to Johnny and Maddie. Scottie had finished nursing and was now asleep on Johnny's shoulder. Any trace of the hard-shelled professional disappeared as she took in the simple domestic picture. "How about you two? Any thoughts?"

Maddie was glowing with excitement. "I've been wanting to put a small one-chair salon behind the house. This will cover the cost of that plus beauty school - and we won't have to touch what's already in savings!"

"Well, hang on to your hats because I'm not finished with you yet. Let me read you this quote from the U.S. Department of State on its Anticrime Rewards Program: *The Department of State manages two U.S. government programs that offer rewards of up to $25 million for information leading to the arrest and/or conviction of members of significant transnational criminal organizations and the disruption of other forms of transnational organized crime.* Maddie," she continued, dropping the formality, "because of the verbal information you provided along with the data on the flashdrive, there is unanimous agreement that you qualify for this reward.

"I don't know what the total amount will be because it will be decided on a case-by-case basis. But the first of the crime bosses made a deal to avoid trial by pleading *guilty* to lesser charges - and probably ratting out his friends - but he was still a pretty big fish."

Everyone laughed at McKenna's unusual use of slang, and she

joined right in. "Anyway, here's the first installment on that reward. You need to sign and check the same boxes."

"Wow!" exclaimed Maddie, and Scottie whimpered a little. "Oops! Sorry, little one. Look at this, Johnny! We can help Mama Shenice and Papa Jaden get the sound system they want for their church, and I think Tatia's mom said they need a new HVAC for their ministry. And I bet that's even enough to get that ultrasound machine Tatia wants." Then she switched to a stage whisper. "But don't tell her. I want it to be anonymous."

"Sounds like you need to talk to your investment manager about a philanthropic trust."

"And we need to discuss your fee," said Jesse. "When we started all this, you took a dollar and said we'd talk details later. I'd say this is later, and you've earned whatever you charge!" Again, everyone agreed.

"No, Jesse. You don't owe me anything. In just eight months all of you have given me something I thought I had lost years ago - faith in people. When you wallow in the filth I've worked in since I took the bar, you forget there is goodness in the world. I've watched you live and love in spite of the filth, and I want what you've got. But I don't think I'll find it here. I've made a lot of money in my career, and I've just signed the papers to sell my part of the law firm to my partner, so I've got more coming. He's bringing in a fresh new face who is brilliant but not yet jaded. I'll make sure she understands everything in your files backward and forward, and once I'm confident that she'll represent you even better than I can, I'm going to Montserrat for a while. I can't practice law there, and I don't know what else I'd want to do. Who knows, maybe Shenice can turn me into that island girl she talked about - and maybe I'll find the God that you're always talking about."

"The Bible says if you seek Him, you'll find Him," said Maddie.

Later, after McKenna had left and Maddie was giving Scottie a much needed change before they headed for home, Jesse and Johnny were standing on the front porch watching the sunset. Finally, Johnny broke the silence.

"Man! A lot has happened in the year since I met you."

"No kidding," said Jesse.

"When I first saw the Fallen Angel Salvage sign, I didn't get all the implications of it. I mean, you guys don't just salvage bikes, you salvage people from their past with your cover-up tattoos, Tatia salvages victims of trafficking, and all of you salvaged me and Maddie with your love. I'll never be able to thank you for all you've done, especially for showing me how to have a personal relationship with God."

"All the thanks we need is seeing you living out what you've learned."

They stood in a comfortable silence for a few minutes before Jesse asked a question. "Do you remember that Sunday after Joy's kidnapping - the night Maddie showed up? We were setting up for the Bible study we missed that week. Do you remember the question you brought up?"

"Yeah, I wondered where the money the kidnappers were paid for Joy ended up."

"Well, now you know."

ABOUT THE AUTHOR

Linda Brendle, a multi-genre Christian author, first began to write during her years as a caregiver. After two memoirs about Alzheimer's caregiving – *A Long and Winding Road* and *Mom's Long Good-Bye* – she ventured into the world of fiction. She has published a three-novel romantic suspense series, *Tatia's Tattoo*, *Fallen Angel Salvage*, and *Salvaged*. She has also published a light-hearted journal titled *Kitty's Story* about the feral cat who took over that Brendle household several years ago. Retired from the business world, Linda now blogs and writes for the weekly newspaper in the tiny East Texas town where she and her husband David live and take care of the needs and demands of Kitty.

MORE BOOKS BY LINDA BRENDLE

Tatia's Tattoo: As a successful D.C. lawyer, Tatia's mission in life is to destroy the sex trafficking trade in small-town America. She knows where to find it. She's been there. Filled with tragedy, crime, redemption, and love, Tatia's Tattoo is a story that exposes the sordid underbelly of small towns and shines a light of hope on how the evil might be defeated.

Fallen Angel Salvage (Tatia's Story, Book #2): Tatia and Jesse have a perfect life in Chicago. Her testimony put Eric in prison in Texas twenty years ago. How could anything go wrong? An old black van. A missing child. Tatia and Jesse race through the city streets with a band of bikers while Johnny and Jade dig through the dark web and Detectives Nelson and Martin pound on doors. Will it be enough? Or will their daughter become another statistic?

A Long and Winding Road: A Caregiver's Tale of Life, Love, and Chaos: This memoir is the story of the hilarity and chaos that happen when four people, two of whom have Alzheimer's, spend seven weeks traveling through sixteen states in a forty-foot motor home. It is also the story of the lives and experiences that led these four people to this particular place and time in their lives.

Mom's Long Goodbye: A Caregiver's Tale of Alzheimer's, Grief, and Comfort: After finishing Winding Road, many readers asked what happened next. Mom's Long Goodbye is the rest of the story. Mom's goodbye began with a red photo album and ended fifteen years later in a hospital bed in the Alzheimer's wing of Southridge Village. This is her story and mine.

Kitty's Story: From Feral Kitten to Reigning House Cat: A four-ounce ball of black and white fur walked out from under the porch of an unsuspecting couple who had no intention of having any pets, much less a house cat. Four years later, she has grown into a beautiful, thirteen-pound semi-longhair tuxedo cat who reigns supreme over the Brendle household.

As the author of **Tatia's Story**, I believe her story is complete - but since I began writing fiction, I have learned that what I believe doesn't count for much if the characters feel otherwise. If Tatia, Jesse, Brush, Shawna, Johnny, Maddie, and their children have more to say, there will be a Book #4. However, until that happens, I have other projects in the works. **City Girl: the Early Days (2011 - 2015)** is in the rough draft stage. This collection of my early City Girl newspaper columns covers topics like gardening, faith, community, country girl stuff, humor, and more as I chronicled my struggle with adjusting to country life after decades in the city. After that, I plan to work on a novel with the working title **But God...** This will be a fictionalized version of the early life of a friend who lived in Holland during World War II and kept the secret of the Jewish couple who lived in his attic for two years. Until then, thank you for reading and coming back for more. You are the reason I do what I do.

LIST OF ORGANIZATIONS

**These organizations fight Human Trafficking
and Offer Support in Crisis Pregnancies:**

For the Silent: https://www.forthesilent.org/
Our Father's Children: https://www.ourfatherschildren.org/
Ink180: http://ink180.com/
Let My People Go http://www.lmpgnetwork.org/
Poiema Foundation: https://poiemafoundation.org/
Be Lydia: https://www.belydia.org/
U.S. Ins. Against Human Trafficking: https://usiaht.org/
Operation Underground Railroad: https://ourrescue.org/
Redeeming Zoe: https://www.redeemingzoe.org/
Saved In America: https://www.savedinamerica.org/
A 2nd Cup: https://a2ndcup.com/
Truckers Against Trafficking:
    https://truckersagainsttrafficking.org/
Raffa Clinic: https://raffaclinic.org/